JURASSIC ARK

Jurassic Ark

A Journey Through Time with Noah

JOHN MATTHEWS

AVENUE BOOKS

Copyright © John Matthews 2009

First published 2009

Published by Avenue Books
P.O. Box 2118, Seaford BN25 9AR.

ISBN: 978 1 905575 09 1

All rights reserved.
No part of this publication may be reproduced or transmitted in any form or by any means, electronic or mechanical, including photocopy, recording or any information storage and retrieval system, without permission in writing from the publisher.

Unless otherwise indicated, biblical quotations are from the New International Version © 1973, 1978, 1984 by the International Bible Society.

Book design and production for the publisher by
Bookprint Creative Services, <www.bookprint.co.uk>.
Printed in Great Britain.

To my wife Pauline:

and to the many others who
knew the truth of
The Jurassic Ark
before I did.

CONTENTS

	Acknowledgements, Apologies and Disclaimers	9
	Preface	11
	List of Characters	15

Part One – When the Children Were Young

1.	Before Dorset Was – *people were . . . marrying*	19
2.	A Dorset Home, 1970 – *there appeared before them Moses and Elijah*	21
3.	Anniversary – *each year . . .*	44
4.	A Very Wet Monday – *the floodgates of heaven were opened*	49
5.	Barren! – *you are no longer to call her (by her old name)*	71
6.	Salmon Special – *people were eating and drinking*	74
7.	Money Matters – *. . . boosting the price . . . and cheating*	101
8.	If You Go Down in the Wood Today – *make yourself an ark . . . coat it with pitch*	107
9.	Acronym – *no longer will you be called (by your old name)*	127
10.	On Fire – *the fury of the flames*	133

Part Two – The Book that Granddad Never Wrote

11.	My Old Camera – *you are to bring into the ark two of all living creatures*	155
12.	They Had Poisoned Ham – *seven days from now I will send rain. Then the Lord shut him in*	173
13.	Footprints in the Sand – *the ark floated*	193
14.	Detectives – *they . . . examined . . . the scriptures . . . to see if . . . (it) was true*	215
15.	Overland by Boat – *all the high mountains . . . were covered (with water)*	223
16.	Land Ahoy – *God remembered Noah*	241
17.	Stones – *Noah built an altar to the Lord*	255
18.	Freedom – *The region where they lived*	268
19.	On the Bottle – *(Noah) became drunk*	280
20.	No Smoke Without Fire – *let's make bricks and bake them thoroughly*	287
21.	Babble – *the Lord confused the language*	301
22.	Rainbow's End – *the Lord scattered them over the face of the . . . earth*	308

Epilogue	315
Notes and Guide to Bibliography	317
Bibliography	328

ACKNOWLEDGEMENTS, APOLOGIES AND DISCLAIMERS

From my youth, secular textbooks on geology had convinced me that the story of Noah, the ark and a global flood described in the book of Genesis was not worth the paper it was written on. Then one day I had idly started to read D C C Watson's popular paperback – *The Great Brain Robbery*. Within ten minutes, that book had shown me that the Genesis story just might be real.

As a geoscientist in the oil industry, I had a unique opportunity to discuss Noah's Flood with Christians and non-Christians alike, and I appreciated the time and effort many devoted to those discussions. Slowly, with the help of J Whitcomb and H Morris's heavyweight tome – *The Genesis Flood*, the penny dropped fully – the bulk of earth's fossils were formed in The Noachian Flood and not by evolution.

Disturbed by the fact that I, like so many other Christians, had fallen for this "great brain robbery" of evolution over millions of years, I felt that the Lord wanted me to promote the reality of The Flood through fiction. This book follows the pattern of the Australian doctor, John Hercus, who in the 1960s had created his *God's Case Books* in which he had brought Old Testament characters to life by embellishing their stories, but without compromising Biblical details.

I am grateful to those who have corrected my factual errors about Dorset, botany and zoology in earlier drafts, improved its readability and artwork, including Tony, Tim, Paddy, Jon, John, Jennie, Elizabeth, Diane and Andy. I accept responsibility for any residual errors. However, the geology herein is mine alone based on updating *The Genesis Flood*.

I have tried to honour the Biblical details of what Noah did, but to flesh out the story, artistic licence has to be used. People's ideas differ as to the shape of the ark, how long Noah took to build it, whether they were a high or low technology society, etc. I pray that my imagination, including time travel for Noah to modern Dorset, will not prevent you from enjoying this story and thinking about the definite Biblical details. The resulting book is very different to fiction written by A R Guyatt and A Provost who have Noah struggling to enter the ark after the rain and Flood had started. This is not the natural reading of Genesis ch 7 v 4.

None of the modern day characters such as Frank and his family bear any intentional resemblance to anyone living or deceased. If anyone feels that there is any resemblance then I assure them that it was accidental. My apologies do, however, go unequivocally to Noah and family. One day I expect to meet them, and learn exactly what happened. So, 'Irene', if I have defamed you by suggesting that you downed tools and abandoned your husband whilst you were engaged on the world's most daunting project, I apologise unreservedly. What I do know is that the world of wickedness that the nine of you worked in to build the ark can only be described as hell, otherwise there was no reason for God to destroy the world that was.

PREFACE

Children are enthralled by the story of Noah's ark. They excitedly ask: 'Will Noah finish the ark before the rain starts?' 'Will all the animals turn up?' 'Will they behave themselves on board?' 'Will there be enough room?' The drama continues with the animals entering the ark drenched. Forty days on, the rainbow appears and the animals scamper out of the ark.

Tell adults the story of Noah, and where children saw excitement, adults shudder. Even if the story wasn't a legend, who would want to spend eternity building an ark? Would a crew of eight, clueless about sailing or looking after a zoo, cope with wild animals cooped up below decks? Could they work as a team without tensions appearing? What about the rain, the mud and destruction that engulfed everyone not on the ark? Was the whole world submerged, or just part?

In the 1920s, archaeologists digging in the Middle East were excited when they found thick layers of clay. This, they supposed, was evidence of a grim flood such as that described in the Bible but their 'eureka' was short lived because the clay could not be traced very far. Other archaeologists have tried to find the relic of Noah's ark on the mountains of Ararat. But the glaciers on these Turkish mountains and the threat of being shot or taken hostage have deterred many explorers from confirming sightings made by fighter pilots during World War 1 that the ark is still there. So the mystery persists.

Few of us want to risk life and limb like these dedicated scientists combing moor and mountain to find the truth about the Bible story. However, if that flood engulfed all, then it would have extended to Dorset, my home county, at the same time as to the Middle East, to Ararat and onto your doorstep, wherever you live.

Crowds flock to the beaches at Bournemouth, Poole, Swanage and Weymouth to enjoy the seaside. Others potter along leafy lanes that link villages with magical sounding names such as Purse Caundle or Sixpenny Handley. Some come to explore its archaeology at Roman towns such as Dorchester (*Durnovaria*) or prehistoric sites like Maiden Castle. Others try to capture the atmosphere created by Thomas Hardy's novels, about places that bore exciting names such as Anglebury Southerton or Aldbrickham Chene Manor. Geologists come to study Lulworth Cove, or the Jurassic Coast, now designated as a World Heritage Site. Many want a cream tea in an idyllic garden surrounded by roses whose scent transforms the humblest of scones into a memorable feast.

Nobody looks for evidence of this Biblical flood in Dorset because they do not believe that they'd find any. Why not? Do the beaches, the forests and the geology hold no reminders of The Noachian Flood? Let us ask Noah to explain what he saw.

Suppose that Noah had finished building the ark ten days before the animals were due. Once he had set a guard on the ark, he'd want a break after years slogging to build the ark and get strength to face the new tasks of becoming a zookeeper and sea-captain. In our imagination, we can suppose that God meets Noah's wants by allowing his family to travel into the future to visit modern Dorset.

At that exact moment, two children at school in Dorset have been told a romanticised version of the story of Noah's ark and they excitedly share it with Mum and Dad (Gaynor and Frank) when they get home. Frank, a historian by training, insists that the story of the ark is a legend. He and his wife agree not spoil their children's enjoyment of the school version of the story by rubbishing it.

Now Noah hadn't reckoned on a zebra turning up earlier than expected. It disrupts his attempts to relax and remain incognito in Dorset. The zebra bolts into Frank's garden. Noah and two sons recapture the animal, but in the process meet Frank. In sharing their life story with him nothing seems to match what is recorded in the Bible. That confuses Frank further. The only way for them to sort out whether the Bible story is true or not, is to talk and walk Dorset, and ask the unthinkable about history, archaeology, geology and theology. That is, until youths set fire to the Jurassic Ark to punish the man they see as a self-righteous, religious nutcase. Noah's life is turned upside down again.

When you have finished the book, visit the places mentioned. Be a tourist and a detective searching for the conviction that The Noachian Flood was a global event. If you cannot come here in person, look at the photographs I have put on my web site (www.jurassicark.org.uk) or at the satellite photographs on other parts of the web. Check out the bibliography and then explore your own county, or even your own country through the eyes of Noah. Finally, tell others.

John D Matthews
Dorset, 2009

LIST OF CHARACTERS

Biblical and legendary characters:

Gilgamesh – a character in the Babylonian legend
Ham – Noah's middle son
Irene – Ham's wife
Japeth/Jay – Noah's youngest son
Katrina – Japeth's wife
Lamech – Noah's father
Nimrod – One of Ham's sons (grandson of Noah)
Sabteca – Older brother to Nimrod
Shem – Noah's eldest son (an acronym for Stephen Harry Edward Martin)
Stonely (Rev'd) – the wedding priest
Tricia – Shem's wife, a shortened form of Patricia
Utnapishtim – a character in the Babylonian legend

20th century characters (Part One)

Frank and Gaynor's family:
Anne – one of their twins
Ben – the youngest son

Tom – the other twin
Adrian – a neighbour
Miss Jones – the twins' teacher
Samantha – the neighbour's daughter
Mr and Mrs Sharman – the couple hoping to buy Frank's house

Additional 21st century characters (Part Two):

Beryl – Frank and Gaynor's granddaughter
Gavin – son in law
James – the grandson
Charles and Jenny – Frank and Gaynor's new neighbours
Dr Ashmore – a radio-isotope man

PART ONE
When the Children Were Young

CHAPTER ONE

BEFORE DORSET WAS
"people were . . . marrying", Mat 24 v 38

The priest did not like weddings arranged at short notice. They were often shotgun affairs, the flower arranging hasty and pathetic, and the organist struggling to cope with an unpractised anthem. This one did not fit that pattern. When the bride told her father that she planned to marry in three weeks time, he gave the priest grief, trying to get him to cancel the ceremony.

"Do you . . ." He looked again at the sheet with the groom's name on it and mumbled it, because he was still half asleep from another spat with the father last night, " . . . take Patricia Elizabeth . . ." The priest hesitated again, wondering who to blame for this predicament. Maybe he should have taken the father's offer of a bribe to declare the wedding illegal.

The groom responded, "I do."

Turning to the bride, who looked frayed in mind, but happy in spirit, he continued, "Do you, Patricia Elizabeth, take . . ."

She smiled at him, but he could not smile back. She was the culprit, defying her father's advice not to marry him. Who in his right mind would want his daughter to marry a man pursuing a crazy mission? So he mumbled on, hoping that after this wedding, he could coast to his retirement, his reputation intact. ". . . Harry Edward Martin to be your lawful wedded husband?"

The sight of the bride's mother glaring at everyone on the other side of the aisle, while their eyes were focussed in admiration on the wedding couple, brought him back to earth again. At the slightest hint that they were looking her way, she would smile, as if she was enjoying the wedding. He knew that it was a china clay smile, so if looks could kill, he would be busy with funerals shortly.

"I do," the bride said proudly.

There were two more vows, which he managed to complete without mistake, and then his part was all over. Thankfully, they had not invited him to the reception.

CHAPTER TWO
A DORSET HOME, 1970
"there appeared before them Moses and Elijah", Mat 17 v 3

The twins burst into the house, breathless from having chased each other home with unbuttoned coats billowing behind them. I could not help seeing the state of their school uniforms.

Their teacher had started reading the story of Noah's ark. Now the class was busy building a papier mâché model of the scene. Words tumbled out of Anne anxious to tell me that her job was to cut out a rainbow shape and colour it, ready for putting it over the ark when the rain stopped and the sun reappeared. The collage was not finished, but before coming home, they had sung a song about Noah and the animals where a monkey kept going in through the door, coming out of the window and rejoining the queue. "Anne giggled," said Tommy, "when Miss Jones told us that Noah was irritated by this bad behaviour. He had to keep recounting the animals."

"Is that when Anne spilled glue down her dress, Tommy?" I asked cautiously.

Without giving Tommy chance to answer she jumped to her own defence, "He nudged me," and then pressed her lips tightly together to indicate that she would not allow further interrogation.

That evening, as I tucked her up in bed, Anne was back to being my open-hearted chatter-box. "Noah loved his animals, 'specially the giraffes. They were too tall to get under the doorway, so he had to saw off the top of the doorframe while the other animals got wet. If you'd been there, you could've helped him, Daddy. You're clever."

"Daddy, the monkey was funny. He kept climbing out of the window and going in again through the door. Noah got very annoyed because he had to keep recounting the animals."

Her remark touched me. Many children believe that their parents can do anything. Granted, there were some do-it-yourself jobs that I excelled in, but not carpentry. I could not use a saw the correct way up, so using it upside down to remove a door lintel was 'no go'. Besides, there'd be animals booting me in the back, anxious to get in before the mud sucked them away, and cold rain trickling through my hair and under my clothes. I'd rather run a mile, though the puffing and panting would bring on a rash.

As a child, I'd loved the story of the ark and the animals. But as a teenager, history, not animals, had become my first love. Let others aspire to the ideals of this legendary character in saving animals from extinction. I wished them success even though they would not be able to repeat his lofty achievements.

Because she could not see my thoughts, Anne pressed me, "Do you wish you'd been there?"

I muttered a reply, hoping that she would not notice that I had dodged her question. Then I turned her light low and went down into the kitchen. My wife had switched the coffee percolator on and it was beginning to gurgle and give off that aroma that prepares your taste buds for the delightful drink.

"Anne's got bitten by the Noah-story. Did she tell you she'd had to use an encyclopaedia to find the correct order of the colours in the rainbow instead of guessing?"

"Yes, and Tommy had had to cut out two cardboard zebras for placing on the gangplank when their classmates have finished their part. Anne now knows the colours of the rainbow, and Tommy knows that there is a striped pattern on a zebra."

"Is that the only purpose behind that lesson?"

"They had fun while learning."

"So while they indulge in fantasy, in the supposed cause of education and mess up their clothes, I struggle at work to ensure that we can pay the bills."

Though not affluent, we managed a holiday abroad each year funded by Gaynor's part time job. The housework did not suffer in any way, and right now she was carefully drying the crocks on the draining board and putting them away.

"But why do you say that the story of Noah is fantasy?" she asked. "There must be an element of truth in it. Moses ensured that the book of Genesis and the rest of the Pentateuch accurately recorded the early Hebrew history."

"Moses was an eyewitness of the Exodus from Egypt, but what about the history of the Hebrew predecessors thousands of years before? There is no evidence of written records from that time. Did a man calling himself 'Noah' travel into his future to see Moses and tell him about how his family built a boat big enough to hold pairs of every animal and ensure Moses wrote it down?"

"Moses visited Jesus on the Mount of Transfiguration, although they lived over one thousand years apart. And Elijah joined them."

"My logical faculties tell me that that bit of the Bible is fiction. Time travel is impossible. Otherwise the next thing you'll be telling me is to expect Noah to visit us, and with a zebra to boot."

"You are being cynical, Frank. You enjoyed the story of Noah as a youngster, so why not play along with the children's belief that it was real and re-live it? There is more to life than a bright brain. We get pleasure out of pretending that Father Christmas is real, and joining in with the children's wonderment."

Gaynor had touched a raw spot in my logic. Christmas Day was exciting for us as well as for the children, but I wondered how long it would last because I'd overheard Anne asking Samantha from next door how Father Christmas entered their houses. Samantha told her that he comes down their chimney. Anne asked how he stayed clean or how he got into our house because two years ago I had dismantled the chimney breast and the fireplace to make the room bigger.

What am I going to tell Anne about Father Christmas' entry when she asks me? What if she asks if Noah was real? I remembered the professor who taught me archaeology years ago recommended three books which explained Noah's legendary origin. Those books were buried in the loft, somewhere. Gaynor had argued that because my college days were long over I should dump them.

I cringed at the idea because I had scrimped and saved from my student grant to purchase them so they now had a sentimental value. The professor's words were etched on the slates in my brain because of his Welsh accent. 'The Noachian Flood,' he said, 'recorded in early chapters of Genesis, is the story of a man and his sons who built an ark to save the animals from a worldwide watery grave. Ussher dated the event as 2,300 BC using strict addition of Bible dates. All that Biblical scholarship was blown apart when a clay fragment, found in a Canaanite stratum at Megiddo which is older than 2,300 BC, told the story of a Babylonian flood. Archaeologists are now united in the view that the story of The Noachian Flood, which Moses accepted uncritically, is a legend based on that earlier Babylonian legend. That legend begat 39 other flood legends.' And he wagged his finger at us to reinforce the point.

One character in the Babylonian legend was called Gilgamesh but the other had a foreign sounding name – utterly unpronounceable. They supposedly took a pair of every animal inside their boat, and sailed on flood-waters for seven days. It was too late to climb into the loft to find those old books to check his name so I looked in the volume of the encyclopaedia that Anne had brought downstairs after she came in from school. His name was there in black and white in a short article headed '**Flood Traditions**' – Utnapishtim.

I wondered if I should show the article to Anne tomorrow. I suspected that she was already asleep, dreaming about rainbows, animals and dads who were perfect handymen. If I did show her it, it would spoil her fun, although she might not understand everything. Gaynor reminded me that this 'Epic of Gilgamesh' had been put to music. Then she suggested that we call the man with the unpronounceable name 'Unhappy Tim'.

"That is better than calling him 'Nappy Tim'," I retorted. "When my brain has had a rest after that recent exertion I might be able to remember something about the other 39 legends."

"Don't tell me that you failed to enjoy working on that business guide."

"We finished it four days late," I said, trying to stifle a yawn, "but when I gave it to the printer he said he can still print one thousand copies by Monday. His next customer phoned this morning to apologise that his copy, due for printing today, is not ready."

"That is a relief. When do you go back to work?"

"Monday week. It sounds a lot of time off but one hour off for every hour overtime is fair but not generous."

"You must deal with that letter from the estate agent in the morning, but how do you plan to relax after that?"

Producing that business guide for the county council had drained me, working until 10pm each night and weekends. Gaynor suggested that I should sleep in tomorrow. In return I offered to collect the children from school, and cook the supper. If I felt energetic, I'd get out my golf clubs and, in the garden, practise my swing. If my confidence came back, I'd phone up golf courses and ask their prices. I used to play with Gaynor's father before his infirmity took its toll. One day my children might join me in the game.

Whilst I was thinking about that letter, Gaynor screamed out, "Frank . . . zebra . . . garden!"

"Stop stuttering! The neighbour's dog gets in occasionally, but not a zebra. It is your imagination fanned into flames by the legend of Noah."

"Frank, quick! My begonias!"

Though I did not believe her, the acidity in her voice drove me to open the back door. In the flower border was a zebra. I pinched myself to check that I was not dreaming.

I could send my neighbour's dog scurrying away with a sharp clap of my hands, assisted by a verbal "Shoo!" This beast looked too large to be bothered by a shoo, however loud. A foghorn might shift him, but if he went, which way would he go? My neighbours would not welcome the beast either. I felt helpless while he pulled up another begonia, tossed his head upwards and swallowed it without enjoying the taste. And they were pricey.

My dilemma was worsened by a scratching noise behind the fence. Not another zebra to add to the rampage or a different animal, perhaps a gorilla, wanting flesh? To my relief, a human face peered over the top.

"Can I come round and rescue our zebra, please?" the face asked. I could only nod.

"What number house are you?" He paused for my answer and then said, "Be with you . . ."

Fear glued me to our doorway, with my heart beating faster than the doctor would approve, watching the zebra devour more begonias. I felt that I was waiting for eternity. Then he appeared with two other men, muttering about how they had got confused by the alleyways behind our house. They must be new to the district. If I had told them about the 'For Sale' notice outside they would have found us easier than by looking for house numbers.

Gaynor's azaleas were flattened in their mêlée of lassoing the zebra. I'd have to do gardening tomorrow, not relaxing.

The older man introduced himself. "I am Noah, and these are two of my sons, Ham and Jay."

"I'm Frank," I muttered, seething with anger at the desecration of my private property. "Nice to meet you."

How did I come to say 'Nice to meet you'? I was used to going to committee meetings, facing people whom I had never seen before and who were expected to be antagonistic about my views of business development in Dorset. I always said, 'Nice to meet you', even though my knees were shaking at the thought of the verbal mauling that would ensue. And when our meeting was over, however awkward and uncomplimentary they'd been to my ideas, I always said, 'It was good to have met you'.

But those names? 'Noah' is an old Dorset name, common until recently but maybe I had only imagined that that is what he had said because my mind was still pirouetting around the story of the Biblical Noah. 'Ham and Jay' sounded so like a sandwich filling that I was not sure I had heard correctly. How could they both be his sons when one was a pale-skinned European and the other had a dark skin and curly hair suggesting an Afro-Caribbean origin? When confused by what someone had said, I had learned to ask a supplementary question to give me time to think. So, whilst angry at this intrusion, I asked him politely if there were other animals about to enter my garden.

He shook his head and asked, "Can you help us, please? This zebra should not have come to us until next week. He wanders in and out looking for food, tripping us up. Do you know what to feed him on apart from expensive begonias? By the way, how much do I owe you for the damage?"

That chink of money helped cool my confused anger. While the darker skinned man escorted the zebra away, out of my sight, hopefully forever, I invited the other two into the house. Noah apologised about the sawdust on his clothes and did his best to shake it off before stooping to get in the doorway.

Gaynor, relieved that the rest of her garden was safe, got out two more mugs, filled them with coffee and offered the visitors the biscuit tin full of her freshly baked Dorset Wiggs. If I could find out what zebras ate, I wouldn't feel embarrassed about giving him the receipts for the begonias and azaleas. She had only bought them last week.

As I climbed the stairs to get the relevant volume of the *Encyclopaedia Britannica*, I realised that the incident bothered me for deeper reasons than the damaged garden and the rude interruption. In the old days, a ringmaster had been allowed to lead elephants along the roads of Dorset. Each subsequent elephant walked in line with its trunk curled around the tail of the previous elephant. This linking gave the illusion of safety, but it had been dangerous, for they could easily have broken rank and gone on a rampage.

I had never seen elephants in the street, but one night last year I had been woken by 30 cows mooing and jostling each other in our tight cul-de-sac. Some had entered my neighbour's garden, because he had not fastened his gates before retiring to bed. The cows had then disappeared, so I had gone back to sleep. My neighbour had slept through it all, but next morning was livid about his lawn that had been transformed from the show-piece of 'The Close' to a rutted muck-heap. Only later did we learn why the cows were on a jaunt at midnight.

Did the Biblical Noah have problems with cows arriving in the night? What about the stench from the waste that they would deposit in the ark? "Don't be silly, Frank, the Bible story is a legend! Concentrate on working out who are these people are." I realised that I was talking to myself. My hope was that those downstairs hadn't heard my mutterings. Talking to oneself could be the first signs of madness.

The volume of the encyclopaedia with the entry '**Zebras**' in it was the last in the series and I rushed downstairs with it. In the kitchen Noah had already explained to Gaynor that if he knew the natural diet of the zebra, he could keep him on the ark. Otherwise, the animal would keep wandering outside when hungry, and come back into the ark to sleep at night.

"What about closed gates?" she asked.

"Look at their back legs next time you see one. The power in their muscles carry them over such obstacles," Noah replied.

Gaynor had apparently not spotted the absurdity of the situation. Had I met someone, complete with animals, trying to re-enact the Bible story? Where had Ham taken the zebra? Was there a zoo or a circus nearby? Would more animals be trampling our garden tomorrow? In my nightmare I could see the estate agent writing to me again: 'Your neighbourhood is no longer a desirable place to live. The asking price of your house will have to be lowered further.' Would we ever be able to sell up and move?

Noah read my confused mind. He knew, as well as I did when clear headed, that there was no local zoo.

"Frank, we are a normal family. Sarah, my wife had a miscarriage and then we had three sons who are now settled in their careers. We would have liked a daughter, but the stork stopped visiting us. We had two fine daughters-in-law that have filled part of that emotional vacuum in our lives. Azaleas and begonias adorn our front garden and we have a vegetable plot at the back. We managed a round of golf every Sunday morning, and one evening each week in the summer. The only thing that was missing was grandchildren. I slept soundly every night, until a vivid dream shook me awake. I was worried that my agitation would disturb Sarah. She needed her sleep because, once the lads had grown up, she had returned to veterinary practice, involving irregular hours and shift working in the animal hospital."

"Her job sounds as demanding as mine. Today I finished a month of overtime. But what did you do for a living?"

"Nothing to do with animals, though you might think so, having met you as a result of a lively zebra. But the dream . . . I had seen a man, holding a clipboard and pen, who told me to build an ark to a design he would now reveal."

"This afternoon, my daughter reminded me about the legend of the Biblical Noah and his ark, though I'd have called it a boat with pointed ends and an open deck."

"Your concept of an ark sounds as vague as mine was before I had the dream. So when I asked the man in my dream what an ark was, he replied, 'Come and see.' He escorted me round a monstrosity, ticking off items as he did so . . . the door, the window, the gangplank, the gallery, et cetera. It was a cross between a million ton oil tanker and an overgrown chest. Banging on the side produced no echo. It was solid wood."

"Since you are not a vet, Noah, you must be a ship builder to understand such matters."

"I should have brought my drawings and then you would see that it was not a traditional boat; there were no sails, rudders or engines, and corners were square. With my visitor's help, I climbed inside to find cells, store rooms, bedrooms and a recreation area."

"Sounds like an old fashioned farm house. So you are not a ship builder."

"I forgot to mention the bilge and control room."

"We are back to boats then?"

"Yes and no. The man in my dreams checked that I had no more questions about the difference between an ark and a boat, and then made me sign a statement saying that I would start building a real version immediately. He then took the signed copy away, telling me that our master needed it as proof that he had told me everything. Then I woke up."

"Although you'd signed a piece of paper in your dream, what made you take the command seriously? And the purpose . . . ?"

"The dream had switched on an autopilot in me, making me replicate the drawings of the ark from memory before I forgot the details. As to the ark's purpose, it was as if I had stumbled on a solitary piece of the jigsaw puzzle of life with a picture of the ark on it. Little did I know, but Sarah had been handed the next piece of the jigsaw right then. At that point she awoke and came downstairs, with hair tousled and pyjamas creased. I can remember the conversation as if it had only happened yesterday.

"'Noah, you look as awful as I feel,' Sarah said. 'I turned over in bed and could not feel you. You might have told me that you had an urgent job that you needed to finish this morning. It would have saved me worrying.'

"'It's not work. I have had a peculiar dream.'

"'So have I,' she replied.

"'Over the years we have been married I have had lots of dreams. But by the time I'm awake, and anxious to share them with you, they have disappeared.'

"'The same happens with me,' said Sarah as she absent-mindedly riffled through the pile of my drawings on the table. I was not paying attention but busy drawing in a lake near the ark to make it look realistic.

"'Hey, what's that? Where is all the window space in the lower floors of your building? It's like a prison. And why is the door half way up the wall?'"

Noah halted his reminiscence.

"Got it at last," I said. "You're an architect, and I thought you were a shipwright."

"Correct, Frank. A stilted conversation then ensued with Sarah and myself trying to swap bits of these dreams. They were like two adjacent pieces of the same jigsaw. In Sarah's dream she had been working normally at the veterinary hospital when a motley queue of animals appeared – a male with each female. The females were all in the early stages of pregnancy, and the males were telling the receptionist that their partners wanted prenatal check-ups."

The details in those dreams had nothing to do with real life, I mused. Animals keep clear of each other's territory and only talk to each other in children's books. Vets sometimes have to assist an animal struggling with a breech birth. A snarl or a bite is a typical reward. And to cap it all, most mates showed no interest in the birth, having forgotten the pleasure when they sired the offspring. So I asked him why he thought the dreams fitted together.

"Each of the animals in Sarah's dream had signed a card thanking me for saving them from the *mabbul* because I allowed them onto my ark."

"What on earth is a *mabbul?*"

"Neither of us knew. It was only later when talking to one of our daughters-in-law that the word *mabbul* took on a meaning."

Jay, who was sitting opposite Gaynor offered to continue the story so that Noah could drink his coffee before it went cold.

"And help yourself to the Wiggs," said Gaynor, having swallowed the story hook, line and sinker, though still confused by the word *mabbul*.

"While Mum and Dad were trying to sort out whether the dreams could be ignored or whether the future of the world depended on their obedience to this project, I added to the daze of the moment by rushing over to their house once I had thrown a few clothes on. Decades after the event, it is as though there is a tape recording in my mind that keeps playing back the conversation of that morning."

"'Mum, Dad! I've had a crazy dream where our whole family built a massive wooden structure. We had to order a ton of timber each day for years. Your wallet bulged with money to pay for each consignment. I could touch the wood, and smell the resins as each plank went through the sawmill. You are no chippy, so what do you want it for?'

"Dad scratched his head, and said, 'I never liked working with wood, Jay. Stone and steel are my forté. My brain is in autopilot mode at the moment, doing what it has to do, not what I tell it. I should be shaving, eating breakfast and going to the office with my suit and tie on.'

"He hesitated. 'Instead I am perched here, having drawn an ark whose details embedded themselves in my brain without my permission. Even worse, I signed the confirmation sheet to say that I understood everything and would carry out instructions to the last mortise and tenon. Your mother, instead of going to work, is telling me about her encounter with talking animals. Then you barge in and tell us how much timber we must order. As for money, I do not have an inexhaustible supply of it. Without going to work, what bit we have saved for our retirement will disappear rapidly. It looks as if we are all on autopilots, heading away to insanity.'

"'That little speech has exhausted you Noah,' said Mum, thinking hard. 'Why not ask your father? He has often been able to understand the complex issues of life and destiny. And we trust his judgement.'

"'He does have an uncanny knack of knowing what to do when life is tough. I know that dreams are important but interpreting them is beyond his experience.'

"'But Jay's dream helps to complete the jigsaw. You have to build an ark whose design you have carefully replicated on paper.' She tapped her finger on the main drawing for emphasis. 'Jay gets the timber delivered and my job is to guarantee the animals' welfare.'

"'It's crazy. Where does the money come from? Trees are more expensive than match sticks. If we go ahead with this floating thingy, will people see us as fools believing in dreams? There is no decent-sized river near here to launch it.'"

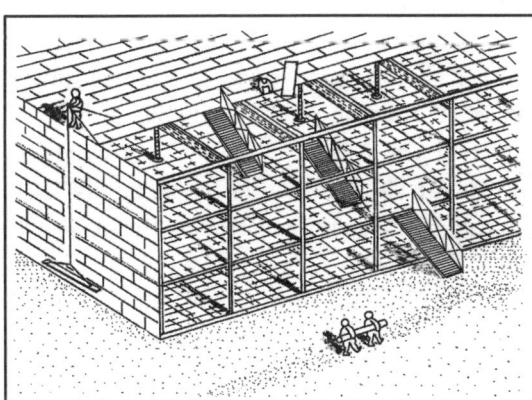

"The ark was huge, Frank. It had to hold a pair of every kind of animal. It did not need a streamlined shape, so corners were square, thus simplifying its construction."

Now zoologists tell us that one species of animals becomes extinct every day and the odds could shorten to one an hour. The main cause is loss of their natural habitats. How on earth, I wondered, do building arks halt extinctions?

"That morning," Jay explained, "the family did not understand why the ark was needed. The word *mabbul* in Mum's dream was nothing but another vague word, implying violence."

"In that case, why leave your comfort zone?"

"Mum would not let the discussion falter, being convinced that the dreams had to be obeyed, whereas we other two members of the family, like you, Frank, were sceptical. Dad was thinking of every excuse to get out of the commitment he had signed. He told Mum that since dinosaurs lay eggs rather than become pregnant, that shows that the dream could not be ignored. Otherwise the staff on board the ark would have to risk their limbs being torn off by these vicious monsters.

"Mum tried to explain why dinosaurs were in her dream," he continued. "She turned to Dad and between sobs said, 'Noah-ben-Lamech, you have taken your dream seriously otherwise you would have not spent two hours drawing rather than going to work. So, why are you trivialising my dream? Every kind of dinosaur was in the queue, even those with teeth a foot long. I don't like what we have been asked to do, but do we have any choice?'"

"ben-Lamech? Please explain."

"Like your surname, it means 'Son of Lamech'. Mum always used Dad's full name when she was annoyed with him, and wanted to get his attention. He sat there looking silent. She continued, 'You cannot refer to it as *my ark*, it's *our family ark*. There are only three of us here but my dream showed that the whole family are to be involved.' Mum's dream was a definite message to tell us to take dinosaurs on aboard."

"But where do you get live dinosaurs from, or are you inventing a yarn to excuse yourselves from wandering around with a zebra and ruining my garden? Although I am no scientist I know that once they roamed this earth, laid eggs, but became extinct when a comet crashed into the earth sprinkling poisonous iridium everywhere."

"Frank, I know nothing about dinosaurs. I'm a chippy, not a zoologist nor a palaeontologist."

"Then you must be a story-teller, Jay."

"I am not. As Dad's comments about dinosaurs had not

changed Mum's view about the need to start the ark immediately, he reviewed his other reservations about the task. He knew nothing about boat building and how they cope with the waves in stormy seas. His forté was concrete, which sinks if you put it in water. He then went as far as suggesting that we sink the whole idea."

I realised that I was beginning to show empathy with Noah at this intrusion into his life. I was living the story as if it were real. A glance at Noah told me that he was struggling to prevent his emotions, which had erupted that traumatic morning, from showing.

"Dad's cynicism was lost on Mum," continued Jay. "Eventually, I was able to bring order by reminding Dad that Granddad Lamech was a carpenter before he retired. As a hobby, he had built a rowing boat, though his daily work was timber carcassing and roof trusses. His experience would allow us to judge whether the structure of the ark would withstand the buffetting. And, for good measure, the whole family could go to carpentry classes if we were still foxed by the intricate woodwork. Dad said that if we were going to take the dreams seriously, we should let Granddad take charge and leave him out."

Jay was now finding it hard to carry on with the story as he mopped his sweaty brow. It gave me a chance to think straight. "So what changed things? You all had individual dreams that mock human experience. You were hesitant about following instructions, although those dreams felt prophetic in some obscure way, but now you have followed them to the last mortise and tenon. Did Granddad support Sarah and Jay's view?"

"We did not have to ask Granddad to adjudicate. Later that day we learnt that he had had a dream. Each member of our immediate family except Ham had dreams telling us about this imminent *mabbul*-disaster and telling us why we were part of the solution. There seemed to be no alternative but to start straight away, although problems loomed in every direction."

"So in your family of eight, seven of you had dreams so vivid that you could remember them the next morning. One person didn't dream. As evidence of the further muddle of knowing whether to treat the dreams seriously or not, only five of you were willing to start immediately. Have you come into my house to spin a yarn not fit for a psychology text book?"

"You make our problem sound like children arguing over a bag of liquorice allsorts. Which one do you pick? This was a serious decision with eternal ramifications!"

"I never liked psychology," I told my visitors. "Every one knows that committees are notorious for not making decisions before it is too late."

"We were not sure whether Ham would join in, but he did promise to listen to us."

"Watching him remove that zebra who grazed my garden bare tells me he is an active partner now. And your father must have been convinced as well."

"They twisted my arm," Noah said, finally finishing his coffee and taking another biscuit.

"But that's a whole story on its own, isn't it Dad?" said Jay.

Three hours ago I was tired, and my garden attractive. Now I was wide-awake, and my sanity like that of my garden – rutted by a zebra. Were legends of animals and arks creeping into the 20th century and convincing these people I had met to do things out of character? Or was there a new prospect of a bad flood? If so, would I need to get on the ark with my family? Where was it? Do dreams have a magnetism that draws the future back into the present so that we can plan ahead? It was worth trying that interrogation.

"Gaynor is a romantic," I said. "On our first date she told me she had had a dream about meeting, falling in love and marrying an academic. I asked her why she thought that she would marry an academic rather than a doctor, a sailor or whatever."

"Did she enlighten you?" Noah asked.

"She told me that most girls have romantic dreams about their future spouses. Though they could not see the boys' faces, they could guess their occupations by what they were carrying. In her dreams, a man carried books rather than a stethoscope or kit bag. I laughed at her wishful thinking and decided I was not going to date this girl, who had me married off before I had proposed, any more."

Gaynor glared at me.

Noah saw her embarrassment and tried to ease the pain I had caused.

"Frank, you were probably scared by the pace of events running beyond your control. I had the same worry about these dreams."

"I guess so." It sounded feeble. "Although I didn't see her for a year, I thought about her many times. So I dated her again, fell in love, proposed and we were married soon after."

"Ours was an arranged marriage, planned years before the event. Even so, we are now deeply in love, and I would not swap Sarah for anybody else. She has been a tower of strength while we have been building the ark."

"I've never heard of an arranged marriage in this country."

"Who said I was from this country, or this century?"

That answer made another hole in my head. He can't be from another century. Time travel is impossible. And what about dreams with definite instructions? Perhaps these visitors had become locked into what I call a 'reinforcement dream'. Maybe they had watched TV programmes about natural history and dreamt about extinctions so often that they convinced themselves that they needed to re-enact, in the 20th century, the story of the Biblical Noah.

"Frank, your experience of dreams is different to ours. If Gaynor will pardon me for saying this, her dream was vague. Each of our dreams came only once and each was like a dagger driven in deep, leaving scar tissue that will remain permanently. They do not fit into a pattern of repetition that drives people to act irrationally."

"Did you take purple hearts? I knew a student at college who took acid and claimed he heard voices telling him to save the world."

"We avoided recreational drugs, so hallucinations were not the answer. The dreams we had were blueprints for action directly from the master above."

"But don't you think you might have made a mistake and wasted your time and energy? Dorset gets flooded occasionally, but not to the extent of needing a floating animal sanctuary."

"I have never seen a flood of any intensity. But the kind of floods that you are thinking about, covering mere miles, are trivial counterparts to a *mabbul*. My description of the *mabbul* is second hand because I did not see it in my dream. We are expecting so much new water that a lake deeper than all mountains will form across the whole world."

"Clouds don't hold enough rain for that."

"One reason why we have never seen a flood of any size is that we have never seen rain, although that is only one of the ways that we expect additional water to arrive on the surface of the earth. Every day our sky is cloudless. Our dreams told of a frightening future where the weather bears no resemblance to the calm that we have had so far. Animals will enter the ark of their own accord soon. Water from the sky and land will then destroy the earth. Being human, we worry about how we will cope. For one year, assuming that the *mabbul* comes, we will be working our fingers to the bone in the ark. It will be the only thing afloat."

"So your family are in Dorset to try and relax before this disaster?"

"Sure. As the ark is finished apart from minor jobs, each member of the family is taking a break on a rota basis. Yesterday, in the library, I scanned tourist information about Dorset. I want to see these places for myself because everything looks exciting. Next week will be too late."

"I'm still not with it," I said. "Where have you built your ark?"

"Frank, my ark is near a town that does not have a name on any of your maps because it belongs to a time thousands of years ago, not the 20th century. It may sound unbelievable to you. As it is late, if you want me to answer more of your questions, why not join me tomorrow whilst I enjoy Dorset?"

I muttered something non-committal, as I had done to Anne hours ago. How could I become a tourist with a man who claimed to believe in dreams, had built a gigantic ark thousands of years ago and was now perched on my kitchen stool in the 20th century?

What could this fellow teach me about Dorset when I had masterminded the production of *'The Guide to Small and Medium Sized Businesses in Dorset'* and lots of other material? I could let him see my new edition next week.

"I want to go to Weymouth. I will get Gaynor some replacement begonias and azaleas while we are out. Thank you for the coffee and Wiggs. It has gone 10pm, so Ham will be waiting to take us back."

"Why Weymouth?"

"In the library I read that Weymouth once had record amounts of rain," Noah replied.

"But Weymouth does not suffer from excessive rain. I've written encouraging words about the place in *'The Guide'*."

"Weymouth is generally dry, but you become conditioned by the dryness, and then fail to listen to any grim forecast. I have never seen this thing called 'rain' before, but our dreams told us to expect 'rain' next week with no other warning."

For a moment I thought I was beginning to understand him. If he wasn't familiar with rain or storms, how could he understand flooding? Nor could I see the connection with Weymouth, which was not an impressive place.

"Does that mean you have been less than truthful about the town in your guides and brochures in an attempt to get more businesses started here?"

My answer was defensive. "There are better places in Dorset than Weymouth. Is that the only place you want to visit?"

"No, but Weymouth is the place to start. Join me at the Memorial Clock, 10am, perhaps?"

With the visitors gone, Gaynor put the mugs in the sink as if nothing unusual had happened. Apart from a couple of questions, she had listened silently to Noah and Jay, although she had puckered her face at my reference to her romantic dreams. Looking at the garden, I could see that I had not been dreaming. The hoof marks were still there and the gaps in the begonia bed. Gaynor brought me to my senses, "Are you going with him?"

I shouldn't have hesitated because she continued, "but whatever, young man, stay where you are for a minute. When you proposed to me you said that I was the princess of your dreams. Why did you not tell Noah and Jay this?"

"I didn't want that lot to get the wrong message."

"So you do not believe in dreams?"

"You admitted that yours was vague in comparison to theirs. Noah received dates, diagrams, dimensions and instruction sheets but you didn't even see a face."

"Though all their dreams complemented each other, did ours not? And don't shrug your shoulders."

"When I answered his question, I was trying to emphasise that I never had any dreams that lead you astray. If you took notice of every dream you would waste time on things that have no bearing on life. It was . . . just a phrase."

"You be careful about what you say, otherwise you will find yourself sleeping in the loft. I did not marry you because I was lonely or because of a dream. I loved you then and still do. So, are you going?"

The heated discussion was over but the invitation to join Noah required a decision. Putting the onus on Gaynor, I asked her if she believed in time travel.

"Why not? There are things beyond our comprehension. Even if time travel is fictional, it still makes a good story."

"*Star Trek* is far fetched!"

"I know that was far fetched, and that is why I stopped watching the TV series, but I thought you liked H G Wells. He made money out of his book – *The Time Machine,* which was later turned into a film. You could do the same, Frank."

"I liked Wells' history, but not his fiction. But the reason I don't believe in time travel is because he never explained how the time machine worked. It was a shed with standing room only with a window so that they could see outside, and a control box with a handle to change the century they were in."

"I know, and Noah made no claim to having such a contraption."

"Or how the zebra got in with them. That reminds me. I discovered last week that Wells' ashes had been scattered off Studland."

"How come, not being a Dorset man?" asked Gaynor.

"He spent most of his life in London. His relatives must've thought well of the county."

"Are you going to keep the appointment? Three hours ago you felt that it would be wonderful if a historian could check his facts by talking with people from the past. And have you sorted their names out? You were puzzled at first by their names 'Noah', and 'Ham and Jay' – the supposed sandwich filling."

I was intrigued by the story that Noah and Jay had spun. I'd heard them address each other enough times not to doubt their names, but what was their provenance? Time travel only features in imaginary stories like the *Dr Who* series or strange bits of the Bible. However, the alternative explanation that they were modern tricksters trying to sell me religion or get money out of me did not fit either. To get to the bottom of this conundrum I needed a two-prong attack. First – to challenge him over the impossibility of time travel. Second – to copy that page from the encyclopaedia and write reams of questions down in my notebook about the legends of arks. I'd need to find my archaeology books from the loft first thing in the morning to refresh my mind about the details. Then I could argue authoritatively with tonight's Noah instead of being caught out unprepared.

"What about your lie-in?" Gaynor asked me.

"I can have it on Thursday when I have consigned their gibberish babblings about *mabbuls* and lakes that cover the earth back to the realm of legend. Then I will talk to Anne, and Tommy if needed, and put them right. Subsequent discussions with Miss Jones at school would be interesting, possibly getting heated about the Bible, and the absurd stories of those two prophets who indulged in time travel."

"But if you do that, you will spoil our children's fun."

"All the accounts have to be legends whether they are Noahs of the Bible, modern day Noahs or this 'Unhappy Tim' fellow.

People think a cubit is 18 inches – that makes the ark 450 feet long. Utnapishtim's ark is square – 180 by 180 feet, and 120 feet tall."

"I can see that 'Unhappy Tim' could not build an ark about the size of Barclay's offices in Poole in two days."

"But although Noah's ark has less volume, it is still bigger than 100 bungalows. Nobody knows how long he took to complete it because the ages are crazy in Genesis; some folk lived 900 years."

"Frank, look at the reasons why he might be the Biblical Noah. Tonight's 'Ham' is the real Biblical 'Ham', 'Jay' is short for 'Japeth', and 'Stephen' is a variation of 'Shem'. And I still believe that the Bible explains time travel."

"The 'Jay' sounds reasonable, but you would need an elastic mind to stretch 'Stephen' into 'Shem'. But he didn't tell us about the names of his daughters-in-law."

"That solves nothing because they are not recorded in the Bible."

"But he also told us about several other people involved with the ark not mentioned in the Bible. Stephen isn't married, and Granddad is part of the story. What's more, the Muslims' Koran casts a shadow over the historical accuracy of the event. Only two sons boarded the ark, although the three daughters-in-law went in. The third son had assumed that going up a high mountain could save him, but Allah judged him to be unrighteous. Of course, we could explain all these 40 legends by saying that once there was a local flood, which happened when someone was on a boat moving a few animals around. It rained a bit more than usual, flooding the banks of the river. And since the water stretched as far as the horizon and people did not travel far, they assumed that the water covered the whole earth."

"For goodness sake, go out with him! At least it will be a relaxation from work."

"My enquiring mind tells me to go, Gaynor. If nothing else, I can find out where the zebra came from."

"Do you think you will sleep tonight?"

"You know something I don't?"

"It is a year to the day that those cows came into The Close, and messed up Adrian's garden."

"I thought they had identified and prosecuted the rogues who deliberately let the cows out of that field and shooed them down the main road and into our village. They'd be mad to try it again. And our gates are closed, so don't ask!"

"I was only winding you up, Frank. And the farmer keeps the field gate locked now to avoid another episode of rounding up his flustered and distressed cows in the middle of the night, and paying compensation."

"I'm not superstitious about anniversaries."

CHAPTER THREE

ANNIVERSARY
"each year. . .", 1 Sam 2 v 19

Her husband loved to make Heath Robinson contraptions, though they often fell apart on first use. Patricia had no option but to help. "Can you pull the end of this cord tight for a moment, please? I am going to connect the cord to that spring over our bed, the one with the bell at the other end. This cord goes over a pulley, out of the window and all around the outside. If any one comes near us in the night they will snag the cord. That will jerk the spring and set the bell ringing and we can deal with them."

"I was hoping for a quiet night on this of all nights."

"Why?" he asked her. "Duty comes first."

"Ten years ago to the day, I had a rotten night."

He looked quizzical.

"You've become so involved in guard duty that you have forgotten that tomorrow is our tenth wedding anniversary."

"I am sorry, Patricia. We have drawn the short straw for guard duty so many times lately I have had no time to think. And where could we go to celebrate at such short notice?" He paused. "But you never told me about that rotten night."

"You must've been such a romantic dreamer not to notice how tired and baggy-eyed I was on our wedding day."

"I was too excited to notice, and relieved that the priest did not burst a blood vessel before the ceremony was over. So?"

"Though it was late, my mother insisted that my father go out on our wedding eve to see Father Stonely again to try to get him to stop our wedding. Father came in around 3am, slamming doors. Mother could tell from his face that he had failed. Whilst I'd heard Mother swear before, it was the first time that I had heard my father utter profanities. I watched the fingers of the clock tick slowly to 5am when I dropped asleep, exhausted."

Fifteen minutes later her husband had finished his contraption that, if all the wires were of the correct tension, would warn them of prowlers. As they undressed, Patricia asked him, "What do you remember about our wedding? Did my mother spoil it for you?"

"I did steal a glance at her, and she was smiling, though my sixth sense told me that I was the last person she wanted you to marry, but it did not destroy my happiness."

"Mother hasn't spoken to me since the wedding. Father is polite, but cold. If I'd had a baby, there would have been an excuse to go and see her and hope that she would thaw on seeing her new grandchild. She dotes on my nieces and nephew."

"Dad said you would not get pregnant for decades marrying into our family."

"What does your dad know about my body?" asked Patricia.

"On gynaecology he's clueless. You know why he said that." He paused to give her time to think. "Did your mother talk to you about married life when you were young?"

"She taught me the facts of life in a brusque manner when I reached puberty, saying that she was glad I looked like a stick because there was less risk of boys being attracted to me and thus casually getting pregnant. Once she knew I wanted to marry you, her brusqueness rose to roof level, and if the roof had been a bit weak she would have gone into orbit. I imagine that she would rather me get pregnant from some casual boy friend, even if he then disappeared when he realised that he had got me into the pudding club, than for me to bear a child in wedlock with you. I felt dumped in the deep end of her emotions before I could swim. My father, I thought, must have had a concrete constitution to survive in the same house. So, on reflection, my own baby would not have healed the rift."

"We need a holiday. I am exhausted."

"I said that weeks ago. You were not listening. You were a million miles away in thought. I said 'Your dad . . .'." But he had slipped into slumber. Aggrieved, she shook him.

"You were saying about my dad before I nodded off?"

"He's trying to arrange a holiday for everybody."

"So late in the day? How come you know?"

Hunching her shoulders, she said, "I'm his favourite daughter-in-law, and privy to his secrets which he fails to share with his sons."

"That's a lie."

"OK. Though I have been on the project a shorter time than the others, he treats us all equally. He reckons that we are nearly finished, and so there is a brief holiday on the horizon, something to do with that shed he built in his garden. Anyway, we need a break if we are to survive the next year."

"Are we supposed to get our passports out, stand cramped together in the shed and have a party after pretending that it has flown us to a Pacific Island with gentle waving palm trees, glistening seas and exotic food?"

"I credit your dad with more intelligence than that."

"So why did you not accept what he said about your pregnancies?"

"You're rude," she said as she lay down with a thud, making the mattress bounce, then rolled over, presenting her back to him, "and insensitive to my desire for motherhood. I've waited in vain for ten years."

Sleep still evaded her, so he had another shaking. "Who drew the short straw for tomorrow's guard duty?"

"I thought you were not talking to me, Patricia."

"I'm not. I am only asking a question."

"If I were not a loving husband, I would refuse to answer you since you turned your back on me. As I am a loving husband, I will tell you the answer, 'Junior'."

"Thank goodness," she said. "At least we can celebrate our last anniversary in this world without this hassle."

"Unless anything goes wrong tonight."

"Goodnight."

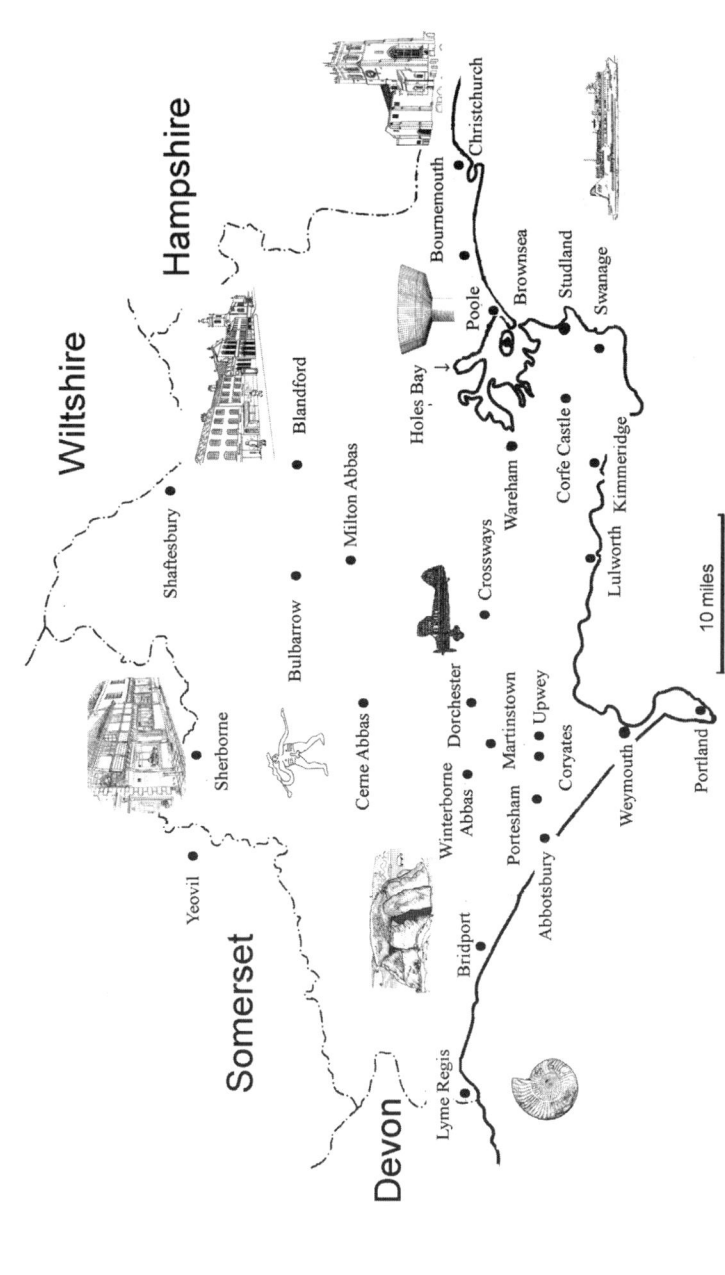

CHAPTER FOUR

A VERY WET MONDAY
"the floodgates of heaven were opened", Gen 7 v 11

"Boo!" said a voice behind me, startling me out of my wits.

First the milkman's clatter of bottles had jarred my dreamless sleep. Then the 6am alarm call had shattered any illusions of drifting back into slumber. I had hauled myself out of bed and climbed into the loft for those books I had thought about last night. Diligence in my student days had made me mark pages with red biro where things did not make sense and further investigation was necessary. So by flicking through the books, I could easily spot issues to challenge my mystery visitors with. Whether any of them would come back was a different matter. Doorstep salesmen could usually be stumped with awkward questions about their wares. They'd tell you that they did not know the answer and offer to come back tomorrow. You'd wait all day in vain.

From the marked pages, I'd written down questions that I hoped would stump this Mr Noah-ben-Lamech. I had many doubts about the story of anybody's ark. Experts agree that they are legends because the dates are not given and the background history is schizophrenic. Even if you know nothing about archaeology, challenge its proponents about the details and the answers are vague. Which adult had not come to a similar conclusion?

The school project was easy. The cardboard ark could be completed in two afternoons, and the tiniest hands could lift the animals in. And they did not need real food, or the stalls cleaning out, or bits sawing off doorways so that the giraffes could enter. If the Bible story were real, how had Noah coped with these practical issues?

So intent was I on writing that I had not heard the children creep down the stairs until it was too late.

Anne, typical for her, laughed the loudest at my reaction to her 'boo'.

Tommy said, "Why have you not gone to work today, Daddy?"

"I have a few days off."

"But we have to go to school," he protested.

"I know; you have to finish your ark."

"Oh yes. I wonder if the glue is dry on my zebra."

"I'm sure it is." The weightier questions on my mind were not worrying him.

"Are you going to mend the garden today, Daddy? Mummy says it's awful."

"I'm going to Weymouth to meet a special man."

"What's his name?"

"It's . . ."

"It's a secret," said Ben.

"Yes, it's a secret," I said. Isn't it marvellous how a five year old can get you out of an impasse? His remark saved me telling his siblings the truth that my mind was unsettled. Until last night, I had never thought seriously about time travel. If historical figures could visit me from the past to clarify mysteries about what happened, that would be super. Even better would be going back in time to be an eyewitness of those events. Let me pick AD43. I'd be famous as the news headlines rolled off the presses – '**Local historian recaptures excitement as Roman soldiers land in Holes Bay, Poole**'. My day-dreaming ended abruptly when I realised the risk of getting hurt or killed by a stray arrow shot by the warring factions if I had gone to watch that battle.

As Gaynor stooped to kiss me before she took the children off to school, she asked, "When will you be back?"

"By 11am, if he's not there. Otherwise late afternoon."

"If he is not there I bet you will go off golfing. The clatter you made this morning tells me that you had mixed motives for going into the loft, searching for golf clubs as well as those books. You have a bit of 'Jekyll and Hyde' about you, unpredictable. Sort out the estate agent's letter." She paused. "One more thing!"

I looked up, expecting a lecture.

"Get some new plants if he is not there."

"Who pays?"

"Bills are your responsibility."

Weymouth is a seaside town, and had been a port for as long as records had been kept. In summer, the ferries ply to France and the Channel Islands. Had you dropped in on Weymouth 200 years ago you would have seen a hive of ship-building activity. The rising popularity of sea bathing and the patronage of King George III convinced the ship builders that there was more money to be made in building hotels, shops and amusement arcades than ships on the Esplanade.

In honour of the new ambience he had brought to Weymouth, a statue of the King was erected on the Esplanade and a figure of him on horseback cut into the hillside overlooking the bay. Occasionally, a restored bathing machine, such as was used by the King, is brought out of winter storage and placed by the statue.

The Memorial Clock Tower, the centrepiece of Weymouth's Esplanade, is where I met Noah.

He had difficulty squeezing his seven-foot frame into my Cortina. As he swung his legs in, I could not help but notice his feet, which I had not done last night. He was wearing the biggest pair of shoes – 15s?

Trying not to be intimidated by his bulk, I said, "Noah, I have been trying to work out whether you are a time traveller, a confidence trickster, or a bully waiting to get me alone in a quiet spot and rob me. I plumbed for a confidence trickster because time travel is fictional."

A bathing machine, like the type used by King George III is sometimes placed for show on Weymouth Esplanade, under his statue. George III first bathed July 8th, 1789. His band also went into the water, but they were fully clothed.

"I was hoping you would say that I was an unemployed carpenter, who has travelled from a previous century, whilst awaiting a new challenge. Confidence trickster? No. They do not have split nails and calloused hands."

"Supposing, for a few minutes only, I accept your story and that you have packed your best clothes and navy-blue captain's uniform, with its epaulettes and insignia, on board this ark ready for your new occupation next week. Why come to 20th century Dorset to unwind?"

"That's a bit of flannel about having a captain's uniform for next week, Frank. Do you flannel other people in your brochures and guides telling people how good Dorset is, and encouraging them to come here when you are not impressed yourself?"

"I want them to come and set up businesses, make light industry tick once more after the decline. Imagine the hustle and bustle of ship building in Weymouth's heyday. You are talking about tourism, which is not on my agenda. We are a third-rate seaside town and it will hardly change because our beaches, unlike Bournemouth, do not all face south."

"Does that mean you do not like Dorset? I want to enjoy it for its own sake."

"Dorset is a place to live in, and there my affection ends. Look at the tackiness of the Esplanade now. But you are still dodging my question. You might know something attractive about Dorset to add to the next edition of my guides."

"I will explain if you tell me where you are going on holiday."

"Gaynor and I went to Spain for our honeymoon and appreciated its dryness so much that we go there every year now."

"Frank, this thing called 'rain' is a mystery to me. I have a shower everyday, and that gives me an inkling of what 'rain' might be like, but I have never seen water falling from the sky. It must be a million times more intense than what my shower sprays onto my body. Nor have I ever seen a puddle form on the roadway, let alone a lake grow during flooding."

"You'll not see any rain today or tomorrow – there is high pressure over the Azores."

"Oh, that is a shame. I will have to be content with visiting places where exceptional amounts of 'rain' fell, and see how they coped with the flooding."

"Noah, your wrinkles tell me you must be 60-65. How can you say you have never seen rain?"

"I read that your modern Sahara and other deserts get less rain than Spain. So what is so unusual about us never having any?"

"Do you come from a desert area?"

"The two of us live in worlds that are as poles apart. I have never seen a desert. All around our towns green grass grows without rain ever falling."

"No gardener or farmer will believe that! Why should I?"

"It is hard for me to explain the reason why. Equally, it is hard for me to understand your world where it rains. The only inkling that a *mabbul* of 'rain', 'storms' and 'flood' was on the way was through our dreams. We were privileged to have those dreams, but that baffled look of yours tells me that you are still missing the plot."

I nodded. "And you didn't call your dreams a privilege – more like marching orders with a knife in your back to make certain you obeyed orders."

"For ages I resisted the idea that dreams could be prophetic. Through them we knew that this cataclysm will eventually come to the whole of our world, destroying everything. I discovered that this part of Dorset has a special association with 'rain', and that is why I want to explore it, feel it, touch it, and then tell the others back in my world."

A peep of a horn behind me told me that I was blocking the road, and needed to get moving. Noah asked me if I would take him on what he wanted to call the 'seven-to-eleven tour'. Bowleaze Cove, a couple of miles eastward would be the first stop. To me it was a non-descript caravan park for low-cost holidays.

"But it has a history that you seem unaware of," he insisted. "Let me digress. I came to Dorset almost by accident. Once here, I went into the library where your tourist literature showed Dorset in splendid light."

"As a local, I'm biased. I see the western counties of Devon and Cornwall as more interesting places."

"Maybe so, but last night I realised that you might be able to help me to enjoy Dorset and I could help you to appreciate it in a fresh way. Nothing to do with your work."

"Then tell me why you gave me the litany of 'rain, rain, and rain'?"

"I wanted to see the world after the *mabbul* when the ark had served its purpose. That would give me confidence that building it had not been in vain. So I needed to see whether 'rain' had fallen, the damage, and how the world had recovered. Now you know more about your modern history than I have time to read about, but when I got here two days ago, I did discover something that you appear not to know. There was a hard winter in 1955, when Britain saw more snow than usual."

"I remember the harsh winter of 1963, but any further back my memory is vague."

"However, the summer of 1955 made up for the bad winter. There were long periods of sunshine and dry weather."

Gaynor and I would always take our holidays in this country if we could guarantee dry weather for a week, though the downside is the need to water the garden daily. Airports are a hassle with children. Last year we hit a low spot. Air traffic controllers had worked to rule the day we set off and we were delayed for 14 hours. We'd told the children stories for half an hour, and then used our free meal vouchers. That left 13 hours to agonise over.

"I am sorry about that," said Noah. "Perhaps better luck this year? In 1955 few people went to Spain, but plenty came to Weymouth, especially during the school holidays. Early holidaymakers had had better weather than those in Spain. There was space on the beach for their daily ration of sun and calamine lotion from the chemist to soothe skin irritated by any accidental sunburn. If you did not go home from your holiday brown as a berry, you could not boast to your neighbours that you had had a holiday."

"Gaynor insists that our children acclimatise slowly to the sun. Half an hour extra per day."

"Local people were desperate for a drop of rain to quench their parched gardens. One inch of rain had fallen in Blandford in 15 minutes but gardeners were angry because that deluge washed the good soil away and rutted roads. A few days later, 2½ inches fell in an hour at Shaftesbury causing worse damage."

"Were Weymouth holiday makers worried? These 'rare' amounts of rain would be in the local papers and the Shaftesbury downpour dramatic enough to have made national headlines."

"Only a few holiday makers bought papers and that was to find out what shows were being performed at the Pavilion theatre, Frank."

"So they didn't know, or care about the weather in Dorset, as long as it was not affecting Weymouth?"

"The rain in towns 35 miles was too far away to affect them, so why bother with that news? For these early holiday makers sober thoughts, that it was nearly time to pack and go home, were their immediate concern. Larger numbers of people would be invading the town the following week. Room on the beach and promenade would then be at a premium. Their suntan had been obtained, and inside their Kodak Brownie cameras were rolls of exposed black and white film that would be developed and printed once they got home."

"I spotted my old Brownie in the loft this morning. But why you are finding our local history interesting?"

"I can see that human nature has not changed. When I told my neighbour that it was going to 'rain', he said that if it 'rained' in our town, there would always be a dry place to escape to."

"He is right. There is always somewhere dry within a few miles of the worst storm."

"Then let me finish the story of summer 1955. School holidays were due to begin. Last full week of July, same as now. So Weymouth, with a plethora of special holiday trains disgorging their passengers, would find its population swollen. Local children were getting their home-made barrows out of sheds where they had languished for the last 11 months, cleaning them up, and oiling the wheels."

I remembered that story. Children waiting at the railway station for those holiday specials to arrive from London, the Midlands and South Wales, bundling luggage on their barrows and leading the holiday makers from the station to their hotels. The fee was six pence. There were few cars to dodge as they made their way to the main hotels on the Esplanade or the cheaper ones in the back streets.

Then plucking notebooks and pencils from their pocket, these children would remind the visitors of the times of trains to go home on and offer to take them back to the station at the end of their holiday. That would be another sixpence. If the holiday had been good, they might get an extra shilling.

That chapter in Weymouth's life had closed for ever. Though a diesel train service to Waterloo had replaced the soot and smoke of the steam engines, I blamed the car. People jump in their motors, and before you know it they have passed through Dorset and landed in Devon and Cornwall. That is why I had special responsibility to encourage light industry in the area to make up for the loss of the tourist trade.

"No one can stop change," Noah told me. "Nor can we always anticipate it. Look, the warmth and the sun lulled those early holidaymakers of 1955 into a false sense of security. No one imagined that within a couple of days, one of your villages would be catapulted into the record books. Disruption and destruction would sweep across a swathe of West Dorset, including Weymouth. It was rain worse than Shaftesbury."

My study of history had concentrated on the 19th- and early 20th-century revolutions in farming, population movements. And although I'd lived in Dorset since graduation, I'd not heard local people mention this tragedy.

"In my lifetime," Noah reminded me, "I have never seen rain. The yarn that Anne told you where the animals arrive at the ark ringing wet and trampling mud on the carpets inside is a million miles from what we expect. Convincing the people who lived around us that there was going to be a flood was impossible because nobody had seen 'rain' or a flood."

"So do they not know about the 'Epic of Gilgamesh', which describes both?"

"I knew nothing of Gilgamesh or the other character that Gaynor called 'Unhappy Tim' until last night. If this story had existed in my day, would my neighbours have believed it? You don't!"

"My limited experience of carpentry tells me that no one can build 'Unhappy Tim's' mammoth ark in two days. Nor can you steer it using punting poles, even with your bulging biceps. The story shouts 'legend' from prow to stern."

"So the Epic was a legend, possibly a corruption of a real story. History easily gets distorted." He paused, knowing that I could only agree. "Any more questions?"

"I'm suspicious of you because you deny ever having seen rain fall from the sky."

"But I know how bad rain can be for you 20th century people. And it is going to be worse for us. I cannot take you back there but I can tell you what I read about 1955. Monday, 18th July was disaster day. It started off cloudy, but by mid afternoon a thunderstorm settled on Weymouth, deluging it for four hours. At teatime things slowed up, but by evening the storm found fresh vigour.

By midnight, the clouds had donated seven inches of rain onto Weymouth's pavements and people alike.

"I have made it sound like a charity collection, but I am sure that no town council would appeal for record amounts of rain in the holiday season creating havoc! A light shower would have met the gardener's needs, but not this. Lakes appeared everywhere. The worst damage was where the rain water channelled into a small area, such as Bowleaze Cove. That is why I have asked you to drive me here. The river Jordan was turned into a raging torrent, destroying two bridges and sweeping caravans onto the beach. All 300 holidaymakers had to be evacuated while caravans were recovered, dried out and cleaned up. That is hardly the holiday of a lifetime."

As we gazed at the caravan park, it was obvious that it had been redeveloped since 1955. The river Jordan hardly justified the title of 'river'. It was so stagnant that an ice-lolly stick that someone had carelessly tossed into mid-stream remained stationary whilst we were there. Two men were fishing on the beach, but their aim was to pull fish out of the water, not caravans. I tried to imagine the scene of 1955, but I could not. Noah suggested that I go into the public library and look at newspaper photographs from that date. I put a 'to do' note in my diary for next week.

Other Dorset caravan parks had suffered, but not as much as Bowleaze. Bridport received a dramatic five inches of rain but the caravans there stayed put because the water level rose gently. With a touch of humour, the camp supervisor borrowed a rowing boat to check that the occupants of the marooned caravans were all right rather than get his feet wet. People living near St Swithin's Road walked on the garden walls to save themselves from the mud and mired lawns.

"I think I would rather your zebra spoil my lawn," I told Noah, "than be inundated with flood-water. It gets indoors, shrinks carpets, stains the walls, and ruins electrical goods."

"It is not easy to clean up after five to seven inches of rain. How is the world going to cope with the amounts of rain that I have been warned to expect?"

"But why, Noah, if you are time traveller, didn't you go to 1955 to see it for real?"

"Until I went into your library yesterday I did not know of this tragedy. Whilst the characters in H G Wells' story had control of their time travel machine, I do not."

"So how did you get here?"

"One day I will tell you. For the moment let us drive further into the eye of the storm. In Upwey they did not get seven inches of rain, but nine. Everybody was caught off guard including the owner of a local rain gauge who realised too late that it had overflowed after recording nine inches. Scientists reckon that Upwey had at least ten inches dumped on it.

"There were no caravans here to be swept away like at Bowleaze Cove. This time it was cars and an unfortunate 11-year-old boy that were swept away by a four-foot mass of water. There could have been more fatalities. I am now beginning to understand what our *mabbul* is likely to bring." Noah paused. "What are you thinking?"

"The scene today seems so idyllic, with the branches of the trees hanging over the road shielding us from the sun's rays, and the river running by. I cannot imagine the violence of that day. I feel sorry for the bereaved."

Upwey is the spring head for the river Wey. It had been a popular spot in the days when George III used visit it on horseback when staying in Weymouth. He drank water from the spring, and wished as he threw the remaining water over his shoulder. The cup he used is now presented at Ascot.

To capture a bigger tourist trade, a railway station was constructed within walking distance and the area renamed The Wishing Well. That was in Weymouth's heyday. Now it hardly throbbed with life, but it did let me muse about the damage that Noah had described whilst we sipped a coffee in the adjacent café. Finally, Noah brought me to my senses. Time to move north.

The road wound slowly up the valley. At the top on the ridge of hills I stopped the car where the inland section of the Dorset

Coastal Path crosses the road. It sounded like a contradiction in terms and so I explained its origin.

"The coastal path is fully coastal, but this alternative path is a sop to walkers. They don't want to traipse around the urban parts of Weymouth and its tacky Esplanade."

"You are sticking your knives into Weymouth today."

"Walkers don't bring much money into the county, just muddy boots. And with this optional footpath, they avoid the town where they might spend money."

"I can see your dilemma. Sure, the shop-keepers get a raw deal because serious walkers like to admire views, not be jostled in crowded shops on dull esplanades. This view is breathtaking because of its beauty. You will have to tell me, a newcomer, what the landmarks are."

To the South there was Portland, famous for its stone quarrying industry and a prison. Across to the North was Maiden Castle, an elongated mound with ramparts, beloved by archaeologists. By letting our eye follow the coastal path westward we could see Admiral Hardy's monument. Alongside that path were circular mounds of earth 20 to 30 feet in width – ancient barrows and tumuli, burial places, from the Stone Age or what is technically known as the Neolithic Period. They range from four to ten thousand years in age. Noah said he had never seen any before so it gave us chance to talk about the supposed time he had travelled from.

The Hardy monument, near Martinstown, is flanked by hemispherical mounds ('Neolithic Barrows'). Frank and Noah differed about their antiquity.

"My family records go back 1,600 years, Frank. Thereon my knowledge ends, except that your newspapers tell me that I am in AD 1970 now."

"Surely you know how many centuries you have come forward? H G Wells had a dial in his time-travelling shed whose pointer told him what year it was."

"Sorry, no. But I am certain that these barrows were made after my time. There was nothing like this in my world. If there had been, they would have been washed away in the flood."

"Even 500 feet up like we are now?"

"We were warned in our dreams that the flood-water would cover all high ground, otherwise, why build an ark? Just nip up the hill like we are now. I guess that the people who dug these barrows were descendants of my middle son, Ham. You were so anxious to get rid of that zebra that I could not introduce you last night."

"I was scared. Zebras in zoos are one thing. Zebras and domestic gardens do not go together."

"Am I pardoned, Frank?"

"When I get some replacement plants. And even if you have managed to travel across the barrier of time, then it must be at least from ten thousand years ago, because you have never seen barrows. That rules you out as the Biblical Noah. I'm confused!"

"There was a copy of the Bible in the library, but as it had 1,200 pages, I put it back on the shelf, intending to dip into it another day."

Although critical of the Bible, I explained that it was a chronicle of Jewish history in 66 shorter books. The first book, Genesis, mentioned a man called Noah who built an ark. Archbishop Ussher added up the dates in the Bible and came to the conclusion that this Noah's flood was 4,300 years ago. That was long after most of the barrows were made, and allowed me to rule my passenger out as the Biblical Noah dumped in 1970 by time travel. Even more damning, those dates ripped apart any residual ideas that stories of floods in the Bible or the 'Epic of Gilgamesh' were anything but legends. To add insult to injury to many religious folk,

Adam and Eve supposedly lived six thousand years ago. Our ten thousand year old barrows killed that story, and much of the other stuff in Genesis, dead.

True, there were no written dated records. We know that the Roman invasion occurred in AD43 in Holes Bay because they kept calendars for over 100 years before they came to Dorset. To go further back in time before written records, archaeologists use radio-carbon dating, thermo-luminescence, and other modern techniques on their finds of bones, pottery and flints.

"I have never heard of these techniques," Noah told me. "But I did spot a book in the library that challenges your answer. Give me time to read it and then I can join the debate properly."

"Even if you are then able to convince me that the barrows are younger than I believe, that will not confirm you as the Biblical Noah. So my mind is still churning over the question – 'are you a modern-day charlatan, or a prehistoric Noah?'"

"When *Doctor Who* went travelling in his police-box thingy people did not keep asking where he had come from. Do you think that you could give me the benefit of the doubt for the moment?"

"The *Doctor Who* stories are pure fiction. How about taking me back to see your ark? That'd convince me."

"If I had permission to take you back to my century, would you stay around to see the flood and help clean out the cow stalls?"

Noah had touched a raw spot in my thinking. Once the rain started, I'd want to come back promptly on the excuse that I needed to earn my living in Dorset with a dry office job.

"Then you would miss the drama," Noah pointed out. "But why can you not believe it without seeing it? You have not seen any evidence of Dorset's storm damage, nor can you travel back in time to see the masses of clouds as they unfolded that disastrous Monday. Yet you believe it happened!"

"You said it was recorded in the newspapers, with photographs. Historians know that, unless reporters are biased, they can trust what they read about the past. Your evidence is like straws in the wind – just old clothes covered in sawdust, and a zebra. I want a full dossier of evidence. As for the 1955 event, there must be many people around who can confirm it."

"I did not mean to bring a zebra. You agree that they are not regular visitors to kitchen gardens, but that should have convinced you that at least half my story is correct. I have built an ark in anticipation that it will rain back in my home century, but at the moment the ark sits there in a dry place. Our neighbours see it as a monument to folly and their view will only change when the rain and flood come."

"You might have used a pantomime outfit for the zebra."

"Was the damage to your garden an optical illusion or real, and did our actors devour your begonias?" asked Noah.

I didn't answer him.

"In which case, turn left into Martinstown."

"That little village! Unimportant."

"Nothing in your guide?"

"The residents would be unhappy to have factories belching out smoke and smell on their doorsteps."

Entering Martinstown, Noah pointed to the house, where in 1955, the occupant had kept a rain gauge that recorded an unimaginable 11 inches of rain during the storm, creating a new British record. It beggared belief that it all fell in six hours. The town that had held the previous UK record for the most rain was Bruton in Somerset with ten inches on 28th June 1917. Dorset had snatched the record from a neighbouring county.

"Sounds more like Dorset got a booby prize than a trophy," I told Noah. "I'm sure we would rather it had not happened here. It's not easy getting people interested in Dorset when they know it is wet, roads flood and lives are lost. Telling people I go to Spain for my holidays was bad enough."

"But it makes the county more interesting than Somerset. You can now tell people about the 'seven-to-eleven tour'. Encourage tourism!"

"Although it is nothing like the Gulf of Mexico, summer storms happen in southern England that spoil a day out. That's one of the reasons why we holiday in Spain. Eleven inches of rain was exceptional and I'm glad I was not around then. Nor do I think we want to be reminded of it. But how do we explain the rain that Monday? Think about the legend of St Swithin. It was dry on 15th July so we should not have had any rain for 40 days, let alone record amounts."

"You live in modern times with clever scientists, but they could not explain why that storm stuck over this local part of Dorset instead of moving to the east and shedding some of its load there that day."

"So we have the 1955 deluge, substantiated by newspaper photographs, but no explanations. How about showing me photographs of the ark to convince me of what you have done?"

"Sorry, cameras have not been invented in our world. However, I do have other family witnesses whom I can call on."

"You could be in this subterfuge together, and your flood has not yet come. You admit it might be a non-event, so let's stick to Martinstown."

"Cut off for days by the waters, Frank. The stream swelled, and spewed over the road making it look like a river, grinding traffic to a halt. It would have been worse and engulfed the houses if the ground had not been dry and porous allowing some of the water to soak away like butter on hot toast rather than make the flooding worse. Toast reminds me – I am hungry."

The door of the pub was open so we entered. As Noah wanted to try a Dorset speciality, we ordered Admiral Hardy's Old English Lamb, a dish that the Admiral loved. His monument was only a few miles to the west of us, on the hills overlooking the coastline and the harbour from which he had often sailed into battle to save the realm. Noah sampled one of Dorset's fine ales, but I had a soft drink.

Thinking about the name "Hardy", I could see a similarity between Thomas Hardy the writer and this man sitting opposite me. Both started life as architects. Both were good at spinning stories. I could imagine 'Noah' becoming a writer of fiction. It wouldn't matter whether he had invented the story about the ark or time travel. Nor, if he were the Biblical Noah, would it matter if the flood never came and he had wasted so much energy building the ark. Even failed men can write memoirs full of fabrications that allow them to sell thousands of copies. I reckoned that that is how the legend was born that crept into the Bible. Feeling a bit aggressive, I told him so.

"The ark is real," he retorted, "and from what I have read in your library I am now convinced that 'rain' falling from the sky will become a regular feature of life for people everywhere. Though the flooding was bad in 1955, it nowhere matches up to the staggering global flood, our *mabbul*, that we expect.

"If I have got the message about a global flood wrong, I might have to get a job writing fiction to earn my living because of this misadventure. But if the rains and floods come, I might feel more like Admiral Hardy. He went to sea at the tender age of 12, raw in experience. Either way I am split down the middle because I am not a natural writer any more than I am a natural seafarer. I have not got a captain's uniform to put on. Perhaps I ought to come back afterwards and get you to write the story."

"Hmm, you'll have to give me more to go on than that if I'm to write anything credible. A book entitled *Noah Builds Ark but Rains Fail to Materialise* won't find many readers. And how much money did you waste?"

"You are rubbing it in. If I weren't relaxing for a few days trying to forget about things that can go wrong and how much we have spent, depression would set in."

"Sorry. I didn't mean to be hard."

"Oh, yes you did," he said as his voice rose in pitch. "You are interrogating me with an unending stream of questions as if I am a murder suspect. And then you suddenly switch to being gentle and condescending."

"That is how barristers do it in court. They ply you with loads of hard questions, which you have to dig deep in your mind to answer. Then they give you an easy one, which only needs a 'yay', or ' nay'.

The sudden switch puts you off your guard, and out comes the truth. Any hesitation in answering exposes you as a liar."

"My answers have been consistent. I can add a sworn affidavit on the Bible if you want."

"No point. It didn't exist in your day if you are from the era of pre-history. Let's go back to the Hardys; how do you compare yourself with them?"

"There is an unbridgeable gulf between myself and Hardy the writer. I have kept up the tradition that was started at the beginning of the world of sacrificing a lamb on the altar each Saturday in worship, and confessing our sins. No one else bothers. Nor did Hardy judging from what Lawrence of Arabia said. He regretted the use of Christian rites at Hardy's funeral. Hardy was an enemy of faith, not one of the faithful. For the deans and canons to refer to Hardy as a 'Brother' was telling lies. That funeral was a mockery to God."

"There would have been an uproar if the clergy had described Hardy as an atheist during that service, thereby consigned to hell."

"Frank, what may have been going through the mind of Lawrence when he made these remarks was the fact that Hardy's testimony to atheism was diluted by having that Christian liturgy said over his corpse. Both of them were promoting atheism. To them there was no purpose in the world, or if there was, it was so vague that they had missed it."

Noah had at last revealed that he was religious – perhaps a Seventh Day Adventist or something to worship on a Saturday. Gaynor insisted that we got married in church and had the children baptised. There my affinity with the CoE ended. As for Hardy, the testimony of the millions of his readers is that he was a brilliant author. Noah would have a riot on his hands if those in his literary circle heard his comments. Those were the supporters who wanted him buried with full church rites.

"How can I follow any kind of religion that you are familiar with? We do not have a Bible."

"Wisdom doesn't depend on religion. Everyday experiences had showed them that religion does not have the answers to life they wanted. Through omens, which any of us can have, the two of them had insight into the future. They were not drifters in a lost world needing the help of the church to find salvation."

"Surely you do not agree with everything they said, otherwise you would never go to church?"

"A bit of the Christian religion helps life along; but that is all I want. I can live comfortably between the two extremes. Any more and I would be accused of being a fundamentalist."

"Frank, when Hardy and Lawrence met their mutual friend, Watkins, at Max Gate, Dorchester, they claimed that they knew he would die that night because the dog behaved strangely. That could have been coincidence, not a tip-off by an omen. The guy was unwell. And no omen stopped Lawrence, in the prime of life, having a fatal accident on his motorbike."

"Until your flood comes I can't be certain that you've glimpsed the future correctly, religion or no religion."

"Hardy and Lawrence's claim to be atheists was inconsistent. They had a god, though they called him 'the angel of death'. Who was the creator that gave them life?"

Noah realised that I was not going to answer his pointed question. To save me embarrassment, he asked the barman if he had lived in the area long.

"In 1955," he said, "I lived in nearby Winterborne Abbas. Although no one had a rain gauge, the pattern of rainfall led the weather experts to declare that 12 inches had fallen there, but without the gauge we could not claim the record."

"You missed a trick, barman," Noah told him.

"But what village wants to be known as the wettest place in England?"

"I take your point."

"I used to come to Martinstown on my bike to see my friend. My wife and I decided to move here when we got married because the heavy traffic that thunders through Winterborne ruins life."

Anxious to understand the demographics of Dorset, I asked the barman "Would you go back there if they built a by-pass?"

"By-passes are rare in Dorset."

I had to agree with him. Most towns and villages that need bypasses in Dorset have hills and vales around them that are not the right shape for bypasses. Long detours would be needed, or excessive earthworks. Dorchester is high on the list for a by-pass, but it will be years before we get it. If the government would pay for them they would boost industry.

Noah continued his conversation with the barman, "Where were you Monday 18th?"

"I'd got home from school as the worst of the rain started. Mum insisted that I stay in. From the kitchen window we watched puddles in the garden grow into a lake and then cascade down the road. Later I heard about that boy at Upwey, so my grounding may have saved me."

Noah turned to me. "There's your first witness to the event." And then to the barman, "Did you take any photographs?"

"No camera. If we had one, was the scene worth taking? Now if we had lived in Coryates . . ."

"What do you mean?"

"I've got a few photographs of it taken by someone else. They show the vicious scouring at Coryates, though it has now been repaired. You can still get an impression of the damage by walking up the gully to the north. It was in that field that the rain water collected and then funnelled ten million gallons of water down the narrow road into the village tearing out the tarmac and gravel, almost undermining the houses and cottages."

With the meal over, Noah persuaded me to visit Coryates. "After this I must depart and check back at the ark that there are no new problems before my sons stop work for the day."

"I thought you were on holiday. Time doesn't mean anything then."

"Nice thought, Frank, but I still need to be vigilant. Call it a commitment to the job."

"Then relax and enjoy the last half hour of our trip. At least I'm convinced of our rainfall record, however unattractive the result was. What to make of you is still my puzzle."

"Thanks, barrister."

We drove along the bottom of the ridge that separates the lowlands of Weymouth from the valley of Martinstown. To the south, the land rolled away towards Weymouth and Chesil Beach. These were outstanding views that I had not appreciated before, and in shame admitted that I was a tourist for 30 minutes rather than an unimpressed inhabitant of Dorset. Then I switched back to being a historian and tried for the second time to imagine how the land would have coped with the deluge of 1955. But the bigger difficulty was to think about the legends of arks and floods, and whether they were real.

Halfway along the road, a thought occurred to me as we passed the Friar Waddon pumping station, a long building of brownish bricks on the left, part of Wessex Water. We could have a discussion about fresh water. The pumping station takes water from the underground aquifer to supply the thirsts of Weymouth and Dorchester. I knew that the rocks beneath us are shaped like a bowl ten miles across and 300 feet deep. When it rains, the rain soaks into the porous earth and fills this bowl.

Pumping stations like the one at Friar Waddon draw water from the chalk aquifer beneath for domestic use. The water level is restored by regular rainfall. In Eden, before The Flood, rain is not mentioned.

"You are getting technical, all of a sudden, Frank. What is your motive?"

"At Friar they pump water out from the middle of this bowl for human use. The spring at Upwey is on the edge of the bowl, so the spring water runs out over a low lip at that point. Without regular rain topping up the level in the bowl, all the water will be drained away by the spring and pumping station. So, Mr ben-Lamech, if you have springs and rivers of fresh water in your land of long ago, you must have had regular rain, not perpetual drought. The contents of these bowl-shaped aquifers are not inexhaustible."

"You have stumped me, Frank. I do not know what keeps our springs and rivers flowing without rain. I will think about it tomorrow. Meanwhile, I am more concerned about getting Gaynor's begonias. Otherwise I will keep Ham waiting to take me home."

As Noah came out of the garden centre, he asked if he could come back tonight with Sarah and give the replacement plants to Gaynor. On the spur of the moment I said "Yes, and join us for our evening meal?"

"Sounds super. Will Gaynor mind?"

I hesitated. "Provided you wait until the children are in bed." I had no wish to confuse them at this stage with meeting Noah even if he came in clean clothes. Inwardly, I wondered whether Gaynor would appreciate cooking the meal when I had offered. I would have to placate her because my appetite for his story had been whetted whether he was charlatan or real.

"I'll wear better clothes tonight."

With that, he was gone.

CHAPTER FIVE

BARREN!

"you are no longer to call her (by her old name)", Gen 17 v 15

An owl hooted, startling Patricia. "What was that?" she said as she shook her husband awake.

"I heard nothing."

"No. You were fast asleep, snoring your head off."

"The bell over our bed has not rung, so there is nobody outside."

"I've known your gadgets to fail before."

"You are getting jittery. Look how carefully I set the whole apparatus up. No one could get near us without snagging the wire outside and thus ringing the bell. Think of something pleasant instead. Then these imaginary noises outside will go away."

"My first baby."

"At least another year away."

"Do you think I will get pregnant sooner if I change my name?"

"I will tell you in the morning," he said indignantly as he rolled over, presenting his back to her.

"I like the name 'Tricia'."

"I am asleep, Patricia."

"You're not otherwise you wouldn't have answered me."

Grumpily he replied, "What is wrong with 'Patricia'?"

"My mother gave it to me. It's part of my old life. I want something to signify a new start."

"OK, Tricia. But what will your mother make of the change or your father think of casting off the 'pa' part of your life?"

"That's an interesting play on parts of my name that I hadn't appreciated."

"Did you never affectionately call him 'Pa' or 'Papa' as a child?"

She shook her head. "The more I mull over the family history, the more convinced I am that Father and Mother thought alike. When I wanted Father's advice he'd always tell me to ask Mother. At first I thought he was hen-pecked, afraid to make decisions. In reality he was a cool customer and businessman who used Mother's temper to get what he wanted. If we have a holiday break for a few days I don't think that we will ever meet again. Pa gave me life, and for that I am grateful. I've told him how to avoid drowning next week and he's ignored me. That rejection of my warning will stick in my gullet for the rest of my life. God gave everyone free will to chose what to do and I cannot change them."

"That family breakdown helps me to understand why you have difficulty sleeping."

Sleep still did not come to her. She was bothered about not getting pregnant. Then she had another idea, and nudged her husband. "If changing my name does not work then I'll change your name as well."

"Do you not like my name, Tricia?"

"I almost had a fit of hysterics when the priest read out all your names that day we got married. Why didn't you warn me that you had four names?"

"I had no desire to change my name. No one has ever called me by anything other than my first name, and I am happy for that to continue, otherwise I will be confused."

"Who picked that string of names?"

"Mum liked one, Dad another. The others came from my maternal grandfather. Now go to sleep."

"I definitely think I ought to change your name as well."

"Why do you keep waking me up, Tricia?"

"It takes two to make a baby."

"I know that, but it is too uncomfortable here. I did suggest tomorrow night."

"It's not the right time of the month."

"You have not become pregnant even when we have made love at the right time in the month."

"I'm talking about your name."

"What does pregnancy have to do with my name?"

"You might have a low sperm count. A new name might boost your hormones."

"What a ridiculous suggestion. Remember what Dad . . ."

"Your dad might be right, but you could've had a test then to check."

"It would not help, Tricia. I know I'm fine!"

"OK. . . . I'm glad I didn't giggle during our wedding ceremony at that list of your names. I think Mother and Father would have walked out. They were only looking for the slightest excuse to create a scene in front of your family."

"I don't approve of shortened names like Ted or Mart so what is your plan?"

"I'll sleep on it."

"I am pleased about that. Maybe I can get some shut-eye at the same time."

"At least I'll try. You're so lucky. You seem to be able to sleep on sixpence stuck to a wavering branch on a tree. Goodnight again."

CHAPTER SIX

SALMON SPECIAL
"people were eating and drinking", Mat 24 v 38

As I opened the door, Gaynor called out, "You have invited them here for a meal!"

"How did you know?"

"Having lived with you for ten years I know that you normally push the door open with force. This time it was done gingerly."

"Did Anne say anything about the school ark when she came in?"

"For her the story is over, Frank. Their ark is complete with the rainbow dangling from the ceiling. Somehow I suspected that your enquiry has only just started."

Gaynor was right. Surprisingly, I enjoyed seeing Dorset in the shoes of a tourist rather than a local worker. And as for the flood of '55, it was amazing that there was little evidence of the damage now left. Noah used that incident to make me think seriously about Genesis.

There was a mystery about him that prevented us rejecting him as a charlatan, but we needed more convincing that he was the Biblical Noah. So we agreed a compact. She'd cook and I'd give the children their tea and put them to bed. Their bedtime story had to be a real one to save arguments about myths and legends. The final agreement was that neither of us would mention love and romantic dreams.

With the children tucked up, I did a rough sketch of the church at Martinstown, and marked the 36-foot height which is as much rain as would fall if the Martinstown downpour continued for 40 days. Noah might have difficulty explaining how that level of water could cover the world.

Noah and Sarah came at seven. He had abandoned his working clothes and wore a sports jacket, and a white shirt. "I had stowed these clothes away in the ark ready for after the flood, but decided to unpack them. Tonight is a special occasion," he said as he introduced us to his wife, who, though shorter than he was, was taller than me.

"And your outfit looks splendid," said Gaynor welcoming Sarah.

Handing over the begonias, Sarah explained that the dwarf one with the bronze and mahogany leaves was a "Devon Gem". She chuckled, "It was the closest we could get to Dorset." Then turning to me, whilst squeezing Noah's hand continued, "I'm most grateful to you for going out with my husband today. The break from working on the ark has taken years off him."

They both blushed, the red sharply contrasting the blue colour in her dress. It made guilt creep over me about that riposte with Noah earlier. Even if he had told Sarah about it, there was no feeling of animosity as she continued, "That mouth-watering smell from your kitchen has brought back memories of the times I regularly cooked for my family. Of late, we have hardly had time to grab a tomato sandwich let alone have a special meal."

"I hope you like my Dorset fare, though mostly straight from the freezer," said Gaynor, anxious to impress the guests with knowledge about her first freezer. "It makes such a difference to preparing meals at short notice. I suspected my husband would invite you here tonight."

While Noah sipped his drink, I revealed my sketch of the church with the waterline. He told me that the ark would float by then, though that depth of water would be too shallow to cover all land, or the tower 55 feet high. He reminded us that Ham's wife had seen most of the details of 'rain' and the flood in her dream.

This is what Martinstown church might look like if the record level of rain were to fall for 40 days. Only the top of the tower would be visible.

"One moment there would be water falling from the sky as if it had come out of giant shower heads, creating enormous lakes. The 'rain' would then ease off temporarily, but the lakes would not shrink and the rain would return a few hours later, enlarging the lakes until the whole earth was submerged. We struggle to believe that what she saw in her dream is possible because we have no experience of 'rain'. Seeing 'rain' for real might help us get over the shock that we expect next week. You are pleased with the dry weather, but we are disappointed that we have not seen rain in the three days we have been here."

"You've been lucky to have three dry days in a row. The weather is bound to break soon."

"Sarah and I look forward to the experience."

"If you've never seen rain, how did you convince your wife and family to join you in building an ark? All your family's dreams were different, and should it rain as ferociously as at Martinstown, but for 40 days, you have admitted that you could escape such a disaster by going up the hill and waiting until the water runs away into the sea. You'll get soaked for a while, but that's hardly a disaster."

Sarah smiled at both of us, and reminded us that the family badgered him into doing it because of the way seven dreams interlocked.

"Why did Ham not have a dream?" Gaynor asked her.

"I don't know, but seven out of a family of eight is a good score which you can't ignore, and none were your 'reinforcement-dreams'."

"My Frank might laugh at me saying this. You said that Ham's wife was forewarned of the rain and flood. It happens all the time. One of our Dorset writers was camping near Martinstown the night before that 1955 deluge. The place was oppressive, and she felt compelled to move to Somerset the next morning and so avoiding having her tent washed away. Women are good at intuition."

I was about to argue with my wife about intuition versus facts when Noah spoke a healing comment. "I doubt if intuition and dreams are the same. In our ancient world we believe that God communicates with us through dreams. Details are dispatched accurately to a single recipient. Intuition can be misleading."

"So you believe this other dreamer, whose name I can now pronounce without a falter, Utnapishtim, had a real adventure whilst obeying the call from the gods?"

"Having had time to reflect on the story, I do not believe that Utnapishtim was real. How could he have built that huge boat in two days even if the timber was already cut and shaped? We needed decades for a smaller ark."

"Both Gaynor and I believe that the 'Epic of Gilgamesh' is a legend."

"Although that story was a fabrication, I could not dismiss the trumpet call in our dreams to provide deliverance from the impending flood."

"I didn't notice that you had stripped like a runner for the starting blocks, ready for the gun to be fired," I said, pointing at Noah to emphasise how uncertain he had been. "There must have been one awful tussle in your mind before laying the keel."

"After our arguments that first morning, the three of us went off to work late, and tried to put the dreams out of our minds. Concentrating was impossible when God had called for such a dramatic change in our lives. Nothing went right that day. I got phone calls from Stephen and Dad, both agitated. That caused me to mislay some drawings. Then I started other drawings that should have been in cubits instead of feet."

"Gaynor and I are unsure of the difference between cubits and feet."

"Look at my arm, Frank. That is how you get the cubit. Elbow to the tip of middle finger when fully extended is 18 inches."

"But not all arms are the same length, surely?"

"We have an industrial standard definition, but it is not significantly different to the length of my arm. To continue, we agreed to meet together that evening at six. Ham called in at the take-away to save Sarah cooking. It was quite confusing for the poor fellow behind the counter because we all picked different foods, and the bags were mixed up."

Gaynor told us to go into the dining room, excused herself and went into the kitchen. There was a chink of pottery, and then came back bringing the soup.

"This is a cosy dining room," said Noah. "It reminds me of the occasion when we met together that evening after those forceful dreams. I had fixed the plans of the ark onto the walls of our dining room so that we could sit around the table with space for notebooks. I asked my family the 64 thousand dollar question – 'I understand the shape of the ark, the arrangement of the internal decks, the staircases, the ramps, the stalls, the storage rooms and our rooms, but do we build it? If we answer 'yes' who will take charge of carpentry?' They all knew that I was hopeless at it. Then, ashamedly I have to say, an agitated free-for-all broke out. I can picture it still.

"Jay had argued that we start the ark the next day. I almost exploded at this idea because of all the problems he had ignored – how could I, Noah, be in charge when I knew nothing about animals, their food, health and sanitation needs? How could the family keep sane, healthy and fed during the time we were building the ark and floating from here to nowhere when all the land had disappeared? Nor could I see many people offering to help on a project that would take decades to finish. And what about woodwork?

"Before I had chance to discuss my first question, my eldest son, Stephen and my father barged in with an answer to my second question – 'we will'. I asked them why they were so positive. They told me that in their dreams they had seen themselves doing exactly that. Everybody else nodded as if to say – 'They were born with hammers and saws in their hands.' Sarah offered to become the zookeeper, the role she had seen in her dreams, while Katrina would concentrate on the animals' food. This was not what she had seen in her dream. She had been shown a calendar that had all the important dates and milestones on it connected with the construction of the ark and the arrival of the animals. Irene would stock our pantry."

"If I've heard correctly, Irene and Katrina are your daughters-in-law. I thought the wives would have strange names like Adah or Zillah that I find in the Bible, not English ones. It makes me doubt you're the Biblical Noah."

"Local women had those names, but not our daughters-in-law."

"Now with them explaining their dreams, it sounds as if there was an immediate majority in favour of building the ark, though you still doubted, Noah."

"Yes. There was a pregnant pause in our conversation that day. I held the trump card and did not know how to play it. The ringing of the telephone shattered the silence and made me jump. Our meals were ready and Stephen slipped out to collect them. By the way, this is splendid soup, Gaynor."

Gaynor blushed. She had prepared cream of watercress soup. With the watercress beds being local, she could buy watercress from the booth by the road at any hour, day and night. And to top it all, she had also made the cream from hot milk and unsalted butter. But it was important not to get too diverted by culinary issues when it was the ark that intrigued me. So I invited Noah, who was sitting opposite me to answer the question, 'Were you pressurised into building the ark by the others or were you convinced by your own analysis?'

"There was a catalogue of issues to sort out before I would

agree to take on the mantle of building a floating zoo. If any of my family wanted to lead the project, they could have the drawings and get on with it."

"I understand your caution, Noah. But you've done it! Who gave you the money? An archaeologist, who went looking for the remains of the Biblical ark on Ararat, reckoned that it would take 80 years to build the ark."

"As we ate our meals, I was writing down our concerns as we voiced them. They were similar to yours, Frank and Gaynor, about time, money, resources, etc. We would be dead if it took 80 years to complete the ark. Then we brainstormed solutions for each concern and came up with ideas, but because some were vague I refused to say 'yes' that night."

"Did you have another dream that finally tipped the balance?"

"There were no 'reinforcement-dreams' that you seem to imagine is the answer to all legends. We slept soundly every night thereafter and were thus able to remain cool-headed, concentrating on the request and on our daily work. Two evenings later, Jay suggested that we re-mortgage our houses up to the hilt, use the money to buy the materials we needed, and hire workmen to speed the task."

"I thought that mortgaging was a modern idea. That suggests to me that you are a modern couple, and not from an ancient world. You're even dressed like my contemporaries with your cravat and jacket, take-aways, use telephones and speak with a BBC English accent."

Gaynor felt that I had overstepped the mark of politeness. "Don't be rude," she told me. Then turning to face the guests, she continued, "You both look very smart."

"Thank you," said Sarah.

By then, Gaynor was in full flow, "Frank! Dress fashions such as the A-line come and go through the years. The same is true of shoes. It's platform shoes one year, stilettos next, open backs next and then back to platforms."

"I don't remember any dresses or shoes in your wardrobe waiting for fashions to come a full circle."

Sarah broke the silence following that second faux pas of mine. "What we are wearing tonight is contemporary for us."

"I love that flower pattern on your dress," said Gaynor. "It's stunning with that gold necklace which gives everything a sparkle."

Finishing his soup, Noah turned to Gaynor and thanked her. Then he turned to me, "Frank, mortgaging and fashions are as old as the hills. Re-mortgaging was one way of testing the waters, if you will pardon the pun. All of us would be unemployed if we threw our lot in with the task. That would justify the building societies turning down our request for mortgages. As long as the flood came, there was nothing to lose because we would not need our houses once we floated away."

"That action sounds like 'putting a fleece out'."

Noah looked puzzled, so I recounted the story of Gideon, in the Bible, but supposedly long after his time. Gideon was told by an angel to lead the army into battle. Being a nervous farmer, a civvy, he'd rather hide from any marauders that came to steal their food and grain than fight them off. To check he had got God's message right, he put fleece out for two days running, calling on the angel to do the unorthodox. The fleece was wet on the dry day, and dry on the wet day. Thus convinced that the angel's visit was not a hallucination, he led a ragamuffin band of men to victory.

"An interesting drama, Frank. Now that I understand your phrase I can tell you that we did put this proverbial fleece out many times. One worry was pregnancies. Two of our sons had got married, and both families were anxious to have children because ages were creeping on."

"Or was it you wanting grandchildren?"

"You read me like a book, but there was a practical side as well. Having to cope with babies in the hubris of the project would have diverted energy away from the ark. Reluctantly, we asked the stork to stay away until the job was over, but without our children having to deny themselves their nuptial pleasures, or the girls reach menopause. Sorry that that is another pun because we expect to take two storks into the ark."

"I'm still struggling to think of you and your family living in the past. If you really are time travellers from the past . . ."

"We are, Frank, though we did not have H G Wells to help us."

". . . then lack of grandchildren sounds a bit risky. I don't want to be rude, but I guess you're both past child-bearing age. If your two married sons and their spouses are not fertile, the human race as you know it will disappear."

Sarah blushed.

"Don't be personal," snapped Gaynor. "You will be telling them about your snip operation next and how long you took to get over it."

It was my turn to blush.

"Please, I am not upset. Top priority has to be our safety during the next 12 months. After that, we hope that the animals will breed, and our children have families. If it does not happen, we have done our best. Absence of human babies on the ark could be a blessing. Exotic animals harbour salmonella which could pass to the babies in the confined space."

"Sorry for getting personal, but I've a dilemma. You might be modern folk from the neighbouring housing estate making fools of us, or you could be from the past. If I go for the most outrageous suggestion – that you are time travellers – issues about this downpour are still not cleared up properly."

"Frank, we have been given permission to travel from our present into our future. It feels uncanny to us, as we sit in your home in Dorset in the 20th century, that we are looking at a world that is real to you. However, if we were back in our own homes then neither you nor Gaynor would have been born. You are part of our future, our descendants."

"So what happened at the building society?"

"It was three weeks before I could get there, but other things were moving forward. Though Dad was retired, he was fit and started his part of the project straight away. His wife had died two years earlier, so he said it would give him a new focus in life. He took the plans away, and copied them, line by line. My three sons and Katrina also handed in their notices at work. They went through less agonising than I did, because if things went wrong, they were young enough to get new jobs. At my age, prospective employers condemn you to the shelf."

"They were pressurising you, Noah."

Breaking into a sweat he said, "That is why I was hesitant to tell you everything last night. One night, I could not sleep. No dreams, so do not ask me again. It was not the physical side of building the ark, though that was stressful enough, but the trauma of the floodwaters engulfing everything. If the ground had not been porous when seven inches of rain fell on Weymouth absorbing half of the water, 300 people might have been swept to their deaths in their caravans. How many people would be lost in a flood that lasted 40 times longer? Everyone not on the ark!"

"So that is *mabbul*, Noah?"

"As I lay there tossing and turning, I knew that I had to hand in my notice at work to confirm my commitment to the ark. My relationship with my boss had been stressful ever since that day of the dreams. He reminded me that I was under a contract that called for three months notice. He could extend it by one day for every day I did poor work, and without pay. A few days later he offered a compromise. If I could finish our current design project in the next two weeks, he would allow me time off to get our ark started. I would then have to work another month to complete a period of reduced notice.

"The boss was pleased with what I did and reminded me that he could not understand why I, as a valuable employee, could leave the firm to embark on a crazy project. Where else could he get someone else so conscientious to replace me?"

"Had you explained about your dreams, and why you were late that first morning?"

"It went in one of his ears and came out of the other without making synaptic connections as the words passed across his brain."

"What are synaptics?"

"The bits of your brain that help you to remember what has been said, and what your response should be."

"What did the manager at the building society think? Did you get a cheque or another blank stare as his synaptics did not work?"

"The receptionist sniggered when Sarah and I told her why we wanted to see the manager. However, he was a poker-faced individual, listening without batting an eyelid. He arranged the re-mortgaging but made it clear that neither he nor the building society were endorsing our belief that this thing called 'rain' would fall so intensely that an ark would be necessary for survival. Water could never rise high enough to cover every mountain. As far as he was concerned, our request for a mortgage was 'business as usual'. The fact that we would be unemployed was not important to him. The society had adequate security in the form of our houses as long as no insurance to cover defaulting on the payments was required."

"We had an impromptu party," interjected Sarah.

"Lack of insurance has been getting me edgy as our expected deluge approaches. If it does not rain we cannot get our money back. I learned long after that visit that when we had left the office, he admonished the receptionist for sniggering at our request. Her job, he said as he looked at her eye-ball to eye-ball, was to encourage business and not laugh at people's reasons, however crazy."

Noah painted a picture of the scene for me. "The receptionist had started to cry under her boss' intense gaze. 'But sir, what they are doing is crazy,' she managed to blurt out.

"Keeping a poker face, the boss said, 'If you think that their story is crazy then what about betting me a thousand shekels that this *mabbul* of a flood does not come and their houses have to be repossessed?'

"'I do not have that sort of money to give you if that flood comes.'

"He laughed. 'Then it sounds as if you believe Noah's prophecy. Why?'

"As a junior member of staff, their relationship had been strained. She would have left, but jobs were scarce, and now he had twisted her slow thoughts around his little finger by the subtlety of his argument.

"He waited a few seconds, and then broke into a smile. 'Really, I'm being unfair. Noah's reading of the future is ridiculous. I'm a big head and can read your mind just as easily as I can read the minds of the other staff here in my office. That is how I came to be manager here. I know that you do not always see eye to eye with me on business matters, but on this occasion we think alike. We will have great delight repossessing their houses soon, and surely you have noticed that those houses are worth more than the mortgage we agreed? Their value will continue to increase further. I'm organising a party tonight to celebrate. Bring your fiancé.'"

"Then this guy Noah turns up and wants to remortgage his house and use the money to build an ark. Says that the world is going to be flooded everywhere. We made such a nice profit out of him that I decided that we could throw a party."

"You weren't there, Noah, so how did you know about this dialogue?"

"Several years later people started bragging. Nothing could then be done about it. Eventually all five families visited their building societies and got mortgages, probably on low valuations. Those house valuations showed how shady commercial transactions pervaded the society we lived in. If people could make a fast shekel by being economical with the truth, they would do so."

"You also took a calculated risk in mortgaging your houses. If the rain and the flood come, the bailiffs will drown so you will have lost nothing. What if your flood does not come?"

"Then we have to live in the ark for the rest of our lives. Soon it will feel like a prison camp. Remember, the ark is not a caravan on wheels that can be moved. Right then we did not know where to build the ark, or if it would have any second-hand value if it all came to nought."

"With your money from the building societies now safely in your hands, did you rush out and order all the wood?"

"While I was still at work, Dad listed the quantity and type of timber needed. The money we raised from the re-mortgaging covered Dad's estimate of the cost with a bit spare. We took it as a confirmation that we were doing the right thing."

"Didn't you want other people to participate, help you with the work and provide company, Noah? It would also offer genetic variation for succeeding generations."

"Of course! As the enormity of what we had to do dawned on us, we spread the word that we wanted help. Most were like the building society manager, whose itch for extra profit was stronger that his itch for God. A few offered us money, miserly sums, given in an attempt to get us off their backs rather than because they felt that the world was doomed. For each person that gave 100 shekels we fixed a brass plaque inside the ark with their initials on. For larger subscriptions, we named an animal stall after the donor. As for full time helpers, most told us that they were too busy with daily life."

My mind flicked back to a photograph that I had seen of a Bedouin sitting in the doorway of his tent at the end of a day tending sheep, playing a one-stringed fiddle. No variety.

"That it not an image of us," said Noah. "We do not have televisions or cars, but in the daytime people will be on the farms, in the offices, schools, market places and shops. In the evening they will head home for a family meal, chatter, paint, and make music. Weekends it is football or the races. Our climate is amenable all through the year, so many have outdoor swimming pools if competitive sport does not enthral you. Life goes on as if everything is predictable and nothing will change."

"The in-thing for the rich is an outdoor pool heated by solar panels. But that does not work in winter in Dorset."

Gaynor interrupted the conversation to clear the dishes away, get the next course and ask about Cain's wife.

Noah replied, "Adam and Eve's sons and daughters married each other. Maybe that is a foreign concept for you in the 20th century, Gaynor?"

"Yes. One reason why people reject Genesis as real history," she said after remembering to fetch the remaining bowl of peas, "is because if people marry close relatives there is a risk of having genetically damaged offspring."

"But since Sarah and I know that God made a perfect Adam and Eve then there would be no genetic deterioration in their children or grandchildren. Deterioration would, however, eventually happen by mutation."

"I get your point," said Gaynor. "After all, I note that Abraham married his half-sister, and I believe that he was a real character, though that kind of close marriage is now forbidden."

"Going back to the construction of the ark, at last we were able to start the carpentry," said Noah. "Stephen's employer did not have the right timber and even if he had, the hassle of transporting the timber to the site ruled it out. We thought about buying a wood of about ten acres, and building the ark in the middle of it. This would minimise the transporting of trees around and also have meant that we could carry on living there if the flood did not come."

"So where is this wood?"

"We did not find one that met our needs."

"Your dream led you up the wrong track there."

"Not quite. As a result of our enquiries we found someone who would sell us timber directly from his forest."

"Your labour-saving idea didn't materialise if you're moving lots of timber around," I said aggressively.

"This forest was owned by a pleasant and trustworthy fellow. He allowed us to build the ark in his forest. Since he owned many forests, he knew that it would be difficult for anyone to find the ark even if they knew that it was being built on his acreage."

"Sounds as if he might have been a candidate to help in the building, but why were you bothered about people not finding the ark? At that size no one could steal it."

"Some of the people we had talked to before we started to build told us that they would rather die than see the ark completed. For protection, we fell in with this gentleman's idea. We could purchase the trees we needed directly from his forest at ten shekels each. That was a discounted price because he told us that other timber merchants would charge 20 shekels. Anyway, 20 shekels was beyond our budget."

"Sounds like a bargain. I'm glad you found cooperative and helpful people."

"Most of the time when we went to his office to discuss each timber order we only saw his wife. She seemed very efficient, always ready to help. When asked to join the ark, she relayed the message from her husband that they would join in the week that the animals arrive. In the meantime he needed to keep his business in top gear to stand the loss he was making on our timber because he was trading it at half cost. We made them a luxury suite of bedrooms in the ark to their design."

"Now, what about planning permission for the ark?"

"Non-existent. The owner of the forest told us that we could build anything we liked provided that it had no foundations and was not higher than the trees. To check, we paid a visit to the planning department."

"Did you not trust his word?"

"He was straight as a die. This visit to the council was an excuse to widen our contacts and seek other helpers. Our request for planning permission was like a bombshell to them. They argued for days over which forms we ought to fill in."

Trying to get planning permission for a bedroom over the garage for Ben had driven me to despair. I'd filled in our forms accurately, but our planning application was thrown out unceremoniously. '*Right to light for the neighbours, over-development and structurally unsound.*' You name it, and our council had found something in the rule book to object to. I had tried getting the expert opinion of a structural engineer, but it had not helped. Apparently, Noah had not thought about the strength of his ark to withstand the violence of the flood. The planning officer had not been able to help. Nobody had ever built anything so big, and even if they had, would not know how to launch it. Unsurprisingly, his planning officer thought that Noah's family were crazy in what they wanted to do, but after weeks of indecision suggested that provided they did not make any noise at night, weekends or local holidays, they could proceed. That was a first-class fudge.

"He and his staff did dodge the issue, Frank. To have said 'yes' would have meant that they recognised that a *mabbul* was approaching – something they did not want to do. By denying permission they knew that I would keep on appealing against their 'no'."

"Getting away without planning permission is unusual. Bureaucracy is rife here."

"What happens now that your house plans have been rejected?"

"We have been trying to sell up and move to a bigger house a few miles away."

"I am looking forward to it, after this cramped place," interjected Gaynor. "Did any one from the planning department want to join you?"

"No. We were building an ark; they were quietly smirking at us. One of the staff sent us a letter saying that the ark would break apart and sink when buffeted by the flood."

To me, building sites are fascinating places. The bigger the project, the better. I wondered if Noah had organised guided tours to encourage people to join.

"We thought about that idea, but God said 'No'. I have already told you that some might want to destroy the ark. Others would use the opportunity to ridicule us. Thus, driven by this need for security we cleared a site deep in the middle of this forest where we could build without too many people accidentally discovering the ark. It also kept the planning department happy since it was away from roads and houses. It is too much to risk at this late stage accidentally letting someone who has resolved to destroy the ark learning where it is."

"You could move it around. That'd fool them."

"You are being facetious, Frank. You have just reminded us how big the ark is. If we could find a low-loader big enough, it would block all six lanes of a motorway. This thing is meant to float, not travel by road. And there are no friendly rivers nearby."

"Seeing is believing. Will you to take me there tomorrow? I'm not at work, and surely you trust me?"

"Too many things can go wrong with time travel for you. I never did discover how the zebra got here."

"You're making excuses again. Suppose I believe that you are from the past, where is this forest? The Middle East, Dorset or what? And what will I find if I go there in today's time?"

"Those are all 64 thousand dollar questions. If a global flood really came, the ark will have floated away and everything at the old site washed away. Even if a flood did not come I doubt if you would find anything because the wooden ark would have rotted away. Then the site would have been built over, bulldozed, or whatever in the intervening years. You have evidence of disappearing sites on your doorstep. What few records existed would have been lost. Remember there was no planning permission."

I remembered that not far from Crossways, where we were trying to buy a house, there used to be a wartime airfield. Should enemy bombers try to attack our ships in Portland harbour, our fighters could scramble and be there in a few minutes. Nothing of the aeroplanes and buildings remain. The site served its purpose before becoming a sand and gravel quarry. Now it's a housing estate. At Moreton nearby, the Anglican Church has Spitfires and other war memorabilia engraved in the windows.

"Frank, I can tell you about another site that has since

disappeared. During World War 2 a thriving research establishment was created in Dorset. The scientists were requested to develop radar that outclassed what the Germans had. People were sceptical that they would succeed."

"Your neighbours must have questioned whether you would succeed in completing the ark."

"There were times when we all doubted that we would finish the ark before the animals arrive. At least we have ticked off that part of the project."

"We are drifting away from the story of Dorset Radar! It's industry. Tell me more."

"Worth Matravers near Swanage was the place chosen for the research centre. The farm owner was obliged to move to Hampshire, leaving only his pigs and poultry at Renscombe, to be looked after by locals."

"You sound like a civil servant, Noah. You said he was obliged to move. Ordinary people would have said he was forced to move, or worse still, kicked out."

"I am not a civil servant, but whatever, it was disruptive for him. Aerials, 360 feet tall, sprung up alongside other buildings on the old farmland. A strict guard was set, with workers forbidden to talk to the locals about what they were doing when they went to their lodgings each evening.

"The place was evacuated in a hurry in 1942. In war, stealing is justified. So Prime Minister Winston Churchill ordered a clandestine commando raid on a German radar station in Normandy at the full moon in February. The enemy was caught off guard and the commandos came back with vital secrets about the German technology. Worried that there would be a reprisal at the next full moon, Churchill ordered all the equipment and staff to go to Malvern to ensure that if a reciprocal raid was carried out by the enemy 29 days later, they would find nothing. We need the ark and since we cannot move it, for its own safety we do not trust anyone else to go to the site. These last few days before the animals turn up are crucial. I could not face years of building a new ark if it were destroyed."

The Westland Lysander was used in clandestine missions during World War 2. No lights were allowed, so it could only be flown when the moon was full. If the night was cloudy, you waited 29 days and hoped that you could still achieve the impossible.

"And you must be exhausted," said Gaynor, passing the hollandaise to Sarah.

"We have neither the time, the energy or the money to build another, and the rains are due."

"I'll visit Worth Matravers one day," I said. "If you are interested in other articles of war, how about visiting the Military Museum in Dorchester? They have Hitler's writing desk as a trophy."

"Just as Hitler must have had a war cabinet meeting daily, writing out the orders at his desk, so did we. Stephen supervised the timber felling and moving the logs into the clearing. Dad helped on the joining of the structural timbers and producing working diagrams so that we could carry on when he was not around. He also taught Jay how to supervise the sawing, knowing that I was all fingers and thumbs. Ham was always the technical fix-it-man when we were confused."

"Did you go to night school?" asked Gaynor.

"Yes, he did," piped up Sarah between mouthfuls. "And I went to cookery classes."

"But you told us you were already a competent cook."

"I was, and so are you. This salmon pie is superb."

Gaynor explained how the puff pastry kept the flavour of the herbs and salmon in the pie. Her brother regularly fished on the river Frome, one of the rivers that empties into Holes Bay. "Every third one that he catches he gives to us," she told our visitors.

"That is noble of him. We are honoured tonight, Noah," said Sarah.

In agreement, he nodded back at his wife. "You must be a close family."

"We are, and I get the impression your family is also close. Otherwise you could not have got this far with your project."

"Do you plan to fish over the side of the ark?" I piped up.

"Would you like to eat fish from water polluted with dead bodies?" answered Noah.

With the main course cleared away, Gaynor wanted to know why Sarah needed to go to cookery classes.

"To learn about new menus, foods, vegetables and preservation techniques."

"In my classes," said Noah anxious not to be outdone, "we learnt about using band saws, and how to keep your hands out."

"That is one of the reasons why I steer clear of carpentry," I told him. "My uncle lost his hand that way."

"I'm sorry to hear it. Dad removed the rusty saws from his old machine shop and brought them into the forest. Once cleaned up and sharpened, we made faster progress. But he did instil in us a routine of safety."

"Bring him over tomorrow, Noah."

"Sadly, he died four years ago."

"I'm sorry. Why did you not tell us before?"

"It did not seem important."

"So you were short-handed unless some one took over his work?"

"Nobody offered. Stephen had learned from Dad how to do the planking and the internal stalls, so that was on schedule. A while earlier we had worried about him. His younger brothers were married but not him."

"I see your problem, always assuming that you are Noah of the Bible. If the flood wipes out all life except those in the ark, the survival of the human race will depend on two families whose fertility has not yet been proven."

"Good summary, Frank. Then a miracle happened. Patricia burst into Stephen's life, and within a few weeks we had wedding bells. It is their tenth anniversary. She is the daughter of the owner of the forest, our timber merchant. That family are coming with us on the ark!"

"How on earth are you going to cope with each other for 12 months in the confined space? And what about the animals? If you take two of every animal, you are going to have many heavy animals on board. There are not enough of you to prevent six ton elephants charging around and wrecking it."

Sarah offered to pick up the story to allow Noah to concentrate on his sweet. "I hate to tell you, but dinosaurs are heavier than elephants. The big ones tip the scales at 80 tons."

"Your husband told me last night that you saw dinosaurs in your dream. But before we get off on a tangent over dinosaurs and their weight, tell me how you are going to cope with elephants."

"Calm people mean calm animals, Frank. So let us start with our well-being in the ark."

"Sounds sensible, but not foolproof. I heard of a tourist killed at a circus in Thailand when an elephant went berserk even with a qualified trainer present."

"We have a recreation room for use each evening to take away some of the emotional pressure whilst at sea, wondering whatever is happening and whether it will ever end. Until the flood comes, we can only guess how it will all pan out, but we have tried to prepare properly."

"What about other domestic arrangements?"

"Each family has its own conventional bedroom. There are several spare bedrooms including Lamech's. He was most supportive of the project. He said on the day his son had been born, he had a vision of him saving the world and that is why he had him named 'Noah'. It's sad that Lamech did not live to see the ark finished."

I thought 'Noah' was an old Dorset name; nothing to do with floods. Noah explained that in his country 'Noah' meant 'relief from a difficult and unbelieving world'. He admitted it did seem odd spending time making the ark with many people around them being obstructive or evil, taking peoples' guts for garters. That was not relief, but their goal was to float away into a new world. Changing the topic, I asked Sarah about their food stores.

"Patricia was wonderful helping me with the stores. I was delighted to have a third daughter-in-law, though she has only been with us a short time. She had taught domestic science at school. Using her knowledge, we have tried hot air drying of food, curing, smoking and pickling various foods and then testing them for flavour a year later. The quality of the preserved food varied from the ghastly, threatening our taste buds, to foods whose flavour and taste was enhanced by preservation. Sadly, strawberries could not be preserved except as jams."

"Deep freezers would have made a difference."

"They are not part of our culture and technology."

"They have only recently become a must-have consumer item in our century, but strawberries still lose their texture," said Gaynor. "Have you tried salting runner beans or candying peel?"

"Or water glass for preserving eggs?" I asked, not to be outdone by the exuberance my wife was showing on the subject.

"I am sure the girls have. The list is so long that I cannot remember everything they have done. The quantities we have preserved are enormous because we will miss a harvest."

"You're on the ball tonight with your explanations, but you're still dodging the dinosaur issue, the ponderous ones you saw in your dream swaying on your narrow gangplank as it bent under their weights. They became extinct long before the time in history that you claim to have come from."

"You are digressing now, Frank. Your vision of them swaying on the gangplank is a product of your fertile imagination, not what I said."

"You were going to tell me about keeping the animals calm in rough weather."

"On each deck we made an exercise space for the animals. Although we expect to take dinosaurs on board, they will not be 80 tonners, but chicken-sized babies. Adult animals will be restricted to farm animals. Dogs will be good company, and help us with controlling other animals when exercised."

"Why baby animals?"

"They eat less, and are easier to control and exercise. We expect to feed many on milk formula. Do you remember Elsa?"

I had heard the story of the lioness. Elsa's mother was shot, so Joy Adamson reared the cub in her home. Elsa grew up tame, and they took her everywhere on a lead. Joy eventually returned her to the wild, though Elsa struggled while she coped with finding her own food. The triumph of the story was when Elsa produced a litter and allowed the Adamsons to see them. If all the animals in the ark behaved like her, Noah would have an easy time.

"What about breeding?" I asked.

"Zoos often have problems getting their animals to breed in captivity. And our hope is that, apart from the zebras and the domestic animals, they will be the only sexually mature ones queuing for a place on the ark. Otherwise we will be like tinned sardines, short of space in spite of the spare bedrooms."

"Dinosaurs became extinct 60 million years ago," I said, waving my spoon at her. "You said you came from a world a few thousand years ago, so are you fraudsters or liars?"

"Neither. We have seen dinosaurs of all shapes and sizes. I was describing my husband's plans not explaining why your scientists wrongly assume that the dinosaurs disappeared millions of years ago. I know the ages of the rocks bothers you but can we clear up one mystery at a time?"

I put my spoon down and ringed the question in red biro in my book. "It's a key question. Failure to answer it means you forgo coffee and mints."

"I will say who can or cannot have coffee and mints, Frank!"

"Sorry, Gaynor," I said to her, "but they do exasperate me with all these ridiculous suggestions."

"Then let her finish. It is interesting, even if the story is out of this world. Go on, Sarah."

"Let me tell them, dear," interrupted Noah. "It will give you a chance to sample Gaynor's Dorset Apple Cake. It is mouth-watering. Gaynor, can you give Sarah the recipe? I hope that she will make some on the ark to remind us of our enjoyable break in Dorset."

"Do you have apples on board?"

"We have picked apples over the last few weeks, and we hope those will last us for six months before they are all eaten."

"Several of our neighbours have apples trees, Noah, and put their surplus crop in boxes by their gates for passers-by to help themselves. I can never keep them from autumn until Christmas, let alone 12 months."

"We have jars of dried apple as a backup if our freshly picked ones do not last. As for fruit trees in our new life, we have to save the pips from all the fruit that we eat, dry them, and plant them in a new orchard."

As a child I had planted pips but the growth was slow. As an adult I had heard about grafting and root-stock. Noah wanted to know about the procedures but I didn't know the details.

Noah's face suddenly lit up. "When I was in the garden centre this afternoon, I saw fruit trees with their roots in tubs for sale at one pound, nine shillings and eleven pence. Planting could not be simpler."

"Don't get carried away with the idea because your dark ark will kill them off in the 12 months that you expect to be hemmed in."

"Worth a try perhaps? Then if we plant them when we land we will not have to wait aeons for fresh fruit."

Sarah, who had now sampled the Apple Cake, beamed with delight at her husband's suggestion. Even I had to smile at the crazy idea, taking trees back into the past to guarantee fruit in the future.

"What about animal food?"

"Sarah and Patricia assessed what they needed and how much, though some was guess work, because the zookeeper was stumped – his young animals are fed by their mothers. Once I had their estimates of the quantities needed, I designed the storage bins appropriately."

"How will you cope with rabbits, moles and other creatures that dig holes? The ark would sink."

"Easy. We have a two-foot deep pit of earth."

"Animal sanitation? I told you about those cows that entered my neighbour's garden and left their smelly waste."

"We have got it worked out, in theory," Noah emphasised, "but the daily clearing out will not be pleasant."

Thinking about it, everything Noah had said was logical, something that my daughter could make up, but to my adult mind the whole thing verged on the edge of nonsense. If he took me to the ark or if someone could show me photographs of that wreck on the mountains of Ararat that the Russian pilots are supposed to have seen during World War 1, I might believe that there was once an ark. What puzzled me was if the ark was on a high mountain, how did it get up there, and how did the Biblical Noah release the animals, especially those that needed warmth?

The Noah in our dining room must have been reading my thoughts. He was silent, looking to Sarah for support, but she was more interested in Gaynor's engraved wedding ring and apologised that hers was getting thin and scruffy. "There was never any shortage of gold where we come from, and so mine, like the one I gave to Noah when we got married, was pure 24 carat."

"That's very soft for a man."

"We did not expect this manual labour for years on end which wore Noah's ring completely away. We did consider buying new ones, but they would have no sentimental values. Changing the topic, tell me about Dorset Wiggs. My husband told me about them last night. I want to make some for the store cupboard in the ark."

"Go for Dorset Knobs instead. Although they are harder to make, they do keep better. Give me a few minutes and I will copy out the recipe for you."

"Thanks. And the instructions for Apple Cake. Can we help with the washing up?"

"Frank and I will do it later. We might leave it until tomorrow. Frank is off work."

"Then may I have a quick look at the garden before it gets dark?"

Left alone for a few minutes, Noah and I continued to chat about whether modern archaeologists would be able to find the ark. Even if the story were true it might have totally rotted away in the intervening years. We discussed the wrecks around the coast. Part of the Studland Bay wreck had been recovered, but most of it had disappeared within 500 years. Then it was time to plan our outing for tomorrow.

"We will head for the woods," Noah said. "Thus, while I continue to enjoy the sights of Dorset, I can introduce you to the feel and smell of building the ark. For now, I must get Sarah and say our goodbyes. Ham will be waiting for us at the allotment, and we want time to check how our lads have been doing this evening. That pesky zebra had been behaving during the day, but he might have repeated his antics this evening. Thanks again from both of us for the lovely meal. Good night."

"You and Sarah had a good natter in the garden, Gaynor."

"She wanted to see the damage that their zebra did," she said hesitantly. "Then knowing that you wanted proof of the ark, I loaned her your camera. So don't explode. I cooked for your guests without complaint."

"But the half-exposed film?"

"I wound it out and gave them a fresh one."

"But today was the first time for months that I had used it."

"In that case you won't miss it for a while."

"But if I go out with him tomorrow?"

"Take your old Kodak Brownie."

"I found the Brownie in the attic this morning, but I haven't got any 127 films, only 620s. Do they still make 127s?"

"She also asked me what the 'snip' was."

"I'm going to bed. I feel pained and giddy at the thought of what you subjected me to."

"It was your passion that triggered the choice."

"Not tonight. It's early travels tomorrow."

"You make sure that you do something about the garden before you go out. And no meals tomorrow night."

"Who does the washing up?"

CHAPTER SEVEN

INFLATED PRICES

". . . boosting the price . . . and cheating", Amos 8 v 5

"Gosh, first light. I have hardly slept a wink, Patricia."
"I haven't slept, but you have."
"How do you know?"
"Your snoring spoke volumes."
"But I am still not getting up."
"But it's your turn to make the tea."
"Give me a minute, then."
"In that case, talk to me. Then I might forgive you for not calling me 'Tricia'. Tell me about your grandmother."
"It will take me ages to get used to your new name. The rest of the family will also be confused. But talking of Grandma, you would have loved her. It broke Granddad's heart when she died. I started popping in to see him on my way home from work each evening. Being in the same trade we could talk about wood. Whilst I did not try to curry favour with him, as I was the first grandchild following Mum's miscarriage, I was special to him. By the way, since you said that you were awake all through the night, did the bell ring?"
"I heard nothing apart from that owl and your snoring."
"Once I have put the kettle on I will check outside."

101

"Sorry for the delay in getting the tea, Tricia. There was no evidence of nocturnal visitors. But why did that owl scare you last night? You told me you were immune to such things."

"I used to camp in this wood as a child with my elder brothers and sisters. We were never scared. Then one evening, when I was 16 and the only child left at home, I got exasperated with Mum. She was screaming so loudly that I grabbed my sleeping bag and fled into this wood. Owls hooted, but I lapped it up."

"What was the wood like then?"

"All the streams flowed gently. Now water is plummeting over that rock ledge in the stream outside like it has no time to waste. It's almost a portent of disaster."

"I noticed that while I was checking outside. What caused that family argument?"

"Shekels and cents, mostly shekels! I'll tell you over breakfast."

"Where is my razor, Patricia?"

"If you cannot remember my new name, I will call you 'Teddy'."

"I am sorry, I forgot again with too many other things on my mind. Remember that I do not like 'Ted'?"

"You are forgiven."

"But where is my razor?"

"You did not bring it with you."

"Why did you not tell me I had not packed it?"

"You ought to grow a beard. I love men with beards and hairs on their chests."

"You are getting personal."

"Look at all the time you would save by not shaving."

"Look at all the time you waste going to the hairdressers. You have booked an appointment for next month!"

"Wendy insisted because bookings were filling up. Somehow I agree with you that I shall not be going. And breakfast is ready."

"Another croissant?"

"Please, Tricia, then tell me about your parents. I know that you did not have much regard for your mother, but you never told me about these money issues that caused you to come into this wood alone that night."

"I slept out here in protest at Mother's awful behaviour. She had bragged all evening about how they had tricked this man into parting with more money than he needed to. She had taken an order for wood from a retired man who wanted to build a boat. She marked the price up by half without him realising that she had manipulated him. Are you ready for a double shock?" She paused. "It was your grandfather."

"Wow, it explains a lot! I know Granddad was surprised at the high price he had to pay, but he never told me who the vendor was."

"When I protested at her overcharging him, she told me to shut up. How else could Father afford to pay college fees for all his children? And one day I would be rich because of my inheritance from him."

"So you toed your mother's money-grabbing line, Tricia?"

"Hold your horses until I've explained! Two years later I went to teacher training college and then taught domestic science in an inner city school. Father was neutral about my vocation, but Mother did not approve. The family had plenty of money, she claimed. Business was never so good, so why should I need to work in a rough area of the country? Back at home one holiday, Mother started bragging again. Told me she had done the deal of the century with a man who had stones in his brain. Our family would never need to work again."

"Who?"

"Déjà vu. Like father, like son."

He went ashen, but then tried to compose himself while she continued, "Mother and Father were defrauding your dad by charging double for the timber. Badbury's, a few miles away would only have charged five shekels for each tree."

"So on our tenth wedding anniversary, you punch me below

the belt by telling me that I have had the misfortune to marry the daughter of a family double-crossing my dad, *Pa*-tricia?"

"That is an unkind thing to say. I did not know much about Noah at the time and thought how stupid he had been not to suspect my family for overcharging. I saw your dad going around with the air of a pious do-gooder, not streetwise. But the shrewd financial deal Mother had done bothered me, though I would inherit a share of this wealth when my parents died."

"What did your father say about our family?"

"That this man, Mr ben-Lamech, had had a dream about a special kind of flood, a *mabbul*. Nobody knew what a *mabbul* was or 'rain' falling from the sky. After cross-examining him, Father felt that the man was so out of his mind that he would buy wood at any price. In the deliberations, Noah offered to put in special panelling in Father and Mother's bedroom. I think that Noah did this to humour him because my father seemed to have been one of the few that had shown interest in the ark. But my father capitalised on it again. He said he would have to import the wood panelling and that would double the price. In reality, Father was growing it locally at a handsome profit."

"And you encouraged this?"

"As far as Noah was concerned, I saw it as self-righteousness a bit too far. Your families had invented the *mabbul*, and then were the only ones doing anything about it. At first Father was pleased with my views. When I asked him why Noah was not suspicious that he had ordered a bedroom for himself and Mother but not the rest of the family, he warned me not to get involved. In the recesses of my mind I guessed that he had no intention of joining the ark when the crunch time came. Furthermore, he knew you were a handsome potential suitor, beard or no beard. He could not bear the thought of our family marrying into your family and me joining the ark construction team. But the more he told me not to get involved, the more interested I became. So I thought of an excuse to meet you and Father unwittingly arranged it."

"I do remember it."

"That was not my impression of our first meeting. You hardly took any notice of me. You probably thought I was too young for you, or you were so wrapped up in the work."

"Wrong! I knew that your mother and father had promised to join the ark when the animals arrive, but I had assumed that you and the rest of your family were at logger-heads. When talking about the extra bedrooms, we had asked your father about space for the rest of his family. He told us that no one else was interested. We emphasised that we had spare space if anyone changed their minds. Obviously I did not realise that your father was charging double for the timber. Why did you never tell Noah?"

"For the last ten years I have struggled with this on my conscience. If I told Noah the truth about my father and he confronted him, the whole of the project could have been jeopardised. Father could forbid access to the forest for Noah, and the building of the ark would grind to a halt. Please do not tell him. It would break his heart."

"I empathise with your dilemma, Tricia. It is too late to do anything about it now. The final bill was settled last week, and Dad warned him that he must start bringing in his possessions. He said he had not forgotten the date the *mabbul* was expected."

"What would you say of me if I told you that I did not want them to come with us?"

"We have to learn to forgive their duplicity. Although we have had to work harder than we needed because of this, we are also sinners in God's sight. What baffles me now is that as your father was not interested in joining us, why did he not tell everybody where the ark was?"

"Father knew that there were many who wanted to destroy the ark. If they had done so, Noah would either go and build another ark somewhere else or give up altogether. Both options would have left Father short of his profit on each tree."

"Let's return to the romantic bit instead of bemoaning what went wrong. How did you fix up that first visit?"

"I worked out the rota your family used to find out when you would be working in the evening. Then one afternoon I asked Father if I could drop into your workshop the list of trees he wanted you to fell next. He knew that that afternoon Noah would be on duty, and you would be at home. Instead of going straight to the ark, I idled the time away taking the dog for a long walk. Only at evening time did I venture your way."

"You were lucky to find me in that night. I had nearly swapped shifts with Ham."

"I couldn't help but be impressed at your vision and concern."

"You were one of the few people who wanted to be shown around, and did not end up laughing at our dreams and aspirations, but I still could not make you out. I am sorry that I gave you short shrift answers to your questions that day."

"Your clinically cold answers did not disturb my vision of the future. I had a dream of marrying you and struggled hard to contain my emotions. But I was frustrated because I knew that I could not make you fall in love with me."

CHAPTER EIGHT

IF YOU GO DOWN IN THE WOOD TODAY
"Make yourself an ark . . . coat it with pitch", Gen 6 v 14

You are never far from a forest in Dorset. In Domesday times timber was grown almost everywhere but with the rising population and the demand for food, the higher quality soils in the west were turned to agriculture leaving most of the present woodland (70%) now in the east.

The Forestry Commission first planted Wareham Forest in 1924. There is good access and many marked routes for walkers, including a Sika deer trail. It was here that Noah asked me to meet him – because it was just like the forest back at home where he had built his ark.

Sitting in the car waiting for him I started to become pensive. My memory had been jogged into thinking about the pleasures of golf, having passed the billboard advertising Wareham golf club. A tap at the window disturbed my reverie. Noah had appeared from nowhere, smiling in a roguish way and looking fresher than he did when I first met him.

"Gaynor's cooking and the pleasant company last night has made me a new man. The chance to relax helped me unwind. Building the ark and coping with criticisms for decades is hard going. Why are you looking glum?"

"If you get involved in hair-brained projects, you expect to be weary. I was thinking of golf, and gardening. And by the way, Noah, you are late!"

"Yesterday you told me that time does not matter when you are on holiday. Besides, I allowed you extra time to finish the washing up and put in the begonias."

"Gaynor did most of the washing up. She does not work on Thursdays."

I started to rattle off statistics about forests in Dorset, but he cut me short. "Statistics bore me but at least we are talking about trees. I expected you to ask if I got the apple trees from the garden centre. They were bargains so I loaded my trolley with several varieties: Fiesta for eating – it crops reliably and heavily and Annie Elizabeth for cooking. The sales spiel says that they will pollinate each other. I also got Conference pear trees, which are self-pollinating, and plum trees."

"Did you know that you need bees for proper pollination, Noah?"

"I am not a biologist."

"I think you mean 'gardener'."

"Have it your own way. I am not an expert in either topic."

My questions continued to flow fast and furious. "Are you taking bees on the ark?"

"Not thought about it. Maybe Ham has."

"Where are the fruit trees now?"

"Ham has taken them back to the ark."

"In case Ham hasn't made any beehives, my neighbour could sell you one."

"But how do you carry it?"

"Empty!" I was tempted to say.

"But surely I only want two bees?"

My mind was arguing with itself. Did Noah need at least three bees – a queen, a daughter worker and a male? Or would a pregnant queen be sufficient? He was not interested and took over the conversation again.

"The biggest forest in the area is Ringwood Forest, but much of that forest is inside the neighbouring county of Hampshire. I only have time to explore Dorset so I suggested that we came here. With the luxury of more time, I am sure that we would be able to find examples of everything in all other counties of England, except for the rain record held by Martinstown."

Then he spotted the police notice on the fence about thieves in the area breaking into cars. "Look at that – 'Thieves About'. Nothing has changed over thousands of years. Back in our world thieves were not our only worry; saboteurs were included."

That comment made me pat my pockets twice to check that I had all my possessions with me. I locked my car and followed Noah, trying to keep up with his long strides. Then the monologue started again.

"The trees here are pines which grow easily in this sandy soil. Did you know that because there are so many pine trees in this part of Dorset that they named an express train after them?"

I shook my head, too breathless to answer.

"You need an active job, or more exercise," he hinted.

"It is your long legs. You've also had plenty of exercise hammering and sawing for years. I have a sedentary job."

"So you believe the ark is real, Frank?"

"Not yet. Possibly I never will, but I grant that you are fit however you have achieved it." I promised myself that I'd start taking more exercise, going swimming with the children now that that feverish pattern of work had finished.

Noah had delved into the history of *The Pines Express*. The train would have been familiar to people in the 1950s and early 60s. It ran from Manchester and Liverpool each morning, and arrived at Bournemouth in the late afternoon. To say that it was an express was an understatement. It struggled to make 30 miles an hour between Bath and Bournemouth. But the name conjured up images of speed and elixir – because the scent from the pines at the end of the line from Manchester or Liverpool was assumed to have a therapeutic value.

"Do you know how high these pine trees that surround us are, Frank?"

"Fifty feet?"

"Spot on! This forest has a many similarities with the one where we have made the ark. You can now see how our ark, 45 feet high, can be hidden by trees until you are close to it."

"Surely this is like a busman's holiday, nothing different to what you have seen for years. In fact, Dorset is not an industrially thriving county, which might give you something new to rivet your attention on. No motorways, few bypasses, slow trains and lumbering tractors that block roads. Why come here?"

"To see a place that had endured heavy rain. But having come here, I find Dorset likeable even though it holds the UK rainfall record. Beaches, country lanes, idyllic villages; they are all things to be enjoyed slowly, like your trains, or even when you are stuck behind a tractor. Count yourself lucky that you now have trains that can go a bit faster. We never had railways, though we did set up a tramway to move timber from deep in the forest to our building site. Donkeys pulled the trucks at a sedate pace."

"Is your building site in this wood?"

"Were you listening last night, or you are trying to get me to contradict myself?"

"Both. I was tired last night, but I'm also barrister Frank again."

"I understand your reservations about my world. Cross-examine me even when I say things that may seem stupid to you. Our building site is deep inside a forest of long ago. We chose a working area twice the size of the ark that was thin on trees otherwise we would have wasted time felling useless timbers and grubbing out roots. There was a stream nearby for our water and power supply. Before starting, we agreed the location with the owner and told our planning authorities, but no one else."

It sounded daft building the ark in the middle of a forest. How would they launch it? They were not sailors, and even if they were they had no rudder to steer it. But then, where would they go? A global flood means no friendly ports anywhere.

"We were following instructions relayed in the dreams."

"That is a contradiction. You said that the site was deep in the forest to avoid accidental discovery. However, the owner knew everything. If he had not been cooperative he could have turned you off his land," I emphasised. "The planning people could also have caused you trouble."

"Total security was impossible because we could not have found the timber that we needed at a low price without telling someone, or building the ark without telling the planning people. Our worries that rogues will discover the site will haunt us until the flood comes."

We suddenly came to a clearing about 150 feet wide by 1000 feet. Noah was excited because it looked like the one he had used to build the ark. The size of it made me realise how big the ark was – larger than the ferries at Weymouth. Sure, he'd told me that the size was governed by the need to carry a lot of animals but many had doubted whether that capacity would hold more than a small fraction of the animal kingdom. I'd research that topic and challenge him tomorrow. I also wanted to photograph the view, but Noah had left my camera with his sons to record scenes at the ark. It'd be a task for another day.

"The first job," said Noah, "in our clearing was to fell some pines to create a temporary floor, like a raft. It gave us chance to pack the undulating surface level without having to grub out too many trees in our working zone. Keeping the ark off the ground reduced the rot from damp and insects that dwell in the soil.

"There was a profusion of other trees besides pines; yew trees by the hundreds for the structure and alder to clad the ark in. Round the corner were ash and beech for furnishings, but those came later. Once we had the raft complete, Dad brought over his saws and drills to speed up progress. The power from the stream was too good to miss, so we built a wooden workshop alongside it to house the band saws and installed a waterwheel. Dad put the tree trunks through his power saws to cut them into straight planks."

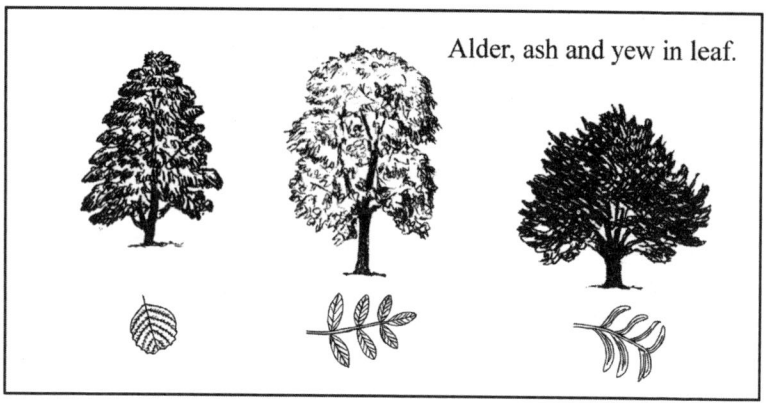
Alder, ash and yew in leaf.

"Are waterwheels that powerful? The stream here has no force to it."

"Our stream produced two hundred horsepower."

"I did not realise that mills could deliver such power. But why straight timbers? Boats need curved timbers!"

"Boats are built with curved timbers for streamlining and speed. We are not hurrying anywhere in particular so straight planks were adequate for the ark, but we did tongue and groove them."

"That sounds extreme!"

"Water-tightness on modern boats is achieved by overlapping or doubling up, such as in clinker boats. To survive a year at sea, we had to make doubly sure that we would be water-tight for that time by tonguing and grooving everything."

"You've repeatedly said that you'll be in the ark for a year. I thought the Bible flood lasted 40 days, and that's much longer than 'Unhappy Tim's' seven days."

"I did say 'a year', Frank. Our dreams told us to expect abnormal rain for 40 days, but the flooding to get worse for another 110 days. A full year will have to elapse before the flood-waters retreat and the ground becomes dry enough to resume normal life."

That length of time cooped up in the ark sounded like a prison sentence, I thought.

"You will laugh at this. We have taken on board Granddad's rowing boat that had curved sides and bottom."

"If the ark sinks, you won't get many animals away to safety in that."

"It was not in a handy location for emergencies. Our dreams told us to put it deep inside rather than on the top deck in davits, as on modern boats."

"I thought you and the rest of your family were intelligent. Surely someone should have spotted the flaw that your lifeboat cannot be launched quickly from there. Or are you winding me up?"

"If the ark sinks, but we clamber into a boat, who will be around to rescue us? And God is not going to enjoy watching the ark project fail. Now you can understand why the dreams were so specific about it being water-tight. Dad's dream told him to write a quality control manual for us all to consult."

"That sounds extreme. Quality control manuals are just appearing in industry."

"They were essential for us because the only thing that we have for emergencies is an extra set of bilge pumps.

"The plans for the ark showed a flat bottom rather than a keel," Noah continued. "We coated one side of each floor plank with pitch. Once that was dry, we laid the plank on the pine raft, pitch side downwards, and cramped it as hard as possible against its neighbour using ropes and pulleys to tension the wood."

"Even with all these precautions against leaks your journey sounds hairy or scary, or both. There are other reasons why boats sink."

"God designed the ark to avoid problems that cause modern boats to flounder. I guess that you know what they are. Water leaking into the boat through the sealing gland on the propeller shaft has sent many modern ships to a watery grave. We have no propeller. Then there was deck space where large quantities of water can be shipped on board during rain and storm. But a deck was dispensed with because we built the ark around the stores. And a deck can weaken the structure, so that is why it was not in the design. Everything had been thought about."

"But don't count your luck yet. Sunday 14th April 1912, the unsinkable Titanic sank because it scraped alongside icebergs which tore gashes in its side below the waterline."

"We expect to be the only thing afloat during most of the flood. Even if not, everything else should be floating in the same direction on the same current so impact damage should not occur. That saved us the labour of making bulkheads in the ark. Bulkheads are vital in many boats so that the crew can close off the damaged section if they are holed. And who wants an ark half full of drowned animals? We concluded that our God knew what He was doing when he designed the ark for us."

"But you have not thought about tipping over."

"It should not happen. We do not have any sails or masts to catch the wind, so however strongly it blows, we will not tip over. Utnapishtim's tall and lanky thing got it wrong. That is why it is a legend."

"OK, I've seen the look-alike forest, but where did your pitch, the rope and the pulleys come from? They are not the sort of things you find here so I'm not getting a feel for that aspect of your project."

"True, but in Dorset, pitch and pine are not far apart. I will tell you about the pulleys in a minute, and the rope is something we can discuss when . . ."

I cut him short. ". . . we go to Bridport."

Noah smiled.

"But why coat the inside of the ark with pitch?"

"Cleanliness. We have to wash the stalls down regularly. Waste water from the top deck will be released into the sea through flaps set into the sides of the ark. The floors on the lower decks will be below sea level. So we will keep as few animals down there as possible. The waste water mixed with urine and faeces from those decks must not come into contact with the wooden floors otherwise it would attack them."

"But you're still going to have to pump it away, otherwise won't the smell get stronger?"

Noah nodded, "An unpleasant job!"

Noah explained that they had bought some old narrow gauge railway lines, sleepers and sets of points and half a dozen tubs on wheels. The lines had been laid from his construction site to several spots deep into the forest where they were felling trees. Two of the tubs had been used as a pair to bring felled trees into the work area. All pulled by donkeys.

I told him that Purbeck was once littered with narrow gauge lines that carried tubs full of clay from the Norden pits to the piers around Poole Harbour or stone to Swanage. In days gone by they were donkey-powered. More recently, small steam engines had taken over. Typical for him, he wanted to see Poole Harbour, and where the Romans were supposed to have landed so we could explore this industrial archaeology at the same time. I was not enamoured.

"Then suggest another attractive place to go tomorrow . . . . We also laid a double track along the two main sides of our pine raft. Using four tubs, two on each side, we were able to make a mobile crane which we could use to lift timber and other items to the upper parts of the ark."

"I wish I could have seen it in action, Noah. Tommy keeps telling me that he wants a model railway for his birthday with some of that old Pullman stock that used to run the Bournemouth Belle and Weymouth boat trains. It was romantic with table lights glimmering night or day, and the carriage attendants in their white and black uniforms, stiff with starch."

"I would like to come back and see that, when the flood is all over and we are settled. But beware, setting up a train set layout is as boring as building an ark. Enthusiasm flags when you find that different bits do not fit together in the available space."

"My father has spent ages in his retirement trying to construct a layout. Tommy is desperate to see it but his granddad keeps making excuses to keep him out of the room. Maybe I'll make one when we move into a larger house."

"The boring stage is over for us. Our ark is finished."

"Did your boredom lead to family friction?"

"What family never has arguments, even about trivia? But at other times we felt at peace toiling to save the world as we got used to being a well-oiled team. Dad was exasperated at the speed at which we were completing the flooring. We were for ever barging into the saw mill and asking for the next piece of timber."

"What was wrong with that?"

"It was not ready. 'Stop!' he said, 'and build a bigger workshop. Then I can keep up with your demands. But this time we'll use concrete and fit a steel door, which can be locked at night. Our tools will then be safer from casual thieves.' The wives insisted that we added a toilet and kitchen. Last year we added a bedroom so that one of us could sleep at the site."

"History shows no use of concrete until modern times, Noah! It wasn't invented until 1824. So you must be a charlatan – a modern man pretending to be from pre-history."

"Whatever did they teach you in archaeology classes? The Romans made concrete, mortar and lime. The dome of the ancient Pantheon, which spans 150 feet, is made of concrete with volcanic pumice as an aggregate. The first building in the Field of Mars was constructed around BC 27. The remains of the present building were erected 140 years later. During that later time, the Romans came to England and stayed for 400 years, bringing their skills with them."

"But there aren't any buildings with concrete sections in Dorset before the eighteen hundreds," I protested.

"Tragically, your Dorset predecessors failed to pass on the skill of making cement from generation to generation. Many archaeologists ignore these human failings when they say that different archaeological sites are the same age because the technology of whatever they were doing was the same. Technology gets lost or forgotten, or develops faster in different places. That is why I laughed when you tried to tell me the ages of the barrows we saw near Martinstown. But concrete – we have an example of two places using the same technology almost 1,700 years apart. Archaeologists would claim that the dates were the same."

"But Noah, you claim to pre-date all that. So how did you get concrete?"

"Right now, our civilisation is 1,600 years old. We have had time to develop many of the skills that you consider belong only to your 'modern' era. We are arable and pastoral farmers, make things of metal and wood, make music and we know the three Rs. We are advanced civil engineers because we can plan cities with first class roadways and water supply. We regularly used concrete. I can go on . . ."

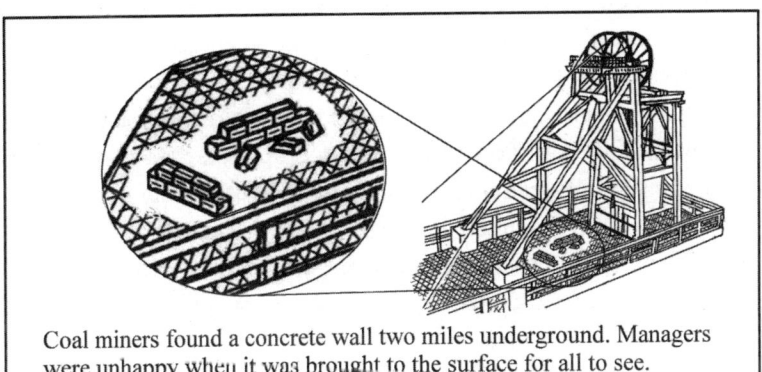

Coal miners found a concrete wall two miles underground. Managers were unhappy when it was brought to the surface for all to see.

I realised that I had to change the topic of conversation until I had resolved this fundamental point that Noah had made about archaeological dating. In the back of my mind I remembered reading that miners found concrete in a coal mine, in 1928. Several sections of a concrete wall two miles beneath ground had been exposed. When the miners told the colliery managers about the wall, they were instructed to deny the discovery. Not only was the story, if true, a problem for archaeologists, but embarrassing for a conventional geologist. If the flood that Noah was expecting did really come, then their houses and factories of his city could have been covered by tons of mud and coal, then buried deep. Maybe the miners found the walls of his workshop. How dreadful! No wonder modern people did not want to believe the story.

I put the thoughts out of my mind and said, "If you are so clever about concrete and metals, why do you have no electricity, no trains, things that we take for granted?"

"Our technology is not on a par with yours. I envy the abundant gadgets and tools you have. A walkie-talkie radio set would have made such a difference to the ark project keeping in touch with each other when on the move. We did not dare put a phone into the workshop because someone could have followed the line from the edge of the forest and found the ark. But we did invent cement. We called it 'Havilah' cement, but it was exactly the same as your 'Portland' cement which has been named after a bit of your Dorset."

I had researched Dorset's archaeological past. Every part of Dorset once had its cement kiln, but the process produced fumes, so all were eventually shut down because of complaints and big factories went elsewhere. It meant less local industry, but cleaner air. Against this background I struggled to reinvigorate industry.

In the midst of our argument about the origin of cement, a lorry coming up behind us startled us. We moved out of the way to let it pass while the driver waved a thank-you.

"That is another bit of technology I would have appreciated. An articulated lorry with a crane on its back able to collect logs from deep in the wood would have been far better than us continually moving the railway tracks."

"That lorry caught me by surprise. I had forgotten they come in here to collect wood. However, it sounds as if we will have to disagree on who discovered cement, so back to your programme of building the ark."

"Laying the base of the ark took a couple of years. For the framework we used uncut tree trunks straight from the forest and lifted into place by the cranes. Thicker ones were split rather than sawn."

"So you abandoned neatly planed planks?"

"Dad's schedule would have slipped behind again. This stratagem was copied many thousands of years later by Dorset boat builders."

"Did you read about this, or have you been to the Poole Museum and seen the maritime exhibits?"

"I have only read about it."

"I've been and enjoyed the museum. I think you'd enjoy it too; it'd be home from home."

"More like a busman's holiday for me, Frank. I came to relax. It might frighten me by drawing my attention to something that I have not thought about. Forget it!"

His remark jarred my memory. The museum showed how ancient ship builders buried water-logged timbers until they needed them so that they did not shrink. If it had taken decades for Noah to build his ark, using mountains of fresh timber, surely some of it would have shrunk, split or buckled, thus ruining the ark's water-tightness.

"Not needed," he commented. "The drying out of wood is a modern-day phenomenon. With an equable atmosphere we were spared of the need to bury our timber or take any other precautions against shrinkage. Our moisture level was constant, helped by the even temperature, between summer and winter, night and day. Besides, we are expecting to be at sea for a year. We trust that the alder, with lashings of pitch on it, will survive attack by boring insects for that time, nor split. What happens after the flood abates is immaterial."

"But they don't make piers and groynes at seaside towns out of alder!"

"There would be uproar from holiday makers if they did. Like all cheap wood, it splinters and soon looks unsightly."

"So in your story you have your flooring done and the framework erected. It would be the sides of the ark next?"

"We only built three sides."

"Three? That's ludicrous, Noah. You need four sides to stop the water getting in."

"It is logical, pure logic because I told you earlier that we loaded our stores as work progressed. On the lowest deck, we made space for things we will not need until after the flood is over. We visited auctions for second-hand farm equipment, buying two ploughs and millstones. We also put in two solid-fuel cookers and enough charcoal to keep them going until trees start growing again after the flood. The final side of the ark was only built after all this had been loaded."

"I see. I fell for that one."

"There was another bonus for doing three sides first. 'Seeing' is the operative word. Our lighting was poor. So, with an open side, as much natural light as possible could get into the ark."

"So you didn't have arc lights, if you pardon the pun?"

"Want another pun? We did not have flood lights either."

"I'm not surprised. The flood hasn't come yet."

"Enough of flippancy! Dad's quality assurance manual was written in stern tones."

"You sound as if it was pompous."

"We did have a play-time. Dad told us to check that the lower part of the ark was watertight by damming the stream. We did that once the fourth side had been built up 15 feet. It took days for the water to rise to the ledge of the fourth side. Then we rowed across our newly formed lake to the ark on a raft, scrutinised the inside, found a couple of leaks, and noted where they were coming from. Then we broke the dam apart and watched the water rush away. Ham then applied more pitch to the problem areas of ark outside. We rebuilt the dam, and created the lake for a second time to check that we were fully watertight. We ticked that part of the project off on the master plan and had a celebration."

Noah wanted to go to Kimmeridge Bay and see the oil well that afternoon, but before leaving the forest, asked if we could go back to the car via the Woolsbarrow Iron Age fort, half a mile to the north. From there he said that I could see how he was able to conceal his ark in the forest. But being warned about the Sika deer trail, I had to ask him if we'd meet any.

"You and wild animals are not the greatest of companions, Frank. I think I can keep them away. This fort is one of the smallest forts in Dorset. No one knows much about it because it has not been excavated properly. Your industry was so anxious to retrieve the gravel that they shovelled away the centre before the archaeologists could look for artefacts."

"I know these things happen so don't blame me for the tensions in society – the battle between curiosity, conservation and commercial pressures."

"It is a splendid place for a picnic if you ever want to bring your family. And hide-and-seek is easy to play here."

"I'll come back with my camera, when I get it back."

"I will pretend not to have heard that remark. But remember to bring the deer repellent spray."

"Deep repellent spray? Is there such a thing?"

"Hardly. I'm pampering to your worry about meeting animals. Now from this vantage point you will see splendid views of the surrounding forest. But even from here you cannot see that clearing we visited an hour ago. The ark would have been safe from prying eyes if we had built it there. Woolsbarrow also reminds me about snakes. An area has been created for wildlife, especially reptiles, that need a quiet sunny spot to make incubators for their eggs."

"Does that mean that you're expecting snakes in the ark that'll drive their fangs into your heels?"

"By keeping them in the cold, they will be inactive. We have been practising handling the snakes. Pythons up to 15 feet long are rather fun."

I flinched at the thought of even a short snake crossing my path, but tried not to show it. That would surely put off other people joining the ark.

"Although most people we asked to join the ark told us that their lives were already overfull, four families came forward and another family, whom I have already told you about will join us shortly. Neither they nor the other families are worried that snakes will crawl all over the ark at night. They chipped in with money and effort. I was glad because you guessed correctly that we would overspend even with that trickle of donations. The books balanced again."

"Who got your budget wrong?"

"The pitch was more expensive than expected."

"The price of our heating oil has gone sky-high lately, Noah. They both come from crude oil, so the prices ride up and down together. It's another reason for wanting to move to Crossways where they've got cheap gas on tap."

"Those wild price fluctuations are the sort of thing that happened to us. Dad also had a memory problem, forgetting that we needed brass nails and screws, not iron. Ten tons of them bumped up the cost."

"Even I know iron rusts in water. So, you boobed on that one."

"But now we had extra money, new helpers and were back on schedule. There was a new song in our hearts as I modified the plans to include four extra bedrooms."

"It seems to rule you out as the Biblical Noah. There is no mention of these extra families in Genesis."

"Arguments from silence are not convincing."

"It's my way of trying to rattle you again, Noah."

"When we were planning on how to collect the animals for the ark we did think we might need a decoy pond to capture waterfowl."

"They do that in the swannery at Abbotsbury."

"They also did it here on the lake in this wood towards Morden village. It is a bit of light industry to cheer you up."

A bird fluttered overhead. We both turned to look at it, and spotted a vapour trail left by an aircraft so high it was impossible to make out what kind it was.

"Frank, Dorset has also given a different slant to the concept of a 'decoy'. In the last war there was an important decoy at Arne and in this wood. Their purpose was to attract metal birds. Drawing enemy aircraft away from the cordite factory by the railway at Holton Heath, crammed with combustible material, was vital to your war effort. Had they bombed it, the place would have burst into flames and your production of the explosives would have ceased."

"You amaze me with the amount of information you have picked up being in Dorset for four days. Did this subterfuge work?"

"First rate. They burnt waste cordite at these decoy spots so that the German air force would bomb the decoy, not the factory. The fire brigade would then spray the blaze with water to produce clouds of steam so that the German pilots would not tumble to the fact that they had bombed the wrong place. For good measure, the Germans would then drop more bombs on the dummy blaze before going home congratulating themselves on how much trouble they had caused to the English. But the subterfuge of the brigade ensured that the factory remained unscathed."

I chuckled. My father had been in a reserve occupation during the war, and had become a volunteer firefighter. He had never told me of any of his exploits. It would have been dangerous whether you were a real firefighter or someone pretending to put out a blaze, for both groups had to dodge exploding bombs. I would ask him about his stories when I saw him next week.

As it was well past midday, food was uppermost in our minds and we headed to the local – *The Silent Woman*. Noah was curious about the legend behind the name. Much of Dorset's coast 200 years ago was a smugglers' haunt. The owner's wife overheard smugglers talking about where they were to land their brandy. They discovered her eavesdropping.

"Hence, '*The Silent Woman*' who can no longer tell the authorities how to catch them red-handed, because they cut out her tongue, I suppose?" he asked.

"Hole in one, Noah, though it is a legend!"

"I do hope that you will be able to take up golf again. Now, you never asked me how things were back at the ark last night, especially the zebra."

"You've hardly given me a moment to catch my breath and think properly. You could talk the hind legs off 20 zebras, though most people could only manage to talk one hind leg off a donkey. So?"

"He is fine. It was not food that he was looking for, but his mate.

Ham tells me she turned up yesterday evening and both of them have been acting passionately with each other. I am worried about pregnancies."

With our appetites satisfied, we drove over the level crossing and into Wareham. We had talked about Lawrence of Arabia yesterday. As his effigy was in the church on the left I suggested that Noah call in and see it whilst I bought some petrol at the garage opposite by the river Piddle. There had been a water wheel there years ago.

"Why is his effigy in a church," he asked me, "when he was an ardent atheist?"

"There was controversy about where to bury him because of his anti-religious views. He ended up in the cemetery a few miles west at Moreton. But to many he was a saint, and they make pilgrimages to his home at Clouds Hill. There was pressure on the church to acknowledge him, though not in the way the writer Hardy was."

"Acknowledge him for what? Frank, if the Christian church can be manipulated by secular society to blur the difference between atheism and Christianity, then it is failing in its duty to stand up to revealed truth. Many tried to manipulate my preaching about the forthcoming flood in an attempt to silence me. Then they tried ridicule. And what was it driven by? Last night you told me about Gideon. From that story we learn that individuals can test God if they have any doubts about Him, what He wants them to do, and how their relationship with Him should develop. Most people refuse to put God to any test, not because they doubt His existence, but because they want to control their own lives. I'd call them theo-phobic."

"That's an interesting word, and you sound very positive about it. Yet over the last three days you've told me about how many doubts you have had over building the ark ordered by this god of yours."

"One reason I was late this morning was because I stopped to read about Gideon. I have compared how God dealt with him and how God dealt with us. God did not suddenly charge up to Gideon and tell him to lead the army into battle. Gideon probably did not know which end to hold a sword. Trust grew from small things, including the time when God told him to break down the altar his father had built to the false god Baal. Gideon knew that he might be lynched for it but trusting God, he destroyed the altar. Having come through the incident unscathed, he accepted a more challenging request – that of leading the army. To check that he had understood this new instruction correctly, he put out the fleece."

"So why are you nervous, Noah, with all these precise instructions?"

"Long before we had the dreams about building the ark, we knew we were being protected by the Lord God as we worshipped each week. Our altar was in our front garden, yet no one touched it. The occasional passer-by would poke fun, but the bitterness they showed and their threats never escalated into violence. So a level of trust had already been built up between God and us. Building the ark is out of all proportion to that level of trust established prior to the dreams."

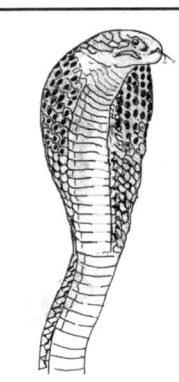

Snake charming was a recognised activity in the Old Testament (Ps 58). Noah would not necessarily have had to learn these skills to control his batch of dangerous snakes. God saved Paul from a viper (Acts 28). Isa 11 vv 6-9 offers us a vision of the future.

Joy Adamson's experience with Elsa the lioness cub 1900 years after Paul is a powerful reminder of how humans can interact safely with wild animals.

Kimmeridge cliff top was our next stop. This was home territory to me. Past the Blue Pool tourist spot, over the ridge of hills at Cocknowle, through Kimmeridge village with its quaint tearoom and down to the toll road, and what did we do? Get stuck behind a slow-moving oil tanker on the narrow road.

The tanker only makes the journey twice a day, and we'd picked the wrong time. But I should not have become agitated. I'd spent months trying to persuade BP to drill another well at Kimmeridge because that first well had produced far more oil than anyone could explain. It was all part of my effort to increase industrial activity in Dorset. The consequence would be many more tanker journeys between here and the loading point in the sidings at Wareham where the railway wagons depart for Ellesmere Port for refining. The road would have to be widened.

We pulled into the cliff car park, and watched the tanker continue its way to the BP compound. "Come on. Let us walk over to the nodding donkey."

"But please walk at my pace, Noah."

As we crossed the ground, Noah tried to explain that they used pitch for waterproofing the ark. In Dorset, the oil pumped out of the ground is sent to the Ellesmere refinery for cracking. One of the by-products is pitch. Ham had set up a little refinery for them. How it worked, he did not know. All he had to do was to use the pitch on the ark.

I admitted that I did not know how it happened either, but inwardly I was still wondering if he had made the whole story of the ark up by flaunting his knowledge of Dorset.

"There are still many gaps in the story that I need to fill you in with, and I hope that that will convince you that I am talking about reality, not fiction. As it has been a busy day, and the afternoon is far advanced, I must head home. I cannot come round tonight and continue explaining."

I thought Noah was presumptuous, but was slow saying 'that's a relief'. However, we did agree that Jay and Katrina could drop in later in the evening. Ham and Irene would still be on duty, and Stephen and Patricia were out celebrating. Katrina might be a bit difficult to handle, but at least there would be no meals.

CHAPTER NINE

ACRONYM
"no longer will you be called (by your old name)", Gen 17 v 5

"Do you remember how I came to propose to you, Patricia?"

"I told you not to call me 'Patricia'."

"I proposed to a 'Patricia'. You are splitting hairs now so forgiveness is not needed on this occasion."

"You win for the moment. Were we both scared of each other on that first meeting?"

"It was the first time I had been alone in the ark with an attractive young lady. But I put you out of my mind because I thought that you had no intention of joining us. What changed your mind?"

"At the end of another school term I went home for the holiday because my contract had finished. The headteacher wanted me back at the school but I dithered. Mother and Father seemed pleased, saying that I could stay at home as long as I liked. They would pay me for doing nothing, but I knew where their money had come from. Then the dreams started. All I could think about was seeing you again and I did it without deceiving Mother and Father."

"I remember Mum and Dad asking who you were, and I told them about that first visit of yours. The future suddenly clicked in their minds. We were drifting together, our chemistries bubbling over, whatever."

"Those are not romantic things to say. Is the word 'love' not in your vocabulary?"

"We did not have a traditional courtship of going out with each other for years, Tricia. But yes, I was in love with you, though scared to acknowledge it. I had almost given up hope of falling in love and marrying. Although I thought that your father was coming with us on the ark, and therefore bound to welcome my request, I found it a struggle to find courage to visit him to ask for your hand in marriage."

"I was listening on the other side of the door."

"You what?"

"I thought you knew what kind of person I was."

"I imagined you to be sweet and demure, not an eavesdropper, Tricia."

"Father did not want to say 'Yes', but neither could he say 'No'. At least he did not pass the buck to Mother."

"No dowry was needed so we shook hands, and I left excitedly, with hormones pounding. It did not bother me that he did not call your mother to tell her the news, or open a bottle of bubbly."

"What did Noah and Sarah say?"

"They were thrilled, not being aware of your family's shadier dealings. They broke open the champagne and some of the food stores that we had set aside for the ark."

"I suppose that they thought that my father was serious about joining the ark. And your mum and dad were so enraptured at our wedding that they failed to notice how aggrieved my parents looked. What did you think of my sisters, Stephen? Prettier than me?"

"I never met them until the day we got married, Tricia. Why do you say that?"

"Come off it, I know what goes through men's minds in the presence of pretty girls getting out their best dresses for a wedding."

"Beauty is in the eye of the beholder. What mattered most was your attitude to the ark. Theirs was dismissive. That is one thing that your father was right about."

"You sound so righteous. I always suspected that you thought I was plain looking. And you did not remember our anniversary until I told you. That proves that you no longer love me."

"Calm down! The way you talked to your father before I met you sounds as if you are also self-righteous."

"So you are not bothered that I am brown-eyed and lanky and both my sisters are blue-eyed and have better proportions?"

"What a thing to say on our wedding anniversary. And your sisters were married when I first met them. Besides, you told me you love men with beards, and yet you married a clean-shaven man. I could feel aggrieved that I was second fiddle to your ideal husband."

"You always have the last word . . . I guess we have been drawn together by a purpose and love. But I'm still worried about not getting pregnant, so I've worked out another name for you – Shem!"

"How did you get that?"

"The first letter from each of your names: S̲tephen H̲arry E̲dward Martin. Do you like it?"

"If it makes you happy. Then what about spending another night away from the family with your new Shem to celebrate? Guard duty is over so we can see more of Dorset."

"How can we do that?"

"I did remember the date of our wedding anniversary, and asked Dad a month ago if we could be spared that day. He deliberately fiddled the draw so that we would get the short straws before our anniversary and the other members of the family would get them then."

"I am touched by his concern. The extra day off sounds a good idea, but you haven't got a razor with you."

"Oh, sucks, I'll have to put up with that."

"I can test your stubbly whiskers for real, and then decide whether to twist your arm to let them grow more."

"Changing the subject, what happened to the Reverend Stonely?"

"He retired and moved away. Before he went we asked him to join the ark. His answer didn't make sense. Strange fellow."

"We never really got any one else interested in the ark. Have we made a mistake that it will come to naught?"

"Or is everybody else outside the family going to perish?"

"Let's forget those worries and enjoy the next 24 hours. Remember what the Lord said – I own this project and the consequences."

"Shem, my newly named, but ever beloved husband . . ."

"Your words of flattery make me feel that you want me to do an unpleasant job, Tricia."

"No, it was only a simple question. Jay married Katrina before I met you. How did they meet?"

"They were childhood sweethearts, courting in the school playground. They never showed interest in anyone else. No one imagined anything other than they were made for each other. Both sets of parents approved."

"But what did her folk think once you started the ark?"

"The family had drifted apart years before that. Her father was a top industrialist, working every hour possible. Grandchildren might have been cohesive by allowing him to see that the world is bigger than workaholics admit. Perhaps it was meant to . . ."

"You seem to be thinking what I'm thinking, Shem."

"I can appreciate what you are saying now. Three girls married into the same family and all infertile for decades. The problem could be with the ben-Noah boys and their low sperm count. We end up working our fingers to the bone for nothing, just like Katrina's father. We save the animals in the ark, but the human race disappears."

"There is a bigger risk with the animals. One pair of each, so there is minimal genetic variation there."

"People will never believe the story of the ark and The Flood, even if we succeed."

"We must write it down."

"Why not keep an ark log, with daily entries, like they do on ships?"

"I'll suggest it to Noah. Now I want to know about your other brother. I presume that that was not an arranged marriage either, so how did Ham choose Irene?"

"He had more girl friends than hot meals; almost a Don Giovanni."

"So with all these girls wanting him, I guess their relationship is a bit one-sided."

"I hadn't thought of that!"

An unfettered view of East Street, Blandford Forum. The Georgian buildings replaced those destroyed by fire in 1731. Some of these have since been rebuilt, though in keeping with the earlier character.

CHAPTER TEN

ON FIRE
"the fury of the flames", Heb 11 v 34

Blandford Forum, an important market town since the mid 1500s, sits on the northern side of the river Stour. It was famous for lace and button making. Now brewing beers takes precedence.

In 1731, a fire started in a tallow-chandler's thatched cottage and spread rapidly to other thatched properties. The church and 351 dwelling were burnt down. Georgian stone buildings now grace the centre of the town where the worst damage occurred.

The town once boasted a railway station on the line used by *The Pines Express*. Now the only evidence of those railway days is a short section of undemolished bridge over the river.

Making my way home from Kimmeridge, a noise behind me made me look into my driving mirror. Bearing down on me was a fire engine, bell clanging and blue lights flashing. I edged close to the kerb to allow it by. I was about to resume my homeward journey when a second engine made an appearance, followed by a police car. Some conflagration, but where?

I pulled into my driveway under the "For Sale" notice. Home never looked better, though how long this house would be ours was a moot question. But for the moment familiar territory might restore my confidence in my understanding of history and archaeology. That point Noah had made about concrete having been invented three times and a wall found in a coal mine rattled me. Archaeologists could only cope with them by sweeping the facts under the carpet or declaring them as fables. Would my contact with another member of Noah's family tonight threaten my opinions about history and the antiquity of civilisation that I'd had since college days?

Jay and Katrina came at 8pm bearing a zebra carved by the family as a memento of our meeting. Jay told me that the fruit trees had been stowed in the ark.

"It is a pity that you couldn't transplant growing corn and wheat to avoid waiting another year for harvest," I told him.

"Sounds as if you are close to believing in what we are doing."

"Doubts flood my mind."

"Who is using a pun now, Frank?"

"It was a slip of the tongue using the word 'flood'. I'm not convinced that your time travel from the past is real. And what about my camera?"

"Katrina got the hang of it. I'll ask her when she stops talking to Gaynor. Now, we had a shock this afternoon when two hundred animals turned up unexpectedly."

"Did your dreams not warn you of early arrivals?"

"Dad got the design of the ark down on paper while it was fresh in his mind. Katrina, during her dream, saw a calendar with dates, milestones and the schedule for everything. She replicated the information on a big wall-chart but that went up in flames in an unfortunate fire."

"Then why did you know that the animals would be turning up this week, and the rains begin next week?"

"Memory helped! We had looked at the old chart many times in the previous years. But then came confirmation and comfort. Two Saturdays ago, we were sacrificing a lamb on our altar when Dad heard a fresh message from above. He wasn't taking drugs, so don't ask.

"'Noah,' said the voice, 'I am pleased with your trust in me and your progress.'

"'If that is you, my master and my Lord God, I am scared,' Dad replied.

"'Why?'

"'That fire burnt our calendar with all the timings on it. The ark is now ready for the animals. Will they be in time? Or worse still, will the rains fail to materialise?'

"'Trust me, rather than being afraid. I can give you a glimpse of the future to show that everything will happen as I told you. That will encourage you to persist in saving as much life as possible. I can also combine it with a break from your labours before the next test begins. Where would you like to go?'

"'All of my family deserve a break, having worked as hard as I have.'

"'I agree, so tell me where you want to go.'

"'Somewhere where they had a lot of 'rain' and a flood, though it might have been only of limited extent, but after it life returned to normal and was enjoyable.'

"'I will do that for your family, Noah. You will also be a witness to an unbelieving world.'

"'I have done that for decades, yet few have taken notice, or stayed with us until the evil of this world won the battle for their souls. They were more nuisance than worth. What happens next?'

"'You have spare wood left. Take half of it on board for repairs during the journey, and build a shed in your garden with the rest.'

"'Repairs? That sounds awful. Is there a weakness in the design of the ark? Tell me, please, otherwise I am not subjecting my family to an ark that might break apart before we see a drop of 'rain'.'

"'I am The Lord of this project, your safety and the consequences; I am not just the master giving orders to save doing things myself.'

"'But the shed?'

"'When you go into it, it will travel across the centuries into the future. There you can enjoy yourself. It will land in a derelict part of an allotment so that it will not attract attention to itself. When you are ready to come home, all you need to do is get back in the shed.'

"Dad heard nothing more," Jay continued, "but by following the instructions we are having a break in Dorset, enjoying ourselves in an unorthodox way. Then you tighten the thumb screws in your interrogation because you think that we are only telling porkies."

"I'm not tightening the thumb screws to put unfair pressure on you. I'm intrigued by your story, but not convinced that it is real. You had dreams, you hear this lord of the project speaking to you. Supposedly there is an ark that you have finished which could collapse at any moment unless you are diligent in repairs. And to cap it all, every other day something else seemed to go wrong. You sound as if you are dancing on a tight rope without a stabilising pole or a safety net in an effort to save the world. I've not even seen the shed."

"There are lots of other things we have not told you. Three of those families that started to help later left us. They were irritated by the fact that we were building the ark in the middle of a forest and could not see how it could be launched."

"Jay, I don't understand why you were building it there. At least Utnapishtim built his boat near the water's edge. Could you have used that lake you created?"

"That lake was too small to float the ark fully loaded. When these three families realised this they downed tools and demanded their money back. Unfortunately we had spent their money on pitch and screws that turned out to be more expensive than expected. They threatened legal action. As we were penniless, they knew that they would never get their money back and so resorted to violence. Dad and Mum got back to their house one night after working late to find their front window smashed in, and smoke pouring out. Although they doused the fire quickly, vital paperwork including the plans of the ark was reduced to ashes."

"Did the police catch those responsible for the attack?"

"Before calling the police, Dad's thoughts were for safety of the other set of plans."

"But you told us that Granddad kept a spare set."

"Remember, he had died, and we had cleared his house out by

then. His copy became the master used at the factory. In panic, Dad rushed back there while Mum tried to clean the house. He found a carbon-copy arson attack – smoke pouring from a gap in the broken glass."

"But I thought Noah's factory was safe from intruders?"

"We had used concrete for the walls, and provided small windows with bars of steel across them. But the intruders broke the windows by poking them with a pole. Then they squeezed in oil-soaked tapers that had been set alight. That is when we lost the calendar on which we kept the dates for project planning."

"With a double attack, I imagine the police would have no difficulty in finding the criminals," I said.

"The police guessed that they were from these three families who deserted us, anxious to extract revenge. However, their last words on the subject were 'There is insufficient evidence to implicate a particular family. And finding witnesses to events in the middle of a forest is impossible.' We came away without justice being done."

It sounded like a replica of the way the Christian church is attacked in some Asian and Middle Eastern countries. Their churches are regularly torched, but the police make little attempt to find the perpetrators. Maybe they were complicit in the attacks because they do not want the Christian witness in their midst. Jay thought that I was getting onto a hobbyhorse.

"I have sympathy with the persecuted church," I told him. "We have full freedom of religion in this country."

"I envy the UK. Long may it continue."

"These fires show that your enemies are getting serious now, determined to avenge your preaching."

"It took Dad several weeks to reconstruct the plans from memory. Each of us checked the bits we were familiar with, but I'm sure there were mistakes in the new drawings. For added security, we then started sleeping at the factory. Finally, since we could not point the finger at any particular family we decided to pay them back, thereby hoping to avoid further trouble."

"But you only had 'buttons to pay them with'."

"Frank, that sounds like a modern English phrase that I do not understand."

In the days before automation, Blandford Forum was famous for making buttons. They were then a valuable commodity, but buttons are cheap now, being made by machine. The phrase 'buttons to pay them with' means that you only have little round objects left, with little monetary value, to pay your creditors with. Automation had devalued the stocks of buttons.

"Yes, Frank, we only had worthless buttons, so we racked our brains for fresh ideas. In the end two of us went back to work."

"That would hold the project up, unless you worked every hour of the day in the office and late into the night."

"We kept it up for two months, but found that we were all losing weight. Then the unexpected happened. We visited a solicitor to arrange the sale of Granddad's house. Whilst its value had gone up a little with inflation, and we did get some benefit from its earlier under-valuation, it still left us in debt. But then came good news. Whilst doing the searches and sorting the deeds out, the solicitor discovered that away to the east was an oil field owned by the Cush Oil Company. There were several oil wells, like the one at Kimmeridge. He spotted the fact that the oil field extended under Dad's house."

"Why was that good news?" I asked.

"In England, mineral rights belong to the crown. But that wasn't so in our land. It isn't true in the USA either."

"With lots of new exploration prospects in Dorset for oil and gas, I guess landowners would like to feel that about the UK."

"I did not realise that you were finding that much oil here."

"I guess I am exaggerating. One day, something big could turn up in Dorset."

"We agreed to sell the mineral rights to the oil company before parting with the house. The compensation was enough to pay off the three families."

"Having an additional family helping is not consistent with the Bible! So who are you?"

"You will have to loan us a copy so that we can all read it properly. I know that Dad has managed to dip into the library copy. Some names match, but until our future unfolds, we cannot argue for or against us being the people that chapters 6 to 9 in Genesis describe."

"I know that the police were not interested in joining the ark. Did you try to convince the solicitor?"

"He did not believe that a flood was due. He just smirked when he took the fee from us for the sale of Granddad's house."

While Jay and I had been talking, our Labrador 'Rover' – who had been lying by my feet – got up, went over to Katrina and started nuzzling himself against her legs. She encouraged him to continue while she fussed him. Then he flopped on the floor with a sigh of contentment.

"Katrina has a way of calming animals," said Jay." It gives us a glimmer of hope that life will not be unbearable on board when the ark is tossed about by the *mabbul*."

"But it will take more than one person to calm a ship full of animals if they get unruly."

"If that is an indirect way of asking me if I'm scared of what could happen, the answer is Yes!"

"You could always toss the unruly or aggressive ones over the side."

"We have to save life, not abandon animals to a watery grave! It would be nice if we had that option because the pressure on us gets worse. The other family that were helping died."

"You're pulling my leg."

He shook his head.

"Let's try a different tack. Did your father talk to you about bees?"

"Ham suggested that I rustle up a hive on the top deck. Although I'd spoken to Dad ages ago about it, his mind was too full to cope."

"But a hive will have more than two bees in it. Your world of make-believe is creaking with inconsistencies. You've lost all of the families who were helping. On board you'll have two of that animal, 14 of this animal, and now an unknown number of other creatures. Where do wasps and scorpions fit into your story? Or are they to be left behind?"

"Bee-collecting is not on our list of things to do, or rounding up other creatures that sting. The idea is ghastly. I am tempted to say that that is the Lord's problem, but maybe I should say He already has the solution because He told us how big to make the ark and how to divide it into stalls of different sizes."

"Suppose one of you can come back tomorrow, where do we go that will help me unravel the truth? I still have time off."

The big towns in Dorset include Bournemouth, Bridport, Gillingham, Poole, Sherborne, Swanage and Blandford. Jay had heard of the fire at Blandford. He told me that because hot stoves are needed on the ark for cooking and warmth, they had a veritable hazard, so he proceeded to explain that they had lined the kitchens with ceramic tiles and installed a sprinkler system fed by a water tank in the roof.

"You've got your quality assurance procedures wrong there," I retorted. "Water worsens fires in the kitchen."

"We know that water can spread burning oil everywhere. Homemade fire extinguishers that produce foam are installed near the cookers ready for those emergencies," he boasted. "It is amazing what you can do with conkers, baking soda and vinegar. We deliberately set a chip-pan on fire and then tested its efficacy with these extinguishers. Sweeping the chimneys is also a must."

"That I don't understand."

"Soot from the fire sticks to the inside of the chimney. When it gets thick it can catch alight and send flames and burning embers out onto the roof of our wooden ark. Using charcoal rather than wood produces less smoke, and fewer problems. "

"What happens if the stalls catch fire?"

"How? No one in the family smokes. Neither do the animals," he added with a mischievous smile.

"I thought dinosaurs did."

"You have been reading about 'Puff the magic dragon' or some other fables."

"Perhaps. Any accidents so far?"

"Dad nearly lost his hand in the band saw. Although he is a splendid architect, he is not a boat builder, and certainly not a careful artisan. I think we are all accident prone." There was nervousness in his voice while he explained. "Katrina broke her leg. Slipped down the incomplete stairway to the lower level. She was off work six weeks. I hate to think what is going to happen while we are stuck in the ark. Am I next on the list?"

Gaynor was admiring Katrina's dress. "I wasn't going to wear it until we have been in the ark for weeks. The coloured flower pattern will help cheer me up in that dark dungeon. But then I thought, it's so beautiful I'll show it to Gaynor."

"Thank you. You would do well on a cat-walk. But what about other clothes, new ones, fresh changes?"

"I've got 20 new dresses untouched waiting to be worn on birthdays and anniversaries."

"I would love to see them all, but will that make up for gazing at dresses in shops, spotting something you might like and then carrying armfuls of clothing into the changing room? One of my treats is going out with my sister when I want a new dress."

"We will miss the shops and indulging in trying on new dresses, feeling the quality of the material, standing in front of the mirror umming and arring much to the disgust of our men folk. I think that is one of the reasons why so many would not join the ark. It would mean turning their backs on the consumer society."

"I hope you do not put weight on before you wear those unused clothes, Katrina."

"Being busy each day, I do not think that I will have to count calories."

"I hope that you do not trip and fall again. Won't the moths over the year get at the clothes that you have packed? And spiders will spin webs in dark corners."

"Yes. That is how I slipped and broke my leg when I brushed against one unexpectedly."

"So you have got used to those creepies?"

"I don't think that I will ever get used to wandering about the spooky parts of the ark. There are no windows downstairs. Would you?"

"I would hate the thought of it."

"As for moths, things have been carefully packed, and we have made liberal use of mothballs. They were easy to make when Ham was distilling the pitch. And the clothes trunks have been sealed with pitch to keep vermin out, only to be opened on special occasions."

"And when things wear out or you get tired of them, or worse still, wish you'd never bought something – what then?"

It was a good job that I did not hear that remark as they chuckled to each other saying, "Both of our husbands would explode if we admitted that such thoughts creep into our minds." Then they turned to serious matters – how do they get replacement clothes?

"Noah gave us strict instructions to learn two different skills essential for making clothes so that we can do everything ourselves. We have a couple of spinning wheels and treadle-powered sewing machines. I've learned how to use the spinning wheel to produce threads. Noah has become an expert at fashion design."

"I wish my Frank would take more interest in that."

"I share the sentiments with you, Gaynor, but I don't seem to be having any more success with my Jay than you are."

"So what triggered Noah's interest?"

"Being an architect, he has an eye for design and aesthetics."

"Where is your wool coming from?"

"We are expecting seven pairs of sheep. A local farmer taught us how to shear them. I don't think we will win any prizes in competitions for the fastest shear, but it will have to be done whilst they are on board. It would have been better if the farmer had offered to come with us, but his excuse was that he'd have to leave his other animals behind."

"So are you confident you'll get 14 sheep?"

"If we don't, woollen clothes will be things of the past. But safely aboard are bins of cotton and linen ready for making into other types of clothes when the need arises. It will be years before we have fresh crops of those."

"But they are all bland colours. Nothing like your dress."

"Cotton grows in four natural colours."

"Now you have caught me by surprise."

"And my Jay has been experimenting with dyes. Most of the dyes come from plants, so Irene and Sarah burned the midnight oil studying seed catalogues to ensure that we had everything important for our new life. There are 300 lockers of labelled seeds on board."

"Most of our modern dyes are synthetic."

"That would have made our lives easier, but we don't have that technology. We've also bought a couple of cloth-printing machines and the manuals. I'm not sure if we will be able to produce printed material such as the dress I have got on, but we will have a go once the flood is over."

"How about washing clothes?"

"A twin-tub like yours would be super, Gaynor, but we do not have electricity to run it. And if it went wrong, who would repair it? So we have to be content with boiling in a cauldron, and wringing in a mangle."

"An outdoor drying line must be one of your other needs."

"This is one of the things that nearly caused grief to the project. Even if we had an open deck, we are expecting a daily downpour, so no drying line. The plan is to dry clothes around one of the stoves that will be kept alight day and night. True, it does not freshen them up."

"Why the near-grief?"

"Irene is so clothes conscious. To her, the idea of indoor drying, no shops for new clothes, and having to wear jeans day by day was too much. She's as bad as I am with cobwebs and spiders. A while back, she deserted Ham and went back to live with her parents."

"You have to be joking. You are such a close family."

"Noah and Sarah were especially fraught. They realised that the survival of the human race was down to one woman – me. I blush to think about it. To make matters worse, Ham had never had a dream about the need to build the ark, so he only joined because of Irene's dream. It was a double worry because we were also in danger of losing Ham. Her parents had always been critical of her marriage to him. Claimed he was a religious nutcase, always ready to help other people and not concentrating on looking after himself and his wife. They were pleased to have her back, saying that at last she had come to her senses about Ham who, for many years, had slavishly trotted behind his parents' perverted view that the world was doomed. They engaged a solicitor to start divorce proceedings."

"On what grounds?"

"The solicitor said that the religious nutcase idea might not work. He suggested that they try and get the marriage annulled on the basis of no consummation because of religious bigotry about sex by Ham. We knew it wasn't true, but the solicitor said that after 20 years of marriage, the absence of a baby was a sign of something wrong. Or he was infertile. It had to be his fault because his other brother had the same problem. The Lonely Hearts' Club found her a new boy friend, recently divorced and looking to re-marry."

"Gossip for the neighbourhood, Katrina?"

"A few new people starting asking questions about the ark and we offered them the spare bedrooms, but there were no takers. Their excuses were pathetic. In reality, they had a hard-hearted spiritual objection to getting close to the God we knew."

Infertility is more common than acknowledged. My sister and her husband had never had a baby. Gaynor wondered if Katrina had heard of the Cerne Abbas Giant – the naked figure of a warrior cut into the chalk hillside north of Dorchester. She thought that he was a warrior with a club in his hand. I explained to her that he is a fertility symbol. The 'club' emphasises his power to sire offspring. Childless couples have braved the embarrassment and English weather and made love on his lower parts in the hope of conceiving, though not my sister.

 The Cerne Giant, cut into the chalk hillside east of Cerne Abbas, is a fertility symbol, not a warrior. His true origin is not known. He was cleaned and restored by a team from the National Trust in Sept 2008.

The spring, near the old Abbey, is woven into the legend of the Giant. Christians were keen to baptise those who repudiated the fertility symbol, but had no water. St Augustine prayed for a spring and got one.

"Knowing English weather I am not sure I would however desperate I am for a baby. I suspect that my other sisters-in-law would think the same way as Frank's sister and husband. Our trust, however misplaced it seems to you, is in the 'Lord of consequences'. Fertility rites are out."

"Were you heartbroken about Irene and her new boy friend?"

"She dated him a few times and then gave him up. It seemed that we hardly had time to say 'pass me the next piece of timber' before she was back with Ham. Since then she has worked hard to catch up on all that she hadn't done whilst she was away. She realised that service to God requires self-sacrifice though she did ask if she could put her gym equipment in one of the other bedrooms. We would have made up a swimming pool if it was the only way of keeping her."

"Gyms are not something that I am into. But every one to their own tastes. Now, nice dresses need a matching handbags, shoes and hairstyles."

"Handbags are easy to make, but not shoes. Everything will be leather with plenty of fresh material to hand. We have been practising tanning it. Obviously we set the vats up outside the ark to avoid that awful smell pervading the ark. We now have sufficient leather to keep us going for two years until our baby cows have grown up. Noah has made shoes for himself. Whether he will ever rise to the skill needed to make ladies' fashion shoes is questionable, but he is trying. Noah offered Irene the first pair, but she said they should go to Sarah because they have the same size feet."

"I admire his talent. Ladies and fresh flowers also go together, Katrina."

"I am envious of your display of chrysanthemums on the table over there. We have put fresh flowers in the ark today. They might last two weeks before we have to throw them away. After that it will be a year without blooms, apart from a few hyacinths. There is not much natural light on the ark to grow flowers."

"Put them by the windows."

"That is not possible. There are special windows at the top of the ark but they are more for ventilation than for light. So we have painted some pretend windows on our bedroom walls with curtains to pull across at night to make it feel cosy."

"You will have no difficulty in getting poinsettias to go red. Controlled darkness for eight weeks before they flower is what they need."

"That is interesting. But don't they need bright light thereafter?"

"Mm, that's true. Never mind, you can have freshly grown mushrooms each day from the dark bowels of the ark."

"You're sweet reminding us of these small blessings that we can get in the dark."

"Perfume! You need perfume. As a child I had crushed rose leaves to put their scent in a bottle. You won't have any handy chemists for toiletries. So have you made your own second-rate stuff?"

"With Sarah working in the vets, she learned the secrets of musk. Making perfume has been one of the enjoyable aspects of the project. As another bonus, Ham converted a coffee blender to grind up magnesium silicate."

"What's that?"

"It makes talcum powder."

"I hope that Frank does not expect me to make my own talc from now on."

"The other three ladies in the team asked about hair-cutting and styling once we leave this world. To surprise them, I got Wendy to give me lessons and I plan to share those skills with the others later."

"You seem to have thought about everything. But why is Wendy not joining the ark?"

"You could ask that question about everybody around us. In her book of life, God did not exist, so why bother putting yourself out?"

"Frank's camera? He was annoyed with me that I loaned it out without his approval."

"I've taken some photographs of the ark, including flash photos of our bedrooms. You haven't got any more films, have you? I've almost finished this first one. I missed the opportunity to take photos of the animals that arrived early, being caught on the hop. We'll bring the camera back tomorrow with the exposed films."

"I have two spares in the fridge because the chemist tells me they keep much longer that way."

While Gaynor was getting them, the doorbell rang. I went to answer it and found Noah there. He told us that a gang of youths had found the ark and were trying to set fire to it. It was scaring the animals and would need more than kitchen fire extinguishers to douse the flames. He wanted Jay and Katrina to return promptly.

"What time will you be back tomorrow?" I asked.

"With so much going wrong, it looks as if we will be gone for good," Noah replied. "I only hope that the rain starts soon so that we can get moving."

"But you can't go. We've not been to all these places that we listed and I have other questions about your activities."

"I am sorry, Frank, it is worse than a fire. Irene has deserted us again and Ham is in a plight. Stephen and Patricia wont arrive back until the middle of the night or even later. Even if they return sober, they will still be useless. The other four of us are in a quandary, emotionally and physically. How do four of us cope with 12 aggressive youths, fire and disturbed animals?"

"What about the helpful owner of the forest?"

"I have just discovered that he went off on a long business trip with his wife this morning. On reflection, we think they planned it this way to avoid us."

"So what do we do?" I continued.

"If you are bothered about the things we have been talking about, why not go to Bournemouth, Bridport, and Swanage yourself. If you are still looking for explanations for the legends, why not ask the archaeologists about cement making or the geologists about concrete walls in mines. I am sure that the flood legends are corruptions of a monumental truth but we cannot give any guarantees that it has anything to do with us. Go and ask some searching questions of your peers and professors. As lives are at stake I must go now."

"But if you're not coming back, what about my camera?"

"Have you never had disappointment? I was looking forward to a longer break in this superb county of Dorset. Events beyond our control have overtaken us. And I am sorry about the camera."

I tried to say that they could not go. The forecast was for thunderstorms, violent ones. Noah wanted to get the feel for rain before he had to face it on the ark. But they had gone. I tried to fold the map up, but I was so exasperated that the creases did not go in the right places.

"What are you trembling for, Frank?" asked Gaynor.

"I thought he was going to ask me to go back with him."

"But you said you wanted to see the ark."

"Being shown over the ark in the middle of its construction is one thing. Facing a blazing inferno is another. Think of the smell of burning flesh!"

"Do you remember awhile ago watching the Pathé Pictorial cinema news when the foot and mouth crisis was at its peak? Farmers were having to burn mountains of animals."

"Yes, that's why I didn't want to go with them. You could almost smell the picture."

"And that time when you dropped a streak of bacon on the hot cooker?"

"It caught fire quickly."

"And then the ceiling tiles started to shrivel with the heat, and bits of hot polystyrene dripped onto the floor."

"They've stopped making polystyrene ceiling tiles. Noah knew they are dangerous and so used ceramic tiles." So where were those fire engines going?

"What are you muttering about, Frank?"

"Something that happened on my way home, Gaynor. My mind will not focus on one thing at a time."

"Remind me how long Jay and Katrina have been married."

"Twenty years."

"With Stephen being the oldest, that would make him in his forties or fifties. And Noah and Sarah would then have to be 70 to 80."

"But they don't look that old."

"Could it be a hoax?"

"And my camera!"

"I will buy you another one. It was my fault for trusting them."

"Let us close this chapter in our lives and I'll garden tomorrow, even if it rains."

"And golf the day after?"

"You can read me like a book."

"Talking about books, did you ever read Virginia Woolf's books?"

"I know they appealed to you, but not to me. Why ask?"

Gaynor explained that in 1910, four high-ranking Abyssinian Princes, an interpreter and a foreign office official asked to visit *HMS Dreadnought*, the navy's mightiest battleship to cement relationships between the two countries. A special train was laid on for them from London to Weymouth. At Portland, the navy swung precision protocol into play to impress the special visitors in a tour of the ship.

Safely back in London, the "Abyssinians" got in touch with a newspaper, and explained that it was a hoax. The princes, who included Virginia Woolf, were English but dressed as foreigners with dark paint on their faces. Their panache in carrying out the hoax was even greater because the Chief Staff Officer on board *Dreadnought* was related to Woolf, and failed to notice her. I had a vague recollection of it because they had immortalised the phrase '*Bunga, Bunga*'.

"I condemn this visitor who claims to be Noah-ben-Lamech as a modern day hoaxer," I told Gaynor. "He is replete with a cooperative family like Woolf who dash in and out claiming to be from 4,300 years ago."

"Are you going to do anything about it?"

"Why should I? People will only laugh at me for being tricked."

"What about the zebra?"

"He could've picked that up in a jumble sale."

"I do not mean the wooden one, I mean the real animal. While you were out this morning, Adrian popped round to say he had seen the zebra come into our garden and the damage he had caused. Knowing that we wanted to sell, he offered to help us get the garden tidy in case a prospective buyer came around at short notice."

"That was kind of him, but that zebra is still a puzzle. And he got the time scale mentioned in the Bible completely wrong. If he is the Biblical Noah he would be 4,300 years old, but he claims to have lived before any barrows were made."

"But he did argue that archaeologists cannot easily tell the date of these things, Frank."

"Who is the historian in the house?"

"You are . . . Let us stop arguing and focus on our pressing matters. If we are going to move house, you can start sorting through the attic tomorrow and get rid of the things we only needed when the children were younger. It will keep you out of mischief while you are off work. There is a jumble sale at the school next week. The pushchair can go for starters."

"If Anne and Tommy's teacher is there I'll give her a piece of my mind."

"And those archaeology books," she added as an afterthought. "Otherwise they'll drive us silly."

I had to agree with Gaynor that some of them were silly, especially one by Navarra, who claimed that he had climbed Mount Ararat and brought back wood from the ark. With his young son, he'd almost been killed in a crevasse. He claimed that he had been lured up Ararat by reports that Russian pilots during World War 1 had spotted an ark in the middle of a glacier.

"Did those pilots believe that Noah dropped anchor in the middle of a glacier high on a mountain? If so, they were hoaxed as much as we were," Gaynor commented.

"Let's put this daft idea aside. What are we going to do about this low valuation of our house?"

"Try and get Mr and Mrs Sharman to reduce the price of the house that we want to buy, Frank."

"Right now I am going to watch the local news on TV. Find out where those fire engines were going."

PART TWO

The Book That Granddad Never Wrote

"Granddad, the monkey kept coming out of the window and back in through the door. Noah said he was a bugbear because he had to keep recounting the animals."

CHAPTER ELEVEN

MY OLD CAMERA

"you are to bring into the ark two of all living creatures",
Gen 6 v 19

Retirement is wonderful. You can enjoy peace each afternoon until the door is flung open and grandchildren burst in. Beryl jumped onto my lap, clasped me tightly around the neck and gave me a kiss. Her elder brother followed her into the house in a split second. He looked around and finding my lap full, jumped up on to Gaynor's lap, pouring kisses onto her. Two chairs creaked in protest.

"It's lovely to see you children, but where is Mummy?"

"She has gone into the hardware store to get curtain hooks and raffle tape."

"I think you mean rufflette tape."

"Granddad," she said as she gripped me tighter around the neck, ignoring my comment about the tape, "we've been doing a project at school about Noah an' the ark to save the animals from drowning. The giraffes couldn't get in because their heads were too high for the doorway. They were holding the rest of the animals up. Rain was fallin'. We are going to have the rest of the story tomorrow. So exciting!"

James looked puzzled.

"He's forgotten the story from last year when they did it," said Beryl, disparaging her elder brother. "I gonna sing you the song about the monkey. Noah told him he was a bugbear going in and out of the window. If he messed around any more, he'd be left behind."

As she sang, something stirred in my memory, though it was disturbed by a gentle tap at the open door. Anne entered.

"Hello, Mum and Dad," she said as she put down her parcels, and gave us a kiss. "I'd love a cuppa if the kettle is boiling, but then we must dash."

Whilst making more tea I said to her, "Beryl tells me they are learning about Noah's ark. I remember another girl who also got excited about it in her childhood."

"Who was that?" asked Anne, frowning.

"When you were Beryl's age you came home from school one summer's day, bubbling over about the story."

"All grown ups know it was a legend, like F-A-T-H-E-R C-...-M-A-S," she said, spelling it out in the hope that the children would not understand her coded message. "Any excitement was a passing thing; normal for a child."

"But I never told you that Noah and his family came to see us that day you made the model of the ark, animals and rainbow. They had finished the ark, and were taking a break before loading their belongings, the foods and the animals. Then a zebra turned up early and got into our garden. They told me the whole story and asked me to write a book."

"Dad, that's crazy! Are you sure you weren't dreaming? Your memory is getting bad these days. You forgot my husband's birthday last month."

"I apologised to Gavin for that isolated incident. I remembered him last year, and the year before. I also remembered your wedding anniversaries, and the children's birthdays."

"My in-laws have not once remembered my birthday, so I forgive you knowing it was a single lapse."

"Forgiveness accepted, but your mum also met Noah. And we've still got the carved zebra in the attic they brought us."

Gaynor nodded but Anne continued to look quizzical.

"Dad, you are getting old and senile. The story of Noah is a legend, based on an older legend of a fellow I used to call 'Umpy-Tim' because I cannot remember his proper name. The claim is that he made a square boat in two days. At least we are not asked to believe that Noah built his ark so quickly. Even if the story of Noah were true, there is no way he could have got into our century. Time travel is only for science fiction books or TV programmes like *Doctor Who*."

"Your dad is not lying. We both met the family," Gaynor emphasised.

"All eight of them? The Muslim Koran offers two different stories. One of Noah's sons did not join the ark and in another place it says that Mrs Noah was consigned to the fires of hell. These contradictions with the Bible show that the Bible tells a legend."

"We never met the third son, Stephen, and his wife Patricia."

"Stephen and Patricia are not Hebrew names, so it sound like a jumble of different legends. Besides, think how big the boat was. Cubits are bigger than feet, making the ark an impossible size. Why have you suddenly remembered this after years of forgetting?"

Gaynor and I looked at each other hoping that the other one would offer an answer to Anne's question but silence reigned. I could have said that it was shortage of time, the demands of being a husband, raising three children and doing my work properly. But she knew that I had written Christmas plays for the school that everyone had enjoyed. The truth was that I did not want to risk ridicule by writing about Noah. I changed the subject and asked her who told her that Father Christmas was not real.

"I worked it out with Sammy when I was six. It was the sooty chimney that gave me the clue. I played along with the story for years for the sake of Tommy and Ben."

"What happened to Samantha? I know that she was one of the first women to be ordained in the Church of England, and a pretty hot-headed moralist, but we lost touch with Adrian and his family when we moved here."

"We still keep in touch. She has finished her curacy and got a parish in Devon."

"At least we had a bit of family fun with the F-C legend."

"You could have written that book if you had played less golf. Even as a teenager I remember that you constantly harped on about this dream-course near Lyme Regis, and wondered why none of us wanted to play."

"Alright, golf was another excuse, but I needed the relaxation. Sadly, part of the Lyme Regis course slipped into the sea. I haven't been there for years."

"How were these visitors dressed?"

"Noah first came in his working clothes with sawdust, pitch and paint on them."

"They were set up to fool you, Dad."

"Later they came in modern styled clothes, but nothing of nylon or other synthetic materials."

"You were suckers. Were you hoaxed like the Admiralty and the railways by this new version of the Virginia Woolf entourage?"

"Whatever our visitors' real identity, Noah had been an intelligent man, knowing far more about Dorset and its rainfall record than I did and used his knowledge to lead me astray. If his story had been true then he would have come back and gloated at my expense once the flood was over. The worst thing was that they stole my camera by subterfuge."

"Ah! That explains why there are no photographs of Tommy and me around the age of seven and eight in the family album."

"I bought you a new camera that Christmas," interjected Gaynor. "Auto-focus and other useful features. 'Too complicated,' you said, 'to learn how to use it.' That is why there were no photos of you children at that age, Anne."

"I think I will keep out of this argument, Mum. So where did your visitors go?"

"One evening, whilst chatting with Jay about places to visit, Noah called them back urgently because arsonists were trying to burn the ark."

"Who was Jay and where did he live?"

"They claimed to be time travellers, and Jay was short for Japeth."

"You'll have to tell me the full story of this hoax one day, but we must go now. Gavin is due back tomorrow. The house is in a mess and needs straightening before he returns."

"You mean my daughter has been having private orgies while her husband was the other side of the world?"

"Dad, what a wicked notion!"

"You baited me to say it."

"As a prim and proper wife," she said standing erect with a defiant folding of her arms, "I have been decorating while Gavin has been away. Lots of things still need sorting out, including fitting the new curtains. Come on, children, say goodbye."

"Why can't we stay? Our house is lonely without Daddy, an' you get worried at night, Mummy."

"No I don't," she said sharply. "We must be going. Neither of you have got any night-time things or clean clothes for tomorrow. Your dress, Beryl, has got glue down it and needs washing. Daddy can bring you round on Saturday to see Grandma and Granddad again."

"Anne gave you short shrift," said Gaynor. "You spoilt her as a child, your little golden girl who could do no wrong. Look how she repays you."

"She's not that bad. But I didn't hear an apology for calling me forgetful."

"Keep your hat on! I reminded you twice of Gavin's birthday. Now you can tell me why you did not write that book and why you told Anne a lie that you had met the Biblical Noah when you did not believe his yarn."

"I had forgotten all about Noah's visit until today, but so had you. You know that I was annoyed because those odd visitors disappeared without answering all my questions. You can't write a book without everything wrapped up."

"But Virginia Woolf wrote many successful books."

"As the perpetrator of that Abyssinian hoax, it enhanced her reputation. As the victim of the Noah hoax, that put me at a disadvantage. South West Trains, or whatever they called the railways in those days, and the Admiralty kept as quiet about the incident as possible. They were as embarrassed as I was."

"They did tell you to go and investigate things for yourself. We both agreed, even if they were not the Biblical family, that they had spotted something wrong with the casual way historians describe old stories as legends when they do not fit our modern way of thinking. You could do that now that you have retired."

"You were more convinced than I was that there was some truth in the Bible story."

"Frank, you never tried to investigate the points that he made that pricked your mind like a pin in a balloon. For days on end it was as if you were trying to stick bits of the shattered rubber together to restore the shape of the balloon instead of rising to his challenge, and researching the topic yourself. Go for it now! It would save you getting under my feet each day. You have not played golf for years. The only excitement you have is when Beryl and James come round. Go and look at the fossils in Swanage tomorrow, like Jay suggested. If you could write a book, you could make us a bit of money to eke out our pension. Then we could go abroad again for our holidays like Anne and Gavin, perhaps see this Pantheon in Rome that Noah told you about, or go and see the Leaning Tower of Pisa. You can go up it now that the civil engineers have stabilised the structure against further tilting. "

"I didn't know you were interested in archaeology."

"I got fed up of the Spanish beaches year after year when the children were young. There is a touch of romance about Rome or Venice. I dream of going to them all."

"Did you dream of me writing a book?"

"You must have produced thousands of brochures and guides for Dorset in the last 30 years. So what is difficult about producing a book? You did not throw away your archaeology books when we moved house. Use them for ideas however crazy."

I'd asked myself this question a million times, and turned it down. There were too many pages to write. And if I did write, would anybody buy the book or believe the story? Even if that Noah fellow had told the truth, all we know is that he had made an ark, some animals turned up early and then there was a fire. Whether they put it out or whether the flood ever came, we'll never know. He could have been a confidence trickster, a phoney, getting free meals out of me, an expensive camera and tours of Dorset. Worst of all, they disturbed my mental equilibrium that had, until then, worked on the principle that my understanding of archaeology was perfect. Even now, in the recesses of my mind doubts continued to lurk that there was a smidgen of truth there.

"If you cannot write fiction prompted by what that Noah-guy told us, how about a critical analysis of archaeology as it relates to legends – pure non-fiction?"

"Too exhausting mentally. I'd rather have tea."

"Food!" she exclaimed. "That is all you think about. Use your imagination on a book. You do not have to admit you were caught out by a clever adult hoax. As a child your parents hoaxed you over Father Christmas, and we told our children the same story, though I was disappointed that Anne twigged it so young. They have got over the deception. Use the Noah hoax as a springboard for ideas that captivate your readers, like you did for those Christmas plays. Invent a new '*Bunga, Bunga*' phrase like Woolf did as a pretence that they could not speak English when on *HMS Dreadnought*."

"When was the last time you made Dorset Apple Cake?"

"You write the book, and I will make it. Fair exchange?"

"The scales are tipped in your favour. You can make Apple Cake mixture in half an hour. It will take me months, or maybe years to write a book."

"It would not have taken long if you had done it while it was fresh in your mind. At least you now know it was a hoax."

"Correction, we were both hoaxed. In fact, you seemed to be on the verge of believing that they were the Bible folk."

"What did you say two minutes ago, Frank? 'Even now, in the recesses of my mind doubts continue to lurk that there was a smidgen of truth there.'"

"Trust you to have the last word. But why did nobody else join them if their story were true? Wendy, the hairdresser, knew all about their activities because she taught Katrina hair-styling."

"And the forest owner knew all about their activities, even ordering his own suite of rooms in the ark."

"But he could have played along with the story in order to sell his timber at a higher price."

"Fools."

Tea and arguments over, we watched the TV news in order to put the subject of Noah out of our minds. The Bank of England had made a statement about the economy. There was a new wave of prosperity in the UK. As part of a special report, there was a focus on Dorset whose industry was buoyant, though oil production in Purbeck was declining. The coastline had been declared as a World Heritage Site. There had been a warehouse fire at Granbury – boring detail to someone not enamoured by Dorset so I struggled up the loft ladder to find that carved zebra, and my old notebooks. Maybe, once and for all, I would settle the issue of the legend. Fifteen minutes later I had the zebra and two notebooks.

"You should have stayed and watched all the news," said Gaynor. "The newsreader announced that a new track of dinosaur fossil footprints have been found in Dorset."

"But dinosaurs were Tommy's interest, not mine."

"Have you forgotten that Noah never explained about the dinosaurs?"

"I told you there were lots of things he didn't explain and that is why I refused to write crap. If you thought it important, why didn't you call me down?"

"Even though you have found those notebooks to jog your memory, will you ever type a single word?"

"You're winding me up. You could've called me and given me the choice about watching it."

"I am winding you up. I did something better than calling you. It would have taken you too long to get down."

"It's your fault that I stumbled up there and almost put my foot through the ceiling. There must be hundreds of old lampshades that I had to step over. You buy new ones every year, and never throw any away."

"You are as bad with your books."

"What was this better thing that you did?"

"Set the video recorder going."

"Now that's the wife I married. Thoughtful and helpful. Thanks," I said, giving her a kiss.

"I'll watch it through once more with you and then start some baking."

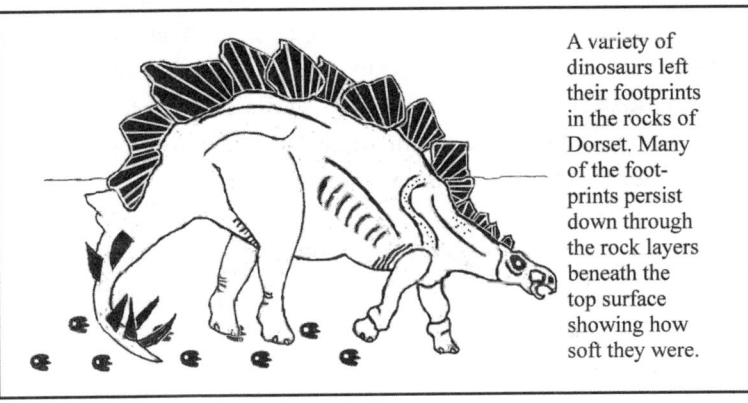

A variety of dinosaurs left their footprints in the rocks of Dorset. Many of the footprints persist down through the rock layers beneath the top surface showing how soft they were.

"In quarrying operations near Swanage," said the reporter as the camera panned the scene, "new fossil footprints have been found. The scientists are excited by this track of footprints, probably made by sauropods, in a shelly limestone layer. The impressions of the footprints persisted into the next layers down. They were made at the edge of a fresh water lagoon that was separated from the sea by a barrier. The beach was not far away."

"I find it difficult to understand how they work that out," I admitted to Gaynor.

"So did I, but in the regional news, the Dorchester museum curator answers the reporter's questions about the footprints in words of one syllable."

Whilst watching the video, the phone rang. Gaynor answered it, but then passed it to me as if it were red-hot. "It's Anne. She's agitated. Wants you straight away."

"What for? I'm watching TV. Is she going to apologise?"

"Dad, there is a giraffe in my garden."

"Stop screeching, Anne," I said, holding the receiver at arm's length. "I'm not deaf."

"He has put his head through Beryl's bedroom window. I can't close it. Do something."

"Calm down. You must be dreaming or you've been thinking of the story of Noah. You are like your mum for being a dreamer."

"Noah is a legend," she added defiantly, "but I need help."

"Can't you ask the neighbours?"

"Dad! I'm scared of going downstairs, let alone outside. I'd have to leave the children up here. I cannot phone anyone else up from the bedroom because the phone directory is downstairs. Yours is the only number I can remember."

When I got to Anne's I could see that the giraffe was too tall to be missed. But it had a bridle over its head and a man holding the reigns. His voice sounded familiar but it was none of Anne's neighbours.

"Hello, Frank. We met all those years ago. I wanted to come back and see you again, and complete the story."

Suddenly, it clicked. "Why, if it's not Noah," I exclaimed. And we shook hands vigorously. "Where have you been hiding? Gaynor wants me to write a book, so I need more ideas from you over the way you hoaxed me, and whether you have fooled any one else. And you must be a brilliant magician to conjure up a giraffe this time because it will not fit into your proverbial garden shed."

"I am sorry about the giraffe. I had hoped to come and see you without any animals."

"I've learned to forgive you about that zebra, and your sudden disappearance 30 years ago, but you'll have to ask for Anne's forgiveness over this intrusion."

"I wanted to see you and Gaynor first. I went to your old house, not knowing you had moved. Then I tried Crossways."

That attempt to buy a house at Crossways had fallen through. Having to repair my roof was an unexpected expense that meant I could not afford the asking price of the house we wanted, though the vendors had dropped it by £500. It was only when Gaynor's parents died that we had the extra money needed to move upmarket. By then, everything on that new estate had been sold, so we went elsewhere.

"Frank, we traced Anne, but then, like the zebra of years ago, somehow this giraffe also got involved in the time travel. I am sorry that he caused your daughter and her children a stir. Let me take the giraffe back, and then we can talk without interruption."

While he led the giraffe away I went in to see Anne, and found her laughing uncontrollably.

"Dad, I doubted your story this afternoon. You got a zebra, I got a giraffe. Is it another hoax, or part two of the same one?"

"Let me phone Mum and tell her we are all right. Then we can get to the bottom of this."

Half way through telling Anne about the rest of the events of 1970 there was a tap at the door. In came Noah, Sarah and Jay. In the bright light I could see that they were showing their ages, but otherwise were much as I remembered them. Jay's hair had gone as grey as had the few hairs I still possessed. I reached for the jar of coffee and five mugs whilst Anne listened to Noah re-capping about the building of the ark and the reason for his sudden disappearance.

"It was early autumn in our homeland, and the ark was complete. With the animals not due for seven days we were hoping to have a long break in Dorset. Then out of the blue, an army of animals arrived baying to get in. So we loaded them."

"But you only told me . . ."

". . . bits of the story, Frank. We did not have time to tell all, and you seemed to have difficulties taking it in."

"When you first came, it was difficult to believe that you had literally popped out of the Bible after making a gigantic ark. Even though you have returned, I'm not going to fall into the trap of believing you. Why wait so long before trying to hoax me again?"

"Other challenges came with the animals."

"Were animals jostling each other on the gangplank, all held up by the giraffe who could not get under the lintel? Lions sinking their teeth into the zebras?"

"Frank, slow down, switch off your imagination which has been fed by books and magazines that have attempted to ridicule the story of the ark. You have forgotten that we took baby animals that were just as easy to look after as Joy Adamson's lioness cub. Our big problem was that local ruffians were trying to frighten the animals and burn the ark. Although I wanted to spend more time with you, safety had to come first. We dared not come back then as we could not risk leaving the animals."

Since 1970, everybody had called me stupid believing in a hoax when I tried to tell them what happened. Even my neighbour, Adrian, who saw the zebra, thought that I'd lost a screw from my brain when I told him about our conversations. Now it sounded as if Noah was winding Anne and myself up for a bigger hoax.

"No, Frank. We were in a real mess. The arrival of a motley collection of animals, nothing like the picture that school children paint with colourful animals in their adult plumage, caused us bewilderment. They were mostly small grey creatures, in stark contrast to the zebra. Sarah, always full of emotions, started to weep. 'It's happening,' she said, 'after all those years of hard work.' We had planned for Ham to take charge of this operation."

"He had a splendid rapport with animals. I watched him handle that zebra years ago. He would have had them settled in no time, even the ones that got out of step."

"Have you forgotten?"

"Crumbs, yes, I'd forgotten that Irene had deserted her husband for the second time."

"Ham was devastated, in a mental fog. We felt ham-strung, if you will pardon the pun, putting the animals in the stalls because we were baffled by what some of the animals were, how big they would be in a year's time or what they would eat. The sight of so many animals made us realise how short-staffed we were."

"I'm still suspicious of the whole story. Or it's got a fiasco for an ending. Think of the headlines in the newspapers – 'Ark Adventure Fails for Lack of Staff, Workers abandon ship', or 'Animals in Ark Zoo Die from Starvation'."

"You are being cynical again, Dad," said Anne. "Would they be here if the story went pear-shaped?"

"This afternoon, Anne, you had doubts that this Noah fellow was anything but a modern charlatan. What has changed your mind?"

"Nothing. Noah might be a hoaxer or a magician, but I am being entertained right now. Once the entertainment is over, if it does not make sense, I shall accuse him of mischief and then expose him for what he really is."

Feeling that he had at least one sympathetic listener, Noah continued, "I expected chaos, but a miracle took over. Most of the animals that arrived early got into their stalls, crawled under a pile of hay and went to sleep for months. This kind of hibernation made our jobs easier. Once we realised that most of these early arrivals would sleep like this, we encouraged the other early arrivals to head to the Cheota – the 'cool end of the ark'."

"Why didn't you call it by its proper name – stern or prow? Nobody would have a clue what the Cheota was."

"The ark did not have a prow or a stern. From the outside, the ark was identical at both ends except for the chimneys. The Cheota was away from our quarters where we had the stoves. We carried these sleeping animals to the Cheota when we realised that we had put them in the wrong stalls."

"Did you keep the animals in pairs or separate them to prevent them from breeding?"

"They came in pairs for company, and we kept them that way. Those that we separated accidentally objected noisily, even though they were only baby animals. Some, like the monkeys, were brought on the backs of their parents to the edge of the clearing in the forest. In other cases, parents came close to the ark and gave birth there. Once their offspring were weaned, they left."

"You had no room for the parents and their babies. Are you telling me that the babies left their parents behind? You must be joking."

"Frank, think about war. Many parents risked their lives for their children, and those of their neighbours. Thousands of children were evacuated to rural parts of Dorset during the war to get them away from the bombs falling on big cities."

I had asked my father, long ago, about Holton Heath and those decoy fires after Noah had mentioned it. Dad said that he had come close to losing his life during one night of intense bombing, which killed two of his mates. They left widows and orphaned children. They paid the ultimate sacrifice.

"It shows the altruism of the human race," Noah told me. "Why should animals be any different when they sense danger?"

"I thought animals were red in tooth and claw."

"That might be true of some species. Others give their lives for their children. The mother octopus dies soon after she has produced babies."

"I was never much good at biology."

"You do not need to be, Frank, to understand the story. And we did have a bit of a laugh."

"Do you mean that the school story was correct and that the giraffes could not get under the door-lintel, or the elk's antlers were too wide for the jambs?"

"I have told you before that all animals were small. Some were so young that they fell asleep on the gangplank. We popped them in a barrow, and wheeled them in. At first we tried ticking each animal that entered the ark off a master list that the women had prepared, but half the time we were guessing what animal was what because of their similarities when young. Towards the end of the year afloat we were able to identify some of them because as they grew, their features became more distinct. Right then, we accepted what came, and hoped we would have enough room.

When Elsa, the lioness cub's mother was alive, she was safe. When mother was shot, Elsa's life was at risk. She was taken into care by the Adamsons and brought up almost as a pet until she was old enough to be released back into the wild. She often returned to see her adopted human family even after having her own litter.

"We had loaded different types of foods on different decks in the ark. Berries and nuts went on the top deck, hay and corn on the middle deck, and things like bamboo shoots for pandas went on the lower deck. There was straw on each deck for bedding. On the lower deck we also put items we would use only after we had left the ark. Outside the ark we had built temporary feeding troughs, each containing a different animal food. One of us stood at the feeding troughs. If an animal stopped to nibble something before heading into the ark, we put a different coloured neckband on them according to what they had eaten. Then whoever was in charge of the gangplank ensured that they went to the correct part of the ark where their food was stored. This saved carting food around different sections of the ark, or moving the animals."

"I'll grant you that that was a good idea but it does not prove the reality of your story. And you still haven't got Irene."

"You are still the same Frank that I remember from all those years ago. Does Gaynor believe us?"

"She's more sympathetic than I am. We did have a discussion about women's intuition, and their greater propensity for religion. It's all down to the female genes."

Anne butted in. "I am not so sure that everyone will agree with you, Dad, in these days of sexual equality." Then, turning to Noah, she continued, "However, telling the story without visible proof isn't going to convince either of us. Unless you have anything tangible, why not carry on telling us about loading the animals. I'm enjoying the yarn and I can see how Mum and Dad got hooked on it."

"The next group of animals came in seven pairs. Some of these would provide us with milk during the voyage and fresh meat over the next few years. I found milking difficult, especially when the *mabbul* was at its height. More milk went over me than into the bucket. Sarah had pity on me and did most of my share of the milking. But I did become an expert in making cream, cheese and butter."

"So you made Dorset Vinney?"

"Delicious, especially with the Dorset Knobs." His smile radiated.

"They have gone out of fashion in Dorset now."

"That is sad because we enjoyed them. On the top deck we had built several aviaries, with perches, sticks and branches to make them as realistic as possible. At first we left the cage doors open. Pairs of birds flew in through the window, found a perch in one of the aviaries, and settled there. Others shuttled in and out for several days bringing their own sticks, twigs and dead leaves to make nests. In came streams of berries and nuts."

Anne was bursting with questions, "What about small creatures like worms, beetles and slugs? Wouldn't they get exhausted climbing up the gangplank and down into the depths of the ark or squashed on the gangplank by you or another clumsy animal? And woodpeckers?"

"The woodpeckers did not peck holes in the ark, if that is the reason for your question. As for the worms, I solved that," said Sarah. "I suggested that Shem make us several trays of wood three feet square and a few inches deep. We filled them with soil, planted lettuces, and put some stones and dead leaves on them. Then we left them outside the ark for three days to attract these creatures. I suspect that when they carried the trays into the ark, they also carried in woodworm."

Woodworm on a wooden ark? That is as bad as corrosion on

an aeroplane. I blame corrosion for that last crash in Asia, and there is bound to be another one soon until they find out the cause and fix it. For Noah, there would be no friendly port to call in to make repairs if they sprang a leak; no beach that would give them a chance to get at the outside to make repairs, refloat and continue the journey. Yes! I thought I could make this story into an interesting book, even if it's pure fabrication. And I could imagine them slaughtering the zebras to feed the lions. They'd be short of animals at the end.

Noah stopped my fantasy. "The animals were young and did not eat meat. No slaughtering, no butchering was necessary. We fed some of them on cow's milk, even the lions. We had also stocked up to the gunwales with dried milk."

"What about fish – safely in a miniature sea life centre? And penguins?"

"We were told not to take fish on board. We did not have to worry about penguins either. Although the ice-caps on which they lived shrank during The Flood, they managed at sea for a short period of time. As the flood-water subsided, the ice caps started to re-establish themselves again, and the penguins went back there."

"There are other animals that now live on the frozen wastes of the Arctic and Antarctic Circles. Polar bears can't swim all the time, Noah. You told us that where you lived it was never cold enough for ice and snow, even in the winter. Did these come to the ark?"

"No one knew how they managed to turn up, but junior specimens came, and we took them on board. To make life comfortable for them, we did have a pool on the top deck for them to use. The pool was central to several stalls that had animals in them who needed to splash and swim around in water for a short period each day. A series of trap doors allowed us to control the entrance and exit of the animals to the pool so that they did not mix, and we took photographs."

"So what happened to my camera?"

"Here it is, with three exposed films. I am sorry that we used up all the exposures before the real drama began."

"I'm not sure we will be able to process them after 30 years. The film emulsion will probably be blackened."

"I hope not, Frank. You said that photographs were the key to you believing our story."

"We have not had any photographs yet, and remember that photographs can be forged, especially with digital cameras."

"The camera that you loaned us was not digital. They have only come onto the market recently."

"I must stop you," said Anne. "This story is captivating, but I am tired and face a busy day tomorrow."

"Why not come home with me?" I asked the three visitors. "You can then try and convince Gaynor that your story is true."

CHAPTER TWELVE

THEY HAD POISONED HAM
"seven days from now I will send rain", Gen 7 v 4
"Then Lord shut him in", Gen 7 v 16

Gaynor could hardly wait for Noah, Sarah and Jay to get out of my car. She wanted to know whether that gang of youths who were upsetting the animals when they left us years ago in a hurry got the upper hand.

"Twelve of them versus four of us – looked like we'd lose," said Sarah. "Like military strategists, they had split into two groups – one lot trying to frighten the animals, the other lot stoking a six-foot bonfire with pine branches against the ark. It was spitting and sending sparks everywhere. We were fearful that our wooden ark covered with pitch would catch fire. Their noise must have woken the zebras, who came out of the ark, rushed down the gangplank, made individual charges at the two groups and chased them away. Relief did not come until we had raked away the fire. Some pitch had melted and the heat had scarred the wood. Noah patched that up the next morning. Then the zebras stood guard outside until all was loaded. We never saw the youths again."

"Elephants, or even tigers would have been better guards," Gaynor commented.

"True, but we did not have room or food for other large animals.

And would they have attacked us or the other animals? The zebras did an excellent job."

"Did you give them a bounty of begonias as a reward?"

"We had no spare ones on board. It made me wonder if your begonias acted as a contraceptive because, being mature animals I was surprised that they never got pregnant. As a vet, I'd never encountered this phenomenon."

"You will be blaming us for having begonias in our old garden that he gobbled up," said Gaynor.

"Those flowers did no long term harm. Zebras are plentiful in the 21st century, I noticed."

"But you also puzzled me when you said four crew members. I know you started with 16 people, some dropped out, others died but I thought that there were still ten people you could rely on."

"Gaynor, just as Frank admitted an hour ago, you have forgotten that Irene ran off. We think that the youths who built the bonfire knew her, and how she had dropped out of the project earlier. Her father might have put them up to it. I know they had insulted her once by calling her 'Noah's female chippy'. Even as Noah's wife, it sent a shudder down me to hear of that comment. The whole thing clearly irritated her and a nerve snapped. And the other two of our family were out celebrating their tenth wedding anniversary."

Settled in our kitchen, Sarah resumed the story. A week had fled by escorting the animals into their stalls, emptying their houses of furniture, personal possessions, books and the encyclopaedias they'd amassed. Their neighbours had seen animals arriving, but adopted an ostrich-like behaviour. Rather than see the procession of animals as confirmation of disaster, many had closed their front-room curtains. Closing your front-room curtains was normally a mark of respect when a funeral was due in the street where they lived. They had not seen the irony of their actions.

Noah had gone round to his ex-workmates and pleaded with them to join, even at the eleventh hour, but no interest was sparked. Katrina had tried her parents, but in vain. Then he'd gone to their prime candidate – the owner of the forest who had even designed his own bedroom. His butler had greeted Noah with the message that his master and mistress had gone off on an urgent business trip. He was under orders to stay in the house until they got back.

"That family had wrapped you around their little fingers," I said.

"Tricia later confessed to us that they had been double-dealing. That was the kind of world we lived in. My parents had died so I did not have to face pleading with them. My husband plucked up courage and went round to the home of Irene's family, but no one would answer the door, though he could hear noises inside."

"Did you throw her things off the ark?"

"We did not have the heart to do that. Ham was going crazy so we had to sedate him."

"Diazepam?"

"We did not need your modern drugs. We used hemlock."

"I thought hemlock was a poison used to kill Socrates."

"If you prepare it properly, you can use it as a sedative, or even a vegetable," Sarah told us.

"Count me out from both," said Gaynor.

"I don't think I would want it in a stew either, but with Ham sedated, or worse still, poisoned, you are down to six able bodies."

"Jay can tell you what happened next because he had the job of closing the ark."

In preparing to close the door, Jay had surveyed the scene in the forest for the last time before its doom. No one could have blame him for shedding his first tear during the project either from a concern about the destruction of life, limb and property that would shortly take place, leaving Irene behind or the possibility that the family had made a fatal mistake.

With his adrenaline rising faster, he had gained supernatural strength to push the gangplank outwards so that it would fall clear of the ark. All 65 feet of it hit the ground with a thud, snapping in the middle. No one could have used it now even if they had come into the clearing. At that point Jay realised that he could not reach out to close the door. Ham had designed it so that it could be closed and locked after work by someone standing on the gangplank outside. Without a gangplank, the door remained resolutely fixed in the open position.

While pondering what to do, he was amazed to hear a voice from the edge of the clearing, "Wait for me," it wailed. A forlorn figure with a suitcase rushed across the open patch of ground and stopped by the broken gangplank. He'd seen this woman before.

Gaynor and I guessed from the way Jay had recounted the incident that it was Irene, but we were intrigued as to whether they wanted her back because of the way she had practically finished Ham off. She was more nuisance than she was worth. She'd loaded the ark with that extra luggage and gym stuff and now another suitcase.

"I didn't think that way," Jay told us. "I was so pleased that she had returned because the purpose of the ark was to save life. Getting her on board with a broken gangplank 25 feet below was now the problem. Telling her to stay there, I went off to find a rope. Lifting Irene's case on the end of the rope was easy. Lifting her took the combined efforts of Dad and me.

"She was shaking like a leaf, cold to the bone and tearful. Flung her arms around both of us. As soon as Irene was safely inside, the door banged shut of its own accord, knocking me backwards in the process."

"Probably a strong gush of wind, Jay."

"There was no wind."

"A door left open could have scuppered you," said Gaynor, "if the flood had turned out to be as intense as you had expected. I remember the ferry *'The Herald of Free Enterprise'* setting sail from Zeebrugge with its bow doors open. Water gushed in, causing it to tilt and then sink. Lives were lost. Passengers and crew that survived were damaged emotionally, and would have given anything for their guardian angel to have closed the door before they departed."

"What brought that incident back to your mind?" Jay asked.

"My daughter and Gavin had gone to Holland earlier that year for their honeymoon, and had sailed in her."

"Do they get nightmares that it might have been them?"

"Gavin soon recovered, but Anne is still nervous, especially in the house on her own."

"I am sorry to hear about that incident. I do not suppose that giraffe poking his head into her upstairs window helped."

"Please do not let it happen again," I said to reinforce Gaynor's concern.

"Now we know where the two of you live," resumed Jay, "it should not happen again. But the story of that ferry reminds me about all those who refused the invitation to join our ark and were now in jeopardy. However, we still needed to protect our human and animal passengers. I checked with Shem and Dad about how to lock the door from the inside to make it watertight. The best idea we had was to brace the door closed by screwing planks across it and against the door-frame. We would ask Ham the next day to check and make any changes if he was unhappy with our efforts. A rubber seal around the door would have helped to keep the ark watertight, but it was not part of the design that the Lord gave us."

"So did it leak, or worse, fly open?"

"It sounds as if you believe The Flood was real."

"I still have doubts. I suspect that Frank feels the same way even though he has not said much."

"In which case, what we are going to say next will cause you even greater difficulties. When we got to the door with the wood and tools we could not find it."

"Easy explanation. You were on the wrong deck. I bet they all looked the same."

"That is a strange suggestion."

"It isn't," I told them. "I had this problem when looking for my car in the multi-storey car park at Poole hospital last week. The levels all look the same in the dim light. You told me how dim the ark was. We couldn't find my car where I thought it should be."

"He was a nincompoop," continued Gaynor. "He nearly called the police, but I suggested that we look on the floor above, and if the car was not there, we try the floor below. He was embarrassed to find it on the floor below."

"We were on the correct floor. Whilst fetching the wood, the door had been altered. Where the door should have been there was now continuous planking, as if we had never built a door into the side of the ark."

Christchurch Priory is home to the famous 'beam'. The legend behind it is that an important beam for the old Priory was cut too short. Another one of the correct length would be difficult to obtain. When the workmen returned to work the next day after a night of sorrow, they were surprised to find the beam already in place, apparently of the correct length.

It reminded me of Christchurch Priory. Thousands of gullible visitors are taken in by it. Supposedly during the construction of the old Priory Church, an important beam for the roof was cut too short. Long lengths of timber were scarce so there was no hope of an immediate replacement. The workmen went home early, disheartened. The next morning they met to commiserate with each other and found that the beam, apparently of the correct length, had been fitted into its proper place. That has to be a legend, so I asked, "Are you sure about your door?"

"Yes," said all three visitors in unison.

"I don't get it. Mind you, I've been questioning everything you have been telling me over the years. Did it bother you that you were now locked in?"

"Yes! How would we get out when The Flood was over – by climbing down the side of the ark on a rope ladder, with the animals lowered in slings? Since you had also told us about where you thought the Biblical ark had ended up, we had an added worry that we might have to do this unloading from the top of a freezing cold mountain called Ararat.

"Except for Ham and Irene, we met in the control room for a family council. We turned to face the four foot wooden altar we had placed in there and Dad said a prayer of thankfulness for our guardian angel for bringing Irene back and sealing the door in an astounding way. We committed our destination, even if it would be on a glacier, to the Lord and decided we would only worry about how to get out when we had arrived."

"What brought Irene back?"

"She had had an argument with her father soon after Dad had made that unsuccessful call. She could not understand why her father would not listen to Dad, even if he did not want to say 'yes' to his invitation. She had been getting ready to go out with a blind date her father had fixed up. Instead, she called her father all the names she could think of, stuffed a suitcase with a few extra things, and still wearing her posh dress, rushed up the forest track, tearing it in the process."

"An hour later," Jay continued, "Ham and Irene came out of their rooms and joined us in the control room. He was wobbly on his legs, though mentally alert. Her tears had streaked mascara down her face and onto her torn dress, but who cared? When Dad told them about the door, Irene was overwhelmed that she had almost missed the opportunity to board the ark and apologised yet again for the distress she had caused, and shed more tears.

"Dad then gently took us through the rota. He would not expect Ham and Irene to do anything for the remainder of the day. He and Mum would look after the animals on the lowest of the decks. Katrina and myself would look after those on the middle deck, and Shem and Tricia those on the upper deck. The next day, Ham and Irene would take the lower deck, Dad and Mum would move up one deck, and so on. For the rest of the day, I was also duty controller. That included filling in the ark's log and dealing with emergencies. It was the job I liked best; animals were never my scene."

I interrupted his account, reminding him that the zebras were used to chasing human beings around and were the biggest animals they had on board with muscular back legs that could vault them over obstacles. "Did they create mayhem?"

"Looking after them turned out to be a pleasant task. They were docile with us as long as they had each other for company. It was as if they knew their duty of chasing ruffians was over."

"With no door, you could not let them out if the ruffians had returned."

"That worried us because they could have rebuilt the bonfire and roasted the ark unhindered as if it were an oven full of fresh meat."

"It must have been your guardian angel again."

"There is no other answer unless they were thinking that the dry weather was laughing at us and that soon we would have to emerge from the ark to be greeted by their jeers. Looking out of the window I could only see blue sky. Even the birds in the branches of the trees were chirping merrily as if the future was theirs rather than ours. An occasional bird would settle briefly on the roof of the ark and then fly off as if to say, 'I have the freedom of the skies, you have a home-made prison with four thick walls.'

"With not a cloud in sight," Jay continued, "doubts began to pass through our minds as to the foolishness of what we had done. I could always turn around and blame Dad if things did not pan out as expected since he had finally accepted responsibility for the leadership."

"That's hard on him because all of you helped twist his arm."

"True, but he was strong-minded, and it was his decision to build the ark. By pinning the blame on him at least I would feel happier about it if it went wrong. It was Ham that I would have felt sorry for, because he did not have a dream confirming his part in the project. He was no sloth though, even when Irene left him and went back home for months."

"More pressures seem to be piling up. What kept the adrenaline flowing?"

"No one could deny that a miracle had happened in the way that the animals had arrived of their own accord and how they had fitted into the stalls."

"What would you have done if other people had turned up?"

"Used the spare bedrooms. Even the recreation room could have been pressed into service."

"Were the stalls big enough for the animals to grow over the next 12 months?"

" 'No' is the simple answer. Our plan was to break down the bins as the food was consumed to create more room. As for the empty bedrooms, it twisted an emotional knife deep in our hearts every time we walked past them. They could have been full of saved people. From our perspective it was wasted space, wasted effort. But the Lord told us to make them to ensure that no one who wanted to join the ark would be turned away for lack of space. We had stored extra food for them so that they would not have needed to bring anything but the clothes they stood up in. Up until the last moment we were expecting at least two additional people. In the earlier years of the project we had hoped for many more."

Noah's story was at last beginning to fall into place. His family had confirmed that the number of people who finally joined his ark was the same as the number in the Bible, but not the Koran. However, consistency does not prove truth. I had already rubbed it in about the archaeologist Woolley who could not find the mud or clay left by this legendary flood, this *mabbul*. He needed to explain where the mud and destruction were if I were to believe him.

"Woolley missed the point," said Jay. "He had not read his Bible and therefore thought that The Flood would have been tranquil. It started that way, but the tranquillity did not last. By mid-afternoon, an uncomfortable stillness had descended on us. The birds stopped singing. I went into the control room and noted that the barometer had fallen by half an inch. For 30 minutes, we all watched as a grey puffy thing grew overhead, grasping at more and more of the open sky in a menacing and unstoppable fashion."

"Your first cloud?"

"We knew what it was because we had seen photographs of clouds when we were last in Dorset. But it was the first time we had seen clouds for real, darting across the sky, and the first time we had seen lightening and heard thunder. While clouds were forming above us, things were happening underground. The ark began to shake as earth tremors developed. The stream became a torrent, and waves developed on the water. Then came the rain."

"You told us last time you came you'd never seen rain."

"The only thing that had given us an inkling into what rain was like was when we took a shower. The noise it made on the roof of the ark was worse than in the timber factory when the band saws were hard at work. It was only when the rain slackened and the noise abated that we heard Shem shouting that there were some leaks in the roof by the Cheota."

"The Cheota is the cold end of the ark," I chipped in for Gaynor's benefit.

"He had put a bucket underneath to catch the water, but the bucket had overflowed within a minute and water was now spreading across the floor and down the stairway. Urgency overtook our careful plans of letting Ham and Irene have the time off – they would have to help.

"Our anxiety hit an all time high as water spread unstoppably across the floor. The event galvanised Ham and Irene into action. Irene now realised that her parents had been domineering and toxic people unwilling to prepare for the future. She apologised many times to us for her behaviour, but from that day on she was 100% steady and reliable."

Now a rainy afternoon and a nasty leak don't mean the end of the world. My house suffered once like this and I'd tell Jay that story one day.

"That opening gambit of the *mabbul* was just for starters," he told me. "We had brought spare pitch on board for emergency use, but it does not stick to wet surfaces. Ham managed to stem the leak temporarily by caulking, but the sense of vulnerability hit us. The downpour was due to get worse according to our dreams. If more leaks developed, they might be too fast for us to cope with using the bilge pumps. That would mean drowned animals on the bottom deck, or worse, that the ark would sink. Fortunately, the rain stopped after two hours, the clouds moved on to shed their rain elsewhere. Us four men were by then soaked to the skin. Brilliant sunlight dried the roof, and so Shem and I were able to wriggle out of the window and climb on the roof to apply hot pitch where that main leak was. In three hours we had found and plugged eight smaller holes.

"I know that you are going to ask what happened to the quality control that we followed to ensure that the ark was perfectly watertight. The roof was perfect when the job was finished. We had had a bit of fun hosing gallons of water onto the roof to check that there were no leaks. What we did not realise was that the roof had been damaged by the burning embers from that bonfire. Repairs involved melting the pitch on one of the stoves at the other end of the ark, carrying it through the narrow passageways, passed agitated animals, and climbing outside. With the job finished, we were on the way back in when the heavens opened again. That new bout of rain lasted for half an hour, but was intense enough to test the repairs. They were perfect. From that day on, no one had to go outside again. Then, as suddenly as the rain had started, it stopped and blue sky returned. The shaking ceased and the animals became quiet. Exhausted, we were able to have a meal together. No one spoke much because we could all sense that a new chapter in our lives was beginning and it would have been trite to say the obvious.

"Ham had put a rain gauge out on a pole through the window at Shem and Tricia's suggestion. Five inches had fallen in those two periods of rain."

"What's that when Weymouth had seven and Martinstown eleven?"

"If that had been all the rain we had had, we would have been too embarrassed to come back to see you. By 8pm, there were more earth tremors and the rain returned. Looking out of the window

I could see that the combined effects of the downpour and the enraged stream had created a lake out to the edge of the clearing. Water now lapped at the sides of the ark. Shem and Dad went down to the lower deck to look for wet patches."

"But hadn't you also checked that the ark was watertight up to 15 feet by damming the stream?"

"That was years earlier. After the fire we had done a visual check of the sides of the ark and reinstated the damaged parts. However, we had not thought to check the under-belly of the ark. Talking together in the control room we had realised that the rogues who tried to destroy the ark could have removed part of the pine raft, crawled into the gap and made holes in the floor from the outside, and then put the pine raft back so that we could not tell during our tour of inspection. They reported no leaks. Even so, we were still nervous about possible leaks because we knew that the ark would not float until the water had risen way beyond our test level."

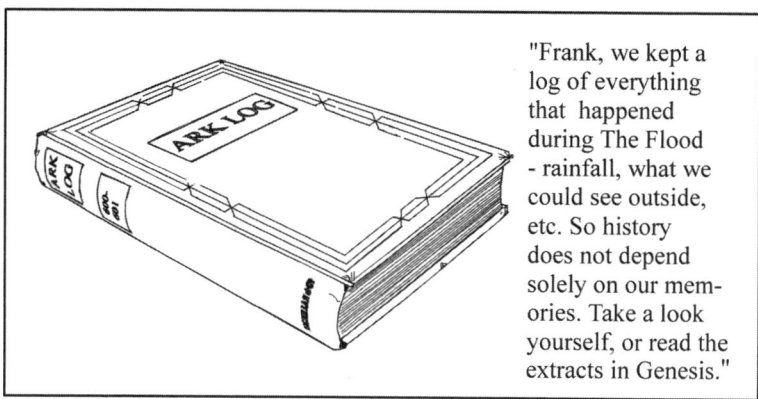

"Frank, we kept a log of everything that happened during The Flood - rainfall, what we could see outside, etc. So history does not depend solely on our memories. Take a look yourself, or read the extracts in Genesis."

At this point, Japeth put a battered book on the table. He told us that at sunset, the rain had stopped. Noah had suggested that everyone go to bed, though he would keep watch through the night for fresh leaks if the rain returned. Before allowing Jay to retire, he had taken fatherly charge and checked that they had completed the ark's log for the day, and with a flourish, had counter-signed it. It was now staring at me.

I was surprised to find that Noah's family had paper books, because people of 4,300 years ago only wrote on papyrus. I'd found the inconsistency in their story at last!

"Come off it, Frank," he protested. "We were not technological wizards like you 21st-century people, but paper is easy to make."

"OK, so why didn't the Egyptians and other early civilisations use paper instead of papyrus?"

"We had taken on board traditional types of books with details of our culture. Maybe the art of paper making was lost 400 years after we left the ark. Check with Ham."

"Paper making was once a major activity in Dorset," chipped in Gaynor. "Our last mill closed in the 1970s. In a few years time, no one in Dorset will have any first hand knowledge of paper making. So what is different to what happened to Noah and family?"

"The Egyptians?"

"Since you ask," Jay said, "the Nile isn't a silt-free river, especially during the annual flooding. That already put them at a disadvantage. Besides, when you have papyrus around, why bother to make paper?"

"Point taken. But you had one wet day: five inches and then two inches later. Weymouth had a wet day in 1955 and it was dry thereafter. Did your lake dry up over the next few days?"

"I was staggered to find Katrina waking me up next morning with a cup of tea. Dad had slumped asleep on duty. Worse still, we had all overslept by two hours from the sheer exhaustion of the previous day. I rubbed my eyes in disbelief because the sun was streaming into the ark through the window. Checking the rain gauge showed that no more rain had fallen in the night. Yesterday's lake had disappeared and doubts began to creep through my mind that last night's deluge was a dream. But the mud outside with a trail of animal tracks in it was a powerful reminder of what had happened. Yesterday was the birth of the *mabbul*."

"Did you see the animal?"

"No, neither could I see anything of the stream. The first earth tremors must have opened a fissure deep into the earth, and allowed the spring to gush out faster than usual. The second tranche of tremors had allowed debris to fall down into the orifice and constrict the flow. The heat of the morning sun dried the mud and cracked it into crazy patterns. At any moment I expected to see people from the town coming into the clearing, forming a ring around the ark, waving their banners, blowing trumpets and shouting, 'Fools! So that was your Flood.'"

"Your flood would then be over like the one-day downpour in Martinstown."

"No one appeared so we set about feeding and exercising the animals that were awake. We stopped briefly for lunch and to share experiences. Dad had struggled with the storage bins on the middle deck. When he opened the first bin, feed gushed out everywhere. He could not push the door back down to close the opening because the feed had formed a mound under the opening. It continued to ooze out however much he tried to scoop it out of the way because the earth tremors had resumed and were vibrating the ark. It spread towards the stairway and other parts of the open floor. There it would have tumbled to the lower deck."

"Leaving you short on feed?"

"That was one worry. The biggest concern was that the feed would rot and gas us out. In a flash of inspiration, we went into the spare bedrooms, tipped the wardrobes onto their backs and filled them with the spilled feed. Animals were baying for their food now so although Shem and Tricia were having their day off, they offered to help get back on schedule."

"Why did you make open lattice floors on the ark?"

"To allow for circulation of the air inside. It also saved time, wood and effort. To make the disaster worst, the first bin Dad opened was in a cramped corner of the ark and he could hardly see what he was doing. The problem was that we had put the hinged door at the bottom of the bin so that we would be able to get all the feed out as the level declined, rather like an old-fashioned coal bunker. What we should have done was to include two doors – one at the top for use when the bin was full so that the contents of the whole bin would not empty onto the floor, and one at the bottom for when the level had fallen below half way."

"You didn't have enough time to build the ark properly, then?"

"The time was not too short. We did check that a bin with a single door would not result in feed oozing all over the place, but we had not appreciated that the vibrations of the *mabbul* would shake the contents out uncontrollably."

"Did anyone accept responsibility for this oversight?"

"Twice we lost heart with the project under abusive pressure from our neighbours and instead of keeping the work going, we stopped and grumbled. We did finish everything that was essential to our survival but at other times we guessed what to do rather than consulting the Lord. The animals did not suffer any deprivation though our comfort and convenience were compromised."

"So you had a catalogue of problems – leaky roof, Irene running off, bins that you cannot close. There must be more!"

"You are rushing things; it is still day two. By evening we had finished attending to all the animals. Once free from the worry of the feeding and exercising programme, our minds drifted to what might be happening down in the town where we had lived, rather than to anything else because the stream in our forest flowed towards the local town."

"I suppose it would have been like Dorset in 1955."

"Did you ever follow the story up from newspapers and books, Frank?"

I had read about the flood of 1955. It was only on the day after the record rainfall that the stream in Martinstown turned into a wide river. The place was cut off for three days, though the records are scanty about Martinstown. Other places have been flooded in Dorset. Although the stories are horrendous, people were supportive of each other. Those living in the area where the damage had been superficial had gone over to their friends who lived in areas that had suffered major damage to help them clear up. Those in the prime of life thought it was a novelty going to see their friends by boat rather than walking. Old people were understandably scared. Broken trees and domestic rubbish jammed under bridge arches, aggravating the flooding. Some bridges collapsed. The army had responded quickly to each emergency, ferrying the frail around in boats and erecting temporary Bailey bridges. When everything was back to normal, the army were given full marks for organisation.

"Did the fact that your rain had stopped worry you?" I asked. "The Bible does not say anything about the rain easing during the 40 days. The Martinstown folk got out and about after three days because the rain ceased. Any one with a boat and wellies could have turned up at the ark on day two."

"In the evenings we had planned to have family concerts to unwind from the trauma of the *mabbul*. That idea went out of the proverbial window that day because of exhaustion. When Noah went to write the log up he was surprised to find that the barometer had fallen another half an inch even though the weather had been marvellous and asked me to check it. He was right, but neither of us could explain why. We went looking for Ham, our *de facto* expert.

"He was staring out of the window watching thick black clouds develop in the sky, which then poured an enormous quantity of rain on us yet again and the earth tremors resumed, causing our cutlery in the draws to rattle. A fresh lake formed outside the ark in a shorter time than it had yesterday. Then, as suddenly as the rain had started, it stopped. That was it for the night. I had a warm bath and tumbled into bed exhausted."

"So the funny barometer reading was not solved?"

"The problem of the barometer reading could wait. Let me read the log for that day. The rainfall had been logged in inches rather than cubits because we wanted to come and show the book to you one day.

"'**Date:** 18/2/600 (day 2).
Duty officer: Noah.
Second in charge: Jay.

Rain that day: nothing.
Total rain: 7 inches.
Barometer: 58½ inches (down from 60 yesterday).'"

"It looks like the one-day wonder as at Martinstown," I told our visitors.

"We felt that way as we got ready for bed. Then the rain started again, but we were too exhausted to watch it. Next morning, unlike the first 24 hours, there was an even bigger lake outside. So we added a rider to yesterday's entry –

"'**Postscript** (added the next day): Heavy rain started at 10pm.'"

"The story starts to get interesting at last. Not like Weymouth, in 1955."

"Not much rain fell that third day, but the barometer continued to fall. Also, water was running down from the hills around us and collecting in the hollow of the land and creeping up the side of the ark. The spring had also come to life again pouring steamy hot water over the closed sluice gates and spinning the water wheel vigorously. It now seemed to be ejecting more water onto the land than was falling as rain. As it poured over the stumps of the trees it was covering them with layers of a whitish substance, rather like the scale that forms in kettles when you boil Dorset water. I now had visions of people overcome by water and mud just like that 11-year-old boy in Upwey. A few brave or foolhardy ones might have tried to get to the ark by boat in the choppy water, but they would first have had to acknowledge that the ark was a sanctuary from disaster. For years they had rejected the invitation."

"Even your hairdresser, Wendy?"

"She did not want to be associated with a family who worshipped the Lord."

"I'm beginning to appreciate that resistance to reading the Bible is not so much due to perceived errors in its record of history, but is driven by an unwillingness to engage with what the Lord wants."

"Our whole family have been saying that ever since we started the ark. People's hearts were hard, and once they were hardened it was difficult for them to change."

That reminded me of the story of Pharaoh, King of Egypt when Moses asked him to release the Hebrew slaves from their burden of brick making. Adamant in saying 'No', nine plagues were rolled out, with each one of increasing severity. You would have thought that Pharaoh would have released the slaves early to save himself and all the Egyptians from the agro that was occurring. When death stalked the land, he released them but then the guy went crazy, and chased after the Hebrews because he wanted them back, making bricks. The Hebrews escaped to the other side of the Red Sea on a temporary dry causeway, created by the Lord. When Pharaoh tried to use the causeway with his army, chariots and soldiers in heavy armour were bogged down in the mud. As the water came back, all drowned. That story had many similarities with the flood Jay was describing.

"Day one," he continued, "had galvanised us more than any other day, except the day of the dreams, because of the sensational way the *mabbul* had begun. We therefore expected the rain to be almost continual. However, we felt deflated because little rain fell over the next few days. It was only when we looked out of the ark and saw the water level rising two or three feet a day up the side the ark that we realised that our dreams had been prophetically accurate. It was uncanny watching the waterline creep up the slopes in the forest as the lake spread its tentacles. The thought of possible leaks in the sides now returned to haunt us."

"Go on!"

"The odd leak started, Frank. There was no way we could add fresh pitch to the outside, so we had to be satisfied with applying pitch and caulking to the inside to stem the flow. A pool of water did collect in the bilge area most days. The team looking after the bottom deck worked the bilge pumps until the area was dry."

"So where did the water making the lake deeper come from if it was not raining all the time?"

"The springs that supplied us with fresh water had flowed steadily and reliably since the foundations of the earth. It was now as if those springs could no longer contain themselves. They were pouring out at twice their former rates, and many new ones had also started flowing. Although the folklore story of the spring at Cerne Abbas is a legend, that legend puts into words what we saw happening on the earth. Fresh springs came into existence of their own accord, and in consequence, the surface of the earth started to sink."

"Oh, come on, now pull my other leg."

"No, I'm serious. Even your scientists agree that land has sunk in times past. Disagreement is only about the speed at which it happened. Sure, they are blue-moon events. Most of the eyewitness accounts come from geologists in America. We do know that it has happened in Dorset."

"What about the dinosaurs?" I asked, changing the subject because of my limited knowledge of geology.

"I will take you to what I call dinosaur land tomorrow if you meet me in Poole, because a picture is worth a thousand words. But we must go now."

For a moment, Gaynor and I were speechless. Eventually she broke the ice. "Here is your chance to put right what you failed to do when the children were young"

"It's a hoax. They are liars, Woolfian-story tellers, religious fundamentalists or magicians."

"I think that they are time travellers."

"But I still don't believe that they are the Noah family of the Bible."

"They had rain of unparalleled proportions."

"So did Upwey and Martinstown and everybody was inconvenienced by the mud and water. All survived apart from that unfortunate 11 year old. Noah still hasn't convinced me that a flood of global proportions occurred destroying everything except those in the ark."

"I have grave doubts about a global flood, but you could go with him tomorrow. I have to cook for the Women's Institute and then go and help Anne with her curtains before Gavin gets home."

"But what have they been doing for the last 30 years? And why did they not come back earlier if all this is true. Did they use another shed for time travel, and where did it land tonight? How have they got back home?"

CHAPTER THIRTEEN

FOOTPRINTS IN THE SAND
"the ark floated", Gen 7 v 18

After the surprise events of last night, and staying up hours writing questions for him, I had had a hard job getting up. I headed to Poole town centre with my new digital camera. What the quality of the photographs would be like, I still had to find out. Gaynor would drop in the three films left by Noah last night at the chemist's for processing.

I could not find Jay. Eventually a stranger approached me and introduced himself as Shem. Apparently Jay had though that his brother Stephen Harry Edward Martin would be more able to answer my questions. I'd been wanting to meet him for 30 years.

Shem wanted to go to Sandbanks. It is the most expensive place for real estate in the UK. Houses worth five million pounds are demolished on the whim of an owner. Even a leaking garage can change hands for six-figure sums. Sand, safe bathing, water sport, sunshine, good access from the hinterland and on into Purbeck Isle, an adjacent harbour and 360 degree panoramic views are its attractions.

We stopped *en route* at Evening Hill, admiring the view over Poole Harbour with Brownsea Island in the background. The spot was a favourite one for wedding couples to have their photographs taken. Then it was back to business with my notebook and pencil poised to record his answers.

"Supposing after you had boarded the ark, beavers dammed the stream," I suggested to Shem. "You would then get a lake 15 feet deep. Was that your flood? I ask that because 40 days of rain as bad as that at Martinstown will not flood the whole earth."

"Point taken. Normal rainwater enters the rivers and runs down into the sea. All the time it is evaporating, so the sea level does not rise. Since normal rain is simply recycled, cloud to ground and back to cloud, that was not the answer to The Flood that engulfed the whole world, not just the forest clearing."

"Then what was different in your world of 4,300 years ago? And if you have a satisfactory explanation for the flood, for good measure, explain where the water went after the flood."

"The Bible tells us where the flood-waters came from. The story of the dinosaurs will show you how severe the effects were. Tomorrow we can talk about your other big question – where the water retreated to after The Flood.

"By day 7," Shem continued, "we were getting thoroughly puzzled as to why the barometer was falling steadily, even after each burst of rain had passed, the clouds cleared and the sun came back out. Ham put his thinking cap on and reminded us that the written records left by Adam told of God creating a water vapour canopy above the sky. There it stayed for 1,600 years. Our rains first started when the vapour canopy was disturbed and it started to feed clouds from above. To use a Biblical phrase – the windows of heaven had been opened, but this rain was on a one-way ticket – only downwards. Apart from its violence, it looked like ordinary rain, but it was new water rather than recycled. There was no way in which it could go back and reform the vapour canopy. So the sea level rose permanently."

"Isn't our sea level still rising?"

"That is caused by global warming, not rain. Your everyday rain is recycled. It goes round a loop. That does not add insight into how The Flood happened. Low-lying countries like Bangladesh will be in trouble because they regularly find that one quarter of their land is flooded. They need to be protected or global warming reversed."

"Thank goodness that the UK does not experience that kind of inundation. For their sakes, let us hope that we can stop global warming."

"I can help you understand the causes of The Worldwide Flood, this *mabbul* by reading the log from day 40.

"'**Date:** 27/3/600 (day 40).
Duty officer: Katrina.
Second in charge: Noah.
Rain that day: 22 inches.
Total rain: 80 feet.
Barometer: 30 inches (down from 31 yesterday).'

"That 40th day was the last day that we had rain exceeding your Martinstown record. The amount of rain was average for the 40 days, and it was the last day that we saw any land, although some places had submerged and rebounded several times over the last 40 days."

"Sounds rather like a drowning person. You must rescue them before they sink for the third and last time. Anyway, 22 inches is an awful amount."

"After day 40 any rain we had was like light showers in comparison to those 40 days. The barometer readings settled around 30 inches of mercury, though the readings dipped occasionally by one or two inches. However, once the showers had died away, the barometer readings would always go back to 30 inches. We concluded that before boarding the ark, a vapour canopy surrounding our atmosphere contained enough water for 36 feet of rain."

"That's 12 years worth for us, yet you got it in 40 days? Ugh! What triggered this one-way discharge of rain from the region above the earth's surface that the Bible calls 'the windows of heaven', which halved the pressure of the atmosphere, and eliminated all evidence of itself?"

"Scientists have suggested that dust from the tail of a comet entered our atmosphere and triggered this one-way rain. Alternatively, it could have been the accumulation of dust in the atmosphere from volcanoes, which littered the landscape before The Flood. The cause does not matter. The key was that we were warned in our dreams of how to cope with the impending disaster."

"I'd have been happier to know the real reason, especially as scientists want to set up a 'comet-watch' to track cosmic bodies that might one day collide with the earth and shatter it to smithereens."

"Whatever triggered The Flood remains a mystery. Recognising that God is the master of His creation, I do not think He will allow the earth to be destroyed by a comet because it would then seem that He has lost control. But let's focus on the harbour and imagine the sea level rising permanently by 36 feet. It would double its extent but Brownsea Island would still be sticking up safely out of the water. We would be on dry land here at Evening Hill though the rest of the road out to Sandbanks would be under water. The other islands in Poole Harbour would disappear."

"All that expensive property on Sandbanks submerged, worthless!"

"Yes, Frank. You get the visual impression of The Flood and the destruction. The Sandbanks of our world lost hundreds of homes worth trillions, and the lives of the inhabitants. But breathe easier. God is not going to send another flood, so present day Sandbanks is safe. But there was more to The Flood than a rise in sea level of 36 feet due to rain from the windows of heaven."

Looking at that page of the log, I had noted that it showed 80 feet of rain in total. Whilst that would cover Brownsea Island, it would not cover the world. Shem therefore invited me to consider how a worldwide Flood could occur without any rain.

"Think of a water bed," he said, "and imagine a puncture in the night."

"You would get wet."

"Exactly. You sink and the water rises. Remember what happened back in the forest where we built the ark? The day the rain started, that stream turned into a torrent as more water gushed from the spring than ever before. It told us that strange things were happening deep underground. The surface of the land no longer had holes through which fresh water emerged from shallow chambers. The earth had now ruptured at deeper levels. In consequence, the surface of our land was sinking fast, as new water was forced out from deep underground making the sea level rise twice as fast as if just one of these events was occurring."

"This is worse than the legend of the spring at Cerne Abbas."

"I am not sure of what you are suggesting."

"Yesterday, Jay tried to use the legend of the spring of water at Cerne Abbas to challenge my rejection of your flood story. The legend claimed that years ago there was no spring in Cerne Abbas. An angel came by and was impressed by the devout nature of the local people. He offered to supply them with wine or water. Their first thoughts were to ask for wine, but then changed their minds. Cold logic told them that while wine would allow them a brief period of merriment, once it had gone, they would still face difficulties drawing fresh water. They asked for a spring, and the angel obliged them. It has never dried up since. Nor, I hasten to add, has anything stupid happened such as the earth sinking."

"All modern day springs are rechargeable, having existed since 2,300 BC when the Flood-waters retreated. They might falter after prolonged drought, and resume soon after fresh rainfall. You should have got the gist of that when you argued with Dad about the spring at Upwey and the Friar Waddon pumping station. Thus the idea that the Cerne spring conveniently opened up in AD 400 is another legend."

"I have no dispute with that single fact, Shem. However, in the world where you first lived you had no rain for 1,600 years. Then suddenly you got aggressive springs and violent fountains breaking forth. How?"

"The written records left by Adam tell us that the world was charged with water beneath the landscape when God made it."

"If you trust the Bible you might believe that, but even though I've told you that I am not a geologist, I do know that the founding fathers of modern geology, such as Lyell and Hutton, put the Bible behind them."

"Adam documented the conversation that he had had with God about how He had made the world. Those documents were kept safe as part of our family records, and we took Adam's notes with us into the ark. Having now read the Bible, I guess that Moses or another important Hebrew knew of these documents that we preserved and incorporated the story in Genesis. Not all the details that we had in Adam's notebooks have been included in the Bible, but there are no errors or exaggerations."

"Who, then, is right in the battle between the Bible and secular geologists?"

"Geologists acknowledge that there is much high pressure water beneath the earth's surface and that provides circumstantial evidence that there was once more water."

"I've got new neighbours – Charles and Jenny. She did a doctorate on the nature of the earth's crust, so the topic ought to be familiar to her."

"I am sure she will be able to confirm the accuracy of what I have said. Thus we can now explain why the Biblical record should be 100% acceptable to all. From the date of creation, enough fresh water was released from shallow chambers for drinking, washing and irrigation. But all the time, bigger and deeper chambers, repositories of hot water, laden with a cocktail of minerals were teetering on the edge of instability, ready to break forth on the earth. We used the word *mabbul* to describe what happened when they could hold back no longer. If geology can only be explained by the ferocious release of underground water, then we have no reason to doubt Adam's record about the created world or our eyewitness record of The Global Flood."

I couldn't imagine Jenny accepting this story but I did promise to ask her. Until that issue had been cleared up Shem had not convinced me about more than an extra 36 feet of water. And even then, I wasn't sure that I believed the story about a vapour canopy that is no longer there for checking, and how it caused the sea level to rise permanently. And in the recesses of my mind was that third question – where did the water go after the flood? If I could travel back in time or could have watched a video recording I might have been able to believe his story.

"Going back to day three," Shem continued, "we realised that the stream in the woods was getting hotter and hotter because the water was now being sourced from deeper in the ground. Steam was being blown into the air like a geyser and this helped the rain clouds to grow in size. That was where that extra 44 feet of rain came from. Since the 36 and 44 feet were both new rain rather than recycled rain, the sea level would have gone up 80 feet. With that rise, Evening Hill would now be under water and Brownsea Island would have disappeared entirely. But, to repeat, there is not going to be another global flood."

"You've wrapped up that explanation to the point that I'm speechless."

"If you had a meteorologist friend, ask them if you still doubt the hydrological cycle."

"I don't know any weather-men, so let's turn to dinosaurs because they are high on my agenda. That news report yesterday of dinosaur footprints being made on a prehistoric beach makes nonsense of your story."

"Then let us visit the beach where we can get to grips with the only explanation – they were caused by the springs of the great deep."

The beach at Shore Road is one of the best in Dorset with its fine, golden sand and safe bathing. From the car park, we walked onto the beach leaving a trail of vague shapes in the dry sand but clear footprints in the damp sand where the tide had just gone out. Shem pointed out that, as that sand dried out, the crisp outline of those footprints would also disappear.

"Near Swanage," he continued, "dinosaur footprints have been found in the rocks that were once loose sandy, shelly or muddy material by a seashore. However, that news report last night did not explain how any dinosaur footprints were preserved. It waffled on quoting one of your popular Dorset writers 'that the dinosaurs were in shallow water, which was rising while they were walking about.' These holidaymakers around us are paddling because it is enjoyable. In contrast, animals do not like the beach. The water is salty and there is no food for them. Bring your dog down here if you doubt it. The odd dog will play in the sea if you encourage it by throwing a ball or ring, but otherwise it will keep out."

"We never took Rover to the beach, though the children implored us to. Now there are notices prohibiting dogs on the beach in summer."

"Those notices were not there when the dinosaurs were here."

"I can believe that. So what were the dinosaurs doing here?"

"The dinosaurs had no option but to paddle. The beach was moving inland, invading their home territory. That news report side-stepped the problem of how their footprints were preserved. For dinosaur footprints to be preserved for 4,300 years, a bank of mud must have rolled across the seabed filling the depressions before they had time to lose their shapes. Start your stopwatch and imagine the scene. There are only a few seconds to spare; any delay and the opportunity for preservation is lost for ever because the next wave is already coming up the beach to scour the imprints away. The unexpected batch of mud preserved the footprints and frightened the dinosaurs so that they would rush about in panic."

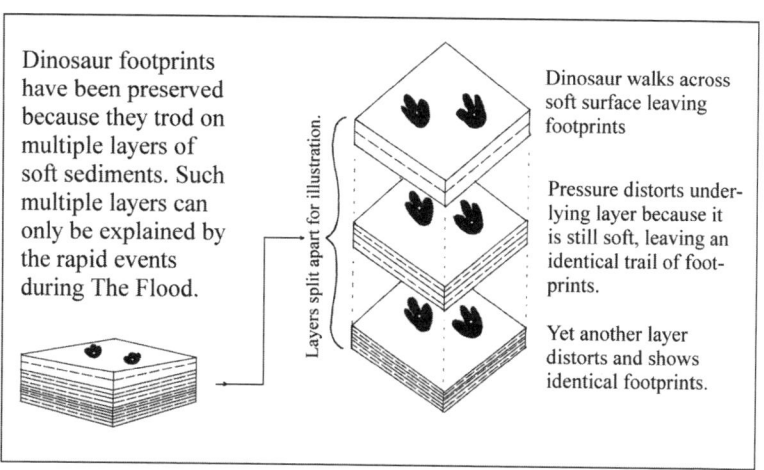

Dinosaur footprints have been preserved because they trod on multiple layers of soft sediments. Such multiple layers can only be explained by the rapid events during The Flood.

Layers split apart for illustration.

Dinosaur walks across soft surface leaving footprints

Pressure distorts underlying layer because it is still soft, leaving an identical trail of footprints.

Yet another layer distorts and shows identical footprints.

"The news report did say that many of the footprint tracks were in chaotic directions that the dinosaurs did not know which way to turn."

"That adds credulity to my explanation. The dinosaurs would be stressed by these events and in fear attacked each other."

"Dinosaurs were always vicious, fighting each other like cats and dogs."

"Not so. Dinosaurs are tame as long as you or another animal do not try to invade their own territories, steal their eggs or harm their young. They saw the carpet of mud as a threat because it covered up the smells that marked their territories."

"Where did the mud come from?"

"These carpets of mud could have slid down the beach because of the heavy rain. Or the sudden opening up of a new spring on the seabed could have brought in a load of ready-made sediment from the depths of the earth or precipitate a cement directly onto the sands and shells containing the footprints."

"Why wasn't this mentioned in that report?"

"Dinosaurs are an enigma wrapped up in a mystery. You have to guess the colour of their skins because they are not alive today. Palaeontologists who try to reconstruct the life and habits of dinosaurs have insulated themselves from the bigger questions about geology. They can spend the whole of their lives guessing what dinosaurs were like, how they walked, and how long they lived and no one can contradict them. They are in love with dinosaurs, not deeper truth, because they have an unwritten rule not to ask awkward questions that begin with the word 'why'."

From what Shem had said I could see that the Biblical view of judgement had been side-lined by palaeontologists. Requests for research grants by scientists who wanted to investigate the possibility that a global flood caused the footprints to be preserved would never get past the committees responsible for approving the money.

Shem realised that human nature had not changed. "Before The Flood, people did not want to know about the impending disaster. Most of the people in this 21st century who say that The Global Flood did not happen do so because if they do not reject it, they also have to acknowledge that God is active in history. As our creator, He has standards of morality that are clearly defined in scripture. To cope with their desire to avoid God, they all fall in line behind sir Charles Lyell, your supposed famous geologist who said that he did not want to know about anything that Moses had written of the history of the world in Genesis.

"The other worry I have is for those who are prepared to accept the existence of God and His moral requirements but are confused by the propaganda put out by humanists and atheists that this Global Flood never happened. They need to be helped so that their faith in God and the revealed truth of the Old Testament is strengthened."

I could see that this area of discussion was the hot potato that would not go away. I could remember Samantha from next door telling me, just before her ordination, that she had met many who tried to live morally acceptable lives based on the last five of the Ten Commandments dealing with stealing, lying and murder. When they failed to live up to their own standards in these matters, rather than admit it, they criticised the Church of England prayer book, saying that it "is rude about human moral pretensions, forcing us to turn to grace as a remedy for disgrace".

Samantha tried to remind them that Archbishop Cranmer had included "comfortable words" in the communion service to tell us that if we confess our sins, God is able to forgive and restore us. To use an illustration from the board game *Monopoly*, we receive a 'Get out of jail free' card. The hot potato arises when people ask what happens to those who do not confess and therefore forgo their free card. One convenient way of avoiding the constant nagging that God will judge is to deny God's existence or his ability to punish, Flood or no flood. It was time for me to change the subject.

"Tommy loved his dinosaurs so we bought him numerous books about them and took him to the Natural History and the Dorchester museums to see the models and fossils. But you are asking me to believe the impossible about this flood. You see it as the only way of explaining their footprints."

"The sea was rising higher and higher each day because of this new rain and the gushing of the fountains of the deep, squeezing the dinosaurs onto smaller parcels of land. Their nests with eggs or young in them would be covered with mud. The mothers would go crazy, and try to dig them out. Other dinosaurs would be trying to defend their own shrinking territory. Hence the battles with each other that feature in dinosaur books."

"And if you hadn't seen it happen, would you still believe, Shem?"

"Lots of people believe in the resurrection of Jesus Christ, even people who would not call themselves Christian, but there is no evidence for us to see now. No one can be sure of where the empty tomb is – near the bus station in Jerusalem or not? Then why is it difficult for them to believe in The Flood when the evidence is still here in Dorset? There is no other explanation for geology."

"If you ever get a chance to meet the Rev'd Samantha she might be able to tell you. And I hope that Jenny can help me on these other technical points for I know that other geologists reject a worldwide flood because there are too many different layers of rock, coal, whatever. A flood should bring a solid sheet of mud or clay, and that's it. Those points are enshrined in a code of archaeological interpretation."

"That is not what we saw. Each higher surge in the water level brought a different mixture of sand, broken shells, pebbles and mud up onto the beaches. Mud banks rolled across the beach, brought down from the hills by the rain. Even steady rain, provided it is sufficiently intense, would cause the layers of mud to arrive erratically."

I wondered why he said that. Wouldn't it have been one violent burst of water rather like what happened when the breach in the dam at Gasper, Somerset, sent its water swirling into Dorset? Admittedly Gasper was a small dam.

"A larger dam collapsed in the USA," he said, "and the

eyewitnesses saw the water and mud accelerate and halt several times in the valley. Many separate tongues of mud thousands of feet long were swept down the valley in an erratic manner. And that was still only a small volume of water compared with The Flood."

"Then Mount Everest must also have been covered with mud. But it isn't; it's all limestone."

"A lot of mud was shifted around during The Flood, because the volumes of water were huge in comparison to the breaching of any dam. Precipitation from the hot water, rich in minerals, discharged by the fountains of the great deep is the answer to every other type of rock except chalk."

"You're getting too technical for me, so can we go back to the dinosaurs in Swanage?"

"Frank, you have asked me not to talk about the religious issues underlying The Flood. If I do not talk about technical matters, there will be nothing else to discuss. I will do my best to think of as many simple analogies with geology and archaeology as possible. Let's recap. The footprints were made by dinosaurs called sauropods. Although the report talks about them being on a beach, it was hardly the Riviera. It was a floodplain filling rapidly with corpses. I imagine that the day that the Swanage footprints were made, the sauropods might have been caught by the surge of water coming in faster and higher than they expected. They left a trail of footprints in the shelly sands, and another layer of mud covered these within seconds, thus immortalising them. Furthermore, several layers underneath the shelly sands were still soft because they had only been deposited a few minutes before. The result was that they show signs of secondary footprints. Multiple layers of different sediments do not occur in normal circumstances. These layers had to be due to numerous fountains of the great deep discharging different sediments every few minutes."

"The reporter used the technical name 'underprints' in last night's news. But if conditions were as violent as that, why do we not find entombed sauropods?"

"Your scientists said the sauropods went north, struggling

through the wet and muddy landscape. The thickness of mud carpets that were rolling over this part of Dorset would not have been enough to trap them, but a strong water current could have swept them out of the area."

One of Tommy's old dinosaur books I rescued from the attic told of a whole herd of Plateosauruses swept away in a flash flood in Trossingen, Germany. Then 20 pages later it mentions a group of Scelidosauruses swept away and drowned when the riverbank overflowed. I considered that both of these were local accidents, minor happenings like the caravans that were swept away in Bowleaze Cove in 1955. There was no worldwide accident to the dinosaurs any more than caravans just a few miles to the east in Bridport were affected.

Shem dismissed my arguments, reminding me that that book failed to highlight where the dinosaurs were found. "They were not swept away by local flood-water surging over a riverbank. They were entombed by tons of mud, stones, shells and sands delivered by a much bigger flood. The tragedy at the coal-mining village of Aberfan in Wales when a school was buried by mining waste in minutes is a better example than the Bowleaze Cove incident, though it still pales into insignificance compared with The Flood. At Bowleaze, caravans weighing tons were swept down onto the beach by the flood-water, but they weren't buried because it was a flood dominated by water rather than slurried waste as at Aberfan. Other caravans in the same field were unaffected.

"If dinosaurs had been at Bowleaze in 1955, Frank, they would have struggled in the water. They might have been battered and bruised, maybe the odd broken leg, but not buried because there were only a few inches of sediment shifted around by the flood-water. Remember, no one was killed at Bowleaze though the caravans were swept away. Here we are saying goodbye to whole herds of large animals buried by sediment. The dinosaurs would not have died in that local flash flood if that was all there was to it. Since they could run at over 15 mph, they could get out of the way of normal floods."

I thought of two objections: that some of the dinosaurs may have died because of the battering and shock that they experienced; second that dinosaurs became extinct over 60 million years ago. How could he have seen it 4,300 years ago?

He accepted that some dinosaurs could have been battered to death, but then pointed out that that no fossils would form. Instead scavengers would eat their flesh once the flood-water had retreated. Skeletal bones would fall apart and be swept away on the tides.

My second objection caused him to stumble. He told me that Katrina had since done a science degree and had been delving into how scientists date the rocks. He'd ask her to visit us tonight. That would be fine as long as she stayed long enough to answer all my questions, unlike years ago when she and Jay left me high and dry.

"I promise. That was Dad's doing, and he had good cause to call the family back. Nothing should go wrong this time. There are no more floods in the queue and no more ruffians waiting to set fire to the ark. Let us board the ferry for Swanage and see the rocks where the dinosaur footprints were found."

Swanage is another seaside town which once relied on stone quarrying. Its development as a holiday town was due to a visit by Princess (later Queen) Victoria in 1835, and the later construction of the railway. The railway had to make a circuitous route around Holes Bay and Poole Harbour from Poole. A ferry across the mouth of the harbour now provides a shorter access.

Swanage has one excellent sandy beach and a bay named Durlston that is exciting for geologists, though hardly for holidaymakers because of the boulders. On a clear day, you can see the Isle of Wight.

We arrived at the Sandbanks Haven terminal as the laden ferry was leaving. It would be a twenty-minute wait for it to get back, but gave us time to admire the view. We spotted boats of every size, from the gigantic Cherbourg ferry to a tiny blue sailing boat. I remember seeing photographs of the flying boats that used to land here. Such idyllic days.

I pointed out to Shem the hotel on the left where Marconi set up the first wireless transmitting apparatus. That was to send messages to and from the Isle of Wight and local ships. Once the technique had been proved, and his equipment upgraded, the next challenge was to send messages to and from the USA. To improve his chances of success, he moved his equipment to the Lizard in Cornwall to be 200 miles nearer the USA. Sadly, that was loss of industry to Dorset, though before my time. Shem turned the story back to religion. Wireless waves, he argued, could help us understand about how prayer works. We cannot see radio waves, but we do know that they are real.

Watching the chain ferry make its way to Shell Bay without us, we could see that the tide had begun to turn. Once the ferry had left Shell Bay, it was being pushed into the harbour by the incoming tide. By the time it had landed again on the Poole side, the positions of the wet tyre marks on the slipway left by the previous vehicles coming from Shell Bay showed that it had landed several feet harbour-side from where it had departed.

Once on board, clanking our way to Shell Bay, we were aware of how fierce that tidal race was in the harbour entrance. Spray broke over the ferry, and we did not seem to be going in a straight line. Fortunately, being a chain ferry it cannot be swept away on the tidal race.

Shem spoke, "On several days in the ark we got caught in a fast flowing current and because we were not tethered to firm ground, we floated away rapidly. We never did a full 360 degree turn, although there were a few gyrations, which seemed to leave our stomachs behind."

"I was never much of a seafarer. Boats leave me sick. Thankfully, this journey is short."

"Interestingly, we could never understand why the Lord told us to make the ark long and thin. It would have been quicker to make it square, which is what they claim Utnapishtim did. To convince ourselves that we had got the design correct, we built several different shaped models, put them in a pond of water, made waves and turned a fan on hard to mimic the *mabbul*. The only model that was stable was the design the Lord gave us.

"On one occasion Dad saw a group of dinosaurs trapped on a sandbank 100 yards from the ark marooned by rising water. For an hour the water level dropped but not enough for them to get back to any of the remaining tracts of land. With no food or fresh water on the beach, some of them turned to attacking each other. In the midst of all this mêlée, we were surprised to see one female dig a hole in the sand and start to lay her eggs."

"That was a silly thing to do when lives were at stake."

"Yes, but nature dictates when dinosaurs and other animals should lay their eggs. Rain and mud do not change that. They were aware of the danger, but not able to do anything about it. When a new pulse of flood-water arrived, the sea crept higher and swept them away in its turbulence. It was traumatic for us watching. For all I know, it might have happened at the spot that you now call 'Swanage'."

It seemed like ages before we got to Shell Bay. Though we were first on the ferry, the buses and the cars in the far lane were beckoned off before us. It allowed me to muse on the sad scene described by Shem. Eventually he broke the silence.

"Not to worry: the Lord said judgement would only be served once on the world in this way. The fountains of the deep and the windows of heaven are closed. Let's go into Durlston Bay."

Dinosaur footprints and remains of insects, crocodiles and mammals have been found in profusion in the rock layers over the last 150 years at Durlston. Most of the mammal bones were found in quarries on the cliff top, rather than in cliff faces. In modern times, quarrying ceased and houses and hotels sprang up, but geologists still make a bee-line for it.

We slithered down the steep path from Peveril Point and into the bay, but it was easier than using the south end close to the castle and Durlston Country Park. There in front of us was a group of geology students with their tutor, all wearing their regulation hard hats and clutching notebooks and hammers.

"Why are those geologists so excited? The bay's a mess."

"They are looking at the insect beds, small creatures. But instead of getting involved in the minute details, I want you to try and take the bigger scene in. Come back another day with a hard hat if you want to examine the cliffs close up. I do not want you to be knocked out by rocks tumbling from above. For now, ask how the cliffs, with their pinky, black, and creamy layers got into this condition."

"You are the expert!"

"One layer would be formed by a carpet of mud eroded from the hills that existed in the years before The Flood. This would sweep small mammals along with it, and so folk living after The Flood would now find their fossilised bones in it. Another layer would be sandy material from an advancing beach, which would fossilise sea-dwelling creatures. Another layer might be clay, sourced from the fountains of the great deep sweeping up ostrocods with it, and yet another layer might be broken shells."

"Ostrocods are . . .?"

"Tiny seashells. Geologists love them because they are a supposed index fossil, but most other people would ignore them."

"Archaeologists use the concept of indexing in a similar way to geologists, so I'm happy with that concept, though Noah challenged my understanding of this."

"Dad never told me."

"It was the story of cement, apparently discovered three times over two thousand years, passing into extinction between discoveries. So the archaeologists' supposed correlation of time across different parts of the country is pure fabrication. But to return to the geology that you are trying to describe, can you draw?"

"I must remember that point about cement in case anyone else asks me about it. As far as geology is concerned, yes, a picture is worth a thousand words so I came prepared with a pad and pencil."

After a few minutes of sketching he showed me the result and said, "Is that not evidence of our flood rather than a local accident, Frank?"

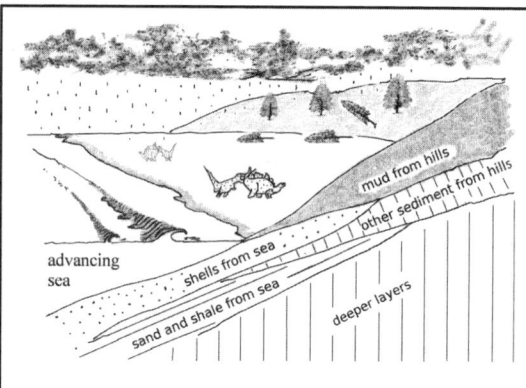

Dinosaurs attack each other on a beach that is rapidly shrinking with mud being swept down from the hills and sand, shale and shells swept up by the sea.

"I'm not a geologist so I couldn't argue with you. I bet that group of geologists over there would not believe your interpretation. And what about all that rubble wrapped up in wire cages in the middle of the bay?"

"It is untidy now, so let me try and reconstruct what happened using an analogy from the kitchen. Imagine that the chef has made a dozen pancakes, and stacks them neatly on top of each other. All those layers of rocks there were once horizontal, just like the stack of pancakes. Now imagine trying to toss the whole pile in one go. Even the best of cooks would be lucky to avoid bending, cracking, sagging and bits breaking off, just like the rocks we are looking at."

"That analogy makes sense of what I see apart from those wire cages full of rocks."

"Those have been placed there by civil engineers to stabilise the cliff where it is weakest. The people who bought flats on the top of the cliffs do not want their homes tumbling into the sea."

"Neither would I."

"Now put the insects into the story. There are numerous fossil insects in the rocks here, dragonflies, grasshoppers, wasps and houseflies. The dragonflies like still water, laying their eggs a few inches under water. Any hint that the water was not calm would send them scurrying from the area. So why were they fossilised?"

"You seem to know all the answers."

"Can I suggest that they were caught out by a massive and unexpected invasion of fast flowing water and sediments?"

We walked back in silence along the beach towards the coastguard's lookout post, and scrambled up the cliff path. The scene in Swanage Bay had changed from the one we had left. A few of the children's sandcastles had not yet succumbed to a watery grave from the incoming tide. Two boats, lying on their sides on the lower part of the beach, started to float as each wave brought the tide higher.

Shem was excited. "That was what happened to the ark. The afternoon of that 12th day, the ark gave a shudder like a lift starting suddenly. Tricia had looked out of the window and came running to report what she saw. Do you remember those pine logs that we put under the ark? Some of them were now floating around us. It was a momentous occasion being afloat for the first time. I had only reached the control room to record it in the log when I was caught off balance by the ark bumping back on the ground. Through the window, we could see the water receding, taking the logs with it. We had grounded after a few minutes afloat, but of course no one thought that was the end of The Flood."

This sequence of events, described by Shem, was being repeated in miniature in front of our eyes. Those two small boats had been grounded again as a result of the changes in the way the tide was coming in. But it was only a few minutes before they were fully floating, and tugging at their anchors.

"We had several more false alarms over the next few days before we floated free of the forest. Each time that we came off the bottom a few more pine logs from underneath would emerge. One day, tree stumps floated free because the soil surrounding the stumps had been loosened and washed away. They formed a tangled mess against the edge of the clearing. Two days later, we had two feet of rain in an hour and the wind hit force 10. We could not see anything until the following morning, but in daylight the forest looked as if it had been exposed to a hurricane. There were a few trees still standing upright, but they had no branches on them. Other trees had snapped at mid-height, some at their bases, whilst others had been uprooted completely. Yet others had been toppled and buried under piles of mud. You asked how far they got, so let us go to where I think they are now 4,300 years later – Lulworth Cove."

I could hardly object.

Driving west through Langton Matravers, Shem pointed out the road leading to Worth Matravers. He asked me if I had ever gone on 'The Radar Trail' that Dad had suggested, but I had not. "If you ever do, also look out for the farm on the left hand side opposite the junction with the road from Harman's Cross, where many dinosaur footprints were found. Others were found in Worbarrow Bay."

As we approached Lulworth Cove, I asked him if he really took crocodiles on board.

"Yes. They were no different to the dinosaurs. When each of the animals came into the ark, 99% were small enough to be picked up with bare hands. We had made up a pool and shower system on the top deck so that those animals that needed it could immerse themselves in water and mud for a while each day."

"Even though you claim to have the answers to all the problems of the animals, you are still cramming millions of years of earth's history into one year. You're also insisting that the whole world was covered with water at the same time."

"That is my bottom line, and my sister-in-law will sort out your problems of the ages of the rocks. But let me ask you a question. Why have the geologists found fossilised crocodiles in Swanage unless The Flood was as intense as I have said?"

"It was flash flood, one day 60 to 100 million years ago."

"I doubt it. Crocodiles are powerful swimmers and can spend hours under water before they resurface for breath. They love wallowing in mud, can eat and even copulate in it. For a crocodile to be fossilised, we are not talking about a few days of rain, and a bit of mud, but the catastrophic destruction of their habitat so quickly that they were not able to get out of the way. They are more difficult to fossilise than dinosaurs because they can swim in mud."

"I'll think about it. But do not pressure me, otherwise I will stop the car, you can get out and catch the bus back to your allotment wherever it is this time."

The penalty for visiting the Fossil Forest at Lulworth Cove is the hard slog across the shingle beach. Along a narrow ledge half way up the cliff at the far end of the Cove are a number of odd shaped hollows, generally circular, two feet in diameter, and a few inches deep. They are surrounded by about two feet of bulbous rock. Other hollows are elongated, but also surrounded by bulbous forms. Inside the hollows are remnants of wood that has been silicified. The fragments identify them as conifers. Shem suggested that they could have been some of the pine trees that they had felled and placed under the ark when they were building it.

"Shem, your imagination runs riot. That notice we passed a few minutes ago said that these tree stumps are in the Dirt Beds and were growing here over 100 million years ago. The bubbly stuff around them, what you call tufa, shows that they were immersed in water for many years."

"You have scored an own goal, Frank."

"I said 'covered in water for many years'. I did not say 'a few days of your flood'."

"I am not convinced. The Dirt Beds do not get that name because there is dirt or soil there, but because geologists assume that the trees were growing there and so they would have needed soil. The rocks have been so named on the basis of an assumed explanation for the trees, but it is all a circular argument and people forget to ask the questions about truth. As for the tufa, that came from mineral salts dissolved in the water ejected by our springs which covered the tree stumps and logs in a matter of hours, not years. I watched it happen."

"But what about the dates of these events? Millions of years ago, says the notice."

"You will have to let Katrina join you tonight and explain. I want all your objections answered."

"I am trying to resist."

CHAPTER FOURTEEN

DETECTIVES

"they ... examined ... the scriptures ... to see if ... (it) was true", Acts 17 v 11

Men and women appreciate diamonds in different ways. To the woman they are a vital part of jewellery, having a clarity that nothing else does, sparkling in the weakest of light. They are also signs of commitment with the giver. To a man, especially a handyman, a diamond-tipped saw will cut through anything because of their unsurpassed hardness.

Diamonds are composed of carbon atoms, bound in a structurally tight configuration. That explains their strength. They are generally found in pre-Cambrian rock, supposedly 600 million years old. There are no pre-Cambrian rocks in Dorset.

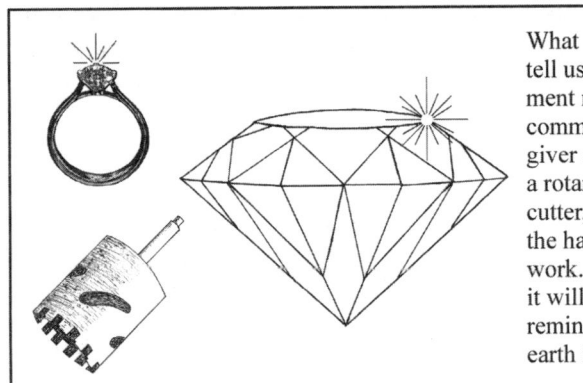

What does a diamond tell us? In an engagement ring it tells of a commitment between giver and receiver. In a rotary masonry cutter, it will challenge the hardest of brickwork. In a sermon, it will be a powerful reminder that the earth is young.

"What about those films?" I asked Gaynor when I got home from Lulworth.

"Anne explained to the staff at the photo laboratory that the films were long past their expiry date, and could they do anything special to compensate for the age? There was nothing they could suggest, so, with fingers crossed, she left them to be developed. Two of the films were completely fogged out, but one has come out. There are eight pictures of groups of small animals going up the gangplank into the ark. There are no full view shots of the ark, but at least it is something to go on."

Looking at the photographs we saw one of a couple of small pigs and one of the zebra, though not recognisable as the one that entered our garden. It could have been a stuffed dummy, made by a taxidermist, posed on a wooden bench. Nothing clinched the story of the ark.

Gaynor wanted to know what Shem had talked about. I summarised to her that 36 feet of new rain had fallen from the windows of heaven and 44 feet of new rain had resulted from steam released by the fountains of the great deep. However, those amounts paled into insignificance from the water-bed effect. Land sank as the fountains of the great deep released water. She found the idea as incredulous as I did.

The next job was to phone up Anne, thank her for getting the films processed and ask about Gavin. He was safely home from a 10-day trip to Texas, USA, attending a conference on radio-isotope measurements. He'd stayed on for three days as a holiday-maker to take advantage of an *Apex* fare. Isotopes weren't the kind of topic that I had much interest in, but out of politeness I asked her how it had gone.

"Being jet-lagged, he's gone to bed early. He took over 100 photographs when he went sight-seeing, especially to the space centre in Houston."

"You shouldn't have any problems with processing them, Anne."

"I hope not."

"I look forward to seeing them and hearing about the trip. And the conference . . . ?"

"Monday and Tuesday were predictable and boring. Run-of-the-mill stuff – lectures, talks, presentations. Wednesday afternoon Gavin took the podium to tell the conference about his new equipment. An American named Ashmore congratulated him and his team on constructing equipment that could measure isotopes to a greater precision than previously achieved. Then he asked Gavin why they had found radio-carbon in diamonds. Gavin was pleased to answer this question because he was able to emphasise how sensitive his new equipment was. In his heart he hoped that Dr Ashmore would want to buy the new equipment.

"Ashmore knew something that Gavin did not," she continued. "He asked Gavin if he knew how old diamonds were. He didn't know, so Ashmore told him that they were pre-Cambrian, nearly 600 millions years old. This titbit produced a twitter across the room as a few of the wiser ones realised the implications."

"I don't understand, Anne."

"Radio-carbon does not stay around in measurable amounts for more than 50 thousand years. So the diamonds are not even 50 thousand years old."

"That tells me that those pre-Cambrian rocks which they came out of would then have to be less than 50 thousand years old."

"But it cannot be true, unless Noah and his family are telling the truth that the world is young. Yesterday, I laughed at you when you told me you had met a man called Noah who had built an ark. Now I've met him, hoaxer or not, and my Gavin has told me about all these problems with the age of the rocks, I feel like a detective – trying to solve a crime that I did not know about yesterday."

"Have you found the answer yet, Anne?"

"No, but I'm further down the road of discovery than you, even though you have had many years start on me."

I argued with Anne for a few minutes, accusing her of unfairness. She reminded me that Gaynor had asked me why I had never delved into the topic and written a book about my experiences. I'd crammed my life with busy-ness, but the reality was a theo-phobic fear – it was what Lyell, Hutton and Darwin did not want to consider – God had been active in history.

"If you had done that, Dad, I would have been able to tell Samantha about changing my view of the historical accuracy of the Bible because until today I had rejected Genesis as real history."

"I'm not ready to think that way, but Shem has given me a migraine over those footprints and fossils in Swanage. I'm struggling to find reasons to contradict his claims that they could only have been formed when those Biblical fountains of the great deep burst open."

"Then join me as we become detectives, with truth at stake. You have more spare time than I do. Put a barrister's hat on. Do a double interrogation on everything they say."

"I'm expecting Katrina any moment now to come and explain about the age of the rocks. I'll keep you in touch with developments. Big kiss for the children, and enjoy having your husband home. See you at the weekend. Bye."

Japeth and Katrina came a few minutes later, apologising for being late. "I spent more time looking at the worldwide web than I planned to," Katrina said. "The library was shut; we had to find an internet café. The discussion on radio-carbon at that conference created a furore."

"Can you explain to me what you know, Katrina?"

"A diamond is a perfectly structured form of carbon atoms, so tightly bound that this accounts for the unsurpassed hardness of diamonds. Many diamonds are mined in South Africa from pre-Cambrian rock that is supposedly 600 million years old. Are you still with me?"

I knew that carbon atoms come in three sizes, 12, 13 and 14. Only carbon-14 is radioactive with a half-life of less than six thousand years. So in that time half the carbon-14 changes into nitrogen, part of the air that we breathe.

"What Gavin's equipment found, though he did not appreciate the significance until Ashmore spoke, was that instead of diamonds being pure carbon-12 there are small amounts of carbon-14 in them. If the diamonds were millions of years old, then all the carbon-14 would have changed into nitrogen."

"Contamination could have caused the spurious results, Katrina?"

"Not with diamonds. The lattice structure of the atoms is so tight that you cannot get carbon-14 into it unless it was already there when the diamonds were formed. If it has carbon-14 in it now, each diamond must have had more in the past. Over millions of years most of that carbon-14 would have changed to nitrogen. Thus, the diamonds in each engagement ring would have lost their strength and crumbled because of the gaps in the atomic lattice. Since they are there, large as life, they cannot be very old."

"The age of pre-Cambrian rocks has been measured by other means. Why do we not take those answers of 600 million years as correct?"

"People have known about the problem of carbon-14 for years. Libby, who pioneered the carbon dating technique, had seen carbon-14 in coal, which is also supposedly millions of years old. Contamination could occur in coal because the carbon atoms are not tightly bound. On that basis, geologists were able to ignore the possibility that the coal was only 4,300 years old – The Flood age."

Katrina had not answered my question properly, but being no expert on radio-metric dating, we agreed that we should bring the subject back to things like archaeology that I was more *au fait* with. "We check all the methods we use to work out how old things are by counting growth rings in trees," I told her, "or to give it its posh name – dendrochronology. You can tell how old a tree is by sawing it down and counting the rings, one per year. The longest living trees are the bristle-cone pines and their pattern of rings tells us that some are up to ten thousand years old. Now if I believe that every forest was destroyed in your flood, there will be no bristle-cone pines older than 4,300 years."

"There are no trees older than 4,300 years. Counting rings to find the age of trees does not work. Do you remember those apple and pear trees in containers that we put in the ark? After The Flood we took them out of the ark and planted them. Within three months they had formed leaves, flowered, grown perfect fruit and lost their leaves."

"What's so unusual about those trees flowering so quickly? The owner of the garden centre never sold anything of poor quality."

"They were perfect trees, Frank. The intrigue started four months later. Each tree had repeated this cycle of growth, fruiting and leaf-decay. Most years we got three, sometimes four crops of fruit."

"Lemon trees produce two crops each year, but not other trees, unless they sold you a super breed."

"If they had super breeds for sale they would have charged more than one pound nine shillings and eleven pence for miracle trees. Part of the answer was the mild and steady climate after The Flood."

"In that case you mightn't have seen any rings at all."

"The opposite happened. Ten years after, these trees had grown so much that they were crowding each other out. Since we could hardly get to the branches, we decided to thin them out by felling alternate trees. On the ones we felled, there were over 40 tree rings for the ten years we had had them."

"But you do not know how long they had been in the nursery, Katrina."

"Two years at the most, so in total, they were forming tree rings at the rate of three or four a year. And only one ring is supposed to form annually. No wonder your dendrochronology is hopelessly confusing."

This was a threat to me as an amateur archaeologist. How could they date everything using the Jewish historical records, which were kept after The Flood even if Archbishop Ussher had added up the numbers correctly? There was no science in that.

"Anne told me to go out with one of you again, but since I am still confused, I wonder whether it will help or add to my confusion. This tree-ring issue could be a yarn, but could be true. How do I check?"

"How about meeting my father-in-law again in a few days time? He has been reading about the chalk land. Apparently it is disappearing faster than any of your archaeologists can understand. Rainwater is dissolving it away and running into the rivers Frome and Piddle."

"Why's it important to us?" I asked.

"Depressions around archaeological sites tell us that three inches of chalk is lost each thousand years. That sounds a trivial amount, but is high enough to worry the archaeologists. Currently the chalk is about a thousand feet thick. It will all disappear in four million years at that rate. But according to the geologists, it has already been there sixty million years. Either the chalk was once three miles thick – that's half the height of Everest – or that the chalk is young. There is no other evidence that the chalk was once this thick, so I am left with the belief that the chalk is only a few thousand years old, and that fits snugly in with the timescale of The Flood of 4,300 years ago.

"There are other reasons why we know that the chalk of Dorset is so youthful. Geologists have no explanation for the Ballard Down fault near Swanage unless they take millions of years off the age of the chalk. Both of these are technical points. Do you want the details?"

"No, it's getting late. You ought to talk to Anne. She worked at the Fresh Water Laboratories as a scientific assistant before James was born when the amount of chalk in the river was being measured."

"I appreciate that we are a long way off answering all your questions. It's a bit like that 40th day of The Flood. We were afloat, but with no land in sight. So do I tell Noah that you want a trip to see how the chalk was moulded by The Flood?"

"Sounds a good idea. It is the bank holiday next Monday. If we can go somewhere that is interesting for children we might be able to take Beryl and James. Anne and Gavin would appreciate a day on their own." Inwardly, I hoped that by suggesting that the grandchildren came, the questions might be less intense.

"What time do you think Anne will go to bed tonight?" I asked Gaynor when they had gone. "I want to phone and ask her about this disappearance of the chalk from Dorset."

"I do not think that Anne understood why they were performing the measurements on the chalk in the river. She was only the lab assistant doing the titration. Why not try the internet instead? The main reports were put up on their web site because the results were higher than expected."

"It's fangled technology that I don't want to know about."

"Then it is time you tried."

Little did I know it until several days later but Ashmore had been hounded at the end of that radio-isotope conference. He had been accused of distorting science by implying that the rocks were only a few thousand years old. But if new understanding leads us to believe that radioactive decay was much faster in the past, why hound the man?

It reminded me of the story in John's gospel about the man born blind. The Pharisees put the screws on him to disown Jesus; to deny that he was God's son. They were not interested in the fact that he could now see, and was therefore one less beggar on the streets. Both groups were theo-phobic because they could see that accepting the truth of those statements would lead them closer to a God who had rules they did not like. I wondered if Ashmore has been driven from science just as the ex-blind man was evicted from the synagogue.

CHAPTER FIFTEEN

OVERLAND BY BOAT
"all the high mountains . . . were covered (with water)",
Gen 7 v 19

What do you pack for a children's picnic? I ducked the issue since parenthood was too long ago for me, left it to Gaynor, and went to fetch the grandchildren.

"Where are we going?" asked Beryl.

"We are going out with a sea-captain," I replied.

"A what?"

"A man who has been on a long journey whilst in charge of a boat."

"We are going to Guernsey for our holidays in a big boat."

"I know you are," I said to her remembering that the children had badgered their parents to take them in a ferry. The last ferry Anne and Gavin had been in was *The Herald of Free Enterprise*. This had almost put them off ferries for good. "This man built his own boat and it was bigger than the ferry you are going on."

"Wow!"

"You seem certain about Noah for a change," interjected Gaynor.

"Not really, but I must say something exciting to the children."

When Noah and Sarah arrived, we wondered how to introduce them to the children. Calling them Noah and Sarah was bound to confuse them so soon after she has done the school project. Calling them Mr and Mrs Lamech Junior was worse. In the end Gaynor and I chose 'Captain and Mrs Captain'. They both had weather-beaten faces.

Sarah had new photographs of the animals taken specifically for Beryl in the last few days. Some of these were the animals that had been in the ark, and were now grown up. Others were the first generation offspring. Noah had brought sectioned drawings of the ark for James, but he was a bit baffled by them.

"Granddad," he said to me, "it looks more like the container on the lorry that has gone by than the ark. Our school ark has pointed ends and an open deck. It is in the school corridor so you could come and see it tomorrow. I can show you what Beryl did."

Noah tried to explain that an ark with square corners was easier to build than one with a prow and a stern, and that the big open deck would have been a hazard during the downpour, but James was not impressed. There was nowhere for the animals to look over the side and smile at people as they sailed by. Noah returned his smile and then winked at me because it reinforced his view that artists often glamorise the story of the ark, especially in children's books. Adults don't have books about mythical legends.

Noah asked to go to the Milton villages because they intrigued him, but did not explain why. As we drove along, Sarah was answering the children's questions about the animals shown in the photographs. They were having a competition as to who could remember the most animals' names, and what foods they ate. The photos of the baby crocodiles fascinated the children but they had not yet thought to ask about dinosaurs. The teacher had insisted that they were extinct in the days of the Noah she had read about in the Bible, 4,300 years ago. Our Noah then told them which sections of the ark he put the different animals into.

By now, Gaynor had tumbled to the reason why Noah wanted to go to Milton. "Wasn't Lord Milton the owner of the park in the mid-eighteenth century? Built a mansion there, and dammed the stream to form a lake, thus submerging the old village?"

"Sounds like we have read the same history books," said Noah. "The people who rented the houses in the old village were annoyed because they were in good condition and they did not want to move. It has parallels with our Flood."

"That sounds like an apocryphal tale!"

"Roads near Milton could only be closed by formal orders. Copies of these orders had been placed in the Dorset County archives."

"Boring place!"

"Frank, you keep telling me to check everything with the appropriate authority. I went and saw them!"

"Have you been in the dinosaur museum while you were in Dorchester? They will tell you that the dinosaurs disappeared 60 million years ago."

"You are baiting me again with this confusing set of dates. I thought you were beginning to accept how so much about geological ages is plain wrong."

"I still need to talk to Jenny." *She will save me.*

"To go back to Milton; new houses were built either side of the valley to the east of Milton Park and people from Milton Park were encouraged to move there. Those who moved complained that the new dwellings were square boxes with no character, too small for the intended families and there were no pubs. People only moved out of Milton Park when their leases expired.

"Slowly, but far more slowly than Lord Milton wanted, because he would be dead before he got his lake, old Milton became a ghost town. He tried to hasten the exodus by destroying good homes as they were emptied, causing further distress to those who had not moved. Mr Harrison, the smart lawyer, was determined to stay put. Since his family lived in Broad Street near the original stream, the lord of the manor took opportunity during a temporary downpour to block the arch under which the stream flowed and thus flooded the area around Mr Harrison's house."

"I bet he was furious, Noah. Sounds a bit like the battle of David and Goliath."

"Although the lawyer managed to get a court injunction against further blocking of the stream, eventually everybody left. Goliath won this part of the battle because of his stash of money, not because of his righteousness. The new houses are now privately owned, but civic pride means that all the owners paint them in pastel colours, which suggests a delightful rural origin, and not a bitter edict of a previous landlord. Since the houses were constructed as pairs of small semi-detached houses, some of them have had the dividing walls removed to create one larger dwelling. Those who thirst for a licensed premises now have a choice of two."

"Sounds as if sense prevailed over the pubs," I said to Noah. "Dorset people always do the right thing."

"Although the stream was dammed, seepage and evaporation restricted the size of the lake. There were other troubles for Lord Milton. As they dug foundations for the new homes, vast numbers of bones were found, thus hampering the construction. Other people were angry when the lake was made. Those living to the south of the new Milton Park objected to their supply of water being cut off by the dam. Mr Moreton Pleydell was awarded £3,000 compensation because, without water to power his mills, he had to close down. That was a huge amount of money in those days. So though your 'David', this Mr Harrison, did not win the right to stay in Milton Park, there was some consolation because the modern day 'Goliath' was short-changed."

"You created a lake, Noah, and deprived people of water. Why criticise?"

He smiled. "Don't confuse motives. Yes, but it was not for my own enjoyment at the expense of others. I created a lake from the stream in the forest to check that the ark was water-tight, but allowed it to drain away afterwards."

"Did anyone sue you whilst there was no water?"

"I could not have paid them if they had."

"And you preached hell-fire and damnation sermons at the street corners each week, encouraging people to leave their splendid homes, with swimming pools and arboretums, and move into skimpy bedrooms in your ark with not a flower to be seen. No wonder why no others joined."

"Your analogy with the events at Milton Park falls short of what we were trying to do. The bedrooms on the ark were tiny compared with the size of houses that people had. However, the flooding of the world was not a deliberate act on our part. We were not muscling in like a big Goliath and shouting obscenities on little righteous Davids, but as servants of these same people, aiming to save as much of humanity as possible. People wrongly assumed that their lives would go on in the way that they wanted."

I had to side with the folk of the old Milton Park and the distress they suffered, but neither of us could deny how attractive this modern lake was, even though only glimpses of it could be had from the road. We had to be content with a walk up the hill to view the whole of the Milton Abbas village.

On alternative years, the folk of Milton hold a village fair. To add colour and ambience, the stall-holders dress in Victorian costumes. There is everything from a pig-roast to pickled onions for sale, and honey to haberdashery if you wanted to make period costumes. Beryl liked the pink cottages and wished they could live there. I tried to explain how small the houses were.

At the top of the valley was a small animal sanctuary and a display of vintage farm tools. Our grandchildren were inquisitive about their functions and why Noah's family had had to take them into the ark. So Sarah explained how they made butter, cream and cheese from the cows' milk. "Even the 'captain' made cheese once I showed him how."

"Mummy buys ours from a shop."

"But we had no shops on the ark."

I think that answer confused the children. Ferries have shops on them.

The highest spot in Dorset is Pilsden Pen. Although it is an archaeological site, the views are not that remarkable. The next highest spot is Bulbarrow Hill, with superb views. Noah wanted us to think about how the ark could have sailed over all the high places in Dorset, and therefore asked us to head to nearby Bulbarrow.

I'd been over this part of Dorset in a hot air balloon, but if Lord Milton could not fill his lake because of evaporation and seepage, how could the whole of Dorset be covered with water? Noah told me that the fountains of the great deep gushed out faster than the Milton Stream, but that still left me wondering how he could state that the whole of Dorset was covered in water at the same time, let alone the whole world.

"The 40th day of The Flood was the last day we saw inordinate amounts of rain. It also marked the last time that we had bumped into solid ground for 110 days. We then drifted one way then another way as the currents swirled around us. On most days, there had been nothing to see out of the window apart from water and flotsam. Boats cast adrift at sea have usually been washed up on some beach within a matter of days. Since that did not happen, we concluded that there were no beaches or land anywhere just as our dreams had said."

"But without flying over the earth, you couldn't be humanly sure that there was water everywhere except for floating vegetation."

"Fair comment, Frank. Some things we had to take on trust. If the flood-waters were insufficient to cover the whole earth, why were we told to build an ark?"

"Don't ask me, but I take your point."

"One morning we awoke and thought that we were in the middle of a wood. In reality, over 30 leafless trees were floating upright around us."

"I thought that trees floated flat like a log raft?"

"Many trees have denser roots than their boles, and so float in a vertical position. From our vantage point, it was as if they were deciduous trees, leafless in winter, but otherwise alive with their roots in the seabed. Later that day we were aware of the eruption of a new fountain of the great deep which swept so much sediment across the sea bed that the trees became anchored by their roots. When the flood-waters rose, the trees failed to unstick from the sea bed and were fossilised in the upright position. Quarry men have found them in profusion on Portland. As far as Bulbarrow is concerned, apart from a few inches of weathered topsoil, the ground under our feet is chalk loaded with fossils of sea creatures that were trapped when this spot was part of the seabed.

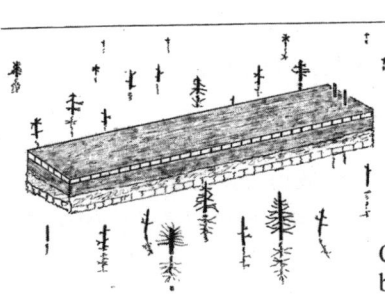

"Frank, one morning we awoke to an almost cloudless day. We thought we were marooned in a very water-logged forest, but the ark and the trees were afloat. Only tree trunks float on their backs. Complete trees float upright because their bases are denser. When the water level temporarily fell, they stuck to the sea bed."

"The chalk is loaded with belemnites that look like long bullets, and ammonites that curl and spiral and vary in size from a few inches to many feet. It is not easy to find any here because the ground has been trodden on and ploughed up many times. The cliffs beneath Golden Cap, near Bridport, are the best place to find them. This chalk covers a large part of Dorset, sieved from the bottom of the ocean everywhere as land emerged from under the sea. Where there are gaps in the chalk cover, there is evidence that it was once present, and has since been washed away."

"You sound very definite about this, Noah."

"Geologists have studied the topic and come to this conclusion. We had the advantage of being eyewitnesses, seeing the chalk being washed away by the retreating flood-waters after day 150. Prior to that, all we had seen was water, water everywhere, or thick mist. That mist made us feel cold and we were glad we had put those stoves on board and had kept them alight constantly. The cold weather was a blessing in respect of the animals. Half of them, particularly in the Cheota away from the stoves, went to sleep for days on end. At first we thought that they might be dead."

"I can't imagine you with a stethoscope checking their breathing and pulses."

"Yes, why bother? If their breathing was laboured, what then? There was no way we could go back for more animals. Fortunately they all recovered from this unorthodox hibernation. In some cases the hibernation lasted for the year we were in the ark. But look, now that we have reached the car park, why do we not take James to see if gliders are being flown today while Sarah and Gaynor take Beryl to Rawlsbury Camp?"

Circling over the nearby hill were four radio-controlled gliders. Their pilots, three men and a woman, were safe on *terra-firma*. A *de-facto* competition was in progress to see who could get their glider to perform the most-extravagant cartwheels, circles, and loop-the-loops. When one owner got tired of showing his prowess at aerobatics, he skilfully brought his glider to a safe landing at his feet. Once the radio crystals had been changed, another person would take his turn, fling his glider into the wind, grab his radio-control unit, and attempt a loftier display of aerobatics than the previous owner had achieved.

To everybody's disappointment, a Beaver Class glider, with a wingspan of six feet was caught by a sudden gust of wind, flipped over in mid air and fell to the ground like a stone.

"Granddad," cried James, "it's broken. Does that happen to real aeroplanes?"

James knew that we were all going to Uncle Tom's wedding by aeroplane. I tried to reassure him about their safety record. In the meantime, the owner went across the road and down the field to retrieve the glider. One of the wings had sheared off. He could repair it, but it wouldn't then fly with such agility as it did before because the repair would add weight to the glider.

Noah turned to me. "You have never asked me about those big flying creatures such as pterodactyls."

"I know that Mary Anning discovered such fossils in Lyme Regis. Until then, we didn't know of their existence."

"How do you think that they flew?"

"Our scientists believe that they used to launch themselves off cliffs or hill tops like these people are doing with their gliders. They would circle around in the updraught and then come back to their nesting sites on the cliffs. We do not think they could fly properly. For food they would swoop on rabbits and hares."

"Then how did they get back to their nests if by catching their food they lost their place in the updraught?"

"You can't walk up a cliff, back to your nest so what's the answer, Dr Encyclopaedia?"

"That is an interesting title to give me, Frank. We used to watch them fly just by flapping their wings. What your zoologists have not allowed for is that our atmosphere was twice as dense as yours. Do you remember about the barometer and the vapour canopy? With this extra air density they were able to lift themselves off the ground simply by flapping their wings."

"Let me guess the rest of the story. You took a pair of pterodactyls into the ark. You did not know the air density would fall below its pre-Flood value. When the ark landed, they couldn't fly any more, so they could not feed themselves."

Noah nodded, "Hole in one. Isn't there a special word for that in golf?"

"Yes, there is, but I've never done it."

"Are you disappointed?"

"The downside is that you have to buy everybody in the club a drink."

"We were sorry about the consequences to these flying creatures. When we evacuated the ark we made an aviary for the large birds, hoping that they would get used to the reduced air density. The two pterodactyls grew in size but sadly they died without flying or breeding. We did have success with other large birds. The albatrosses grew to adult size with a wingspan of 12 feet. The Andean condor, which is only slightly smaller, also survived and bred."

"Changing the subject, Noah, I have been told that those sea monsters called ichthyosaurs lived at a similar time to the pterodactyls. Their fossils have been found along with pterodactyls at Lyme Regis. Their extinction would not have been caused by reduced air pressure."

"We were not told to take ichthyosaurs into the ark. Being fish-like, they should have been capable of surviving The Flood. Maybe some of them are still alive, but I am not a betting man. Ask the crypto-zoologists. Large numbers of sea creatures died because there were many mudslides, which took millions of tons of sediment down into the sea where it buried them. Those that were not entombed this way got caught when the fountains of the deep erupted so that mud and sand came from the other direction, burying them rapidly."

The women had returned from Rawlsbury and had started to unpack the picnic, so I was spared the embarrassment of asking what a crypto-zoologist was. Sarah pointed out the hill forts in the area, including Hod and Hambledon. She had told them that hillocks like these were the first islands to show after the flood.

"As the water swirled away it eroded the soft chalk, thus dredging out wide valleys that are now either dry or contain shrunken streams. The new Milton Abbas village is an example of a dry valley. In contrast, the ramparts on the hill forts are man-made, long after The Flood had gone."

I was not sure Beryl understood the meaning of that. She commented, "It's a beautiful view across those fields. I saw all the way to Somerset in the North, and the Purbeck Hills in the South. And if you listened carefully, you could hear tractors, miles away, though we could not see them. An' Granddad, we saw some badger-holes."

"But did you see any badgers?"

"No. They sleep in the daytime, silly."

That reminded me to ask Noah, "How did you take badgers and moles into the ark? Like Beryl says, they only appear at night."

"We made a deep box, filled it with soil and left it outside for

48 hours. Many burrowing animals made it their home. Then we carried the box into the ark. We never saw the badgers, though we knew they were there because the food we left out for them each evening had gone the next day."

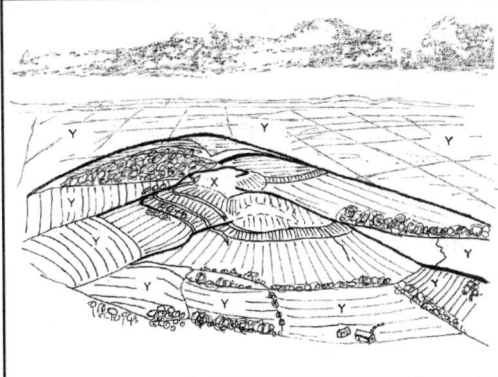

The crest of Hamblen hill-fort (marked X) is 300 feet above the surrounding farmland (Y-Y-Y), which is a further 300 feet above sea level. This suggests that The Flood retreated in at least two separate major episodes in this part of Dorset.

"The long nights were the hardest to cope with," said Sarah during a lull in our conversation. "After getting into a routine with the animals, time seemed to stand still."

"So what favourite radio or TV programmes did you tune to?"

"If we had a TV, where would they have been transmitting programmes from?"

"I was being barrister Frank again, trying to trip you up with a trick question, and expose you as modern people."

"You have tried that approach often, and our answers will always come back to haunt you – that Global Flood that I have described obliterated all vestiges of life. For our entertainment, celebrating birthdays was a must. Katrina's came first. Japeth, knowing that his wife liked my gold necklace, went and bought one before he boarded the ark, ready to present it to her on her birthday. However, the day before he came and told me it was not in the place where he thought he had packed it. We all joined in the search, except for Katrina, and although we hunted everywhere, it didn't turn up. In the end Japeth reluctantly accepted that he had dropped it outside the ark while loading stores."

"Couldn't have been much of a birthday party!"

"I had made a cake."

"Told you – routine stuff. That would not make up for a missing present."

"The best was still to be – a surprise game of skittles which my husband engineered."

Noah proudly told me how they did it. "Katrina was fond of skittles, and also a good player. She had given the game up whilst working flat out on the ark, but had always hoped that one day she could play again. In fact we were all feeling jaded the week before her birthday because life in the ark had settled into a dull routine of cleaning out stalls and feeding animals. Japeth came to me with a suggestion that we knock down the walls between the spare rooms to create a bowling and skittles alley. After checking that the ark would not be weakened if we did that, I did some re-drawing then told him to go ahead, but in secret. The ladies did keep asking what the noise was about as we did the carpentry. Our excuse was that the animals needed wider exercise space as they were getting bigger."

"What about all the wardrobes full of animal feed – and the real reason for taking spare wood on board – repairs?"

"Many of the wardrobes were empty by then, Frank. As for repairs, nothing went wrong."

"So why, if the Lord knew everything, did He tell you to take wood on board for repairs?"

"The Lord must have a sense of humour. He also wanted us to learn to trust Him. His words about repairs made us fear the worse, but the reality is that He is a God who delights in giving us pleasure. He wanted us to take that wood on board to make the rooms into a skittles alley. In the bowels of the ark we had stored a lathe for use after we had disembarked. We went down there and used it to turn off-cuts of wood into skittles.

"As a birthday present, Katrina was presented with a key although it was only a symbolic one because nothing on the ark was lockable except for the bathrooms. The toilets in them did not flush away like yours. Ours were portable, emptied over the side."

"Oh, we have them when we go camping. Funny blue smell," Beryl said, wrinkling her nose.

"That is the idea, Beryl. Then we escorted Katrina to the door but she was hesitant to go in. I think the trouble was visions of the ghost of her beloved granddad inside. We assured her that there was no such thing, so she opened the door gingerly and then exploded with joy at what she saw inside. That first game is etched on my mind, every individual score. We had so much pleasure, though the ladies won, that we agreed to make the whole thing a weekly event. And this is the best news yet. Since coming to Dorset, we have learned that someone may have found our missing gold necklace."

"Not here at Bulbarrow?"

"Although this wasn't in Dorset, in 1891, Mrs Culp of Morrisonville, Illinois, broke a large lump of coal into smaller pieces so that it would go into her stove. In the lump of coal she found a gold necklace whose ends were still buried in smaller fragments that had split off the larger lump. Without seeing it, we cannot be certain that it was the same necklace, but the discovery is circumstantial evidence for our story of The Flood."

"Touché! I read in a Dorset magazine that there was a brewery here in the 1800s. While digging a trench in 1825 to improve drainage following a local flood, a workman found two gold items a few inches beneath ground level – a solid gold armlet and a gold torque. Experts said they were from the seventh century BC."

Noah looked at me as if he were reading my mind. We'd had this discussion about archaeological dating before. So I admitted, "I am stuck, unable to defend what I have just said. Go back to telling us what you did on the long nights when not playing skittles."

"None of us had had much time for hobbies since starting to build the ark. We now taught each other our skills and hobbies. Tricia was the best musician so often gave us recitals, and encouraged us in sing-songs. I had flute lessons from her. It was a struggle for me at first, but once my fingers started to obey my brain, I enjoyed it. My standard wasn't great, even after one year but it did provide me with an alternative interest for the long nights at sea. She also started to write her own music. On one occasion, she and Katrina set the story of the ark to music. When they performed it at one of our weekly concerts, we thoroughly enjoyed it, though it could hardly be called a classic."

"Dorset has produced a few musicians, and we now have our own resident Symphony Orchestra and a Sinfonietta. The hymn 'Jerusalem', written by a Bournemouth man, is my favourite," I said. "Several hymn tunes were named after local places – Bournemouth, Studland, and Wareham, but with the exception of 'Wareham', they have fallen into disuse. But being an architect, Noah, I thought that you would have taken to writing like Thomas Hardy."

"None of us felt inspired to write fiction. The life we had left behind had been hard work, and it was difficult to envisage the future. Whilst we all shared the task of writing up the log each day, Sarah became the official historian. Japeth took up conjuring. He offered to teach one of his sisters-in-law some tricks. Then one night they entertained us, changing the suits of cards. Then he pulled five rabbits out of an empty hat. Sarah went mad. She thought that there were only two rabbits on board. Now we had five."

You'd have to be naïve not to expect rabbits to breed in the ark. Noah told me that Japeth had kept quiet about the rabbits so that he could play the magician to maximum effect. At the end of the show Sarah insisted that they fix up separate cages until they were old enough for them to establish their sexes.

"The star performance of the evening," Noah went on, "was the sawing of Irene in two. She climbed feet first into the narrow side of a long empty box Jay had laid on a table. There were two ankle-sized holes at the far end for her to stick her feet out. Her head stuck out of the end of the box, so Jay placed a square piece of wood, with a large hole in it, over her head against her shoulders. He then taped it to the box. All we could see of Irene were her head and legs sticking out of opposite ends. Then Japeth twisted the whole box long-side towards us, and proceeded to saw across the middle of the top surface."

"That is stupid. He could kill her."

"Ham realised that. He turned white as his brother sawed through the upper part of the box. As the saw went deeper, and down the sides, Irene started screaming and wiggling her legs like mad, shaking her head. Blood dripped off the saw."

"This is madness. No wonder we have never met Irene. You were killing your family off."

"Ham passed out, and slumped out of his chair. Japeth put his saw down, Irene climbed out of the box."

"You what?"

"Irene climbed out of the box, and they both rushed over to Ham. She cradled his head in her lap, and managed to bring him back to the land of consciousness, saying, 'It's all part of the act. Remember it's a trick. I'll be alright.'

"Once she was sure he had recovered, she climbed back into the box, and Japeth resumed his sawing. Finally the saw went through the bottom of the box, Japeth wiped the remaining blood off the saw, and Irene climbed out, unharmed. The animals must have wondered what all the fuss was about, so loud was the applause and stamping of feet when he had finished."

I'd heard of the trick, but never seen a performance. It could be done using a special table, and an assistant. The second assistant lies under the far end of the table, hidden by a cloth draped over the table. When the lady to be sawn in two climbs into the box, she brings her knees up to her chest so that her body only goes half way along. At the same time, the assistant pokes her legs up through a flap in the top of the table and another flap under the far end of the box and out through the ankle-holes. When the audience sees the legs coming out, they think they belong to the assistant because they wear identical shoes. The box can then be sawn in two without either of the assistants being harmed, as long as they keep still, because of the gap between them.

Noah confirmed that Japeth did not have an assistant because they pulled the table apart. "Ham soon got over it," he told us, "but the incident did show how tense we had become under the pressure.

We needed much more relaxation to prevent us from becoming psychiatric patients before the end of The Flood. From then onwards we had a weekly concert with everybody contributing something, however small, plus a skittles match."

"Did you have any other ill health or problems with the animals or yourselves?"

"No is the simple answer. The weather was cool, and that kept illnesses under control. Sanitation rules were rigorously adhered to and this contributed to a trouble-free time. Fresh straw was regularly put down in the animal stalls, and the old straw, food scraps and waste all dumped over the side. Toilets emptied daily overboard."

"How disgusting. They do not do that on ships today."

"What else could we do? If we had not done that our vessel would have become a breeding ground for all sorts of nasties. We did not dare burn the straw and scraps because of the fire risk in a wooden ark. We had nothing in the way of animals' medicines with us and we could not go back for fresh animals if we lost any."

"So none of you caught any disease. But what about the rough side of the job like accidents?"

"I fell down the middle stairway on the ark. Carrying too heavy a bundle, I missed my footing in the gloom and broke my leg. Couldn't do anything useful for six weeks."

"He was silly, Frank. We all agreed that we would share burdens, especially the heavy ones," said Sarah.

"You treated me like a baby. I was not the only one to have an accident."

"Yes, but you should have learned from Ham," she said to him. "Ham was on his own one day in the factory before we had finished the ark. We had agreed that we would never work the band saw unless someone else was there as well. He broke the rules. Said it was only a short job. Nothing could go wrong. Staggered outside with his arm and hand wrapped in old cloth, bleeding profusely, calling 'Help!'. Fortunately, Katrina was around and able to apply a tourniquet. If not, he could have passed out and bled to death. He was lucky not to lose his hand."

"I cannot stand the sight of blood. Let's change the subject to your food."

"We made crisps, like the ones in this picnic."

"And these crimpy things with the red line that Grandma has packed."

"No Beryl. Those are difficult to make and they have lots of E-numbered food additives in them. We all took turns to cook, including the men."

"Say that a bit louder, Noah, so that Frank will hear," said Gaynor.

"I'm not taking sides. We all have different domestic abilities."

"Even if I learn to cook crisps, they alone will not make a balanced diet."

Noah used the last few minutes of our picnic to explain geology using analogies from cooking. "Until we left the ark we had been vegetarians," he said, "but we still had a wondrous variety of foods. My favourite meal was lasagne followed by apple and raspberry turnover. While making these I could imagine the geological processes that were going on under our ark."

"Don't get too technical. I'm not another Jenny or Gavin."

"Fair enough. Let us imagine that we are making a lasagne dish. You start with a basin. That represents a hollow part of the earth that has sunk because water has escaped from beneath. The cook first puts in a layer of lasagne filling. In our case it was nuts and vegetables. They would be already chopped up, and in a pile on the right of the basin. Then a layer of pasta from the left would be placed on the filling. Then another layer of filling, and so on would be applied. The sauces poured over the dish could represent the chemical effects of the flood-waters. The baking of the dish would represent the hardening of the rock."

"Can you turn a pudding making session into an analogy with geology, Noah?"

"How about flaky pastry, especially when it is made for apple turnover? You roll out a thin square of pastry. Then you smear it with more fat or butter, fold it over and roll it out again. Then you repeat the process again and again. This would represent the stretching and folding of the earth's strata. That is a kiddies' version of geology."

"Maybe one day I'll try some cooking."

"Welcome to the club, Frank."

"I did say one day."

"I'd rather you write a book explaining to the folk of the new millennium the reality of The Flood."

"You are pestering me again. I have to get the children home. It's school tomorrow."

CHAPTER SIXTEEN

LAND AHOY
"God remembered Noah", Gen 8 v 1

With the grandchildren returned to their owners we completed the journey home. As I pulled into our drive we could smell the barbecue that Charles, our neighbour, was trying to light. The couple had moved in two years ago. We'd had them round to meals a couple of times, and learned that she was a retired geologist.

"Jenny," we heard Charles shout to his wife, "the barbecue is hot enough to start cooking now."

"While you were blowing hard on that pile of charcoal and going red in the face you did not hear the phone. Peter and Jane are not coming."

"Why?"

"She is not well."

"If I had known that I would not have bothered to light this contraption."

"Her sickness only started in the last half hour. Since the food is thawed already, there is nothing to stop us from having our own barbecue."

"What about inviting Gaynor and Frank over?"

"It's no good. They went out early today with the grandchildren and some other folk."

"I heard them come back a few minutes ago without any children."

"They might not want to come if they have visitors."

"But we have enough food for an army."

I was hesitant to accept the invitation because it seemed as if we were being treated as second fiddle. Then there was the question of Noah and Sarah – to send them home (wherever that was) or ask if all four of us could come. And how would we describe our relationship with them?

Jenny and Charles said all of us could join them. We left it to Noah, not normally lost for words, to explain who he was. The attraction of going to our neighbours with Noah was the prospect that Jenny might be able to call Noah's bluff over his adventure. So with Shem's sketch, we joined them for a repast of sausages, pavlova, kebabs, wine and salad, but not in that order.

"These kebabs of yours, Charles, are super," said Noah. "Did you know that we did not eat meat until after The Flood?"

"Why did you do it the wrong way round? Usually folk are meat eaters and then become vegetarians."

"I suppose I am getting the story out of order. Can you wait for the answer, while we go back to the time in the ark?"

"As long as you talk geology to Jenny. My wife has never heard such preposterous ideas about the earth only being as old as Ussher suggested, a mere six thousand years."

"Hey, I did promise that I will answer everything in the proper order if you can only be patient. All I have to do is tell you four Dorset folk about the last months on board the ark and then I will answer Jenny's questions.

"Five months after the *mabbul* began, water started to retreat. Cleaning out stained and sodden straw from stalls for days on end is not pleasant especially when the ark would suddenly twist around in the current, or heave up and down in the waves."

Jenny and Charles listened intently as I interrupted Noah, "That would make cooking challenging. And don't say you had unintentional scrambled egg for every meal."

"We had put the stoves in the kitchens on gimbals so that they kept reasonably level. When the motion was excessive, we abandoned cooking for an hour."

"And came back to burnt offerings and smashed crockery?"

"We had plenty of burnt offerings. Cupboards and tables all had lips and ledges around them so that crockery would not slide off when the ark was heaving and dancing, exactly as on a modern boat. Some items broke when it was really rough. The broken bits went overboard, and we replaced them with items we had packed for Dad."

"You didn't take any clay on board to make new ones?"

"We had a potter's wheel and oven in the stores ready for use in the new world but the additional fire risk ruled out that idea."

I imagined that with the ark pitching and tossing that they would have found that hammocks were the best things to sleep in. However, Noah pointed out that they are uncomfortable especially for older folk because they do not support your back in the natural posture that your lordosis requires. I took his word for it.

"Our beds had lips on them," Noah told me, "solving the problems of sliding out most days. On the other days sleep was impossible with the ark rocking and the animals making a din."

"Did you have to go and right upturned sheep?"

"As all farmers do. But by day 150 an additional worry had raised its head – we were running short of fresh water. The tanks that we had filled before The Flood began were almost empty."

"Couldn't you have filled them up with rainwater?"

"We had fitted a collecting system on the roof, but the rain until then had been poisonous because much of it had come from the fountains of the great deep. Even when it was not raining we could watch this foul water bubbling up from the seabed. Then on day 150 we had this comfortable feeling that we had not been forgotten. That evening the water was as calm as a mill pond. We watched an orange sun set, but the mist, instead of forming a thicker bank as it did many nights, lifted. Clouds scurried overhead, and produced a light shower of rain – just what we needed for our tanks and soft enough to wash your hair in. For the first time since boarding, I caught a clear glimpse of the moon, yellow and full. Obviously it had risen several hours before, but the mist and then the clouds had obscured it."

"With the old man in the moon smiling at you?"

"It was the Lord whose grin must have been broad that evening. After having suffered uncertainty for five months, we decided to have an impromptu party to celebrate the change that was happening. Tricia brought out her violin, and we danced in the recreation room for hours.

"At the end of it we were exhausted but very elated. We were in no hurry to turn in, and because the clouds had finally disappeared, we had an uninterrupted view of the moon sending its shimmering shaft of light across the waves, just as at harvest time.

"We were baffled, Frank. We had boarded the ark in the autumn, five months earlier so why were we now seeing another harvest moon? A bigger surprise occurred when the moon sank beneath the horizon. An enormous number of stars came out, twinkling as if they were winking to each other to celebrate the fact that the retreat of the flood-waters had begun. Even before The Flood you could count the number of stars that you could see on your fingers and toes. Now there were millions. Nor could we recognise any of the constellations. We reckoned that before The Flood, we lived about 60 degrees south of the equator. Because of that we had only seen southern constellations."

"These are not so interesting or as numerous as those we have in the northern hemisphere. No south-pole star."

"I now know that there are more stars in the northern hemisphere than in the southern hemisphere, but there was more to it than that. Obviously while the mist hung around it had hampered visibility, but neither had we seen much before The Flood started. You remember the problem with the barometer?"

"The pressure plummeted, and never went back up."

"That vapour canopy could have acted as a diffuser, obscuring the fainter stars. With its demise, we could see all the stars."

In his younger days, Ben had been interested in the stars. I'd had to take him to the remoter parts of Dorset to get good views of the heavens, otherwise all we saw was the odd bright star and an orange tint hanging low in the sky caused by the street lights. At least the air was clear. A small telescope had added to his enjoyment, and he had learnt to identify most of the constellations.

"Although we studied the sky carefully and compared the star patterns with the sketches in our notebooks, we could not identify any of the constellations. Tricia came up with a suggestion – that we had drifted into the northern hemisphere."

"So you saw a new set of constellations – Leo and Hydra?"

"No, remember it was autumn when The Flood started. We had drifted mainly in the southern hemisphere through what was their winter. If we had stayed in the same spot it would have been the spring. Having drifted to the north, we had entered the opposing autumn. Hence another harvest moon half a year later. The whole thing was confirmed by the fact that the days had shortened when we had first entered the ark, as autumn progressed into winter. Then they became longer for a month, like a false spring. Finally they became shorter."

"What a disappointment – two winters in a row. But then you would see the constellation Orion – the Hunter, with his sword."

"Correct. The two winters meant that it was cooler, and so many creatures did a double hibernation. We hardly had to bother about feeding them and that saved changing the straw."

"What about the snakes? I never understood why you took them in. The world would have been a better place without them."

"We were told in our dreams not to be selective. They came to the ark so we let them in. It was a pleasure having this wide range of creatures with us. What did one of your modern zoologists say? 'There is a human need for variety, individuality and the challenge of understanding the non-human world – it nourishes awe, compassion, reflectiveness missed when we encounter each other in the impersonality of the traffic jam.'"

"They are brave words. I visit a zoo occasionally, but everything is under careful control there."

"Our biggest worry was the state of the food stocks going down faster than expected. So would we have enough food for the next 12 months?"

"The answer, Noah?"

"I am not going to satisfy your curiosity about that now. I will tell you what happened later if I can persuade Charles to let me have another sausage, please, with a dab of that superb barbecue sauce on it."

For a moment, six of us ate in silence before Noah continued, "We overslept that next morning, but when we finally got the feeding programme going and cleaned out the stalls, none of the animals seemed to mind. Their sixth sense told them that open spaces would soon be back on the agenda. It was Tricia's turn to write up the ark log that day. She pulled in the rain gauge – it was empty. She checked the barometer – it was steady. Then she looked outside at the water. It was calm and flat and had been like that for the whole day. The gushing and bubbling that we had experienced for the last five months had stopped. The fountains of the deep had finally closed up, although we could not be sure of that for a while. The mist had gone for good, blown away by the wind. Then she rushed out of the control room to find me. 'Noah,' she said, 'did you notice that the ark has not twisted around during the last 24 hours?' The pole star had remained in the same direction since last night and I had not realised it."

"What was special about that?"

"Prior to that day, the ark would rotate several times in the swirl of the water each 24 hours because the water was deeper than our draught. The water was now shallowing and we had rested on the bottom of the seabed. Lowering a rope with a weight on it over the side to check confirmed this. Day after day we checked the depth of water hoping that it would go down the rest of the way. Nothing changed. Time dragged. We had light showers of rain. What more can I tell you about being stuck in the middle of the ocean? Five of us were to have birthdays. Had it not been for those celebrations, our regular worship of the Lord and our weekly concerts we might have all become psychiatric cases. On a human level it was tough. We feared that the ark might slowly disintegrate and everything slip into the sea."

"But I thought it was an adventure."

"This was not a glamour story. The ark was a prison. The inmates were the animals."

"But you were the warders."

"Frank, we were the warders, but we were also prisoners, free to move about, but not leave. Think about Alcatraz, that prison on an island in the middle of San Francisco Bay. Far from shore and with currents too strong to swim against, it was escape-proof. However, it was closed in 1963 because its isolation created problems for staff and inmates."

Musing, I realised that Noah and Sarah would not be here now in Jenny and Charles' garden if they had died in the ark from starvation. As they claimed to be listening to God, I wondered what He had got to say about this delay.

"That impromptu concert and seeing that myriad of stars were medicines for our sanity. The animals that were awake were also very friendly. Some days the wind would rise in force, but in our prayers and worship before the altar we were told that the wind was part of the drying-out process.

"For seventy-three days we were stuck on the bottom. That evening, as the sun set, Irene spotted a black speck on the surface of the sea many miles away. She called us all over to see it before the light failed. Alarm clocks were set early for the next day. Katrina, up first, could see three small islands about 20 miles away. As the day drew on, several other islands appeared, and those first three grew in size. We were not yet 'home and dry', but after those days of anxious waiting, there could hardly have been a more excited crew."

"This is where you could have done with an engine. Get you there in an hour."

"We did not have that technology."

"You could have set up sails."

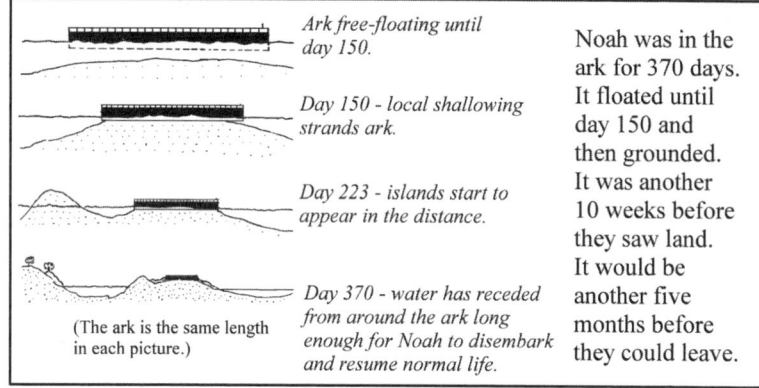

Ark free-floating until day 150.

Day 150 - local shallowing strands ark.

Day 223 - islands start to appear in the distance.

Day 370 - water has receded from around the ark long enough for Noah to disembark and resume normal life.

(The ark is the same length in each picture.)

Noah was in the ark for 370 days. It floated until day 150 and then grounded. It was another 10 weeks before they saw land. It would be another five months before they could leave.

"We were grounded on the seabed, Frank. In a moment of aberration, we hoped that the tide would free us from the bottom and we would drift towards one of these islands. Thinking about it afterwards we realised how many things could have gone wrong. Would the island have been big enough to sustain our animals? How would we have got out of the ark with a draught of 20 feet? There would have been no friendly jetty waiting for us. Anyway, we didn't have a gangplank or a door."

"But you had a boat, Noah."

"We had not worked out how to get it out of the bowels of the ark. The lads were all for releasing the birds because they could fly to the islands. I insisted on patience for 40 days because birds need trees and bushes to nest in, so they had to start growing again."

"But grow from what?"

"When we had been totally surrounded by water we had seen tangled tree branches floating alongside us. They would have been impaled on land as it rose from beneath the water and the seeds would have germinated."

"Seeds do not germinate in salt-saturated soil!"

"There had been enough fresh rain to wash the salt away in those 40 days since land had appeared. As ravens are not particularly fastidious birds, we released the male. He could feed on any seeds that he found or dead fish caught on a beach or stream as the water levels fell. He knew that he could always come back to the ark for food, but never did. A couple of nights later, when the air was still, we could hear him calling his mate though we could not see him. This gave us confidence that at least one of those islands could support life, so I released the female.

"It was exciting to see that the water level was falling. Then it dawned on us why we were told to build the ark with a flat bottom. A curved bottom would have caused the ark to keel over. Stuck on sloping decks for days on end would have been uncomfortable. There would have been problems with the cooking because although the stoves were on gimbals, there was only a limited angle through which they could swing. Nor would the animals have been comfortable on a sloping floor.

"Seven days later, Ham released a dove. It came back the next day, famished. Since they only eat seeds and insects, we inferred that seeds and berries to satisfy the dove had not yet grown.

"We tried again with the dove seven days later," Noah continued. "In the evening she came back with a fresh olive leaf. Our jubilation was tempered by the fact that the bird was still hungry. However, in the night the water had gone down the last ten feet, exposing the ground around the ark."

Although we were all itching to know how they got out, Jenny got in first with a question about the olive leaf. "I see an olive leaf as a sign of peace rather than food and safety," she said, "but I find it impossible to understand how it grew so quickly."

"Four months is enough for the olive leaf to have sprouted from an asexually propagated branch impaled on the surface of the soil. It had been exposed to sunlight as the water receded. After all, rolled leaves were found in the cliffs at Bournemouth, east of Durley Chine. Those leaves and palm remains were probably trapped at the end of The Flood in the same way that the olive branches were. Do you have a convincing alternative explanation for them, Jenny?"

Jenny was now stumped. "As a less than enthusiastic gardener, I am amazed at how quickly weeds grow in my garden. They seem to creep around my begonias when I am not looking. I know that Frank has the same problem."

"You have reminded me of Surtsey. In 1963, a volcanic island emerged off the coast of Iceland. Within months, the barren mound was covered in vegetation and nesting birds."

"I am beginning to see that your story has hints of truth in it," she replied.

"Then let me tell all four of you the events after the dove left us. Sarah can bear me out. The mud outside was slow to dry, so we stayed put. Three days later we watched as a new ridge of land pushed its way up through the surface of the sea a couple of miles to the north in just a few hours. It caused a huge wave of water to come our way, almost like the Severn tidal bore. Had we been outside, we would have been swept away. But when the water finally retreated, we could see a network of dry valleys that had been scoured out by the sudden burst of water over the soft earth. I found carbon copies of these valleys on the road between Dorchester and Yeovil. More spectacular are those near Durdle Door, near Lulworth where you can enjoy the coastal views at the same time."

"Us geologists have puzzled over dry valleys. Some of them were formed during the ice ages. Are you saying that this could be true of these in Dorset, Noah?"

"No one believes that the ice sheets came as far south as Dorset. And the fact that the dry valleys are in an opposing pattern shows that it was rapid uplift of the land from beneath the sea that formed the dry valleys."

"Let us go back to dating the rocks, while I mull this point about the dry valleys over in my mind, Noah. If I use a standard method to date pre-Cambrian rocks, then I get an age of almost 600 millions years. Now you say that the diamonds from that rock are not even 50 thousand years old. Why the difference?"

"The reason seems to be that radioactive decay was faster in the past than it is today, Jenny."

"Your evidence, Noah?"

"Helium retention, radio-halos . . . "

"We are getting too technical for a barbecue, especially when not all the guests are geologists," she said. "I will look into your evidence tomorrow. For the moment, finish entertaining us with your story. I wish that I had met you when you first visited Frank and Gaynor."

"We waited another week, and then released the dove for the third time," said Noah. "We never saw her again so I released the male a few days later. Squelchy looking mud was still present around the ark so it was not advisable to let animals leave. It was another month before the ground was dry out to the horizon. We did talk to the Lord about the risk of leaving the ark in view of that sudden engulfing by that blast of water. He gave the signal to remove the top covering from the ark. Some birds flew away, but others stayed."

"I'm waiting for you to tell me how the rest of you got out."

"We had ideas, but we stayed our hand. But knowing that the end was nigh, it liberated our spirits and our family concerts got much better."

"Tell us some of Jay's new tricks. Did he saw someone else in two?"

"Magicians never repeat the same trick twice. But one of the new tricks he did was linking together of eight separate solid steel rings."

"There must be gaps in them."

"No, there were not. We all tugged and pulled but there was nothing."

"I know that Frank would like to learn another trick to show to his grandchildren."

"Another day, I promise. Today has also been wonderful, going to Bulbarrow, and now this barbecue. With it getting dark we must bid farewell. Do any of you want to go out with Ham tomorrow? You can pull his leg about fainting while his wife was sawn in two. He will tell you about leaving the hulk that had been our home for a year."

Gaynor and I stayed to help Charles and Jenny clear away. It gave me a chance to ask Jenny whether she believed Noah that the whole of the earth was once covered with water. She agreed that geologists were puzzled by the Cretaceous period, when most of the earth was covered with water. I asked her where it was not covered.

"We do not know, Frank. The only reason we say that part of the earth was not covered with water is because there would have been nowhere for the animals to live."

"And Noah made the point that representatives of all the animals were safely in his ark," chipped in Charles. "That puts him one up on us."

"But the Cretaceous period was 60 to 120 million years ago, not Noah's few thousand. And many animals and sea creatures have become extinct over those 60 million years. He is pulling your leg. You have been hoaxed, Frank. Did you ever hear about Virginia . . .?"

"But Jenny, he has made serious inroads into your understanding of geology. I'll go out with him tomorrow even if you are reluctant."

"He has challenged much of what I thought was true," she said reluctantly.

"Do you or Charles know what a crypto-zoologist is?"

"It's the name given to those zoologists who go hunting for animals that are thought to be extinct," said Charles.

"Why do they do that? Are they trying to find evidence that the story of Noah's ark is true?"

"It is a way of life, disappearing into the jungle, talking to the natives about unusual animals and then trying to find them. Others squeeze themselves into midget submarines and go hunting in deep waters."

"How often do they find new species?"

"You ought to read their books. I don't know much about it, though I did hear about an accidental find. A Japanese fishing boat was trawling 900 feet down near New Zealand. When they hauled the net up they found that it had caught a huge creature. It was dead and partly eaten away. By coincidence, a biologist was on board. He wanted to take it back to port because he'd never seen anything like it before. However, it stank and there was a risk of it infecting their catch of fish. They dumped it overboard because money from the catch was more important than satisfying the curiosity of the solo marine biologist. However, they did take photographs, measurements, and saved a portion of cartilage."

"How come you know all this, Charles?"

"Now that I'm retired, I allow myself the luxury of trawling the internet, if you pardon the pun, for 15 minutes each day. Back in port, whilst talking to the authorities and other trawler men, there was a lot of argument about whether it was or wasn't a basking shark. They are common in that part of the ocean and have damaged many a trawler's nets. The photographs gave lie to the idea that it was a basking shark."

"So what was it?"

"A plesiosaur."

"A what?" said Jenny, "I thought they died out in the Jurassic period."

"My darling, have you forgotten that you have married a Scot from Inverness? Most people have heard of the Loch Ness monster. Said to belong to a prehistoric age, it has often raised its head tantalisingly above water since 1900. Occasional glimpses of the unusual have been observed using underwater cameras and sonar."

"But the crypto-zoologists who go looking for these things in odd lochs in Scotland are not reputable geologists. Even if it were true, there is nowhere in this part of the UK for such a beast to hide."

"Have you not heard about the Dorset writer, Sheila Bird, and her brother, Dr Eric Bird, a geologist? They are among the folk who claim to have seen Morgawr, the huge Falmouth Bay sea serpent, which could be a descendant of the ichthyosaur."

"I'll darling you. Whose side are you on?"

After thanking them for the barbecue, Gaynor and I left Charles and Jenny to their war of words.

The Hellstone near Portesham is a Dorset example of how large local stones left after The Flood can be turned into a monument.

CHAPTER SEVENTEEN

STONES
"Noah built an altar to the Lord", Gen 8 v 20

Mention Stone Henge in Wiltshire and you have spoken about one of England's best-known ancient monuments. Its origin and purpose are shrouded in mystery. Was it a place for worshipping some unknown god?

Dorset has a mixture of lesser-known man-made and natural stone monuments. Agglestone, near Studland, and the Pulpit Rock at Portland are examples of naturally occurring features, though legends abound about them. Hellstone, between Martinstown and Portesham is man-made, and was probably the framework for a burial chamber. The mind does boggle at how 20-ton stones were lifted six feet up with primitive technology. However, there is a different enigma about the Nine-stone Circle one mile west of Winterborne Abbas. It was supposedly built in the Bronze Age for religious purposes. But what were they? None of the stones line up with equinoxes of the sun like they do at Stone Henge.

Ham appeared before I had finished breakfast. I ragged him on his fainting when Jay sawed his wife up into chunks of bloodstained flesh.

"Scared the life out of me. I still cannot work out how he did the trick."

"Never mind."

"What do you mean, 'Never mind'? I'd almost lost the girl twice before."

"I'm sorry, that was a touchy remark."

"I'll forgive you."

"Your father promised that you'd tell me how you got the animals out of the ark with no door."

"Dad delights to keep you in suspense."

"And you have to tell me about Jay's other tricks."

"Although the ark had been grounded for weeks, no one felt it was right to let out the animals. We bit our nails as time dragged. Two months later four of us had dreams about disembarking. We held a family council next morning and decided that the moment for exit had come. It was an exciting time hammering and banging out the side of the ark on the bottom deck."

"A hole in the side of your boat sounds ludicrous. However would it float again? Anne's school picture never showed a hole in the bottom. Nor did Beryl's."

"The children's story has been glamorised," Ham reminded me. "I guess her picture showed the gangplank against the door, half way up the side. Our method was easy because we would never need to float again. But once outside we were in for a shock."

"Did you sink into soft ground as they feared the first astronauts might do on the moon?"

"No. It was the ark that scared us. Bare wood was exposed in large areas because the pitch had been worn away. If The Flood had gone on much longer, I doubt if we would have remained seaworthy."

"But wooden boats have lasted at sea longer than that."

"Frank, it wasn't sea water that we sailed through. Corrosive hot waters came up from the fountains of the deep. The roof had lichens growing on it, showing that the pitch was no longer a perfect coating.

"Before letting any of the animals off," he continued, "Dad knew that the first thing to do when we got outside was to build an altar of stone. Inside the ark, we'd had a wooden one, but had never dared burn anything on it."

"I don't understand why you would want to worship a God who foresaw a disastrous flood, yet was powerless to stop it or encourage everybody to get on the ark. Even more of a problem is that if God made the world in the way that He told Adam, He must have placed the water under the earth waiting to release it on an unsuspecting world."

"You have raised a touchy point, Frank. We cannot alter what God is like. But you are making the mistake that Darwin made. Although God designed the earth with judgement in mind if humans chose to go their own way, He also offered salvation. For us it was from a watery grave by boarding the ark. Your New Testament tells that He has another kind of judgement reserved for ungodly people who have lived since The Flood – by fire."

That sounded like the Victorian image of religion – the devil had power to send you to the flames of hell. It reminded me of the Agglestone Rock near Studland.

In the 1960s the Agglestone Rock was like a 20 foot anvil and difficult to climb up because of its overhang. Then suddenly, because the softer part at the bottom was being eroded away, it toppled sideways. The legend of Agglestone Rock was that the stone was thrown by the devil from the Needles in the Isle of Wight and was aimed at the monastery at Bindon Abbey near Wool. The devil was either short of strength or his aim was bad. The rock only reached three-quarters of the way to its target. I thought that that was a crackpot idea and asked Ham how it fitted into his theology.

"That legend was devised by people who were not geologists. However, they did recognise that the devil is real and he will try to destroy Christian witness, however weak that witness is. On this occasion, why not put your question about Agglestone to the geologists?"

"Why did Shem not make that suggestion when we saw geologists in Durlston Bay and we started arguing?"

"He said that you didn't ask the question."

"I am now, Ham."

"Your neighbour, Jenny, might explain thus – 'There was once a layer of hard sandstone across the heath with a softer layer beneath it.' I would agree with that. Then she would add, 'Large areas of both layers were eroded and washed away by a huge river; it's been called the proto-Solent. Smaller areas such as Agglestone were left untouched by the swirling water. Technically these are known as outliers.'"

"Whatever was proto-Solent?"

"We wouldn't have called it a river, Frank. The water running off at the tail end of The Flood was responsible for the erosion. It was a single drainage event, almost like emptying a bucket of water, exposing whole areas of what is now the heath. God wanted all the flood-waters to be cleared away in a few months so that our lives could get back to normal. It was not a traditional river because the amount of water needed to fill the valleys that this proto-Solent occupied would have required as much rain in a day as you see in a year."

"OK, Jenny would be stuck without a plausible explanation, Ham. So with that aspect all sorted out, what did you do with your altar?"

"Once completed, we sacrificed one of each of the ritually clean animals. For firewood we used broken parts of the ark."

"So that is where the phrase 'burning your boats after you' originates."

"And the Romans copied us after they landed in Holes Bay."

That was AD43. In those circumstances, the captains ordered the boats to be set alight so that the soldiers would fight to the end and not retreat, knowing that they would only get home by first winning the battle. In modern warfare, the boats go back for more soldiers, and evacuate the wounded. How things have changed, I noted.

"Going back to this idea that there is a devil, Ham, surely because he is only mentioned in the first few and last few chapters of the Bible we can ignore it. He isn't mentioned in the big chunk in between, which tell of God's universal love."

"There are two sides to God's character – what you might call carrot and stick. The Victorians focussed on 'stick' which they saw God using to punish people. The 'carrot' is the love of God, which shows itself in the way He gives us those things that we do not deserve, including forgiveness."

"Could He not have made theology simpler?"

"God could have made us like animals. Their brains are hard-wired, so that like robots they can only have a rigid pattern of behaviour and therefore cannot be held responsible for what they do. We cannot hibernate, migrate, run fast or fly unaided any more than they cannot stop themselves doing these things. Our hallmark is that we were made in the image of God with free will. When asked, our family chose to build the ark to save ourselves. Others refused to join. God warns, gives time for reflection and action, and then judges. What clinched our wish to worship Him that day we left the ark was not the negative side of life – destruction of the world except for those in the ark – but that once we had a plan of action, He did things that we could not do. It was not a boss-servant relationship but a cooperative loving partnership. Having now had chance to read all of your New Testament, I found that the Apostle Paul summed it up with the words, 'Work out your own salvation, because it is God at work in you.'"

"Sealing the door was one of the things he did for you?"

"You have heard of many other things where He saved us from disaster, so we built a stone altar to Him. We had no building materials so we collected big stones from around the area using our trolley and fitted them together as best as possible. Later we would build an altar of hewn stone."

I needed to ask him where the stones had come from. Surely a flood only leaves mud around?

"As the water ran off the land when it lifted like a submarine surfacing, the water washed away the top soil, exposing what were originally embedded sarcens. The valley of Stones near Portesham is a good example. There are more stones in the field than sheep. Across the other side of the road the stones have been cleared from the valley and made into the Hellstone, though it is not as impressive as Stone Henge. Before we go to Portesham to see them, stop at Bere Regis, Frank, to see a couple of big examples of sarcens. That will give me chance to get some watercress from the cress farm. Dad and Mum told me how superb your wife's watercress soup was that she served up years ago."

"It's very nutritious. Full of iron."

"Just up the hill from the water cress sheds is the school, with a sarcen outside. At six feet wide they are some of the largest ones around."

"Ham, even your family, with its bulging muscles, would need more than a barrow to move that."

"We did not try and move those giant objects – concretions is their technical name, formed by the mineral rich waters that poured from the fountains of the great deep during The Flood. They have become exposed as a result of the flood-waters washing away the top layers of soil.

"It was a calm day when we began the sacrifice and the smoke rose vertically. God spoke to us during the sacrifice that the earth would never experience another watery grave. Furthermore, we were told that we could now eat meat."

"You'd been telling me that you were vegetarians before the flood."

"From that point in time, it was essential to eat meat. Several of the vegetables that we had had in our old world struggled to produce crops after a few years. These would have been important parts of our diet if we had not had meat."

"Anne became a vegetarian in her teens. Though it worried us, the doctor said it should not cause any ill effects provided she ate dairy products. So why was it a problem for you?"

"We had no fresh fruit or vegetables in the ark. It would be months before they grew again, so eating meat made sense now. Is Anne still a vegetarian?"

"Anne stopped being a vegetarian when she met Gavin. She saw how much he enjoyed meat and he was part of her generation, not part of the fuddy duddy parents' generation who tried to impose their values on her."

"That is an interesting phrase."

"Lots of teenagers go through a phase where one day their parents know everything and they turn to them for advice, and the next day they know nothing. Then we get accused of being 'fuddy duddies' because we are lost in the past."

"Most of the things that you taught your children are exactly what good parents should do. But do I detect that you are hedging your bets on some things, Frank? You told us that you enjoy singing the hymn 'Jerusalem', and that you had your children baptised. But Christianity is more than songs of praise and a moral code that only covers our relationship with each other and ignores the first five commandments that deal with out relationship with God. Where does the 'stick and carrot' side of God's character fit into your thinking?"

I had read about Charles Darwin. He was supposed to have become a church leader, but one thing after another knocked his faith. His brother rejected Christianity and so, when his brother died, Darwin realised that Christianity, which is supposed to be a religion of love, had condemned the brother to hell. Christianity therefore seemed to be an irrational religion. After a trip on *HMS Beagle*, wearing a biologist's hat, he came up with the idea of evolution. God disappears from the scene.

"Why did he invent the idea of evolution when it did not happen?" asked Ham. "Why was it difficult for the brothers to accept that God had placed the whole of the human race under judgement, but in tandem with that, God offered love and mercy? Why, to use a famous quote, are people loath to look a gift-horse in the mouth? And, of course, Darwin had already decided that he liked Lyell's geology that avoided mentioning The Flood."

"I am thinking about these theological points that you are making, maybe too slowly for your liking, so can we continue where we left off? Why did these other vegetables not continue to grow?"

"Maybe it was caused by the loss of the vapour canopy, Frank. The pre-Flooded world was also warmer than the new one we inherited and this could have been a factor in the failure of those crops to thrive. In the old world we were forbidden to eat meat because of a serious health issue. In the warm climate, many animals harboured diseases that were fatal to humans, and these could not be eradicated by cooking."

"Like BSE?"

"BSE is serious because cooking does not destroy the dangerous prions that cause the brain damage. But our problems were more like those you have with pork. Until the advent of refrigerators, you only ate pork if there was an 'R' in the month. The simplest of folk then knew that they should avoid pork in the summer months. The heat encourages the growth of the bacteria. Beef was now on our menus, but I still do not eat pork."

"So you've never tasted bacon. You don't know what you were missing. Your father loved Jenny's pork sausages the other night."

"As soon as the sacrifices were complete," he responded, "a heavy burst of rain started. We ran for the shelter of the ark feeling scared. The prospect of another watery disaster and having a big hole in the side caught us off guard."

"You'd had only normal rain since the 150th day of the flood?"

"When we calmed down, we remembered that God had said that He would not destroy the surface of the world by water again. We had not trusted Him. Knowing that we were mortal and would forget again, He reminded us of His promise. Although it was raining, the sun was out, and there, facing away from the sun was a double multi-coloured bow in the sky, something we had never seen before."

"We see plenty of rainbows but we do not always see the second bow, because it is fainter. The inner bow is called the 'water gull' in Dorset. If the inner bow is missing or imperfect, then folklore says that you will be unlucky."

"Seeing a double bow, we were enthralled. We took it as a sign that we could now let all the animals off the ark. That meant enlarging the hole in the side of the ark. We did not let the domesticated animals off until we had erected stalls and pens for them outside. No one was in the mood for running round trying to capture animals for food or the animals attacking each other as they grew in size."

"The picture you have just painted must have been a strange sight, Ham – the ark being broken up, never to be used again, with a motley collection of animals around it. There are several grounded boats in Poole harbour, with the useful parts removed and the remains slowly disintegrating. You can see them from the road or the railway. One of them was once a tea-boat."

"It sounds like the owners subconsciously copied the idea from us because we took the feeding troughs out of the ark first and ensured that they were refilled with food each day so that animals could come back for food if they could not find their own. Then we opened the stalls of the unclean animals and shooed them away."

I thought back to 1970 when that zebra had appeared in my garden. I was too startled to shoo him away. Ham then explained that the families had then stripped the inside of the ark for timbers for their own homes. It was all legitimate, and not quite like the Portlanders, who, as late as 1903, were known to salvage and re-use the timbers found on the beaches. Most of the ark was thereby broken up, with parts for animal pens and fences. The idea of dinosaurs, especially the meat eating carnosaurs, growing up and coming back to haunt the families at night in the future was not something that they wanted.

"What did they eat then?" I asked him. "Killing other animals that you had carefully tried to save sounds the worst ending to what would otherwise be a successful story."

"For a while they were content to eat vegetation. As the animals' population increased through breeding, they became carnivorous again."

"Changing the topic, Ham, I guess that if you were breaking the ark up, it would make it difficult for archaeologists to find it."

"That certainly will be one problem for your 21st century archaeologists."

"But you must have built houses and roads in the area which you would recognise again, Ham."

"We do not live there now. I'll explain when we've finished talking about altars."

"You sound like a politician being interviewed about a touchy thing."

"No. I'm just having a bit of fun with you. After all, you turned the barrister charm and aggression on us many times."

"But I was after the truth."

"I'm helping you to find it, Frank, but I am also warning you that you might be hounded like Ashmore for pointing out how ridiculous many modern ideas are for ignoring the Bible. I am grateful that you have stayed and listened to the story."

"What about visiting Dorset's mount Ararat, Ham?"

"Nothing there. I would rather go west today, not east and show you some big stones. Once our ploughing and planting had been completed for the spring, we decided to build an altar of hewn stone. It had to be the purest we could find – free from blemishes. Our choice was a creamy-white stone similar to what you would call 'Portland Stone'. It's very durable and workable."

"I remember that discussion with Noah years ago over Portland Cement."

"Do you mind taking me to your quarry to see the stone masons at work? I am curious to compare what you have now with what we had."

It took us ages to get to reach our destination. The slowest part of the journey was through Weymouth. Whenever will they build that Weymouth relief road? Will the Olympics in 2012 be enough to turn the need into reality? But now, as a retired man, it was no longer my responsibility to promote it as an aid to the local economy. Finally, it was up the hill into Portland and turn right at the Portland Heights Hotel towards Tout Quarry Park.

Tout Quarry used to provide stone for the building and sculpting industries. Rufus Castle was made from the Portland Stone. Although the castle was centuries older, Portland Stone rose to fame when it was selected for the Whitehall Banqueting Hall around 1620. Since then it has been used in many other famous buildings – St Paul's Cathedral in London and the UN building in America. Sadly, the industry had declined apart from a small portion of the quarry to the south still operating with drift mining.

Ham did not agree the precedent I believed that Portland Stone had set. Whilst they had not mined in Portland, their stone was just as pure a quality as ours. And so in honour of the Lord, the first thing they had made from it was an altar.

The Portland Sculpture Trust has turned the Tout Quarry into an open-air museum. Here, people ranging from novice right up to advanced standard have the opportunity to indulge in sculpting in summer workshops. Gaynor wanted me to take it up as a hobby because she said I kept getting under her feet during retirement, but I declined.

Ham reminded me that another famous place in Dorset for stone is Swanage. Most of the stone produced from the old quarries there is not as durable as Portland Stone, but is more decorative because it can take a polish. "Maybe that kind of stone working would interest you more, Frank," he said. "The effigy of Lawrence of Arabia in St Martin's church at Wareham is made from this latter stone."

"Ham, I'm not interested in sculpting. However, I don't think that I shall forget that interesting discussion about Lawrence and his anti-religious views."

"I am not the best person to talk about his theology to you. But what I can do while we are in Portland is to take you to see the raised beach near the lighthouse. It is hardly a place to swim – its claim to fame is that it helps to understand how the water retreated after The Flood. One day the land would lurch up out of the water 20 feet. Then nothing would happen for a fortnight, when the land would suddenly come up another 10 feet. Beaches were shifting back – just the opposite of what happened when The Flood started."

"I understand that. That is what produced the dinosaur footprints."

"For months, the Isle of Portland had been totally under water while the sediments were deposited and hardened into Portland Stone. Abruptly one day the whole island was lifted sixty feet. At the edges a beach formed. We will only see a bit of it because quarrying has been quite intensive around the area, and much has disappeared, so it is necessary to consult records left by geologists from the 1800s."

From the car park it took us about ten minutes to cover the quarter of a mile to the raised beach northwest of Portland Bill.

As we stood looking at a pile of shingle, Ham said, "There was once a beach here, though only for a few days. High tides and violent onshore winds deposited the shingle, loam and rubble around us. A few days later, the land lifted up again. The sand and shingle that was part of a beach was thereby stranded up on the cliffs."

"I don't think any modern day geologist would doubt your explanation, except for the speed at which it happened."

"You still believed it happened over millions of years, whereas I saw it happen in a matter of days."

"So what is wrong with objecting? You know I'm not satisfied with your explanations."

"Even if I had not told you that the beach was formed in only a few days, there are three things that point to how quickly it happened."

"Ham, that sounds very technical. All these technical people list their three points, A, B and C, and for good measure, slam on point 'D'. Before you have chance to complain about their explanations to points A, B and C, you sink under the weight of the argument."

"If I trivialised the explanations, you would not believe me. Even the words 'The Flood' fail to convey the calamity and global nature of what our family watched through the window in the ark. There is no simple English word to describe the event, and calling it '*The Mabbul*' means nothing to most people."

"I wish that the story of what you call 'The Flood' or more precisely '*The Mabbul*' were simple. I can visualise a bit of water and mud everywhere but not a fully submerged earth or neolithic beaches. You leave me speechless, though you have not spelled out point D, let alone A, B and C. Let's go to Rufus Castle. At least there is no geology there."

"But what about the archaeology?"

"What do you mean?"

The Bow and Arrow Castle (Rufus) on Portland overlooks The English Channel. Archaeologists have difficulty reconciling its name with its apparent military function.

"Rufus Castle is shrouded with mystery, Frank. Some claim it was built around 1080. The puzzle is that the windows are shaped as gun ports, with splayed embrasures. Those are hardly things for the age of bows and arrows."

"Ham, the mystery may be explained by suggesting that the first castle was built around 1080, and called 'The Bow and Arrow Castle'. In 1460, it may have been rebuilt by Richard, Duke of York with reshaped windows. Rufus is unlikely to have been the builder."

"But Frank, you are trying to turn archaeology into an exact science when most of the time it is pure guesswork."

CHAPTER EIGHTEEN

FREEDOM
"The region where they lived", Gen 10 v 30

Lyme Regis is a small harbour town at the western end of Dorset. There was a nasty incident during World War 1. A sharp-eyed German submarine captain spied the British ship *HMS Formidable* just inside Devon waters and attacked it. His torpedo blew a hole in the ship and it started to sink. In mountainous seas, dazed and injured crew members of *Formidable* struggled to get into the lifeboats and row to shore. The local rescue team helped the injured out of the lifeboats, realising that some were barely alive, while others had passed into eternity during the journey from the stricken boat.

In the Pilot Boat Hotel the rescuers started the gruesome process of sorting out the living from the dead. One mariner, identified as Seaman Cowman when his pockets were examined for personal items, was put in the pile of those to be buried within the hour. However, the owner's dog started to lick the face of the man. Half an hour later, he showed signs of life. Another 30 minutes and he'd have been buried alive. Hollywood, with ears like a hawk, picked up on the story and used the idea of a dog's sixth sense to produce films centred on the rough-haired collie. *Lassie* films were born.

Lyme Regis reminded Ham of the first taste of freedom after a year incarcerated in the ark and so he asked me to take him there.

To me, it was only a tiddly town hemmed in by two narrow valleys, claustrophobic not free.

As we drove west he told me that it had been hard suppressing their interest in exploring outside the ark for three days whilst they got the animals out. The bulk of the animals then disappeared; others came back once or twice a day to feed at the ark. As they were not eating half as much as they did when they were in the ark, they had concluded that they were finding their own food. I wondered if some were dead.

"With few exceptions like the pterodactyls, they all lived and started to breed vigorously. With the domesticated animals safely in their outdoor pens, Dad suggested taking the day off. We had a second purpose in exploring – for a fertile area to start our spring planting. Any delay would mean no food for winter.

"We had a discussion," he continued, "whether to follow the stream up towards its source, or downstream. The majority verdict was to follow the flow of the water and try and find the sea. It seemed strange to say that we hankered after the sea when its destructive power is all we had witnessed for months but our feelings of revulsion had not lasted long once land had emerged. We enlarged the hole that we had used to exit the ark and removed the boat. Being too wide for the stream we put it on the trolley with our picnic baskets and set off. The ground was sandy and slightly soft, but the wheels of the trolley did not dig in so we made good progress, singing as we went along."

"You had some horses on board. Couldn't you have hitched one of them up to the cart?"

"That was our intention, until we noticed that they were trying to make love. We were excited about the prospect of the first pregnancy."

"Apart from the rabbits."

". . . apart from the rabbits that bred in the ark, before we decided to cage them separately."

"You never told me about Shem's other tricks. I want something that is easy to impress the grandchildren."

"I've some weighted dice that always turn up sixes; you can buy them in any magic shop."

"Being unwilling to use the horses, how would you get your ploughing done? Your oxen?"

"Because weeds had not colonised the ground yet, ploughing by hand was easy. In places we broadcasted the seed by hand, primitive but workable. It was Lamech's prophesy about the ground coming true."

"But wasn't the ground saturated with salt from the retreating sea? That would hardly fit in with his prophecy that the curse on the ground would be lifted and that farming would be easier after the flood."

"Two months of normal rain, Frank, had cleansed the topsoil. After an hour of taking turns to push the trolley, we had covered three miles and there in front of us was a sandy beach with the tide receding. The stream cascaded over a series of small rocky ledges into the ocean beyond. It was much like Lyme Regis, though there was no sea wall or large rocks to dissipate the fury of the winter storms.

"Japeth and Shem launched the boat from the beach and deftly rowed away from the shore to explore the surroundings. Give us an hour, they said and we'll also try and get you fresh fish."

"So that spare boat was purely for pleasure?"

"The Lord is not a kill-joy and so gives us a time for pleasure. Irene and I went searching for crabs, limpets and seaweed in the rock pools. Dad and Mum went off arm in arm, even after 500 years of marriage, in the opposite direction."

"What did you say?"

"I said 500. Dad was 600 when The Flood began."

"But those ages are crazy. People are lucky to live till 100, let alone waiting until they are 100 to get married and have children."

"Did you not see the dates on the Ark's Log and realise the significance?"

"I though it was a mistake. You told me the world was 1,600 years old when your flood started."

"But the Ark's Log counted from Dad's date of birth."

"Gaynor and I had tried to work out your ages when you first came to see us. We guessed mid to late thirties."

"And all the other years!" he retorted.

"You must have cheated by having a shorter year than we have."

"Our years had 365 days. Why should I deceive you?"

As I could not think of a response, he continued, "By the time the boat was back with the fish the fire was hot enough and free of smoke to cook the fish. Dad and Mum were also back and showed us how to cook crab and limpets."

"I thought limpets were poisonous."

"They are safe to eat though not high in food value, but after a year of dried and preserved food, this was a meal from heaven, three capital Fs – Fantastic Fresh Food. It was the best barbecue we have ever had. If you have doubts about limpets, count yourself lucky. We never got around to visiting Maiden Castle, where archaeologists found numerous limpet shells in a pit. I think that the occupants ate limpets regularly."

"The reason they ate them is obvious. They were primitive people, or under siege that stopped them from growing crops."

"How did they collect them if they were under a siege? Even if they were not under siege, no one can understand why the occupants would go five miles to the beach and carry them in their shells when they have such low food value. Why not cook them on the beach, and throw away the shells?"

"Simple! When Maiden Castle was occupied, the beach was nearer, perhaps a hundred yards. The raised beach at Portland does support this idea, though you might still think that that particular beach was formed millions of years before Maiden Castle was occupied."

"You seem to putting what I considered to be odd pieces of a jigsaw together. The raised beach and the limpets fit together though I still have many other doubts about your story like the length of your years. Did you eat the seaweed as well?"

"Yes. Dad took it over to the stream, washed it to remove the sand and then shredded it. It was like fresh salad. We took some back to make crisps."

"Surely the stream was polluted by those fountains of the deep that you said discharged poisonous water and sediments?"

"No. They were now closed."

"Why did you never fish when you were on the ark?"

"Dead fish floating around the ark warned us off doing such a thing. Now it was time to resume fishing, and we started fossil hunting. It was a new hobby to us because there weren't any fossils before The Flood. Fossils are only created when conditions are violent. Mud by the million tons is needed to entomb living animals."

"Sure, fossilisation requires a sudden impulse of mud on unsuspecting animals. Many geologists realise that the fossil record is a series of snapshots of how life developed on earth, though there are many gaps."

"Frank, evolution did not happen. All of the fossils were produced during The Flood."

"I don't think that Mary Anning or authors of geological text books would agree."

"I admit that the fossils show artificial layering but why does that confirm evolution? Find one exception to a perfect order, and evolutionary ideas are blown up. Evolutionary ideas are only promoted by those who put their heads in the sand like the ostrich to avoid seeing the exceptions."

"Ham, you cannot get away from the fact that the fossils are ordered."

"Ask Jenny how often the roles of ecology and viscous drag are introduced into the discussions when considering the fossil order. You'll get no answer."

The cliffs at Lyme are unstable. Some fossil collectors lost their lives, but Anning was lucky, though it was sad that she died of cancer. More recently, so much of the cliffs had wasted away and more deaths were threatened that the town council built a seawall to stabilise the cliffs, preventing further fossil collecting. As with Durlston Bay in Swanage, the needs for safety and housing were deemed more important than palaeontology.

Anning was the first person to discover an ichthyosaur. The museum on the sea front has a pristine example. Ham told me that he had never seen an ichthyosaur, though his dad had seen one in his youth when he was yachting with his elder brothers. The creature bumped the boat so badly that it nearly tipped up. They were lucky to escape.

"Did the brothers not want to join the ark?" I asked.

"Even their father, Lamech, had out-lived them. Their children, our cousins, were not interested in what their uncle Noah was doing."

"We did talk about the ichthyosaurs and plesiosaurs a few days ago. I remember now why you told me that so many were killed. There might be plesiosaurs around, but why no ichthyosaurs?"

"Why do you say that there are plesiosaurs around?"

"Charles told me about fishermen near New Zealand finding one. It created a family uproar with Jenny strenuously trying to reject the idea. But why no ichthyosaurs? "

"In a moment I will try and explain why there are no ammonites now. Can you wait until we have gone a bit further onto Monmouth beach so that I can recapture for you something of what we saw?"

"But if we go as far as you want, we will be out of Dorset and into Devon."

"Do you remember what you said to Dad years ago? 'I find the counties to the west more interesting than Dorset.' Have you changed your mind about the delights of Dorset?"

"Dorset has grown on me, especially during retirement when I could relax instead of fretting about its economic lifeblood and prosperity."

"Even if you had not changed your mind, I could tell you that you were trying to split hairs again, Frank. This area is still technically part of the Dorset Coastal Path. Anyway, steep cliffs hamper access to this beach from Devon."

Monmouth beach, named after a famous battle, has no sand or shingle on it. In geological language it is a wave-cut platform of hard rock. Embedded in that surface are marine fossils, ammonites and nautiluses of all sizes.

"Ham, one of the reasons why people object to the idea that a blanket of water flooded the whole earth is that they cannot understand why all these sea creatures such as ammonites should have been fossilised."

"You remember what my brother said in Swanage? Rain on its own did not cause The Global Flood. Our Flood was only global because overwhelming quantities of water came from the fountains of the great deep. The mud moving about on the seabed caused a lot of trouble for sea creatures, burying whole swarms."

He picked up a greyish lump of rock full of fossils that had broken off from the cliff behind us. Holding it the right way up, it showed lots of fine banding at the bottom. Then there was about two inches of pure mudstone with a load of fossils, mainly ammonites in it. Then there was another layer of banding without any fossils in it. The middle part, Ham claimed, was deposited quickly, rolled out over the seabed like a carpet. In the process it covered up ammonites so fast that they could not swim out of the way. Since young and old were buried together, the collection of fossils is called a 'living assembly' even though they are all dead now.

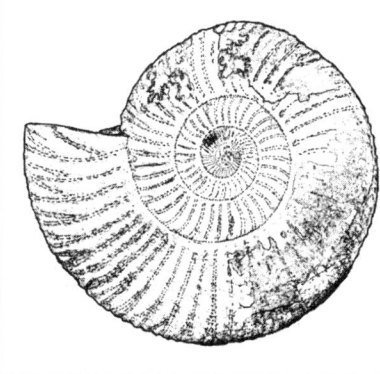

A profusion of ammonite and nautilus fossils can be found in Monmouth Bay. The cliffs consist of a greyish mudstone. The fossils occur in horizontal bands which are separated from each other by fine streaks of light and grey mudstone. These alternate periods of fossilisation and banded sedimentation show the episodic nature of the fountains of the great deep.

Ammonites belonged to whole groups of common species of all ages, living together for company. Once the high-speed carpet of mud had been rolled out, there would have been the slow settling of finer mud particles that formed the banding like dust settling after a carpet is laid in a hurry.

"Why are there no fossils in the banded part of the rock?" I asked.

"Because the settling was slow enough for sea creatures that were not caught by the first tranche of mud to get out of the way. Then there would be another earth tremor, and another carpet of mud would arrive. Ammonites were unlucky. As for ichthyosaurs, they may have all been buried in mud, but could have been killed by humans. I know that whales came close to extinction because of over-zealous hunting, but ichthyosaurs could still be alive, swimming in the depths of the ocean."

We wandered back to the car, with me in contemplation, and Ham reliving his first day of freedom.

"By the time the three of us had got back to the barbecue, it was mid afternoon," said Ham. "We discovered two members of the family were in agony."

"I bet those limpets were poisonous."

"No, it was sunburn. Sarah and Shem were deep red all over. Dad was bathing them gently with water from the stream to cool them, but it hardly helped."

"I can understand the sun burn. You had been cooped up in the ark for 12 months, hadn't seen much sun, and your bodies were not acclimatised to it."

"So why did it not affect the rest of us?"

"You're naturally tanned. If I had met you for the first time, I'd have said you were from the West Indies."

"But Noah is my father and Sarah my mother, both are white skinned."

"The genes must hop a generation."

"That is only half the story. Before The Flood all the family could spend hours out in the sun any time of the year without going red or brown. Before The Flood that extra layer of water vapour above the earth filtered out the harmful ultra-violet radiation. That had now gone so the earth was now bombarded with u-v. Fair-skinned people have to be careful of the strong sun because their skin is slow to produce the melanin that pigments their bodies a brown colour, but also protects them against sunburn. This is another feature that seems to confirm the collapse of the vapour canopy.

"We put the two of them on the cart, and pushed them back. Dad remembered that you had told him about calamine lotion long ago."

"It's an old-fashioned remedy. We now prefer to use sun-blocking creams before venturing out."

"It was another two days of agony with lashings of lotion before they felt well enough to help with the ploughing and planting."

Back in the car, Ham asked me to drive up the hill and out of the town. We headed towards Charmouth, whose fame had been assured by the author, Jane Austen. She had started to write the novel *Persuasion* in 1803. Any moment now I expected Ham to try again to persuade me that the flood was real, but he was silent as we drove up the narrow road to Stonebarrow Hill, now owned by the National Trust.

He had convinced me that I ought to see the effects of massive earth movements. Although I had been to Lyme Regis before, I had not been to this part of Charmouth. Some call it Fairy Dell, and others Cain's Folly. Whole sections of cliff had slipped away towards the sea. The disruption is about one mile long, and up to 400 yards from the sea to the top of the cliff. To the rabbits we could see playing on the slopes below, it probably was Fairy Dell with no human intrusions. But to human beings it was a 'Folly of a place'.

I had to agree that the scene was a dramatic enough example of what is called 'mass movement', taking everything with it. It is a natural equivalent of the Aberfan disaster. Houses, trees, and fields: you name it and it slipped down the slope. But the disaster was worst on the west side of Lyme Regis. "I'm sure that you are going to try and convince me, Ham, that during The Flood, the earth would have been shaken with events of this magnitude, and larger, almost every few minutes."

He nodded.

The last stop on the way home was Bridport. Hundreds of years ago, Bridport may have been a true port, with ships able to come up the lower reaches of the river Brit at high tide. Marshy ground now dominates the area, making it prone to flooding once the rains start or there is a southwesterly gale. In 1960, twice as much rain as usual fell. Bridport suffered badly on the 22nd October when five feet of water flooded the main road. Water burst through the door of one house and carried off a cot containing a sleeping infant in it. To the great relief of all, he was rescued unharmed. That same day, in neighbouring Beaminster the floods swept a car away. Local school children were delighted with the flood because they were given two days off while their classrooms dried out.

However, the area, especially Bridport is better known for its rope-making history. Hemp was grown along the sides of the river because the plant likes the rich alluvial deposits found there. Flax would have been planted overlooking the town. After the central fibrous parts of the plant had been removed, a number of them were twisted together to form strands, and the strands twisted together to form rope. The long streets of Bridport were useful for making rope, because the workers could start a new rope at one end of the street tied down to a post, and walk to the opposite end of the street paying out the strands, and twisting them together as they walked.

"All this talk about Bridport reminds me, Ham, that the words marijuana and hemp are linked. Innocuous plants become the source of hallucinary drugs."

"I doubt if much marijuana would have been made in Bridport. It needs a hot and dry climate to produce potent quantities of the drug."

"Yes, but the land you left behind was hot. Did you not have the drug?"

"Our family never used it, though I know many did. It may have salved their consciences about the evil they indulged in. We did use the seeds to produce oil, paint, soap, varnishes, and to add to our collection of food for birds."

"I am amazed at your inventiveness."

"Many of the things that God created can be used for good and evil purposes. Otherwise free will has no physical meaning."

"I see that. Now, what about your own ropes?"

"With no rigging, our needs were minimal. The lengths that we needed to tighten the planks together were bought in the local market."

Bridport had a lot of public health problems 140 years ago from bad sanitation. There were too many cesspits adjacent to wells that supplied drinking water. The council wanted money to pipe fresh water into the town and dig new drains. They could only do that if people would accept higher rates. Those who did not suffer health problems objected to paying more since there was supposedly nothing in it for them. Poems appeared in the local newspapers appealing to the good Christian people of Bridport to agree to a shilling rate to improve the public state. The hint was dropped that they were not as charitable as the healthy folk in neighbouring Dorchester and Weymouth where there were no health problems. The higher rate was eventually agreed. Pipes were then laid from Little Cheney in 1872 to bring into Bridport the much needed fresh water. Drains were then redug.

I thought of how Ham had tipped waste over the side of the ark but that would have only been appropriate while they were surrounded by water. How did they cope in those months that they waited on board with dry land outside? And did they get plenty of fresh rain?

"One of the things we had to build on the ark was a big tank on the lower deck. We could not understand why it was in the plans we got from the Lord. Suddenly it made sense. It was for the foul water and waste once the sea had retreated. There was no more tipping overboard. When we came out of the ark we dug a cesspit 200 yards from the ark, made a gully to it and let the contents flow into it. As for rain, it came in normal quantities."

"You've thought of everything."

"No, it was the Lord."

CHAPTER NINETEEN

ON THE BOTTLE
"he (Noah) became drunk", Gen 9 v 21

It is a strenuous walk up Chapel Hill near Abbotsbury. But from there you can see the 15 miles of shingle that make up the graceful curve of Chesil Beach. On that same beach, the individual pebbles create a din as even the gentlest of waves cause pebbles to clatter against each other. Many parts are covered with flotsam of plastic bottles, old rope and wood – just like a landfill site. So I had no love relationship with Chesil Beach, but Japeth wanted to see it. I agreed to take him because he had the happy knack of making even a grubby location interesting.

"Don't ask me how the rubbish gets there," I said.

"Swept off passing ships, I guess."

"You are one to talk. You dumped rubbish overboard from the ark."

"Everything we tipped overboard was degradable except for the broken pottery. Was that not allowed?"

"I guess so. At least the seeds helped to get life started again on land."

"Thanks for forgiving us. Chesil Beach is the perfect setting to talk about its history, which is even the envy of the saga of the Inchcape Rock."

"That means shipwrecks?"

"People know Chesil as a graveyard for ships caught in a storm. It is also a haven for wild life, so access is forbidden during the breeding season, but the story today is also about demon drink."

"Pardon?"

"What I have to tell you is embarrassing for Dad. He wants me to tell you what happened, but I cannot do it glibly. So I will start with the beach.

"This 20 mile stretch of open water from the tip of Portland to Bridport is a nightmare for any boat caught in a storm with damaged rigging, broken rudders or faulty engines, and too easily the shingle can become their graveyard."

I'd read *Moonfleet*, based on the story of the floods of the 1820s, which swept part of the church at Fleet away. So I knew that winds, storms and shingle were a recipe for disaster, even inland.

"Each shipwreck in this bay," he continued, "has a different story to tell of the heady mixtures of damage, salvation, heroism, shame and remorse. The majority of boats that are stuck against the Chesil Beach end their lives there. With timbers stressed by the uneven support of the shifting shingle, the boats crack up. Once there is a hole, you can say goodbye to everything except flotsam.

"The attitude of the locals to shipwrecks was varied. In 1824, the 80-ton *Ebenezer* was caught in a storm. She struck the Chesil Beach but the storm was so ferocious that the boat was flung over the top of the ridge of shingle 50 feet high by a huge wave. It hadn't quite made the full 200 feet across to get it into the water the other side, but the local folk dragged it down the remaining few feet and into the Fleet."

"They could not get it out of the Fleet now for there is a low bridge at the exit into Portland Harbour."

"But at that time there was only a rope ferry, Frank, and that vanished one day in another storm."

"Weren't you worried about being blown onto the rocks that would have shredded the bottom of your ark to splinters? Everybody got off *Ebenezer* safely. People in other boats that were stuck on the windward side of Chesil were not always so lucky.

As their boat broke up, individuals were battered to death by the waves. *Moonfleet* is a story of a lucky escape for only one person."

"Not having masts or rigging on the ark meant that we were not seriously affected by the wind. But we are not comparing like with like. The Flood bore only a limited resemblance to a storm – water lifted us up from the bottom, and torrential rain doused us from the top downwards, but we were never washed sideways onto rocks."

There was little wind today, just a slight southwester. So he told me of the Guernsey to Weymouth mail boat, set six years later than *Ebenezer*, which he claimed would make me weep and rejoice at the same time.

"That boat ran aground on the shingle near Church Hope. All on board were saved by the use of ropes thrown from the beach to the boat by locals. The mail was recovered successfully and postmen, professional to the tee, rushed to deliver it so that it would not be delayed any longer. In contrast, the locals then blotted their copy-books and proceeded to steal the passengers' luggage and possessions."

"That event only makes me sad. Why are humans like that?"

"Why did people not want to help us build the ark? It has to be that there is a deeper purpose to this world than eating, drinking and giving in marriage. The world is a theatre for playing out the battle of good versus evil. We are all actors, but some prefer to slumber in the wings rather than learn their lines and contribute to the play. Others want to disrupt the play."

"But no one is naturally evil, are they? There is good in everyone, religious or not. Excusing themselves of giving assistance in building the ark because they are busy with other legitimate things is not evil, surely?"

"Cain asked the Lord God if he was his brother's keeper, Frank."

"But wasn't that after he had murdered him?"

"Before he murdered Abel, God had warned Cain that sin was crouching at the door of his heart. There was no loving relationship between them. If we, like Cain, become disobedient to God's direct instructions about worship and helping others then brutal events, like that murder, follow."

This was an interesting theological point. Can altruism flourish unaided, or to continue the analogy with the theatre, do we have no option but to learn the lines in the play that God has written? Can we not make up our own lines as we traverse life's way and still produce an acceptable play? God should have accepted Cain's sacrifice of fruit as well as Abel's lamb.

"From a human perspective, that seems reasonable. However, there is a '*Jekyll and Hyde*' in all of us because of The Fall, and we cannot control either. Think of what happened on 25th November 1872. The iron built clipper *Adelaide* heading for Australia became hopelessly trapped in West Bay. She was dragging her anchors, and heading inexorably for the shingle beach. The locals gathered to watch and try to help rescue the 69 on board as she grounded close to shore. A breeches buoy, erected by the locals, carried 60 people to safety above the waves that were pounding the shingle and creating an under-tow that no human could survive."

"Saving 60 people was altruism!"

"You said that quick enough, Frank, but the story does not stop there. The ropes then snapped, the ship parted at the seams and spilt its cargo of hundreds of barrels of rum, wine, brandy and schnapps onto the beach. A drunken orgy took place on the beach though soldiers from the Verne and the coastguard station tried to stop the plunder. Daybreak revealed how humans lack self-control. Three Portland men and one boy had died in the night of drunkenness and exposure."

"OK, so some Portlanders could not shake off the '*Mr Hyde*' in themselves. But you are a pure and righteous family. You saved the animals and anyone else who wanted to be saved. Does that not prove my point that some people are perfect? Maybe the story of Adam and Eve, and the way Cain killed his brother are bits of legends rather than truth."

"Frank, they were my ancestors, and yours. Why should they have lied when they recorded history?"

"But there is natural good in many people. Think about lifeboat men. Whilst the locals turned out onto the Chesil Beach to help the rescue people from disaster, their safety was hardly compromised. At worst, they'd get soaked. It takes a different kind of courage to join the lifeboat service, step off the security of land and go out into the raging storm."

"The bravery of lifeboat men is not fool-hardy or particularly risky, although to land-lubbers it may seem so. Simple marine technology makes the job much safer. Before there were modern lifeboats, the Portland rescue teams used a 'lerret' boat because it was never known to capsize even in the mountainous waves that pounded Chesil Beach. The boat had a great beam and a flat floor about 20 feet long."

It sounded like a miniature ark with the copyright going to Noah, or if I wanted to be more precise, the plan goes to God. The ark that Noah had built was long beamed, and flat-bottomed for the express purpose of riding out The Flood. That made me ask him why modern lifeboats are thin.

"Flat bottomed boats do not go very fast, so if you have to batter your way miles against the storm to reach people on a stricken boat, you need every aid to speed your arrival. There is no point in going if you arrive too late. Modern lifeboats have buoyancy tanks in them to keep them upright whilst their thin sections make for speed."

"So what is this about your dad?"

"Um, well. Dad seems to have hit a low spot in his life after our 'shipwreck'. We stripped the ark of useful items and used the wood for building new homes."

"What is wrong with that? The wood was yours, unlike the Portland Islanders you told me about who stripped wrecked boats of good wood even before they fell apart. And you'd paid over the odds at ten shekels for each tree because of that scrooge who owned the forest."

"For several years we laboured to get the farm established. It was not particularly difficult though our own babies started to arrive.

Dad planted a vineyard, made wine and drank too much. In his drunken stupor, he took his clothes off and dropped asleep in a tent. In simple words he was ashamed. Reviewing it afterwards, both of us were intrigued by the words Cranmer wrote for the Church of England's communion services, 'We acknowledge and bewail our manifold sins and wickedness that we from time to time have committed.'"

"The enforced use of those words is one reason why I don't go to church often."

"Have you noticed that the modern services have less emphasis on sin?"

"Yes, but it's still in the liturgy."

"Dad asked me to tell you about this incident because he does not want you to think that he, or any part of our family, are a race of sinless humans, devoid of any *'Mr Hyde'*."

"Surely getting drunk once in a lifetime is not an unpardonable offence? *'Mr Hyde'* committed murder in Stevenson's book."

"Like Cain before he offered his sacrifice, it was what went before it that mattered."

"What went wrong with your father who for years had shown himself a true model of compassion and thoughtfulness, always anxious to please the Lord even when his actions did not appear to make sense?"

"Our whole family searched our hearts to understand what went before. Maybe Dad was unaware of what he was doing, just like the boy and those three men who drank too much alcohol. Do you remember that the intense rain may have come from a vapour canopy that surrounded the earth? Whilst the water was still in the heavens, the air pressure was higher than it is now, which allowed those pterodactyls to fly. It also meant that wine fermented slower. So the wine and beer that Dad had brewed before The Flood had never matured to such a high level of alcohol as the new batch."

"I don't know how you can make that suggestion. When I went to Martinstown with him 30 years ago, he drank Dorset ale, the real stuff."

"But on this occasion after The Flood, God warned Dad to drink less even while he was planting the vineyard. You might think that God was being unfair on Noah, telling him what not to do but not explaining why. It comes back to the invitation to trust. You can obey God and get the big things in life right, like building the ark, which everyone in the community knows about. People can join any rescue service, police, fire or ambulance, and find their names splashed over the newspaper headlines for their bravery in pounding seas, cliff-edge rescues, collapsing caves or blazing factories. Then you ignore the simpler instructions from the Lord and blot your copy-book exactly as Dad did. This is where '*Mr Hyde*' slips back to control our lives. And the more often he comes in, the harder it is to eject him. This is what The Fall did to us."

"I guess that you did not get drunk, otherwise you would have kept quiet about the incident. What about the rest of the family?"

"All stayed sober, but Ham went into Dad's tent by accident."

"What was wrong with that?"

"He treated Dad's drunken stupor as something to joke about. Self righteousness is another sin."

"Are you suggesting that someone who is a pillar of society and always doing charitable deeds is at risk of incurring God's wrath?"

"I will let you think that one out yourself in the quietness of the tropical gardens at the bottom of the hill."

CHAPTER TWENTY

NO SMOKE WITHOUT FIRE
"let's make bricks and bake them thoroughly", Gen 11 v 3

After spending a day washing clothes without anything other than a washtub brought to the boil by a coal fire, a blue-rinse bag and an arm-breaking mangle, a housewife could be forgiven if she complained that the washing she brought off the line when it was dry was dirtier than when it went into the tub. Such were the experiences in parts of Parkstone and Poole during the 1950s.

I had uncovered this complaint whilst preparing a business guide for Dorset years ago. It was an industrial area, and lots of chimneys were responsible for discharging black smoke and soot into the air. On Monday 27th May 1957, the midday smoke seemed worse than usual. Workers at the local pottery knew that smoke from their kilns could be bad especially when the stoker had just lit a fire with poor coal. So they continued to eat their lunch unconcerned except for the realisation that their wives would be full of moans when they got home. Monday was always washday.

Noah met me at the pub on the Ringwood Road, Parkstone, opposite where the pottery had stood. The area is now covered with modern warehouses selling window frames and plastic items, builders' yards, car repairers and auction compounds. There are no longer any signs of kilns or chimneys although the builder's yard sells bricks.

Back in 1957, when six fire appliances rushed to the factory with bells clanging, it dawned on the workers that their pottery was on fire. It was the largest fire in the Poole area since the war. I asked Noah why he had wanted to come here.

"Two years after The Flood, grandchildren started to make their appearance. Twins and the occasional triplets were included."

"That must have pleased the whole family."

"When the grandchildren were old enough to understand, I enjoyed sitting them on my lap, and telling them the story of how their parents had helped us build the ark. Once they had grown up and had their own children, the family was so large that I could not keep in touch with them all. I therefore built a museum as a reminder of the ark and The Flood and filled it with memorabilia."

"Sounds a good idea, Noah. Something tangible for a change."

"The mortgage deeds and the encyclopaedias from the pre-Flood days also went in the museum. I found one of the old stoves still in one piece, though badly chipped. In went our set of skittles and the box that Shem had used when sawing Irene into two. Our years fled by."

"Why did you not come and see me then? I would have loved to visit this museum."

"Such a lot to do getting life back to normal. One day a pleasant fellow, exuding confidence, came to see the exhibits. I guessed from his swarthy looks that he was one of Ham's grandchildren. By then I had so many great-grandchildren that I had lost track of them, and some I had never met. He introduced himself as Sabteca."

Hearing that name for the first time I thought it was another short title for part of the ark like 'Cheota', but it was a person's name.

"After looking around and taking notes, Sabteca said he wanted to ensure that he was safe should the flood re-occur. 'But I also want to be remembered for doing something special in life, just as you have done, Noah,' he said to me. I told him that there would never be another Worldwide Flood, because conditions had changed, but that did not satisfy him.

"He had thought about building a high tower that he could

retreat to if a flood ever threatened again. I re-enforced the point that that was not necessary. There were no large quantities of water under the earth waiting to spring forth any more than there were more huge quantities of water in the sky waiting to fall. I tried to explain about the barometer readings but he was deaf to it."

"Those technical points about the extra water took me a long time to understand. Now I realise that there can't be another flood like yours, covering the earth."

"Our museum and family records were not being consulted about where the flood-water had come from or and why such a catastrophe could not happen again. People went about distorting the story."

I would have called that the Chinese whispers problem. He'd not heard the phrase so I enlightened him that it was a super game for children, but it shows how easily we can get things wrong. Child number one has a story whispered into his ear. He then has to whisper it to child number two, and so on. The more children, the better. The last person then tells everybody what they heard. There is an amusing mismatch between what the first child was told, and the end story.

"I imagine that legends are born in this way," he told me, "when people forget to consult the written word, or do a double check by repeating the story back in their own words to ensure that they had grasped the details. That is how 'Unhappy Tim's' and the other 38 legends came about."

"Then with 40 legends to pick from, children's books can pay scant attention to whether any of them were real. Your animals smile from the open deck, the monkey climbs in and out of the window. Even you, Noah, are shown as waving to someone."

"I have seen those pictures in children's books. Who I was supposed to be waving to baffles me. You don't smile and wave at floating corpses."

"And there was that BBC TV documentary where you were supposed to have loaded reluctant animals onto the ark in the pouring rain, and then got drunk. Whilst sleeping it off you had lost track of how far the ark had drifted."

"I do not deny my drunkenness, but that was after The Flood. But unlike the presenter of that programme who produced a 'mockumentary' not a documentary, Sabteca finally got the message about the seriousness of The Flood and that there would be no new flood. Sadly he still insisted that if he built a tower in the centre of a big city, he would be famous. He wanted to put his name on every brick, so that people will remember him for generations to come, just as people remember me. It disappoints me that I am remembered for saving animals rather than being an actor in a play written by God about judgement."

"Did you see that thing that looks like an umbrella turned inside out in a gale just behind the pub?"

"Whatever is it, Frank? It stands out for miles."

The water tower in Parkstone serves a purpose, but the others (Clavell Tower, Moreton obelisk and Grange Arch - shown clockwise) are curios.

"It's a water tower. Made by civil engineers, it stores water so that should the pumps fail, water can continue to flow to essential services. It sounds a bit trite to say that it has given the name 'Tower Park' to the nearby shopping and leisure centre. And don't say that by building it, we had disobeyed God."

"You would not get many people up on the top of it if the sea level rose dramatically."

"That would be a joke, Noah, because the top is already full of water."

"I must tell that one to the rest of the family, maybe Sabteca if he comes back. Since I felt that I could not win the argument with Sabteca over his tower, I suggested that he build it with stones. He told me it would take too long to cut and shape the stones. Knowing that the museum was made of clay bricks baked in the sun, he wanted to know the secret of making better bricks. I explained to him how to identify clay deposits beneath the ground, and the different types that he might encounter, how to mould the clay into the correct shape, how to dry the bricks, and finally how to fire them. Then we briefly discussed mortar."

"I know about the pottery here in Parkstone, but not much else. My neighbour's father worked there and often yarned about it. There were days when he seemed pleased to show his family how dirty he was."

"Trying to convince people that he had worked hard?"

"Yes, but what was I supposed to make of you when we met for the first time? Overalls, covered with sawdust, pitch and paint."

"I rushed over to try and catch that zebra that was being a nuisance. Did you want me to stop, shower and change into something decent while he tore up more of your garden and then moved on to Adrian's? That busy time working in wood and sawdust has gone. Our new challenge is working with clay and making bricks to build a new world."

"Forgive me for saying this, but many people consider that the Romans were the first people to use clay."

"Frank, we had used it for two thousand years."

"Yes, but small quantities of broken Roman pottery have been found all over Dorset, but nothing older than that. Go and visit the County Museum, Dorchester where you will see a restored tiled pavement."

"But they did not make bricks, Frank. And since the Romans were eventually ejected from England before they had tutored the locals in the art of pottery, nothing further was made of clay until the rediscovery of the craft in the 15th century. The lack of bricks did not matter when the population of Dorset was small. People were able to find enough stone from the fields around to build their houses. Exponential growth in the population changed all that because there was a shortage of good stone to meet the rising demand for houses. Villages grew up where they could find clay for bricks. You can find lumps of clay on the beaches near Osmington. There is a rich variety of clays: fireclay for making chimney sections, ball clay for fine pottery, and lots of low quality clay, which is still good enough for making bricks."

"This new house we moved into had so much clay in the garden that digging was heavy work."

"Yes, but where you lived when I first knew you it was sandy. Meant that you had to water your begonias regularly."

"Such days!"

"As the population in Dorset expanded, so the demand for housing grew."

I suspect that the improvement in public health was one reason for increasing populations. Dorset, a small rural county, has a splendid track record when it comes to medicine. Benjamin Jesty, buried in Worth near the old radar headquarters, discovered that by deliberately infecting someone with cowpox saved them from smallpox. Francis Glisson became renowned as a physician on rickets and the liver, and to cap it all, a shy Dorchester boy became the surgeon, Sir Frederick Treves. He operated on Edward VII for appendicitis, though the coronation had to be postponed while Edward recovered.

But we'd also had people who, having time and money to burn, built towers and follies, which have no function other than to stand there like stuffed dummies. Maybe they saw them as monuments rather than challenges to the Godhead. Grange Arch hidden off a minor road by a row of trees, and Moreton obelisk in the middle of a thick, private wood came to mind. Whilst Clavell Tower was also built on a whim, at least it served the secondary purpose of being a lookout for the lifeboat station that existed at Kimmeridge. Though the lifeboat station has long since gone, the tower became a county monument. Having been built so near the crumbling cliff, it has now been taken down brick by brick and rebuilt away from the collapsing cliff edge.

"Frank, with better and longer life, increasing numbers of people turned to making brick to meet the demands for the basic materials."

"But there are lots of homes, some fairly modern, that are made of stone."

"Yes, but they are the exception, rather than the rule. The earliest record of houses built with brick is Edmonsham House in 1589, with Witchhampton House, part of Sherborne Castle – a close second in 1594. Staggeringly, 104 brick making sites have been found in Dorset. That means that almost every inhabited part of Dorset was within four miles of a factory. Until the railways came in the middle 1800s, transport was only by plodding horse and cart, so villages often grew up where clay had been found and the bricks made on the spot."

"You made your first houses from wood, broken off from the ark. But after that?"

"We started to use stone. Then we turned to clay bricks. The clay was everywhere just for the taking, deposited conveniently near the surface of the ground during the last stages of The Flood. In mid Victorian times, people had learned once again how to make bricks of different colours by mixing different clays, and adding rare earths to the clay before moulding. A splash of coloured patterns, unique to each builder, could then be added to different parts of the houses. The Dorchester examples are fantastic."

"I do know that in recent years in the Poole area, there were three large potteries. The Parkstone one caught fire. There was one at Hamworthy, south of the railway station, and one at Branksome. In earlier years the last two sites benefited from the closeness of the railway. There were mixed feelings when they all disappeared in the 1960s. Local supplies of clay were exhausted, good quality coal became expensive and plastic pipes took over for drainage. The housewives were pleased about the effects this had on their washing, but the resulting unemployment was not something that was welcomed by the bread-winners in the families."

"We faced similar problems to those you had in Dorset. Using a telescope, we could see right down the valley of Shinar and how Sabteca was progressing with his kiln. Once it was completed, there would be an interminable number of days when the valley disappeared under a blanket of black smoke. Other days there would be a white mist hanging around when Sabteca's workers stoked the kiln with salt to glaze the pottery.

"Twelve months later, we stopped seeing smoke and mist in the valley. Sabteca came up to see us again and explained that the first pit of clay was exhausted. However, they had discovered another lens of clay about ten feet below ground level. Digging away the over-lying sand was hard work, slowing up their production of bricks. He wanted to know if there was an alternative method of speeding up production. The management at the pottery in Parkstone faced the same query. They decided to make sand-lime bricks with the spare sand following a method patented by the Germans in 1894. But I knew how to do it and shared the answer with Sabteca."

"I don't think that you will get any money from the Germans for patenting some process that was really yours. Are the bricks as good as those from clay?"

"Depends. You can only use them in the foundations of buildings or on the insides. The ingredients are simple – sand and lime squeezed into a mould. The danger is that they have to be baked in a steam oven at high pressure. I warned Sabteca that because the steam oven and the boiler had to withstand high temperatures and pressures, he would need to learn the specialist metallurgical skills to make the oven safe. In the Parkstone pottery, the whole steam oven, 60 feet by 6 feet, had exploded one evening in 1905. The noise could be heard as far away as Poole Park. Six men in the workshop at the time had a lucky escape. They had noticed a sudden rush of steam from the oven and knowing that the three-and-a-half ton door was about to give way, they hurled themselves flat on the ground fractions of a second before the door flew past them. It came to rest 50 yards away, having first knocked large trolleys laden with bricks out of the way. The cause of the explosion was put down to metal fatigue in the hinges and catches. The survivors were thankful that they were not killed.

"I could tell that Sabteca had built additional kilns, Frank, and once more the valley was filled with black or white smoke on alternate weeks."

"And the tower continued to grow?"

"A little bit crooked! I suspected that as they were mining clay, sand and lime in the area, subsidence was affecting the foundations of the tower, and it started to lean. Just like the Leaning Tower of Pisa, the workmen tried to straighten their tower out as they added course of bricks to course of bricks, to increase its height.

"One year later Sabteca came back to see me with his younger brother, Nimrod. Nimrod, he told me, was also interested in building a city, and he was already constructing kilns five miles further down the valley. Nimrod was not interested in building a tower, but he wanted to make a name for himself through hunting."

"I guess that his elder brother had put him off with all the problems that he had experienced."

"Yes, but Sabteca had not slackened his work force. Nimrod, however, wanted to know about all the animals I had brought safely through into the new world and how big they were. I told him that the animals left before they were fully grown."

"But you said you saw fully grown animals before your flood."

"I did, but I did not tell him that because I detected that his motives were sinister. But I could not stop them pouring over my encyclopaedias in the museum. They laughed and joked, slapping each other's backs and deep in conversation as they unhitched their horses for the journey back down the valley. I have not seen them since."

"So did they complete the tower and their cities?"

"The tower grew in height and width at an alarming rate, though its lean made it look unstable. Houses were destroyed as it progressed across the area. Extra homes had to be built in Nimrod's city to accommodate the displaced persons and these new dwellings rapidly encroached into Sabteca's town, blurring the boundaries."

"This enforced move sounds a bit like Milton Park all over again. As for the two towns encroaching, it is all too familiar a story. At the turn of the 19th century Poole was a hamlet near the harbour and Bournemouth was a little place on the sea front near the present pier. Today they are one continuous mass of offices, homes, hotels, shops, hospitals and factories. You can't tell where Poole ends and Bournemouth begins."

"I am confused about boundaries as well. It is one of the reasons why I found it rather uninteresting to explore that part of Dorset.

"I heard rumours that both Sabteca and Nimrod were driving their workforce to greater efforts to make bricks, get the tower higher, and build more homes. One day, the inevitable happened. The valley was not just covered with black smoke, but flames lit the sky. In a moment of carelessness the door of the steam oven had not been closed properly in the workmen's haste to meet more demanding productivity targets. Like an overgrown bullet, it had blown out so fast and furiously that it had knocked large holes in the Hoffmann kiln. Since the kiln was operating at full power, fire erupted and spread rapidly engulfing the whole of the factory."

"More loss of life?"

"Nobody lost their life, but everybody was scared. Men lost their jobs at the pottery. Builders working on homes and the tower lost their jobs because the stock of bricks was quickly exhausted. Sabteca's workmen then went on a rampage, heading straight for

Nimrod's pottery. They did not see why his men should have work, and they had nothing, so they destroyed his site, lock, stock and barrel.

"In fear of reprisals and counter reprisals, whole families packed a few of their most precious things and scattered from the towns and into small communes. It was mass exodus.

"It was several days before the fires in Shinar burned themselves out naturally, and the smoke cleared away. At that point Sarah and I paid the town a visit. It was ghostly. Apart from smouldering embers and broken bricks, we saw nothing. In our hearts we considered that the disaster was due to God's judgement on people who were trying to protect themselves from things that were God's responsibility. He wanted them to trust Him."

"This sounds all rather callous of God. He put the clay there, the sand and the lime. What did He expect them to do with it? They could not do without homes."

"They were building a tower as an altar to their own self-sufficiency."

"Aren't we supposed to be self-sufficient?"

"Sure, God expects us to do things for ourselves, like building the water tower at Tower Park so that the water supply will not be interrupted when the pumps fail, but we are not to do things that challenge God and His purposes."

"What was the purpose of the tree of the knowledge of good and evil in *The Garden of Eden* if the fruit wasn't to be taken? Wouldn't it have been better if Adam had chopped it down before Eve spotted how attractive its fruit was?"

"People have rattled their sabres at the story of Adam and Eve and the Fall many times. Denied it, criticised it, said that it was pictorial theology, whatever."

"Why did God do it? People do not want the '*Mr Hyde*' character in themselves."

Noah hesitated. "People need to learn obedience."

But I was quick in response. "That temptation was so strong that God must have planned that Adam and Eve would take the fruit from that tree. And if any temptation is so strong, how can He justify punishing those who do wrong? Wasn't that what Darwin complained of when his brother died?"

"To look at punishment without considering redemption is short sighted. It is like the two separate sides of the same coin. One side shows punishment. Neither of the Darwin brothers turned the coin over to see the face of redemption."

"How were the people of Shinar disobedient?"

"God told Adam and Eve and their families to spread out throughout the whole world. God reiterated that instruction to us when we left the ark. What Sabteca and Nimrod had encouraged the people to do was to stay close to each other."

"People want safety in numbers and amongst people they know and trust."

"And what was in last Sunday's Gospel reading?"

"How did you know that I went to church last Sunday?"

"I notice that you are softening to the story of The Flood, Frank. The rest was guesswork."

"It was the 'great commission' from Matthew 28. 'Go into all the world'."

"Does the quote not continue with the words '. . . and preach the Gospel'? That is equivalent to turning the coin over so that the side that shows how human disobedience can be hidden from sight and exposing the other side showing the face of Jesus covering the sin. To go back to our '*Jekyll and Hyde*' analogy, Jesus is the potion that keeps the '*Hyde*' part of our nature at bay."

"I see the two sides of the picture now. However, there are people who go to that church every week and they dispute the historical accuracy of Genesis and The Fall and thereby reject the need for the sacrifice that Jesus made."

"Then you must challenge them, Frank.

"Sarah and I tried to return to normal life near our museum," he continued. "No one came to see us, and the weather got steadily colder year by year. Things that had grown easily in our kitchen garden stopped growing. We knew that we had to move further down the valley in the hope that it would be warmer there. I suspect that the same cold weather that made us move was pushing the other families that used to live in Shinar further and further apart.

"The ark had landed on a spot that we called 'Ararat'. At first it was hardly more than 100 feet above sea level. There were hills to the north. As the years progressed, the beach also rolled further away and the plain where we were living continued to rise. In winter, snow started to fall on the hills. We changed our address from 'Ararat' to the 'Hills of Ararat'."

Snow is rare in Dorset except on high ground. Older people remember the cold winter of 1947, but 1963 was colder. In fact, if you want to stand any real chance of seeing snow lie on the ground, you need to stay in Shaftesbury, because it is 700 feet above sea level and well inland. In 1963, the snow stayed around for 60 days in Shaftesbury. Another bad time for snow was the great Victorian blizzard in January 1881. It resulted in deep snowdrifts all over the county. But, by summertime, the warm weather had returned.

"I believe that our weather turned colder where we were living," said Noah, "because the sea was continuing to retreat. Or to put it another way, the land on which we were living was rising. The effects of The Flood were not all over once and for all in a few days. This rebounding effect, isostatic readjustment to give it its geological name, continued for hundreds of years. Our mountain was growing higher and we were being carried up into the colder and rarefied atmosphere. That is why the remains of the ark are now high on the mountains of Ararat whereas once it was at beach level. We had to get further down the valley. With tears in our eyes we said goodbye to the hulk of the ark and the museum. It was our plan to try and go back later and rescue the artefacts and documents, but for the moment, survival was uppermost in our minds."

Both our glasses were now empty. I offered to get him another pint.

"No, I must not fall into the same trap as in my embarrassing vineyard experience. Moderation is now the by-word."

"You have told me that if you confess your wrong doings, they will be forgiven."

"That does not give me an excuse for deliberate indulgences. But before going, you wanted to know about Mount Everest, now six miles high. During The Flood it was below the sea, like the mountains of Ararat. You would not have recognised it then – it was a shapeless mass of limestone. As the sediment accumulated, it also entombed marine fossils. After day 150 of The Flood, the seabed started to fold and up came the limestone whilst other parts of the ocean deepened. Jenny would use the word 'orogeny'."

"She says that it took millions of years. You said it happened in a couple of decades."

"Obviously she has not realised the significance of finding carbon-14 in diamonds. That makes the rocks on top of Everest quite young. If you want further evidence for how quickly the land emerged from beneath the sea, think about these tilted bowl-shaped hollows called corries, or cirques. There are many in Snowdonia and Scotland, huge hollows whose sides are covered with ice and snow in winter."

"The uneven melting of the snow has hollowed them out, says the geology books, Noah."

"Are you impressed by the explanation? These hollows were formed by the scouring action of water running away rapidly at the end of The Flood. Only as the land rose higher and higher have they become filled with seasonal ice and snow like our mountains of Ararat or Everest."

"Why is this not discussed in the geology books?"

"As one modern creationist said, 'If the story of The Flood were not in the Bible, people would have no difficulty in accepting it.'"

"But since it is recorded in the Bible, with an unadulterated explanation for it, nobody wants to know about it because it reminds them of The Fall."

CHAPTER TWENTY-ONE

BABBLE

"the Lord confused the language", Gen 11 v 9

A screech of tyres and a sharp blast on a horn outside startled me. Three seconds later the door bell rang, and Japeth stood there shaking like a leaf in a gale with Katrina at his side.

"We have nearly been run over. A red car came round the bend on the wrong side of the road. Missed us by a hair's breath. I've got his number. How do I report him?"

"You both witnessed it, so I'll get the phone. Then a cup of tea for the two of you would not come amiss. It helps to calm frayed nerves."

"I thought you English drivers were all so careful."

"Are you sure it was an English driver?"

"Why?"

"There are many continental holiday makers in the area at the moment, plus loads of students from abroad learning English. Dorset is an attractive place for visitors from all over the world, not just England."

"You did not always think that way about Dorset, did you Frank?"

"It was your father that kindled my interest in the first place. He loved Wareham forest. But going back to that near-miss, what was the registration number?"

"AT-170-KG."

"That's not English, though I'm not sure what country it is. He would drive on the right in his own country, and so it could have been a momentary lack of concentration on his part."

"Actually, we had come to talk to you about foreign languages."

"I never asked you what your mother tongue was and where you learnt English and your perfect diction. It fooled me at first and added to my uncertainty that you might be charlatans. Besides, it seems to have been months since I saw any of you."

"Mum and Dad are finding that travelling back and forward to your century is very tiring, and they might not be able to come back and see you again. Farming is getting more difficult because of the worsening weather, and they are thinking of moving yet again at their advanced age. To add to it all, they have also been knocked about by unfortunate news. Nimrod has shot the last pair of dinosaurs. All that trouble we went through to build the ark and save the animals is wasted."

"Trouble descends in threes on me."

"Another disappointment is that because there are now no dinosaurs left, people won't believe that we ever saved them from The Flood."

Inwardly, I had to admit that the story was growing on me. And I might get around to writing that book.

"We have been trying to encourage you for years," Jay said.

"Yes, but now I have an additional incentive to get it done. Tommy phoned to confirm that his wedding is going to be in Australia next spring. The whole family will be going. Ben is to be best man. So I have got to move fast with this book to have it ready for the publisher by then."

"I was beginning to despair that you would ever write that book that Noah and I wanted you to do," said Gaynor. "I have bought you a new computer and a laser printer to drop hints. But you have not started yet."

"I will tomorrow."

"That is what you always say, Frank."

"I've struggled for hours learning to use this word processor. At work I had a secretary."

"When I see page one, I will believe that you have started."

"But Nimrod, why did he do it, Japeth?"

"He likes to think of himself as a brave hunter. He was always on the look-out for bigger animals to bag and add to his collection. When a farmer came to him with a story of a roaming dinosaur spoiling his crop, Nimrod needed no further excuse to go after him and his mate. They were dispatched, dead, with two bullets. These last two dinosaurs were big beasts, but they were only vegetarians."

"They should've been captured and put in a wild life park or a zoo. Dorset fails in this respect of not having a zoo. Do you?"

"No wild life parks or zoos. We need to be much more proactive in this respect before more animals disappear. Sadly, Nimrod is such a pillar of society that it will be an uphill struggle to create a wild life park without his cooperation. Hunting runs in his blood."

"Every generation seems to produce people who are happy to hunt or invade the natural territory of animals with zero thought about the consequences. Whales, elephants and other large animals have almost disappeared in consequence."

"I am glad you appreciate the dilemma. I thought I would have difficulty convincing you."

"No you don't. I've joined an association that cares for wild life. Let's get back to language."

"We never named our mother tongue since everybody spoke the same language before *The Tower of Babel*. It was 'communication'."

"Did you have different dialects?" I asked my visitors.

"There were some dialects, but they were all minor."

"I love dialects. I can understand a Cockney, but I find it tiring to listen to too much of it. I love the old Dorset dialect."

"That's something we have not encountered."

"William Barnes and Thomas Hardy popularised it. There are lots of simple words that you would understand immediately. For instance, if someone said 'zunsheen' you would immediately recognise it as 'sunshine'. Some words get longer pronunciations, such as, 'woone' is 'one'. Some words are just shortened when they are spoken, like 'wi' is 'with'."

"Occasionally, Frank and I go to a dialect poetry evening," interjected Gaynor. "They were popular before the days of television. The point about dialects is that the words are still written in the same way as standard English. An old Dorset person would still write 'sunshine' for 'sunshine'."

"Tell me why you learnt English."

"When we first came to see you before The Flood, we were not conscious of varieties of language. We talked in our mother tongue and you understood us. You talked in your mother tongue, and we understood you."

"But Noah told us about *The Tower of Babel* and how people were scattered. New languages came into existence overnight. Are you telling us that you spoke English before The Flood? If so, you were lucky not having to struggle to understand the words with the letters 'ough' in them. Many foreigners get tongue-tied with the words 'though' and 'thought' although there is only one letter difference."

"Do you blame Dr Samuel Johnson?"

"No, I see the problem he faced when he tried to standardise English. Words pronounced differently in certain parts of the country meant the same thing. He was then faced with the difficult task of picking a unique spelling for each word. We still pay the penalty for this diversity. However, it appears that English is slowly loosing its identify and being replaced by Americanese. This is a consequence of the larger population of the USA and the increasing use of the world wide web for international communication."

"Dad counted six thousand languages in your world. So that we could tell the story of the ark to as many people as possible, I tried to learn Chinese because more people have Chinese as their mother tongue than any other language. I failed abysmally."

"Let me lift both of your spirits, Japeth and Katrina. I now know that the Chinese have a flood legend. Not every part of your story is recorded in that legend, but it does describe the construction of an ark, the destruction of earth by water, human seed saved on the ark, and the sending of birds out of the ark before disembarking."

"That is interesting to hear. It worried us that when God scattered people and confused their language that they would not remember The Flood."

"There is a legend of a calamitous flood in every major country. I checked that out before Frank and I met any of your family. The details vary, but the core of each one of them is similar. So they must be derivatives of one common story. The story of your Flood is known throughout the world."

I was able to give them further encouragement.

"As far as language is concerned, native speakers of English are the fourth biggest group of people, but if you include people who speak English as a second language, then the group becomes the second biggest."

"So although I never learnt Chinese, you are saying that telling the story in English reaches many people?"

"That's the implication. But did you tell the story of the ark to the world of your day, Jay?"

"In the pre-Flood days, newspapers took up the story of building the ark, and those papers had a worldwide distribution unhampered by different languages that cause trouble in your modern world. So everybody knew about the ark. There were no photographs, but enough eyewitnesses of the construction of the ark and drawings galore."

"But security was a problem for you, wasn't it?"

"It was difficult getting the balance right between the openness we needed to encourage people to join us, the ability to preach good and bad news and the security of the ark from those bent on disrupting our work. Indirectly, the owner of the forest did us a favour over security."

"With a bit of help from the zebras."

"Agreed. But who sent the zebras to us, and who put the owner of the forest in that unique position to keep the site of the ark away from prying eyes?"

"You want me to say that it was the Lord. I appreciate that He calls on us to stick our necks out to do things that seem at first to have no rationale behind them."

"Years after The Flood, Frank, we printed brochures about the whole story and sold them in the museum."

"But surely everybody would know about it without having to read. After all, they were descended from you."

"You would have thought so, but some parents did not bother passing the story onto their children."

"And that was when there was only one language?"

"Yes. Then came the tower, and the fire. The world seemed to go off on a tangent from there. God used people's propensity for arguments, bitterness, and recrimination to force them to spread out."

"But I thought the whole point of such a dramatic flood was to cleanse the world from the degradation it had slipped into."

"The Flood was responsible for bringing many things to an end. Before The Flood, farming was a nightmare. If you think you have a profusion of weeds and thistles today, you should have seen the hassle we faced. Many of our weeds ceased to grow after The Flood, and that made life much easier."

"And I seem to remember that it also prevented the successful growth of other vegetables and fruits that were part of your diet before the flood."

"We could have done without that disadvantage, Frank. Fortunately, after The Flood, meats were safe to eat and this made up for this missing part of our diet. The keeping of livestock was beneficial. Many of them could graze on grass and modern weeds, which would otherwise be useless to human beings. So we are better off."

"Those decades of conscripted labour on the ark were worth it, then?"

"Without the ark no one would have survived *The Mabbul*. During it we were reminded of the awful power of water when it was out of control, and our own mortality. But we did appreciate the fact that we all must cooperate with God in the theatre of life, rather than be part of the audience, or worse still, not bother to turn out to watch the performance."

"That answer has religious overtones to it. Were there any other practical benefits of The Flood?"

"I have lost count of the number of minerals that were brought closer to the surface of the earth during The Flood. – coal, gypsum, limestone, sandstone, and oil. How can modern life survive without these things that give us heat, plaster, garden lime, building material and fuel for cars, boats and planes, Frank?"

"Once ancient man could do everything with wood and flint, but these minerals make modern life so much easier, but it does not solve our mortality. Yet you folk seem to live for ever."

"Hardly. Dad is feeling his age. It also focussed our minds on the needs to listen to the truths from God above."

"The building of that tower was a direct contradiction of what you were instructed to do. People stopped listening, so it all ended in disappointment?"

"No, remember that though mankind was scattered, and many new languages came into existence, you have reminded us that practically every language and culture retained a residual knowledge of The Flood."

"And that's how the legends were born?"

"That is how the legends were born, but Noah's ark was no legend. Without it, the earth would be a haven for fish and other sea creatures but that is all. But they are no fellowship for God."

"I can accept that now. So come and see my new computer on which I'm writing this book."

CHAPTER TWENTY-TWO

RAINBOW'S END
"the Lord scattered them over the face of the . . . earth",
Gen 11 v 9

"Granddad, what's that circle over there?"

"You'll have to move your head forward, Beryl, so that I can see. These windows are so small."

"Can you see it now, Granddad?"

"It's a rainbow."

"It can't be. Rainbows are like bows, not circles."

"If you doubt me, ask your mummy then."

"I cannot see it from this aisle, darling. But it had been raining when we were in Brisbane, though the sun was trying to come out. The conditions were right for a rainbow."

"But why is it a circle, Mummy? And now I can see two circles. One is inside the other, 'nd they are such pretty colours."

"That definitely makes it a rainbow. Rainbows are circles, but you only see the top half if you are on the ground."

"Did you know, Granddad? I thought rainbows had pots of gold at their ends. Circles don't 'ave ends."

"Yes, I did know it, and I'm sorry to tell you that there are no pots of gold there. The story of gold is a legend."

"What's a legend, Granddad?"

"It is a story that is exciting but might not be true."

Leaving Beryl to her window view, I turned to Anne again. "Talking about rainbows reminds me that an intense storm hit our village one week after Noah's visit in 1970. An inch of rain fell that morning. All roads with the slightest of dips in them were flooded. In our garden, the goldfish pond floated away."

"Did you say 'the pond' or 'the goldfish' floated away, Dad?"

"I said 'the pond'. With all of that overtime I did in the days before Noah's visit, I had ten days flexi-time credited to me. I was quite happy to spend them with Noah and his family. He only turned up on three days and then left me in the lurch. So I started to do some gardening. Your mother wanted a goldfish pond in the garden."

"Even though you were hoping to move?"

"We hadn't been able to sell the house at the price we wanted. Two more couples interested in buying the house had dropped out that day. We hoped that by tidying up the garden and putting in a fish pond, this would just tip the balance in favour of our asking price."

"You couldn't drop your price any more?"

"We'd reached our limit. If we failed to sell at this valuation, we'd stay and enjoy the garden graced with a new pond. So I went out and bought one of those pre-moulded plastic ponds that are so big that you struggle to get them home in the car, dug a hole in the middle of the garden and placed the plastic mould in it. Being exhausted with digging, I put off the job of cementing it in and sealing the edges until the next day. The rain that morning was so intense that the water on the garden ran into the hole, and floated the mould out of the hole."

Anne shook her head to tell me that she did not remember the incident. Her junior school was on a hill, so it didn't suffer. And I could not photograph the mess in the garden for posterity because Noah had my camera.

"That must have been exactly the day Noah's rain started, Dad."

"I realised that and it put the wind up me. Out in the road other awful things were happening. Manhole covers were lifting at the edges and disgusting dirty water was pouring out."

"So those were your fountains of the deep! What caused them?"

"Piles of debris had been swept into the local drains by the downpour. This then blocked the sewer pipes further down the road. The excessive water pressure in the sewer system lifted the manhole covers, and out flowed huge quantities of sewage. The cover in our back yard also lifted. The health hazard worried me so much that I tried to phone the council up to come and get it rodded clear. Thousands of others found themselves in a similar predicament. I dialled the number at least a dozen times, each time getting the engaged tone."

"And this polite lady's voice that says 'the line is engaged, please try later'?"

"This event happened long before British Telecom introduced 'the recorded voice' as well as the traditional engaged signal. These awful conditions lasted about two hours. There was so much of this disgusting water, domestic waste and other debris on the lawn that I refused to go outside."

"Cannot say that I blame you."

"We were worried about collecting you from school. Then the rain stopped until evening. We watched as the amount of water coming out of the displaced manhole covers slackened, and the water in the garden slowly soaked away. The lawn was a mess, and I promised your mum that I would clean it up the next day if the ground had dried out. It was only later that evening when we went into our bedroom we found the bed and the carpet soaking wet."

"Why?"

"A brown stain on the ceiling over the bed betrayed the cause; water dripped from its centre. We pulled the bed aside, and placed a bucket under the drip. We didn't get much sleep that night. The rain started again, and the leak in the bedroom began to drip faster. The bucket was inadequate to cope. I plucked up courage, put on my wellingtons and made my way across the messy garden, brought the pond mould in and placed that under the leak. That coped through the night without overflowing."

"Where did you sleep, Dad?"

"Your mum went and slept on the floor in your room. I did the same in Tommy and Ben's room."

"It was uncomfortable, Anne," called out Gaynor, sitting next to James and Gavin. I didn't sleep any more than your dad did."

"Your mum's right. Fortunately, during the night, the rain ceased, and we were woken by sunshine and a rainbow."

"Noah had to wait a year for his rainbow. You got yours the next day, just like the ark we made at school."

"I felt sorry for Noah. What we had had to tolerate was nothing like what he had experienced."

"What caused your ceiling to leak? Normally you can solve a DIY problem like that."

"My second name isn't 'Ham' so it wasn't something that I could work out or solve easily. It was ages before we could get a roofing contractor to come in. It was perished roofing felt."

"You mean, it was old and worn out."

"I suppose that's a nice way of putting it. The roof tiles were adequate most of the rainy days to keep the water out, but when the rain fell so fast that day, water was blown up between the gaps in the tiles, and found its way through the perished felt."

"But was any other part of the house affected?"

"No. Our bedroom was the only place to suffer though the felt had cracked across the whole of the house. Our bedroom was underneath the gully that takes the water from two opposing parts of the roof. We threw the bed away and got a new one, but the worst news was that the value of the house tumbled and so we stayed put for much longer than we had hoped."

"Granddad," said Beryl, tugging at my sleeve, to encourage me to look out of the aeroplane window again instead of talking to her mum, "the rainbow has gone."

"It means that the rain has stopped."

"What did Noah do after the rain had stopped? Did he build another ark?"

"He didn't need to. He resumed normal life."

"What does 'normal life' mean?"

"It's like going back to school. You haven't been there for two weeks."

"I am looking forward to going back to school. And when I go into the school shop I can ask for an ice-lolly rather than an ice pole without confusing them. I thought Australian language waz the same as ours."

"You are right, Beryl," called her mum from across the aisle. "I could not get used to asking for the 'comfort room' when I wanted the toilet."

"There was one phrase that caught me out was when we tried to go for a swim on that beach. The guard stopped us, saying that there was Noah's ark out there. It's their way of describing sharks."

"I remember you telling us about sharks, but not the way the locals describe the menace."

"I shall be glad to leave all those funny expressions behind," said Anne.

"So did you not enjoy going to Uncle Tom's wedding, Beryl?"

"Yes I did, but I want to tell all my friends about it, and how pretty my new Auntie Dawn looked on her wedding day. I shall tell everybody at school, especially my best friend, Jane."

"Isn't it Jane's birthday next week?" asked Anne.

"Yes it is. And if she 'as asked me to her party can I wear my bridesmaid's dress again? You said I'll be too big for it next year."

"Certainly, darling and we'll take a photo for Auntie Dawn for when they get back to England." Turning to me, Anne said, "What's 'normal life' for you Dad? Golf?"

"Golf doesn't enthral me now, and don't say it was all to do with being beaten by the vicar. My publisher promised that my book would be printed by the time we got back from Australia."

"So what do you plan next? Start another book?"

"Maybe a fictional story, this time about dreams and travel. Before you and Tommy were born, I had a dream about my family going to the ends of the earth. But after a few years I could not treat it as true because Ben grew up to be such a stay-at-home lad."

"You know why, Dad? All of us children got tired of going to same Spanish beach each year, especially after that occasion when we were delayed 14 hours."

"That was a nightmare."

"When you had that massive storm, Dad, and your drains burst forth, did it change your attitude to the story of Noah?"

"From my student days I believed that it was a legend. After those first visits by Noah, I went into the library to look at the newspaper clippings about the Martinstown deluge. Other things then took over my life and I never went off exploring in the way he suggested. If I'd done so, I might have acknowledged that the Bible story was true earlier in my life. But since his recent visits, and our subsequent conversations, I realise that it is no legend."

"And what about the British rain record?"

"That is still intact after half a century, though there is no guarantee that it will not be exceeded somewhere, sometime."

"But you had an adventure like Noah. First the rain, then the garden flood, then the leaky roof, and now the dispersed and well travelled family."

"I never had to do any carpentry, Anne. All round I guess I got the better deal from our creator Lord. Mine was only a local flood, whereas his was worldwide. What did he call it – *mabbul*?"

"It is a pity that we do not have an English word that conveys the true horror and destruction of what happened as the whole surface of the earth was covered with water. *Mabbul* is hardly a word that I can talk to my hairdresser about."

"Then when the 40 days of the *mabbul* were over, Noah still had to float on those same waters with nothing to see for months. I've never done that. That could not have been a comfortable part of his adventure, wondering if the waters would ever subside."

"You are flying over large expanses of water with nothing to see, being waited on hand and foot by the cabin staff. There are no animal stalls to muck out."

"And although we are flying near the deepest part of the ocean

– the Mariana Trench – which helped the flood-water to retreat, I know that we'll see land in 30 minutes."

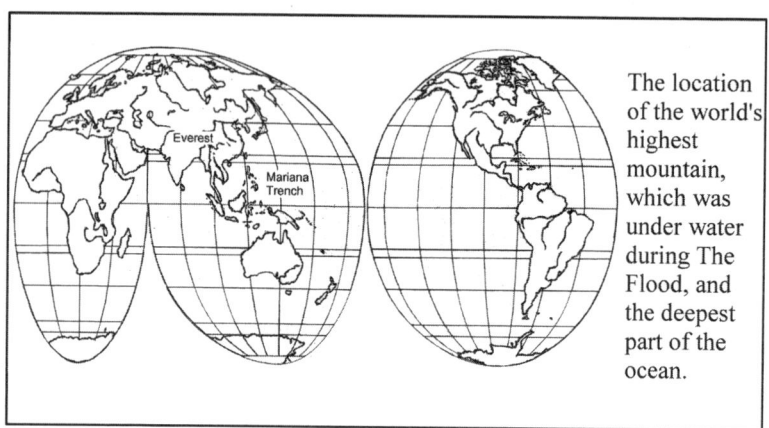

The location of the world's highest mountain, which was under water during The Flood, and the deepest part of the ocean.

"So for us, Lamech's prophecy has a ring of truth. In fact, if it were not for The Flood, we would have no fuel for this aeroplane."

"And do you know what Ben told me before we left him in Brisbane to stay on for a few days?"

"He muttered something about changing jobs. But I didn't hear where."

"He's joining a London brick company."

"As long as he keeps on speaking our language, I will not mind."

"Or becomes a big game trapper."

"I don't think I would forgive him for that."

"Or becomes an artist glamorising the Biblical story of Noah rather than telling it as a warning?"

EPILOGUE

The reason for writing this book was not simply to produce a work of fiction about Noah. Rather, the aim was to invite the reader to take the story seriously. Modern historians, geologists and archaeologists treat the history of the Old Testament casually. But the reasons for treating the Old Testament in this way avoid the unity the Bible has, and the claim God has on our lives.

This image trivialises the story of Noah, the animals he saved, The Flood and the destruction that occurred. We ignore the story at our peril like those who did not join the ark.

As a retired geoscientist, I know that few of my peers accepted that our world is only a few thousand years old, or that The Noachian Flood was responsible for the majority of geological rock sequences. It is only when you press geologists for explanations for common geological features that they obfuscate, dodging the simplest explanation available, namely that The Noachian Flood did it. My bibliographical list allows the reader to delve into specific examples. That does not mean that we can explain everything, for our knowledge will always be partial. However, The Flood can explain enough so that it is wrong to accept text book ideas about geology.

And once The Noachian Flood is accepted, the fossils no longer support evolution. Not that they ever did. This book is not the place to tackle the conflict between the creation of the world in six working days and the theory of evolution, which supposedly required billions of years. A few relevant books are mentioned in the bibliography. To get more details about Jurassic Ark, visit my web site www.jurassicark.org.uk. For the broader details of creationism, contact any of the creationist groups such as the Answers in Genesis or Creation Science Movement which has an exhibition in Portsmouth.

Finally, what about the other aspects of history in the Bible, such as Daniel? We have to credit the Jews with being much more careful historians than those who chronicled the other events in the Middle East. Few would doubt the exodus of Israel from Egypt after the years of slavery even though non-Jewish literature does not mention it. So why dismiss the rest of the Old Testament? Are there not enough doubts about dating archaeological events to leave room for a fully Biblical view of history?

And if the Bible history is true, doesn't it have something accurate to say about our destinies? Noah's ark, salvation for just eight, floated on the flood-waters. Thus, what saved those in the ark, simultaneously destroyed others. There is hope for us in the ark of salvation that 'floats' on the Blood of Christ The Lamb. But to ignore that Blood guarantees destruction. Read the last chapter of Peter's second epistle.

NOTES AND GUIDE TO BIBLIOGRAPHY

Bold type indicates the book that is being referred to.

Acknowledgements, Apologies and Disclaimers

Many evangelicals take view that the earth is old, and therefore only tentative schemes can be used to place the story of Noah and The Flood described in Genesis in a real historical setting. I have divided the duration of The Flood into three periods (in keeping with works such as **Wenham**, p183), though its aftermath rumbled on. The book of Genesis uses the Hebrew word *mabbul* to describe the first 40 days of The Flood (that is my period *one* where the Biblical focus is on a unique type of rain). However, additional water continued to reach the surface of the earth for another 110 days (my period *two*). Finally the waters subsided at least locally to the marooned ark (my period *three*). Period *three* ended at day 370 when Noah left the ark. Clearly, intense geological activity (like mountain building) would have taken place after Noah had disembarked. The family could not have got out of the ark if it had stuck on the mountains of Ararat at the height they are now.

The word *mabbul*, used in the Hebrew to describe the first 40 days of The Noachian Flood, is only used in one other place, namely Psalm 29. This makes it difficult to find an appropriate English word or short phrase for use in this book. The Septuagint uses the word 'cataclysmos'. To make this novel readable, I have used phrases like 'Worldwide Flood' or 'The Flood', but I recognise that this is not always adequate to convey fully the meaning of the word.

Chapter Two – A Dorset Home, 1970

P21 – For songs about Noah, see **Junior Praise** and **Someone's Singing Lord**.

P24 – **Sandar** provides an account of the Babylonian clay tablets and a translation of the 'Epic of Gilgamesh'. Gilgamesh is two-thirds god, and one-third man. He finds a companion, Utnapishtim who was born a mortal, but was immortalised by the gods for saving the earth from a disastrous flood.

P24 – **Hill** discusses Ussher's work and the Biblical dating.

P25 – Both **Navarra** and **Nelson** provide details of 40 other flood traditions and argue that on the basis of comparisons with the stories there was once a global flood, and that the story of Noah is the only one that contains physically robust details. **Wilson** (a secular writer) agrees that there must be significant substance to the Biblical story of The Flood because of the numerous other references to it, particularly in countries remote from a coast. However, he is only looking for a flood over a limited area. The potential flooding (in Eastern Europe), which he describes, came after the Noachian Flood.

P27 – **Custance** describes the differences between Noah's three sons, Shem, Ham and Japeth, from a Biblical point of view, and develops a relationship between them and the table of nations.

P28 – Wiggs were made in the famous bakery at Morcombelake, see **Moore and Moore** for the recipe for the biscuits.

P33 – The frequency of extinctions quoted is from **Cherfas**.

P34 – **Raup** lists the suggestions why the dinosaurs became extinct. The one mentioned by Frank is due to Alvarez. That iridium would surely have caused many other species to become extinct.

P40 – Wells' science fiction book, *The Time Machine* was first published 1895.

P42 – There are various estimates of the length of a cubit from 17.6 to 20.8 inches (**Whitcomb and Morris**). **Fasold** considers that the cubit is 20.8 inches. This would make the ark one-third more voluminous that Frank's estimate, but **Fasold** considers that the ark was tapered.

P42 – The comments about the Koran are in Surah 11, verses 42 onwards, English translation.

Chapter Four – A Very Wet Monday

P49 – See **DNHAS 97** for a brief history of Weymouth from 1699. King George III was a regular visitor to Weymouth and his patronage boosted the town's development long before large towns like Bournemouth were established.

P50 – Whilst only one site of the Roman invasion of Britain in AD43 has been positively identified, the numerous Roman settlements and battle sites in and around Dorset suggest that they might have used the quiet waters of Holes Bay as a landing spot. It would have been a sheltered harbour, free from silt and sand, see **Falkus and Gillingham**.

P54 – Bowleaze Cove is two miles NE of Weymouth at grid location SY 704-891.

P54 – **Ching and Currie** provide an illustrated summary of Dorset weather. This includes the 1955 downpour.

P55 – Dorset people were involved in developing photography. Thomas Wedgewood, son of Josiah Wedgewood the famous pottery maker, discovered that silver iodine could be used to make light-sensitive paper. He lived in Eastbury House (near Tarrant Gunville) until his death aged 34 in 1805, see **Chandler.**

P56 – The railways are described in **Maggs**. The barrow boys were common in the 1950s and '60s until British Railways stopped running holiday specials. When the Waterloo to Bournemouth line was electrified in 1967, coaches continued their journey to Weymouth hauled by diesel locomotives. By 1988, the whole line had been electrified.

P57 – There is no hint in the Bible of rain before The Flood. Hence Noah may never have seen clouds. Noah would see, just as Adam had done, streams that issued from the ground (Gen 2 v 6) and this would have supplied their essential water.

P58 – For fuller details of the 1955 rain record, its analysis and photographs of damage at Weymouth and Bowleaze Cove, see **DNHAS, 1955**. There are also brief comments about what happened to Martinstown in **Hearing**.

P59 – The Coastal Path crosses the Martinstown road at grid location SY 663-865.

P60 – Portland is described by **S. Morris,** and Maiden Castle by **Sharples**.

P60 – The conventional archaeological timetable for the barrows is taken from **Knight**.

P62 – For a discussion of the conventional dating methods, see **Aitken**. **Smart and Frances** provide a critical review of many of the methods, (including radio-carbon and thermo-luminescence), highlighting the problems with individual methods. **Magee** and **Wilson** are other secular writers who recognise the problems archaeologists have with relative dating.

P63 – **File** provides the data on the Martinstown and Bruton rainfall records. **Hearing** tells us how Martinstown was cut off during July 1955. The Bruton story is given in **Crocker.**

P63 – For a discussion on the various types of rain, and how they move, see **Ward and Robinson.**

P64 – For fuller notes about both of the Hardys, see **Chandler**.
P66 – The quotation about T. Hardy by Lawrence and the story of Watkins is in **Legg (1997)**.
P68 – The book with the photographs of Coryates is **Ching and Currie**. The flood damage in Coryates was caused by the rain collecting in the open, but gently sloping field south around Corton Down (SY 63-86) and being funnelled into the village through the narrow valley.
P69 – For a general discussion on aquifers and springs, see **Price**.

Chapter Six – Salmon Special

P77 – Monica **Hutchings** was the author who moved from Martinstown, 18th July before the storm began.
P79 – There is a large watercress farm at Bere Regis taking advantage of natural springs to supply mineral-rich water.
P80 – The word 'brainstorm' was not politically incorrect in the 1970s, see **Watson**.
P80 – The estimate of the time needed to build the ark is by LaHaye, see **Fasold**.
P90 – **Dawson** describes the wartime operations of Warmwell airfield. The only thing left now to commemorate the site is a plaque in Crossways village hall. Laurence Whistler engraved the windows at Moreton church with their wartime images.
P91 – Worth Matravers is on the B-road between Swanage and Corfe. Renscombe is at grid reference 966 – 775. The story of Dorset radar is given in **Batt** and **Penley and Batt**. Says Batt, "One whistled in amazement at what was expected of us. What kind of mad house had I joined?" See also **Legg (1990)**.
P92 – Hitler's desk is mentioned in **Poole and Williams.**
P92 – Until the 1990s, salmon catches on the Frome were 250 per year, see **The Frome and Piddle CMP.**
P94 – **Thulborn** suggests that Triceratops were up to 8 tonnes in weight, and Sauropods up to 80 tonnes. It could take them over 40 years to attain these sizes and weights.
P96 – The story of Elsa the lioness is in **Adamson**. **Durrell** also sheds much light on how to handle animals safely. Animals can be very variable in their ability to relate to humans, from outright aggression to positive friendliness, see for example, **Hooke**. Ultimately, God, who was the creator of all animals, would have instilled in the individual pairs in a supernatural way the need to board the ark and be cooperative during The Flood.
P96 – **The Good Zoo Guide** points out that it is difficult to get animals to breed in captivity. From a human perspective, this would have helped

Noah to avoid an increase in complement in the ark, but the ultimate responsibility for ensuring that animals did not breed in the ark would have been God's.

P98 – **Navarra** reviews the sightings on the mountains of Ararat of what might have been Noah's ark. **Roberts** describes one of his searches for the ark which included him being taken hostage but he was not looking in the same place as Navarra recommended.

P98 – Details about Dorset Knobs, see **Moore and Moore.**

P99 – The Studland bay wreck is described by **Ladle.**

Chapter Eight – If you go down in the wood today

P107 – **Mahon** describes the woods and forests of Dorset. He suggests that at least 34% of Dorset was woodland hundreds of years ago.

P109 – Details of *The Pines Express* are in **Mitchell and Smith.**

P111 – There are several places to enjoy Wareham Forest. There is a nature trail starting at SY 905-894. The narrative describes Frank and Noah meeting at 888-916 and following the track east. Woolsbarrow fort is at 892-925.

P111 – The uses of UK timber are taken from **Mitchell and Wilkinson.**

P112 – **Greenhill** discusses boat construction and the sheer labour of shaping wood and creating masts. Noah did not have to bother. See also **Greenhill and Morrison.**

P113 **Hood** discusses safety at sea, and the problem of water leaks in boats.

P116 – The reference to the Pantheon comes from **Doran.** For the reference to concrete in a mine, see **Magee.**

P118 – For Portland stone industry and cement, see **Stanier.**

P119 – Exhibits in Poole Maritime Museum, Poole Quay explain about boat building and shrinkage.

P121 – Pythons are not poisonous, see **Durrell (60)**. I'm not suggesting that Noah took a 15-foot python on board, but that humans can safely handle a wide range of animals. **Durrell (53)** criticises the story of the ark on the basis that he thinks Noah could only have got one-fifth of the necessary animals into the ark. Noah would have no need to take large animals and would also therefore be able to save on food stores. The Bible also tells us that Noah took on board every *kind* of animal. It does not use the word *species*.

P120 – Sika Deer and the trail are mentioned in the **OS Landranger Guide.**

P123 – **Dawson, Forty** and **Legg (1990)** give details of the cordite and decoy operations in Dorset. For the latter also see **Prendergast.**

P124 – Lawrence's effigy is in St Martin's church (SY 922-877). He is buried in Moreton cemetery (805-893). His old home is at Clouds Hill (824-908).

P126 – The well at Kimmeridge found limited quantities of oil when it was drilled in 1959. Other wells were drilled in the area but they produced no oil. For a technical description, see **Evans** *et al.*

P126 – **BP Exploration** issued a booklet in Feb 1991, entitled *Hook Island – Poole Bay*, which described the proposal to remove oil from the Wytch Farm reservoir using an artificial island.

Chapter Ten – On Fire

P133 – There are many tourist books with details about Blandford and the fire in them, for example **Cox**. Or visit the museum and see a model of the old town.

P140 – When mixed together, vinegar and baking soda produced a gas. The conker solution provides the surfactant to sustain the bubbles.

P144 – The Cerne Giant can be seen from the A352 road (Dorchester to Sherborne) at location SY 662-015. Its antiquity is not known (**Warren**). During the war it was covered up to ensure that enemy aircraft could not use it as a navigational aid. For a brief while a female figure, made of plastic, accompanied the fertility male, **DNHAS**.

P150 – For the "Bunga-Bunga" Woolf hoax, see for example, **Strange Stories, Amazing facts**.

P151 – **Navarra** describes his attempts to find the ark.

Chapter Eleven – My Old Camera

P157 – The story of 'a' flood in the Koran/Qur'an leaves one of Noah's sons off the ark (Surah 11). This creates serious problems with explaining the table of nations and the spread of humankind across the earth after The Flood. This is not a problem for the Biblical account, see **Custance** and **Cooper**. In Surah 66, Mrs Noah is declared as having been an unbeliever, like Lot's wife, and consigned to the Fire. It is not clear in the English translation whether she is supposed to have boarded the ark or not.

P163 – Discoveries of dinosaur footprints are recorded in **DNHAS 1962**. See also **Legg (2000)**. They have been found at Durlston Bay, Worbarrow Bay and Swanage.

P166 – During the tsunami in Asia, 26th Dec 2004, animals seemed to sense the impending danger and retreated to higher ground. Tsunamis are sometimes preceded by small-scale vibrations, see **Bryant**. For a historical survey of the effect on animals, see **Gold and Soter.**

P167 – For an introduction on how animals cope in winter, see *Nature*, but for specific details see **Smidt-Neilsen**. I offer these references, not because I believe that the story of the survival of animals in the ark through The Flood relied exclusively on the natural physiology of animals. Rather, the point is that there is so much variability in animal behaviour and because the animals joined the ark of their own accord, looking after them was made easier for Noah. See a specific Dorset example of the variability of seals in the presence of humans in **Hooke**. Before the arrival of the playful seal, an older vicious seal, which attacked dogs and humans, had been in the bay.

Chapter Twelve – They Had Poisoned Ham

P175 – The various ways in which hemlock can be used from vegetable to poison is described in **North.**

P176 – At the time of writing, short notes and diagrams can be found on the worldwide web about *The Herald of Free Enterprise* disaster.

P178 – Christchurch Priory's famous beam is described in **Cave.**

P185 – For details on paper making in Dorset, see **Stanier**, and **Cullingford (1980)**.

P188 – Books describing the exploits of the Army in Dorset during floods include **Wright** and **Legg (1990)**.

P188 – Boats appeared in Bournemouth Gardens (normally a grassy picnic area) one year during major flooding, see **Ching and Currie**.

P191 – The stunning details about land lift and fall are recorded in **Frampton** *et al.*

Chapter Thirteen – Footprints in the Sand

P193 – Evening Hill is a viewpoint at grid location SY 042-894, overlooking Poole Harbour and the islands.

P194 – Beavers have a propensity for constructing dams in rivers so that the entrance to their homes is beneath the water level.

P194 – The details of the hydrological cycle are taken from the **Open University** Book, *Seawater – its composition, properties and behaviour*.

P196 – The highest part of Brownsea Island is around 70 feet.

P196 – Land only occupies 30% of the total of the earth's surface. Its average height is 2750 ft. The average depth of the ocean is 12500 ft. Thus if you squashed all the land down into the ocean, the ocean would still have an average depth of 6740 ft.

P197 – The Cerne Abbas spring is described by **Warren**.

P197 – For a discussion on the water beneath the present earth, see **Bowden**.

P202 – The quote on 'moral pretensions' comes from **Morris (1980)**.

P202 – **Legg (2000)** writes about the dinosaurs.
P203 – **Erikson** describes the collapse of the USA dam, and the subsequent flooding.
P204 – **Lambert** describes the dinosaur fossilisation.
P209 – For brief details about the geology of Durlston, and its ostracods, and Fossil Forest at Lulworth see **Arkell** and **House**.
P209 – The details on the crocodiles comes from **Levy**.
P210 – A book on dragonflies is that of **Gibbons**.

Chapter Fourteen – Detectives

P217 – **DeYoung** explains about the discovery of radio-carbon in diamonds. On the basis of carbon-14 content, diamonds are not older than 50,000 years, and even if they were that age, they would have no strength. Note that the general problem with radiometric dating has been known for many years, see for example **Dillow** and **Milton**.
P219 – **Aitken** also notes that false and missing tree rings can occur in dendrochronology studies, causing confusion in respect of the correction needed. Varves, see **Whitten and Brooks,** are a sedimentary equivalent to tree rings – supposedly one per year. **Brown** shows this to be erroneous.
P221 – **Groube and Bowden**, describe the loss of the chalk in Dorset. Measurements were made of the mineral content in the rivers at the then Fresh Water Laboratories, East Stoke.
P221 – When the Ballard Down fault was first noticed by geologists, it was thought to be an unconformity. Later, when it was discovered to be a product of the Tertiary period (which came after the Cretaceous period by many millions of years) new explanations were sought. Different suggestions have been made such as various types of over-thrust faulting, but these also have to be rejected, see **Arkell**. However, the first explanation still holds valid if we condense the supposed history of the last 100 million years into a few thousand years.

Chapter Fifteen – Overland by Boat

P224 – The story of Milton Abbey is given by **Wansborough.**
P230 – Rawlsbury, and other ancient Dorset earthworks are described by **Osborn (85)**. The location is ST 767 – 057.
P231 – **Dillow** discusses the effects of double air density on large flying creatures, but see **Denton** for a general discussion about the supposed evolution of flight.
P232 – An interesting book on crypto-zoology and its relation to Dorset monsters is that by **Shuker**.

P235 – The unexpected find of a gold necklace is described by **White**.
P236 – Details on Dorset music come from various sources, including **Ashley and Ashley**, **Cullingford, (1988)**, and several hymn books.
A number of smaller animals hibernate in the winter. These include hamsters, dormice and bats. They first gorge themselves full of food, then curl up and go into a torpor. In this way, the food they have eaten lasts them through the winter because their metabolism is low. Bears sleep a lot in winter, but this is not true hibernation, see **Smidt-Neilsen**.

Chapter Sixteen – Land Ahoy

P244 – **Dillow** explains how his interpretation of the vapour canopy may have obscured many of the dimmer stars from human view. More recent studies on the canopy interpretation suggest that it is smaller than he assumed. See **Jones B** for the night sky identifier.
P244 – For details on the 'Harvest Moon', see **Whitcomb and DeYoung**.
P245 – The quote about how animals add to the rich variety of life is from **Evans H E**.
P248 – For a comparison of the raven and dove in behaviour and eating habits, see **Welty and Baptistic.**
P249 – For a discussion on the propagation of the olive tree under conditions of flood, see **Whitcomb and Morris**. The fossilised rolled leaves in Bournemouth are described by **Melville and Freshney**.
P250 – Several books on geomorphology (the shape of the land) point out that present amounts of rainfall cannot explain the formation of many valleys, for example **Gregory and Walling**. A good example of a dry valley is Scratchy Bottom by Durdle Door. The filling of this valley by water would have required land to lift at rates in excess of 10 feet per day from under the sea. **Goudie and Brunsden** discuss this valley, but fail to provide a satisfactory answer to its origin within their conventional geological paradigm.
P252 – The maps which Jenny describes showing that most of Europe was under water during the Cretaceous period are in **Ginsberg and Beaudoin.**
P253 – The sightings of Morgawr and other crypto-zoological creatures are reported in **Shuker**. The plesiosaur carcass is described in **Bowden**.
P253 – For a general discussion on giants in the sea, see **Bright**.
P253 – See **Campbell** for details on the Loch Ness Monster.

Chapter Seventeen – Stones

P255 – See **Osborn (1985)** for details of the Hellstone
P255 – For a fuller list of sarcens in Dorset, see **Knight**. However, the

sarcen in Branksome library came from Parkstone. Workmen found it when digging 8 feet down for a drain, see **DNHAS, 10**.

P257 – **Warren** describes the Agglestone rock and the legend about its origin.

P261 – Of his main work, **Darwin** said (p2) "I am well aware that scarcely a single point is discussed . . . on which facts cannot be adduced, often apparently leading to conclusions directly opposite to those to which I have arrived." If that is his strongest argument for evolution, then it shows that Darwin's desire to promote the theory of evolution was driven by a desire to put God's nose out, rather than to discuss whether observed facts support evolution or special creation. He explains at the end of chapters 8, 9 and 10 why the facts that he has found do not support his theory. **Bragg** claims that Darwin's book has changed the world. It has, but only by promoting a lie. Lyell carries much of the responsibility for this. His book, *'The Principles of Geology'* originally carried a sub-title, reminding the reader that he was looking for ways of explaining geology by processes that operate now. He thereby ruled out (without checking) the applicability of The Noachian Flood for explaining geology. See **Whitcomb and Morris** for fuller details.

P262 – In a collection of folklore from East Lulworth, we are told that the inner rainbow is called "the water gull". If it is absent or imperfect, you will be unlucky. But it is only lore – **DNHAS**.

P263 – For grounded boats in Poole harbour, see **Attwooll, Legg (1984)** and **Smith**. The destruction of boats on Chesil Beach for their timbers is recounted in **Morris S.**

P264 – Portland stone is described by **Arkell**.

P265 – Swanage is described in **Lewer** and the mining of the stone in **Benfield**

P266 – The explanation for the Neolithic beach being young is A) – the stony material is all from local places, though some do suggest that bits came from as far as Devon. If the beach had lasted millions of years, bits of the stony material would have come from many places in the world. B) – the sharp edges on those angular fragments of stone would have worn away with all the washing back and forward in the tides. C) – the shells would have been fully crushed.

P267 – Rufus Castle is described by **Wilton**.

Chapter Eighteen – Freedom

P268 – For details on Lyme Regis, see **Fowler**, and **Gosling and Marshall**.

P268 – The story of 'Lassie' is recounted in **Attwooll.**

P269 – The geology of the Lyme area, including Greensand and Blue Lias, are given in several books including **Perkins.**

P271 – **Mabee** provides a list of free foods, from field and beach. The findings of limpet shells at Maiden Castle is described by **Sharples.**
P272 – **Ager** is one of the geologists who recognise that the rocks were not deposited in a uniformitarian way.
P272 – For some of the details of Mary Anning, see **Perkins** or visit the Philpott Museum at Lyme Regis.
P276 – Austen's books and adventures are described in **Lloyd.**
P276 – For a map of the landslip in Dorset, see **Cooke and Doornkamp**. The book also gives examples of even larger landslips in other parts of the world, for example 15 by 20 km.
P277 – The details on West Bay and Bridport come from **Short and Shales**.
P277 – The details about the flooding at Bridport are from **Ching and Currie**.

Chapter Nineteen – On the Bottle

P281 – For data on shipwrecks, see **Attwooll, Smith** and **Legg (1984)**.
P284 – The story of lifeboats and their floatation aids is given in **Hawkes**. The "lerrets" are mentioned in **Morris S.** along with the details of Portland shipwrecks.
P285 R. L. Stevenson wrote *The Mystery of Dr Jekyll and Mr Hyde* in 1885.

Chapter Twenty – No Smoke Without Fire

P287 – The story of the Parkstone pottery is given by **Stout. Young** in DNHAS 1971 gives other details of brick making in Dorset.
P292 – Dorset people's contribution to medicine is mentioned in **Chandler.**
P293 – The curiosities and follies of Dorset are described in **Osborn (1986).**
P299 – The cold winters are described by **Ching and Currie.**

Chapter Twenty-one – Babble

P304 – For details on the English language, see for example, **McArthur.**
P307 – **Jones A** provides a useful discussion on how science could be taught recognising God's work in designing the minerals we need for life.

Chapter Twenty-two – Rainbow's End

P312 – See **Bickerton** for the equivalence of English and Australian words and phrases.

BIBLIOGRAPHY

Adamson, J. *Born Free – a lioness of two worlds*, Collins and Harvill, 1960.
Aitken, M. J. *Science Based Dating in Archaeology*, Longman, 1990.
Ager, D. V. *The New Catastrophism*, Cambridge University Press, 1996.
Arkell, W. J. *Geology of the County Around Weymouth, Swanage, Corfe Castle and Lulworth*, HMSO, 1947.
Ashley, H. and Ashley, H. *Bournemouth*, an official borough council publication, 1988.
Attwooll, M. *Discover Dorset – Shipwrecks*, Dovecote, 1998.
Batt, R. *The Radar Army*, Robert Hale, 1991.
Benfield, E. *Purbeck Shop – a stone worker's story of stone*, Ensign, 1990.
Bickerton, A. *Australian – English, English – Australian*, Abson, 1997.
Bowden, M. *True Science Agrees with the Bible*, Sovereign Press, 1998.
Bragg, M. *12 Books that changed the world*, Hodder and Stoughton, 2006.
Bright, M. *The Giants in the Sea – monsters and mysteries of the depths explored*, Robson Books, 1989.
Brown, W. *In The Beginning – compelling evidence for Creation and the Flood*, 8th edition, CSC, 2008.
Bryant, E, *Tsunami – the underrated hazard*, Cambridge University Press, 2001.
Campbell, S. *The Loch Ness Monster*, Aberdeen University Press, 1991.
Cave, P. *The Romantic Story of Christchurch*, published by the Hampshire County Magazine, 1980.
Chandler, J. *Great Characters in Dorset*, Book Guild, 1991.

Cherfas, J. *Zoo 2000, a look beyond the bars*, BBC, 1984.
Ching, M. and Currie, I. *The Dorset Weather Book*, Frosted Earth, 1997.
Cooke, R. U. and Doornkamp, J. C. *Geomorphology in Environmental Management*, Clarendon, 1990.
Cooper, B. *After the Flood*, New Wine Press, 1995.
Cox, B. *Blandford Forum – a pictorial history*, Phillimore, 1995.
Crocker, P. *Around Gillingham in Old Photographs*, Alan Sutton Publishing, 1992.
Cullingford, C. N. *A History of Dorset*, Phillimore, 1980.
Cullingford, C. N. *A History of Poole and Neighbourhood*, Phillimore, 1988.
Custance, A. C. *Noah's Three Sons*, Zondervan, 1975.
Darwin, C. *The Origin of Species – by means of natural selection – or the preservation of favoured races in the struggle for life*, sixth edition (1872) facsimile, Studio Editions Ltd, 1994.
Dawson, L. *Wings over Dorset*, Dorset Publishing Co, 1983.
Denton, M. *Evolution: A Theory in Crisis*, Adler and Adler, 1996.
DeYoung, D. *Thousands not Billions*, Master Books, 2005.
DNHAS – Volumes of the Dorset Natural History and Archaeology Society.
Dillow, J. C. *The Waters Above – Earth's Pre-flood Vapour Canopy*, Moody Press, 1981.
Doran, D. K. *Construction Materials* – Newnes Pkt Book, 1994.
Durrell, G. *The Overloaded Ark*, Faber and Faber, 1953.
Durrell, G. *A Zoo in My Luggage*, Penguin, 1960.
Erikson, K. T. *In the Wake of the Flood*, George, Allen and Unwin, 1979.
Evans, J. et al, "The Kimmeridge Bay Oilfield" in *Geological Society Special Publication*, 133, Edited by Underhill, J. 1998.
Evans, H. E. *Life on a Little Known Planet*, Airlife Publishing, 1993.
Falkus, M. and Gillingham, J. *Historical Atlas of Britain*, Kingfisher, 1991.
Fasold, D. *The Discovery of Noah's Ark*, Sidgwich and Jackson, 1990.
File, D. *Weather Watch*, Fourth Estate, 1990.
Forty, G. *Frontline Dorset – a county at war 1939–1945*, Dorset Books, 1994.
Fowler, J. *A Short History of Lyme Regis*, Dovecote, 1982.
Frampton, C. et al. *Natural Hazards – causes and management*, Hodder and Stoughton, 1996.
Gibbons, B. *Hamlyn Guide to Dragon Flies and Damsel Flies of Britain and N Europe*, 1986.
Ginsberg, R. and Beaudoin, B. *Cretaceous Resources*, Kluwer, 1990.
Gold, T. G. and Soter, S. *Fluid Ascent through the Solid Lithosphere and its Relation to Earthquakes*, PAGEOPH, 122, 1984/5.

Gosling, T. and Marshall, L. *Towns and Villages of England – Lyme Regis*, Alan Sutton, 1993.
Goudie, A. and Brunsden, D. *Classical Landforms of the East Dorset Coast*, The Geological Association, 1997.
Greenhill, B. *The Evolution of the Wooden Ship*, Batsford, 1988.
Greenhill, B. and Morrison, J, *The Archaeology of Boats and Shipping*, Conway Maritime Press, 1995.
Gregory, K. J. and Walling, D. E. *Drainage Basin Form and Process*, Edward Arnold, 1973.
Groube, L. M., and Bowden, M. C. B., *The Archaeology of Rural Dorset – past, present and future*, DNHAS Memo 4, 1982.
Guyatt, A. R. *The Day the Sky Opened – a novel of the Great Flood*, Scripture Union, 2006.
Hawkes, A. *Lifeboat Men Never Turn Back*, Poole Historical Trust, 1995.
Hearing, M. *The Book of Martinstown*, Winterborne St Martin Parish Council, 2000.
Hill, C. *The English Bible and the Seventeenth Century Revolution*, Allen Lane, 1993.
Hood, J. R. *Safety Preparations for Cruising*, Waterline, 1997.
Hooke, N. W. *The Seal Summer*, Arthur Baker Ltd, 1964.
House, M. R. *Geology of the Dorset Coast*, Geologists' Association, London, 1989.
Hutchings, M. *Inside Dorset*, Sherborne Abbey Press, 1968.
Jones, A. *Science in Faith – A Christian perspective on teaching science*, CST, 1998.
Jones, B. *Night Sky Identifier*, Bdd Promotional Book Co, 1992
Knight, P. *Ancient Stones of Dorset*, Power Publications, 1996.
Ladle, L. *The Spanish Shipwreck off the Dorset Coast, Studland*, Poole Museum Heritage Series.
Lambert, D. *The Ultimate Dinosaur Book*, Dorling Kindersley and Natural History Museum, London, 1993.
Legg, R. *Guide to Purbeck Coast and Shipwreck*, Dorset Publishing Co, 1984.
Legg, R. *Dorset at War – diary of WW2*, Dorset Publishing Co, 1990.
Legg, R. *Lawrence in Dorset*, Dorset Publishing Co, 1997.
Legg, R. "Summary of Dinosaur Footprints, Purbeck", *The County Magazine*, Spring 2000.
Levy, C. *Endangered Species – crocodiles and alligators*, The Apple Press, 1991.
Lewer, D. *The Story of Swanage – a history of earlier times*, Harewood, 1986.
Lloyd, P. *Legends of Dorset*, Bossiney Books, 1988.
Mabee, R. *Food for Free*, Harper Collins, 1996.

Magee, M. *Who Lies Sleeping – the dinosaur heritage and evolution of man*, Ask Why Publications, 1993.

Maggs, C. G. *Branch Lines of Dorset*, Sutton Publishing, 1996.

Mahon, A. *Dorset Wildlife*, Dorset Books, 1990.

McArthur, T. *The Oxford Companion to the English Language*, Oxford University Press, 1992.

Melville, R. V. and Freshney, E. C. *The Hampshire Basin*, HMSO, 1982.

Milton, R. *The Facts of Life*, Corgi, 1993.

Mitchell, A. and Wilkinson, J. *The Trees of Britain and Northern Europe*, Collins, 1988.

Mitchell, V. and Smith, K. *Bournemouth to Evercreech Junction*, Middleton Press, 1987.

Moore, R. and Moore, G. *Biscuits from a Dorset Village*, from the shop in Morcombelake.

Morris, B. *Ritual Murder*, Carcanet Press, 1980.

Morris, S. *Portland – an illustrated history*, Dovecote, 1985.

Navarra, F. *Noah's Ark – I touched it*, Logos, 1974.

Nelson, B. C. *The Deluge Story in Stone*, Bethany, 1968.

North, P. *Poisonous Plants and Fungi in Colour*, Blandford Press, 1967.

Osborn, G. *Dorset Curiosities*, Dorset Publishing Co, 1986.

Osborn, G. *Exploring Ancient Dorset*, Dorset Publishing Co, 1985.

Penley, W. H. and Batt, R. *Dorset's Radar Days*, The Purbeck Radar Trust Museum.

Perkins, J. W. *Geology Explained in Dorset*, David and Charles, 1977.

Poole, A. and Williams, M. *Unknown Dorset*, Bosiney Books, 1989.

Prendergast, E. D. V. *Dorset Decoys, Abbotsbury and Morden*, The Friary Press, reprinted from DNHAS, vols 106 and 107.

Price, M. *Introducing Groundwater*, Chapman and Hall, 1985.

Provost, A. *In the Shadow of the Ark – a love story from the dawn of civilisation*, trans Nieuwenhuizen, Simon and Shuster, 2004.

Raup, D. M. *Extinction – bad genes or bad luck?*, Oxford University Press, 1991.

Roberts, A. *Arksearch*, Monarch, 1994.

Sandar, N. K. *The Epic of Gilgamesh*, Penguin Classics, 1960.

Sharples, N. M. *Maiden Castle*, English Heritage, Batsford, 1991.

Short, B. and Sales, J. *The Book of Bridport*, Barracuda Books, 1980.

Shuker, K. P. N. *In Search of Prehistoric Survivors – do giant 'extinct' creatures still exist?*, Blandford, 1995.

Smart, P. L. and Frances, P. D. *Quaternary dating Methods*, Quaternary Research Association, Technical Guide No 4, 1991.

Smidt-Neilsen, K. *Animal Physiology – adaptation and environment*, Cambridge University Press, 1994.

Smith, G. *Hampshire and Dorset Shipwrecks*, Countryside Books, 1995.
Stanier, P. *The Industrial Past – Discover Dorset*, Dovecote, 1998.
Stout, V. *Around Kinson Pottery*, BAS Printers Ltd, 1992.
Thulborn, T. *Dinosaur Tracks*, Chapman and Hall, 1990.
Wansborough, R. *The Tale of Milton Abbey*, DPC, 1974.
Ward, R. C. and Robinson, M. *Principles of Hydrology*, McGraw Hill, 2000.
Warren, D. *Curious Dorset*, Sutton Publishing, 2004.
Watson, D. C. C. *The Great Brain Robbery – Creation or Evolution?*, Walter, 1975.
Watson, O. (Ed), *Longman Modern English Dictionary*, Longman, 1980.
Weld, W. *Historic Landscapes of the Weld Estate*, Lulworth Heritage Ltd, 1987.
Welty, J. C. and Baptistic, L. *The Life of Birds*, Saunders College Publishing, 1991.
Wenhan, G. *Word Biblical Commentaries, Genesis 1-15,* Nelson, 1987.
Whitcomb, J. C. and DeYoung, D. B. *The Moon – its creation, form and significance*, Baker, 1978.
Whitcomb, J. C. and Morris, H. M. *The Genesis Flood*, The Presbyterian and Reformed Publishing Co, 1961.
White, A. J. Monty*, What About Origins?*, Dunestone, 1978.
Whitten, D. G. A. and Brooks, J. R. V. *Dictionary of Geology*, Penguin, 1972.
Wilson, I. *Before the Flood*, Orion, 2001.
Wilton, P. *Castles of Dorset*, Published by the author, 1995.
Wright, P. *The Village that Died for England*, Vintage, 1996.

The Frome and Piddle Catchment and Management Plan, NRA 1995.
The Good Zoo Guide, Harper Collins, 1992.
The Holy Qur'an, (Koran) Translated by Abdullah Yusuf Ali, Wordsworth, 2000.
Hook Island – Poole Bay. Private Bill – Environment Study, BP Exploration, 1991.
Junior Praise, Marshall Pickering, 1986.
Nature, Reader's Digest Family Guide, 1984.
Ordnance Survey (OS) Dorset Landranger Guide, Jarrold, 1987.
The Piddle Valley Cook Book, Barrie and Jenkins, 1978.
Seawater – its composition, properties and behaviour, Open University, 1989.
Someone's Singing, Lord, A and C Black, 1973.
Strange Stories, Amazing facts, Readers Digest, 1975.